Let a Pillar Arise

A Novel of the Revolutionary War

William Guerrant

This is a work of fiction.

Cover images "Colonial Kitchen with Woman Spinning" from *A Brief History of the United States* by Joel Dorman Steele and Esther Baker Steele (1885) and "Tory Refugees on Their Way to Canada" by Howard Pyle (1901). Back cover image "Battle at the Cowpens" (1877) by Felix Octavius Carr Darley, courtesy of the New York Public Library

Cover design by Kyle Griffith

Rough Branch Publishing
Keeling, Virginia

ISBN-13: 978-0-578-36775-0

To Ransom Colquitt, John Watts, George Dodson, Jacob Moon, Michael Gilbert, Robert Walters, Henry Eanes, Arthur Eanes, Edward Eanes, Moses Hall, and especially James Gillies.

Shall they be unremembered,
Those heroes of old?
Their graves all forgotten,
Their glory untold?
Shall Time, in his flight,
Bear their prestige away?
And the deeds they have done,
Be the thought of a day?

Ah! no, from this spot,
Let a pillar arise,
And the gray of the stone
Pierce the blue of the skies.
Let the evergreen spring
Where their ashes repose,
And plant o'er them sleeping,
The lily and rose.

From "Guilford Battle Ground" by Ellen Dowdell Hundley (1892)

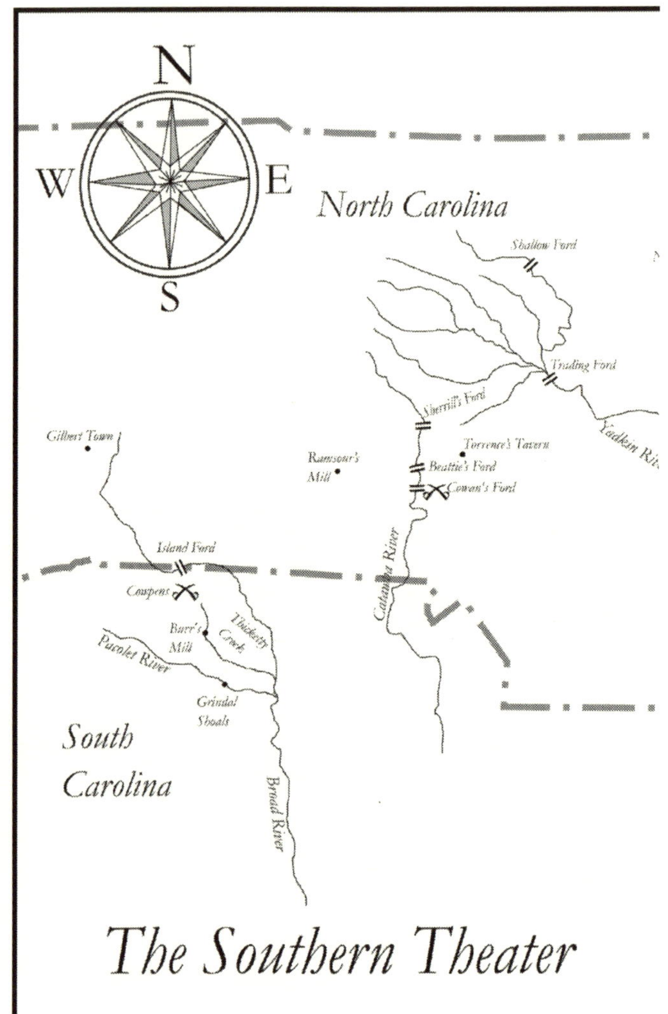

The Southern Theater January-March 1781

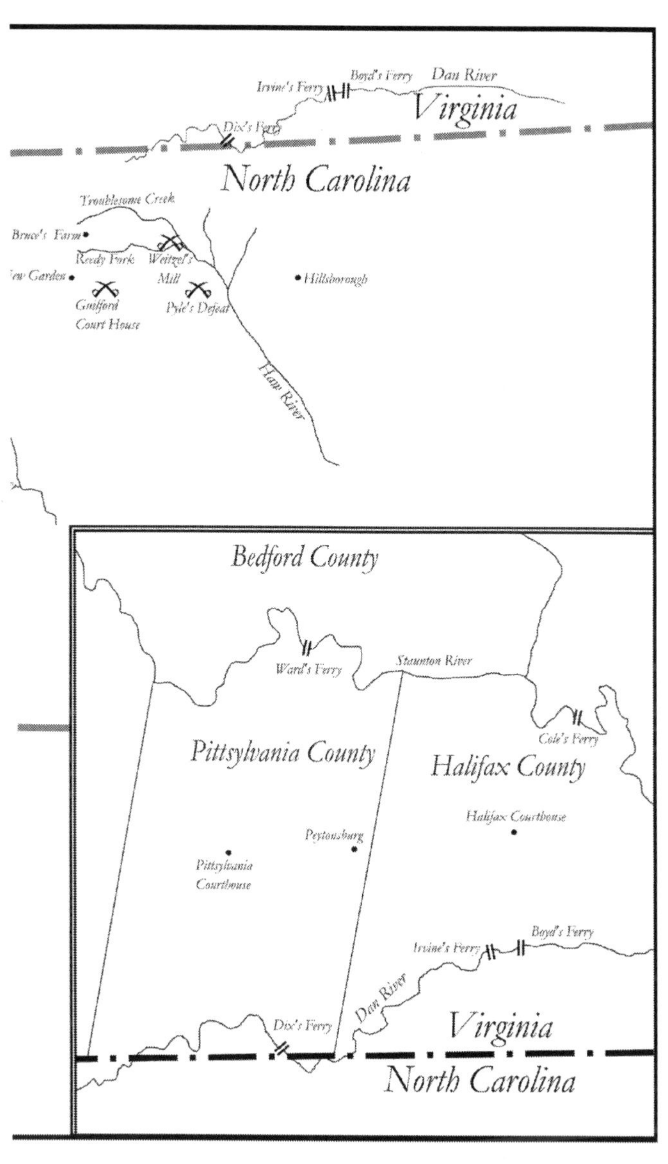

Irvine's Ferry
Boyd's Ferry
Dan River
Virginia
Dix's Ferry
North Carolina
Troublesome Creek
Bruce's Farm
Reedy Fork
Weitzel's
Mill
Hillsborough
Guilford
Court House
Pyle's Defeat
Haw River
Bedford County
Ward's Ferry
Staunton River
Cole's Ferry
Pittsylvania County
Halifax County
Halifax Courthouse
Peytonsburg
Pittsylvania
Courthouse
Boyd's Ferry
Irvine's Ferry
Dan River
Dix's Ferry
Virginia
North Carolina

1

Martin's Tavern
Peytonsburg
Pittsylvania County, Virginia
January 5, 1781

Wynn Bayard dragged his boots over the scraper outside the entrance to the tavern, then pushed the door open, pulling off his hat and gloves as he stepped inside the smokey room, crowded with boisterous men. Nodding in response to the several greetings called out to him, Bayard scanned the crowd, his eyes stopping when he caught sight of a man in the far corner who was raising a pewter tankard to get his attention. Bayard nodded and smiled, pushing his way toward the man.

"Happy New Year, Henry," he said pleasantly, extending his hand.

Henry Lawton stood as Bayard approached. "Happy New Year, Reverend," he answered, taking Bayard's hand and shaking it firmly. "Here," he said, gesturing toward the bench on which he had been sitting. "Join me, sir."

"Obliged," Bayard said, as he lowered himself onto

the bench. Still standing, Henry caught the eye of the young man who was scurrying among the crowd, collecting and refilling the tankards. Henry raised two fingers and pointed at his tankard. The young man nodded, signaling that he understood and began to work his way toward the bar. "But I must say, sir," Henry said as he sat down next to Bayard, "so far this year there has been little to be happy about."

Bayard nodded gravely.

"What brings you to Peytonsburg?" he asked. "Surely not John Martin's ale."

"I've come seeking two things that are increasingly difficult to find in Bedford County these days," Henry answered. "Provisions and reliable news."

The bartender approached and set two full tankards of ale down on the table in front of the men. Henry handed the young man a crumpled note, then turned to Bayard, his face clouded with concern. "Are the rumors about Arnold true?" he asked.

"I'm afraid they are no longer rumors, Henry," Bayard replied. "The express carrier confirmed it this morning. Arnold is marching on Richmond as we speak."

"Damn!" Henry muttered, quickly adding, "Pardon me, Reverend."

Bayard responded with a sympathetic smile. Raising his tankard, he said, "To your health, sir."

"Cheers," Henry responded, decidedly uncheerfully.

Both men took long swallows, then set their cups on the table and sat silently for a few moments.

"The governor will be calling up the militia then?" Henry asked.

"He has done so," Bayard replied. "He has ordered

one quarter of the militia to report to Petersburg as soon as possible."

Henry took another drink, then shook his head solemnly. "These are hard times, Wynn. We're going to get pressed between Arnold in the north and Cornwallis in the south. There are no provisions for our militia in Bedford County. We're short of everything—guns, powder, flints, shoes, blankets, wagon grease. There's hardly a team fit to pull a wagon to be found, and hardly a wagon to be found to pull. The paper they call money these days is hardly worth the ink it takes to print it. And on top of everything else, we're crawling with Tories. Arnold's presence is going to make them bold."

"I've just come from a meeting of the Committee of Safety," Bayard answered. "I think the Tory threat may be exaggerated. But we must stay vigilant, Henry. Is there anyone you suspect?"

Henry shook his head. "No, not really. But I think the snakes are going to start showing themselves soon."

"If you see or hear anything suspicious, let me know," Bayard said. "I can get that information to our committee, and we can handle it. Like we did with those three Tories we nabbed in October."

Henry nodded. "Did they ever confess?"

"Of course not," Bayard answered. "But there can be no doubt of their guilt."

"I didn't realize Halifax County still had a Committee of Safety," Henry said.

"Well, the official term now is 'Court of Inquiry,' but we've never been able to stop calling ourselves the Committee of Safety," Bayard replied. "It seems we are as busy as ever. These are dangerous times."

"Indeed," Henry said. Lifting his cup, he added, "Well, here's to Benedict Arnold's head in a noose."

Bayard laughed. He lifted his tankard, bumped it against Henry's and said, "To justice."

They were interrupted by a loud commotion from the center of the room. "General Arnold is gathering the Loyalist militia," they heard someone say. A large man, dressed entirely in black and wearing a powdered wig, stood suddenly and boomed, "*Loyalist* militia?" His shout silenced most of the men in the room. "Loyalist?" he repeated, more loudly. "What does that mean, 'Loyalist'? Loyal to what? Loyal to tyranny? Loyal to oppression? Loyal like boot-licking lackeys? Loyal like my hounds? Say no more of 'Loyalists,' sir. Call them what they are! Tory dogs! And the sooner we start stretching their Tory necks the better." Among the crowd there were scattered laughs and shouts of agreement.

"Who is that?" Henry asked, leaning forward.

"The Reverend Mr. Charles Clay," Bayard replied. "A fire-breathing Patriot," he added, with mock sincerity. "And a friend of the governor."

"Where is Mr. Jefferson now?" Henry asked.

Bayard shrugged. "On the run from Benedict Arnold, I suppose," he said.

Henry drained his mug. "Wynn," he said, rising and picking up his hat and gloves, "it's been good seeing you. Please give my regards to Ruth. Come see us the next time you get across the river."

Bayard stood, reached across the table, and shook Henry's hand. "Will do, Henry. Tell Martha I send my best wishes. By the way, how are your boys?"

Henry laughed. "Stephen is 15 now. Thinks he knows everything. The other two are still as hard-headed and wild as ever."

"Haven't found wives for them yet? That's what will settle them down," Bayard said with a grin.

"I think Will is just waiting for Lucy Soblett to come of age," Henry answered lightheartedly. "As for Arthur, I'm beginning to wonder if there's ever been a woman born who can tame him."

Bayard chuckled. "Well, sir, give them my best wishes as well. Send them to me if you want to make Baptists out of them."

Henry smiled. "Wynn, as you know, I have no great regard for Baptists, present company excepted of course, but that is an indignity I would not visit even on you poor misguided souls."

Bayard laughed, pumped Henry's hand again and said, "Take care, my friend."

"You too, Reverend. Good day, sir," Henry said, before turning and pushing his way toward the door.

As he watched Henry leave, Bayard took up his tankard and worked his way toward the group of men in the center of the room. Seeing him approaching, Charles Clay stood and exclaimed, "Mr. Bayard! How are you, sir?"

"I am well, sir," Bayard answered pleasantly, extending his hand to Clay. "For an old man, that is," he added, as Clay shook his hand firmly.

"Mr. Bayard, you look to me to be as fit as any man 40 years younger," Clay said, as he sat down.

"Well, sir, if there is any truth to that, I attribute it to clean living, and an occasional tankard of ale," Bayard said.

Clay laughed and shook his head, "I have never imbibed spirits. You would do well to shun them too, sir."

"I am of the opinion that they have a beneficial effect on me, sir," Bayard replied with a laugh. "I take them in moderation, and while I may not be as stout as you, for a man of 62 I believe I am reasonably constituted."

"So you are, sir," Clay conceded, with a chuckle.

After a pause Bayard said, "The news about the traitor Arnold is alarming."

Clay scowled and shook his head with disgust. "No greater scoundrel and blackguard has ever been born, sir. It grieves me to know that such a villain is breathing the sacred air of Virginia, while adding even more theft, arson, and murder to the long list of sins for which he will soon be burning in hell."

"The wages of sin is death," Bayard replied, lifting his cup and taking a swallow.

"Our militia is being assembled and I have good reason to believe General Washington is dispatching a portion of the army to our defense now. Let us pray that Arnold's ignominious career will end in Virginia," Clay said.

Bayard nodded. "I trust then that the governor and the legislature have safely evacuated to Philadelphia," he said.

"Philadelphia!" Clay exclaimed. "Mr. Jefferson would on no account leave Virginia, sir. Until the crisis has passed, I am certain he will be in Charlottesville, as he should be. As for the General Assembly, I believe they have adjourned temporarily.

"Philadelphia," he added with a contemptuous snort.

Bayard answered with a nod, then said warmly, "Come and have supper with us this evening, sir."

Clay shook his head. "Thank you, sir. I appreciate

the invitation, but I am only here to sign some papers. I will be returning home this afternoon."

"Well, next time then," Bayard said, rising from his seat. "I must take my leave, sir. Please give my warm regards to your father."

Clay stood and extended his hand, which Bayard took and shook firmly. "Thank you, sir. And please give my best wishes to Mrs. Bayard."

"I will do that," Bayard answered with a smile. "Good day, sir."

"Good day, my friend," Clay replied.

Bayard crossed the room, pulled open the tavern door, put on his hat, and stepped out onto the porch, the crisp winter air causing him to pull his coat tight to his neck. Main Street—the red clay road running before the tavern, was crowded with horses, wagons, and shouting teamsters. John Martin had built the porch of his tavern right up to the edge of the road, so that patrons could step from their buggies or carriages directly onto the porch, and in so doing had narrowed the road so that it was difficult for waggoneers going in opposite directions to pass by each other. Thus, on busy days things were always lively before the tavern. And it seemed that every day was a busy day, now that the governor had made Peytonsburg one of Virginia's nine official military supply depots. Another consequence of the heavy traffic, and of John Martin's oversized porch, was that Main Street pedestrians had to walk across the tavern porch to get down the street—even those who would otherwise never deign to be seen on the threshold of a tavern, persons such as Tabitha Wiatt who nearly collided with Bayard, moments after he stepped out of the tavern and onto the porch.

In the momentary confusion they both muttered "pardon me," before recognizing one another and exchanging pleasant smiles. "Why, Mr. Bayard. Good morning, sir," Tabitha said, with a dip of her head.

Bayard quickly pulled off his hat and answered, with a slight bow, "Good morning to you, Mrs. Wiatt. Are you going this way?" he asked, gesturing down the street. "May I walk with you?"

"Yes, I am just going to my chaise yonder," she replied. As she stepped forward and down the steps of the porch, Bayard walked alongside her.

"I believe it is more crowded than usual in town today," Bayard said. "Have you any recent news from your son? I pray he is well."

Tabitha's face lit up as she replied, "Why yes, sir. I came in hope of a letter in today's express and, praise God, I have one. Ransom is well."

"I am very glad to hear it," Bayard answered pleasantly. "I trust he is safely tucked away in winter quarters somewhere warm."

Tabitha's smile vanished, a concerned look spreading across her face. "Would that it were so," she said. "His regiment is in South Carolina, supporting the Patriot militia there. I am worried sick, sir. Will you please be so kind as to include Ransom and his regiment in your prayers?"

"Of course I will, Mrs. Wiatt. Of course I will," Bayard answered, his voice expressing concern and sincerity. "Where in South Carolina is his regiment? Perhaps one of my congregants has family in the area and can help provide for Captain Wiatt and his men."

"Thank you kindly, sir," Tabitha, looking into Bayard's face with moistened eyes. "Ransom's letter says they are in the upcountry, camped with General

Morgan on the Pacolet River. Oh, Mr. Bayard, we live in such troubled times," she said, her voice trembling.

"Let us stay strong in our faith, Mrs. Wiatt, as God's people have always been asked to do in times of trouble," Bayard replied. Taking her by the hand, Bayard helped Tabitha up into her chaise, then unhitched the horse for her.

"Thank you for all your kindnesses, sir," Tabitha said as she pulled the reins and set the horse in motion.

"Good day, Mrs. Wiatt," Bayard answered with a slight bow, as she drove away.

As Bayard turned and began walking back toward the tavern, he noticed a young man leaning against the wall at the bottom of the porch steps, reading a newspaper. When he reached him, Bayard slowed his pace and, without looking at the man, said softly, "Tonight. Captains only." Bayard then stepped up on the porch as the young man folded his newspaper. They walked away, in opposite directions.

2

Camp of the 3rd Light Dragoons
Grindal Shoals, South Carolina
January 5, 1781

After stretching his black top boots over the bottoms of his tan leather breeches, Ransom Wiatt slipped on his white uniform coat, buttoning it at the top. He was brushing his coat when interrupted by a commotion outside his tent.

Ransom pulled back his tent flap, stepped outside, and turned toward the source of the noise. About fifty yards away, among the tents of the rank and file, one of the soldiers was berating Collin. "If it won't burn, it ain't worth a damn as kindling, boy! Now go back and find something that ain't so green and wet." As Collin turned and began walking away, another voice called out from one of the tents. "Get some for me too, Collin!" And then another voice shouted, "Us too, Collin. Bring plenty!"

Collin was looking down at the ground, muttering to himself, as he walked past Ransom's tent.

"Collin," Ransom said firmly, startling the boy. He looked up suddenly and snapped to attention.

Ransom smiled appreciatively. He had long been impressed with how the boy—thin and slightly built, barely five feet tall—paid careful attention to proper military deportment. "Yes sir, Captain Wiatt?" the boy said, staring straight ahead.

"Collin, your duties do not include gathering firewood for the men," Ransom said.

Collin dropped his eyes. "I don't mind, sir," he said.

"Well, I would mind if I were you," Ransom replied. After a pause he continued. "Don't do it. I'll order them to do it themselves."

A concerned look swept over Collin's dark face. "I don't mind doing it, Captain," he said.

Ransom looked at the boy curiously for a few moments. "You don't want me to tell them to get it themselves?" he asked.

"No, sir," Collin answered. "I'd rather get the kindling myself."

Ransom furrowed his brow and bit his lip. After considering the situation for a few moments he said, "All right, Collin. Carry on."

"Thank you, sir," Collin said quickly, before hurrying away.

Ransom shook his head as he watched the boy walking rapidly toward the wood line, behind which the sun was beginning to rise. He stepped back inside his tent, buckled on his belt and saber, then remerged and walked briskly toward the largest tent in the camp. Standing outside, he called out, "Colonel Washington, sir."

"Enter!" a loud voice responded.

Ransom removed his hat, pulled back the tent flap, and stepped inside, just as Washington was buttoning his coat.

"Good morning, Captain," he said.

"Good morning, sir," Ransom answered, at attention.

"At ease," Washington said. "What is it, Ransom?"

William Washington was not a physically imposing man. Portly, round-faced, and already balding at age 28, he was not nearly as tall as his famous second cousin, the commander in chief. Seeing him, one might reasonably suppose Colonel Washington to be soft and weak. But Ransom knew better. Having fought alongside him for almost five years, the last three as captain of one of the four 20-man troops in Washington's 3rd Light Dragoons, Ransom knew his colonel to be bold, fearless, fierce in combat, and as skilled a horseman as he had ever known. Both men had joined the Continental Army in 1776 at age 24, Ransom as a private after withdrawing from the College of William and Mary, and Washington as captain of a company he had raised in his native Stafford County after abandoning his study for the ministry. Two years later, on the recommendation of then-colonel Washington, Ransom was elevated to captain. By then Washington had been wounded twice, while Ransom, despite being in the thick of the same fights, had never even been scratched in combat, although a bout of smallpox had left him with sight in only his right eye. The two men had come to trust, respect, and, when necessary, depend on each other.

"What is Collin's status, sir?" Ransom asked.

"Collin? His status?" Washington responded, puzzled. "He is our regimental trumpeter."

Ransom nodded but remained silent.

"Beyond that, Collin is my servant," Washington added, to which Ransom again nodded, without speaking. After a pause, Washington said, "He is also my property, if that is what you are asking."

"It is," Ransom answered. "Perhaps you would do well, sir, to let the men know that he is not *their* property."

"Speak plainly, Ransom," Washington said.

"Sir, I believe some of the men are bullying Collin, treating him as if he is their servant," Ransom said, noticing that his remark caused a flash of anger to cross Washington's face.

"I will put a stop to that immediately," Washington said, composing himself, then adding, "Collin has said nothing to me about it."

"I believe he is afraid to, sir," Ransom said.

"Afraid to? Why would he be afraid to?" Washington replied.

"I believe Collin wants to be accepted by the men, sir. I suspect he thinks complaining to you will hinder that. Did you notice how he joined the charge in that fight last week? He wants to be regarded as a soldier, sir," Ransom said.

"He *is* a soldier," Washington answered quickly. After a pause he added, "Of a sort."

Washington turned aside for a few moments, seemingly in thought, then pivoted and looked directly back at Ransom. "I believe I understand the situation and I believe I know how to resolve it," he said. "Thank you for bringing it to my attention."

Ransom nodded.

"Sit down, Ransom," Washington said, gesturing toward one of the two stools in the tent, as he pulled the other one over and sat down on it. Ransom stepped to the stool and sat down.

"What do you think of General Morgan?"

Washington asked.

The question surprised Ransom. "I beg your pardon, sir?" he said, uncertainly.

Washington laughed. "You heard me. Tell me what you think of Morgan. Speak plainly and candidly."

Ransom nodded. "I admire him," he said. "He's a fighter. It feels good and right to be taking the fight to the Tories here. He clearly has the respect and admiration of the men."

"Right," Washington replied. "I am in agreement, Captain." Washington stood and began pacing as he spoke, his hands clasped behind his back.

"We've been bloodying their noses, Ransom. They're going to come after us," he said.

"Good," Ransom replied.

"Tarleton is looking for us now. We know that from the reports we're getting from locals," Washington said, continuing to pace around the tent.

"Good," Ransom said.

"General Greene does not want to risk a major engagement out here, but I do not believe General Morgan is going to run away," Washington said.

"Good," Ransom said.

Washington stopped pacing, turning to face Ransom. "It's brutal down here. Whigs and Tories murdering each other in their sleep, burning their houses down on top of them, plundering each other like savages." He paused, before adding, "Tarleton is an animal. He will give no quarter. You know that."

"So be it," Ransom said, sternly. "And he shall receive none."

"We're going to have a fight here, Captain. Soon. I'm sure of it. And when we do, everything will be at stake. We will win, or we will die," Washington said.

"We will win," Ransom replied.

"I've been thinking a lot about this, Ransom. Probably thinking about it too much. I am convinced that if we lose this fight, if we are defeated, if this army is destroyed, we won't just lose a battle. We won't just lose our lives. We will lose the war, Ransom. The Tories will rise up and overwhelm the Patriots here. Cornwallis will march through North Carolina, and then through Virginia. If we are defeated, the cause will be lost. I feel sure I am right about that," Washington said.

Ransom pondered Washington's words. It was strange for the colonel to talk this way, to reveal how troubled he was, to admit his concern. "We will beat them, sir," Ransom said, meaning it.

Washington dropped into the chair, facing Ransom. He slapped his knee and said, "Yes. I believe we will. We will because we must." He paused, then looked directly into Ransom's face. "Have your men ready, Captain. Overlook no detail. Impress on them the significance of what we are facing. Make sure they know that Tarleton will give us no quarter."

Ransom knitted his brow, his mind going to the slaughter of Colonel Buford's surrendering Virginians in May, an event on all their minds these days, an event that seemed to make an appearance in nearly every campfire conversation. He thought also of the fight at Hammond's Store a few days earlier—when they had overtaken a body of Tory militia from Georgia, men they regarded as arsonists and thieves. He thought of how many of those Georgians had taken their last breaths with their guns on the ground, their hands in the air, and shouts of "Tarleton's Quarter!" and "Remember Buford!" ringing in their ears. "The men know it, sir," Ransom said. "Tarleton's victims are not forgotten. They will be avenged."

Washington nodded. "Very well, Captain Wiatt. See to your troop."

Ransom stood and turned toward the tent flap. "Do not repeat what I said about General Greene," Washington said, as he too stood up. "I share General Morgan's preference for a fight—especially a fight with Tarleton. I don't expect that General Morgan intends to admit taking more risk than the commanding general desires," he added with a chuckle.

"Understood, sir," Ransom said, as he stepped toward the flap.

"Ransom."

Ransom turned to face the colonel.

"Why did you re-enlist?" Washington asked. "You put in your three years. Fought honorably. Gave an eye. You did your duty. Why come back for more?"

It struck Ransom as a strange question. He had never known Washington to speak this way.

"I reckon I want to see it through," he answered. "Even if I only get to see it through with one eye."

Washington laughed. "Yes, I understand that." After a pause, he continued, "I've rarely heard you speak of home, Ransom. Did you leave a girl behind?"

Ransom hesitated before answering. "No, sir," he said. "Not really."

"I see," Washington said, looking away wearily, thinking, Ransom assumed, of Jane Elliott, the pretty young South Carolinian, now behind enemy lines, who had the prior year presented them with the crimson damask square they called their flag, and with whom the colonel was plainly smitten. "It's been so long," Washington said, looking away. "This war, I mean. So long."

Ransom squirmed, unsure of how to respond. After a few silent moments, Washington shook his head quickly and turned back to Ransom.

"Pardon my musings, Captain. It seems this impending showdown with Colonel Tarleton has me waxing philosophical," he said with a grin. "I will not let him beat us, beat me, again. I would rather die first. We cannot allow ourselves to be taken by surprise."

In his mind, Ransom filled in the rest of that sentence: "…as we have been before." He nodded. "I understand, sir. The men will be ready."

"Very well," Washington said, his professional and disciplined demeanor having returned. "Notify the other officers that we will drill the men in an hour."

"Yes, sir," Ransom said.

They exchanged slight bows and Ransom stepped outside.

3

Lawton Farm
Bedford County, Virginia
January 5, 1781

When the horse came to the narrow road that led to the Lawton farm, it was not necessary for Henry Lawton to tug the reins. Caesar knew the way home. The chestnut stallion veered right on his own and ambled up the knoll, the last one he would have to climb on this trip.

As they reached the crest of the hill, a log house came into view in the distance, smoke curling from its stone chimney. It was a sight Henry had seen countless times, but it never failed to give him a sense of satisfaction. Forty-four years earlier his father had arrived here with a group of Presbyterian immigrants from Pennsylvania. They found only one person living within 15-miles of the area—a decrepit old man who traded whatever dubious claim he had to possession of the land for a promise to care for him in his final years. The bargain made, the settlers had spread out across the area, each family claiming a share of the wilderness and proceeding to transform it into a farm. Henry's parents planted themselves on a spot by the creek, near the Staunton River, and Henry had been born in a tent there, while the logs hewn from trees his father had felled on the site were drying. The next year, his father had built the house, and its two rooms had been the family's home ever since. In the years that followed, they cleared the fields and added a barn, a corncrib, a smokehouse, and four daughters. Thirty years later, after the girls had married and moved away, and after Henry's parents had taken their places in the graveyard at the church, the farm became Henry's farm. He wooed and won the hand of Martha Thomas, his neighbor and childhood sweetheart, and in time she bore three sons—Will, Arthur, and Stephen. Upon her mother's death Martha inherited a man named Squire and his young son George, for whom another, smaller house was built. Together the family had improved the land each year, and it now comfortably sustained them all. Henry knew that the cellars beneath both houses were well-stocked with provisions for the winter and that the carcasses of four large hogs were hanging in the smokehouse. He knew there was a fat cow in the barn which provided their milk, cream, and butter, and a fat sow in a pen out back, which come spring would provide the piglets they would slaughter as hogs next winter. He knew that Martha's spinning wheel and needles would transform into their clothing the flax from their fields and the wool from their sheep, that the woodlots would provide them with fuel for cooking and warmth, and with game to help keep them fed, and that the tobacco curing in the barn would bring them the little cash they required for things they were unable to make or raise themselves. It all gave

Henry a sense of accomplishment. He found life here comfortable and satisfying. And now this place he loved was in danger—threatened by war, a war that had always been a distant affair, but that was now approaching his own doorstep.

As he drew close to the house, Henry saw that Will, Stephen, Squire, and George were splitting wood by the barn and that Arthur was emerging from the woods behind the house, with his rifle on his shoulder. By the time he reached the barn, George had come over to meet him, taking the horse by the halter while Henry dismounted.

"Thank you, George," Henry said, weary from the long ride. "Wipe him down but don't turn him out. I'll be going out again right after supper."

"Yes, sir," George answered, as he led the horse away.

Henry climbed the steps to the porch, pushed the door open and stepped inside, greeted by the powerful aroma of stew. Walking into the room to his left, he saw Martha stirring a large pot hanging over the fire. Arthur was standing at the table, preparing to clean some game. "That smells delicious, dear," Henry said, dropping into a chair before the fireplace. "Arthur, come help me pull off these boots."

His son, tall and thin and crowned with a mop of jet-black hair, put down his knife and came over, arriving at the same time as his mother, who bent down and kissed Henry on the cheek.

"Did everything go all right?" she asked, as Henry stretched out his legs and Arthur began pulling off the boots.

"There's no flour, salt or coffee to be had," he answered. "We're just going to have to make do without."

Martha nodded. "We will be fine," she said, returning to her pot, concealing the sense of dread she had been feeling ever since the rumors of approaching armies had arrived.

"Before things get better," Henry said, "they may get a lot worse."

As Arthur pulled off the second boot, Will and Stephen entered the room, having shed their coats at the door.

"Well look who's here," Will said, glaring at his brother. "Now that we've got all the wood split, you decided to come home."

"I expect you won't mind so much when you're eating these rabbits," Arthur replied, with a toothy grin.

"This is no time to be wasting powder, Arthur," Henry said, as his son walked back toward the table.

"I ain't wasted a grain of it, Pa," Arthur answered. "I never miss."

Will groaned and rolled his eyes.

Henry let it pass. There were more important subjects on his mind. "We need to begin making plans," he said. "It's confirmed. Benedict Arnold is in Virginia and is marching on Richmond. And…"

Arthur interrupted him, bolting up and exclaiming, "Then let's go join up with the militia there! Right now!"

"Settle down, son," Henry said calmly. "The governor has called up a quarter of the Bedford militia. I don't know yet if our company is included. I'll find out tonight."

"Aw, Pa," Arthur said with a whine. "If we get called up Colonel Lynch will probably just make us go and guard his mines again."

"I don't think so," Henry answered, gravely. "Not with Arnold in Virginia, Cornwallis marching up from Carolina, and Tories springing up all over the place. There's going to be a fight."

"What's next?" Will asked. "What do we need to be doing?"

Henry turned toward Will. A stranger might not guess that he and Arthur were brothers. Although Will was almost two years older, Arthur was three inches taller. And while Arthur was dark eyed and black haired, Will, like his mother, had blue eyes and sandy blonde hair. As different as they were in appearance, the brothers were equally different in temperament. Will was quiet, serious, and deliberative; Arthur was impulsive and reckless. The boys had been in a ceaseless state of competition for almost 20 years now. Neither one liked to lose.

"For one thing," Henry answered, "we need to prepare to get called up. If not in this call, I expect our turn will soon come, and when it does it may be for three months or more. So we need to get as much work done around here before then as we can."

"I don't want to wait," Arthur interjected. "I want to go now."

Henry ignored him. "If that stew is ready, I'd like to take my supper early," he said to his wife, with a smile. "I suppose I ought to go and see what news Jacob has."

"Are you taking Caesar?" Will asked, sounding distressed at the possibility.

Henry chuckled. "Yes, I am. I'm not much for walking in this weather. I reckon you will have to take a day off from courting."

Arthur laughed out loud. "Oh, but can't you hear Lucy Soblett's poor suffering cry? 'Romeo, Romeo!

Wherefore art thou, Romeo?'" he said mockingly, finishing with an affected dramatic pose.

Will started angrily across the room toward his brother, his mother gently extending her arm to block him. "You boys behave," she said calmly. "Arthur, shame on you. Apologize to your brother."

"I don't want an apology," Will said, glaring at Arthur.

Arthur smiled disarmingly, "Aw, come on, Will. I was just horsing around a little. No need to get all worked up."

Henry reached for his boots. "I think I'll just ride over and see Jake now," he said. "Caesar will be at your disposal after supper."

"Father, that's not necessary. I…" Will began, haltingly.

Henry lifted his hand and interrupted him, "I would prefer to go now," he said. He pulled his boots back on, kissed Martha on the cheek and stepped toward the door. "I'll be back shortly," he said as he left the room.

The ride to Jacob Thomas's farm was easy. Living only about two miles away, the Thomas's were among the Lawtons' closest neighbors. As Henry approached, he saw that Jacob was forking hay down from his barn loft. "Hello, Henry!" Jacob hollered down to him.

Henry rode up to the barn and dismounted. As he was tying the horse to the hitching post, Jacob emerged from the barn, smiling, and extending his hand.

"How are you, sir?" he asked with a smile, taking Henry's hand and shaking it warmly.

"Just fine, Jake. And you?" Henry asked, releasing his hand.

"Very well, thank you. How are my sister and nephews?" Jacob asked.

"We're all well," Henry said.

"That's good. What can I do for you, Henry? Want to come inside and have something to drink?" Jacob asked.

Henry shook his head. "No thanks. I can't stay long. Will wants the horse so he can go see his girl tonight."

Jacob laughed. "Ah, young love. I remember it well. They're a good match I think."

"We'll see," Henry answered, then changed the subject. "Jake, what about this business with Benedict Arnold?"

Jacob's smile vanished. "I don't know much about it, Henry. I've heard he's got a large force. They landed on the James. Seems to have taken us by surprise. I expect he's doing a lot of damage."

"Have we been called up?" Henry asked. "In Peytonsburg today I heard that the governor has ordered a quarter of the militia to Petersburg."

"You heard right," Jacob answered. "But I got word a little while ago that the Riflemen aren't included in the call."

"Why only a quarter, Jake?" Henry asked. "Shouldn't we all be going?"

"I wondered the same thing," Jacob answered. "Best I can tell, there are two reasons. One is that there aren't enough supplies and arms to provision all of us. The other is that there's a good chance we'll be sent to General Greene instead. Cornwallis may be a bigger danger to us than Arnold."

"So, for now…?" Henry asked.

"For now, we wait," Jacob replied. "It's not our turn yet, but it's coming."

Henry looked down and shook his head, thinking of how much was at stake. "This is going to be the militia's fight, isn't it, Jake? Us against redcoat regulars?"

"Not entirely militia. There are some Continental troops with Greene and Morgan. But I don't think we'll get much help from General Washington. His army is too far away and tied down in New York. So yeah, a lot is going to be asked of the militia."

Henry shook his head again, still looking down. After a few silent moments he lifted his eyes and said, "Well, Captain Thomas, I reckon we ought to start getting ready."

Jacob smiled. "Yes, Sergeant Lawton, I expect so."

"Thanks, Jake," Henry said, stepping into his stirrup and remounting. "Send over word as soon as you hear anything."

"Of course," Jacob answered. As Henry turned his horse, Jacob added, "Be vigilant, Henry. There are Tories hiding among us and these events are emboldening them."

Henry nodded, gave the horse a little kick in the side and trotted away.

4

Sandy Creek Baptist Meetinghouse
Halifax County, Virginia
January 5, 1781

It was a dark night, the light from the half-moon only dimly penetrating the thin winter clouds. But after tying his horse by the creek in the woods, where it would not be visible should anyone be on the road at this hour, and after trudging up the hill from the creek bottom, Gus Johnson was eventually able to recognize in the distance the outline of the small, windowless log building where the handful of local Baptists held their weekly worship services. When he reached the front of the church, he saw beneath the door the faint evidence of a single candle burning inside.

Gus knocked once on the door and was answered quickly by two knocks from within. He knocked twice more and a voice from inside said softly, "Romans."

"Thirteen," Gus replied.

The door opened narrowly from inside, he slipped through the opening, and it closed quickly behind him. Gus glanced around the room and saw in the flickering candlelight that they were all there.

"Did y'all start the prayer meeting without me?" he asked with a grin, as he was pulling off his hat and gloves.

"Welcome, brother," Wynn Bayard answered, with a smile. "Come in and receive the word of the Lord."

Gus bowed slightly in Bayard's direction, then shook the hands of the other three men in the room. "In case you're wondering," he said, looking back at Bayard, "Tommy is at his post, awake and alert. A devil of a night to draw sentinel duty."

"Good," Bayard said perfunctorily. "Now let us get down to business," he said, as he sat down on one of the four rough-hewn benches below the crude pulpit. Gus and the other three men sat down too, facing Bayard.

"Things are developing rapidly, gentlemen," Bayard said. "The hour we have been patiently awaiting is fast approaching. Please listen carefully.

"General Arnold is in Virginia and is moving west from Williamsburg toward Richmond. There is nothing to oppose him but rebel militia, and not much of that. There are reports, I do not know how reliable they are, saying that he has a large army and will sweep across Virginia. Whether in our direction or not, we still don't know," Bayard said. Looking directly at Gus, he asked, "Gus, can you get away for a few days without attracting any suspicion?"

"Yes, sir," Gus answered. "I believe so."

"Good," Bayard said. "Then you need to go and find General Arnold. Get instructions—orders. Tell him we need powder and arms and determine what we are to do. Ask him if we are to cooperate with his command, or with that of Lord Cornwallis. Impress upon him that our mission must be more modest than last time, if we are to have any hope of success. Seizing the lead mines or freeing the prisoners in Charlottesville—those things are beyond our capability."

Gus nodded. "Yes, sir," he said.

"Tell him," Bayard began, before stopping abruptly. "Can you remember all this, Gus?"

"Of course," Gus responded quickly, feeling insulted and not trying to conceal the fact.

Bayard smiled gently, then continued. "Tell him there is a rumor that Washington is dispatching Continental regulars to oppose him. I do not know how reliable that rumor is. Tell him that Jefferson has retreated to Charlottesville and the rebel legislature has disbursed. Tell him that William Washington's dragoons are attached to Morgan's army and are now camped on the Pacolet River in South Carolina, cooperating with the rebel militia there. Got that?"

"Yes, sir," Gus answered with a nod. "But wouldn't it be better to send that last bit to Lord Cornwallis instead?"

"Too dangerous, and the message would not reach him in time to matter," Bayard answered. "General Arnold likely won't be able to use the information either, but this will help show what kind of intelligence we have access to." Bayard paused to make sure Gus understood, then continued, "Tell him the rebel militia here is short of essential provisions and draft animals. Their paper money is increasingly worthless. I suspect they will have to begin aggressively impressing food and supplies from the citizens soon, which will generate resentment that will work to our favor.

"Tell him that until a sizable body of the King's men are near us, our best role may be sabotage and intelligence. Once armed and properly supported, we can rise in force."

Gus nodded thoughtfully. "Got it," he said.

"All right, Gus. Be careful," Bayard said.

Bayard looked at the other three men, the flickering candlelight throwing shadows across their faces. "Tell your men to make ready, gentlemen," he said. "With Lord Cornwallis marching through Carolina and General Arnold liberating Virginia, our time to rise is fast approaching. The rebels are being whipped. They will get more desperate now. They will intensify their efforts to find us. Instruct your men that while we are waiting, they should be careful to keep their loyalty concealed. At all costs. Tell them to sign whatever the rebels tell them to sign, to take whatever oath they demand. Done in the service of the King, these are not sins. Remember, Captains, that it is crucial to our success that we protect against betrayal and forced confessions. Your men are to know the names of no Loyalists other than those in his own company. The other officers are known only to us in this room, and we must take that information with us to our graves if need be."

The men answered him with somber nods.

"It is time to change our signals," Bayard said. "The new sign will be 'Psalms,' countersign 'five-ten.'"

"Psalms 5:10?" one of the men asked quietly. "What does it say?"

Bayard smiled and answered, "Destroy thou them, O God; let them fall by their own counsels; cast them out in the multitude of their transgressions; for they have rebelled against thee."

The men chuckled. "Amen," one said.

"You're going to make Bible scholars of us yet,

Reverend," another added.

"Remember it, gentlemen. Sign: Psalms. Countersign: five-ten."

They nodded. "Got it," one of them said.

Bayard then looked directly at Gus. "When can you leave?" he asked.

"In the morning," he answered. "First thing."

"Very good," Bayard said. "God be with you. And God save the King."

"God save the King," the men answered.

5

Pittsylvania Courthouse
Pittsylvania County, Virginia
January 8, 1781

Dodd Lightfoot's horse snorted and pawed the ground impatiently. "Steady, girl," he said, leaning forward in the saddle and patting her on the neck, while keeping his attention focused on the porch of the Cherrystone Meetinghouse, the county's temporary courthouse, where stood a tall black-clad man wearing a tricorne hat, waving his arms while delivering an impassioned speech to the several dozen people standing at the base of the steps.

"The cause of liberty is the cause of God!" the man shouted. "This is not a time to sit idle, depending on others to do your fighting for you. This is the time for men to plead the cause of their country before the Lord with their blood! Cursed be he who would keepeth his sword from blood in this sacred war!" he thundered, drawing scattered cheers from some in his audience, while a few others turned and walked quietly away.

Another horse and rider ambled up beside Dodd. "What's all that about?" the rider asked.

Dodd turned to face the rider, Billy Lewis, a neighbor from Maple Grove. "Hey Billy," he said. Turning back to face the courthouse, he continued, "Mr. Clay is preaching up a storm. I think he's fixing to start calling down the fire and brimstone."

"And yet," Clay boomed, "there might be some persons present who would rather bow their necks in abject slavery than to face a man at arms! Such men will never deserve the liberty won for them by braver men."

"Listen at him," Billy said dismissively. "Maybe *he* ought to enlist. You here for the draft?"

"Yep," Dodd answered. "First one since I came of age. I figured it would have gone off by now, but Reverend Clay is trying to drum up volunteers first."

"Maybe our numbers won't get pulled," Billy said.

"I think I'm going to volunteer," Dodd replied, while Clay continued his exhortation.

"Ain't no sense in that, Dodd," Billy answered. "If they need you, they'll draft you. I had to go in last year and let me tell you, it ain't nothing but a lot of drilling, eating sorry food, and marching around till your shoes are plumb wore out."

"I don't know," Dodd said, distantly. "I think it's different this time." He nodded toward the courthouse, "And the things he's saying make sense to me. I want to do my part."

Billy sighed, listened to Clay for a few moments, then said, "Looks like this windbag is going to be a while." Turning to Dodd abruptly he said, "Want to race?"

Dodd looked back at him and beamed. "Heck yeah!" he answered.

"Let's go then," Billy replied as they both turned

their horses out into the road and trotted away.

The quarter mile stretch down Court Street was a favorite for races, but today was far too crowded with horses and wagons, so they rode instead toward the end of Mountain Street, where it joined Court Street from the west. "We got a race!" Billy shouted, as they crossed the busy street, causing many in the crowd to drop what they were doing and hurry over.

They stopped at the intersection, facing west, Billy on the left and Dodd on the right. Billy stood in his stirrups and shouted again, "We got a race!" and a few people scurried off the road and took places to watch.

As they waited for the road to clear, they heard someone call out, "Hold on, boys!" William Short, the owner of one of the taverns on the street, hurried over. He stepped in front of the horses, giving them a quick look over. "I'll spot," he said. "Wait for my signal." Stepping out into the street he hollered, "Even odds!" as he walked briskly away.

Dodd chuckled as he watched Short moving down the road, darting from side to side to take bets from the bystanders.

Billy leaned over and asked, "So, what's the wager, Dodd?"

"How about a round at Mr. Short's?" Dodd answered.

"Winner's choice?" Billy asked.

"Sure," Dodd said, with a grin.

Billy stuck out his hand, "You're on," he said.

Dodd shook his hand with a laugh. "You might want to keep your eyes closed, Billy. We're fixing to be kicking mud into your face."

Billy snorted. "I'll be waiting for you at the finish line," he said, smiling.

As they watched Short marking a finish line a quarter mile down the street, Dodd leaned forward and patted his horse on the neck. "Dig hard, girl," he whispered, as Billy pulled out a little switch from underneath his saddle. After a few moments, Short turned and faced them, his right arm raised and holding a handkerchief. Dodd and Billy took racing crouches, and the horses began to squirm restlessly. Then suddenly Short thrust down his arm and both boys shouted and spurred their mounts.

The two horses surged forward in an instant, going from standing still to a full gallop almost immediately—both being descended from animals that for generations had been bred as sprinters, easily able to run a quarter mile in less than 30 seconds. At the start Dodd's horse had pulled slightly to the left, causing her to brush against Billy's horse. Dodd quickly pulled her back straight, but by the time he did Billy had gained a half-length lead.

The horses thundered down the street, kicking up little clods of red clay mud, and the boys could hear the shouts of the spectators as the buildings rushed by and the finish line drew closer. Shouting encouragement and giving a little kick with his spurs every few seconds, Dodd saw as they reached the half-way mark that he wasn't closing the gap with Billy.

As they passed the mark, Billy quickly glanced to his right and saw nothing but the other side of the street. He knew he had a lead but didn't know by how much. Fighting the urge to turn and look over his shoulder, he decided that he should prod his horse, to assure that she kept full speed. Releasing his right hand from the reins, he reached back with the switch to swat the horse's flank, not realizing that Dodd's horse was only inches to his side, so that when he reached back, his hand brushed the front flank of Dodd's horse, surprising both Billy and the horse. Billy fumbled his grip on the switch, and it fell to the road as Dodd's horse surged forward, pulling nose to nose. With a hundred yards remaining, both riders crouched low, lightly spurred their horses again, and galloped to the finish, sprinting across the line side by side.

As soon as they crossed the line, both boys stood in their stirrups and loosened their grip on the reins, signaling their horses to wind down. When they had slowed to a trot, Dodd called out with a laugh, "Looks like you owe me a round, Billy!"

"You wish!" Billy exclaimed in response. "I beat you by at least a head."

As they both wheeled their horses back toward the street, Dodd answered, "You must have had your eyes closed. We beat you plain as day. Even with your interference."

"Interference?" Billy answered, incredulously.

"You hit my horse," Dodd replied.

"I barely touched her," Billy said. "And you should be glad for it. That's the only reason you were able to close. The only interference was when you bumped me at the start."

"Ha!" Dodd said, as they ambled back toward the finish line. "That was barely any contact at all. And it was the only reason you took a lead."

Billy laughed and shook his head. "Well, let's see what Mr. Short says," he said.

As they slowly approached the finish line, the boys saw that Short was standing in the middle of a tumultuous crowd of shouting people, trying in vain to calm them.

"Looks like it must have been close," Dodd said with a laugh.

"Hey, Mr. Short!" Billy shouted. "Who won?"

Without looking at them, Short raised his left hand, palm toward them, while he continued arguing with the crowd. It seemed as if they were all speaking at once and neither boy could make out what they were saying.

They watched the argument for a few more seconds, amused. "It appears that there is some disagreement among the citizenry," Dodd said with a chuckle.

"Yes," Billy answered playfully. "And I predict the controversy will not be resolved any time soon."

"Well," Dodd said, turning his horse. "I reckon we ought to go check on the draft."

"Might as well," Billy answered, as he shook his reins to start his horse. After they had ridden for a few seconds he added, "I should have carried my whip in my other hand. I would have beat you easy then."

"Excuses," Dodd said, choosing to let it drop.

As they approached the courthouse, the boys could see that the crowd was gone and that John Wilson, the County Lieutenant, was standing on the porch, tacking a piece of paper to the courthouse door. They rode slowly up to the bottom of the steps. Without dismounting, Dodd spoke.

"Hey Colonel Wilson, we just come to see if our numbers got pulled."

Wilson turned around and looked at the boys for a moment. "Are you old enough, Dodd?" he asked.

"Yes, sir," Dodd answered. "I just had my birthday."

"So you are in Captain Wrenn's company?" Wilson asked.

"Yes, sir," Dodd answered.

Wilson shook his head. "No. No one was drafted in that company. Your company's quota was all filled by volunteers."

Dodd let out a disappointed sigh.

"What about me, Colonel Wilson?" Billy asked.

Wilson stood looking back at him for a few moments, as if trying to place him.

"William Lewis," Billy said. "Captain Morton's company."

Wilson nodded, "Right. Lewis." He looked at the sheet of paper on the door, running his finger down a column of names. Turning back, he said, "Yes. You were drafted. Report here Wednesday morning at eight o'clock."

Billy groaned at the news, as Wilson turned back around and continued tacking up the notice. "I can't go, Dodd," Billy said softly. "I can't go. My sister needs my help, and I can't leave her."

"Tell Colonel Wilson that," Dodd answered. "Maybe he'll let you off."

"It don't work that way," Billy replied.

"Well, it's too bad they drew you instead of me. I wouldn't mind going myself," Dodd said.

Billy turned to him and spoke rapidly, "Then take my place, Dodd. Substitute for me."

"What? Substitute for you?"

"Sure! You just said you wanted to go in. Then substitute for me. All you gotta do is tell them you agree to take my place," Billy said, pleading.

"I don't know, Billy," Dodd answered, dubious. "I reckon I ought to stay with my company."

"Come on, Dodd. You want to go, and I don't. It's doing us both a favor."

Dodd shook his head. "I'll reckon I'll just wait till it's my turn."

"I'll pay you!" Billy said, urgently.

Dodd looked at him, curiosity in his eyes. "Pay me what?" he asked.

"I'll pay you to take my place. Substitutes always get paid," Billy said.

"Pay me what?" Dodd repeated.

"I'll pay you fifteen hundred dollars," Billy said. "That's twice the enlistment bounty."

Dodd laughed. "Fifteen hundred dollars?" he asked, laughing again. "Paper?"

Billy nodded.

"The only thing that's good for is wiping my arse," Dodd replied. "What else you got?"

Billy hesitated a moment, then blurted out, "How about this horse?"

Dodd looked surprised. "Your mare?" he asked. Nodding to the horse Billy was sitting on he said, "Her?"

"Yep," Billy answered. "She's worth at least fifty dollars in hard money."

Dodd hesitated, and Billy could see that he was wavering.

"You've seen how fast she is, Dodd," he said.

Dodd looked carefully at the horse. After a pause, he said thoughtfully, "Yeah. She seems like a good horse."

"Take my place and she's yours," Billy said.

Dodd weighed the transaction in his mind. Remembering that he had been on the verge of volunteering and thinking of the foals Billy's horse might someday produce, he pondered the offer for a few seconds, then suddenly stuck out his hand. "Deal!"

he exclaimed.

Billy grabbed his hand and shook it, "Deal," he answered.

Dodd glanced back at the courthouse and saw that Wilson was walking down the steps. "Colonel Wilson!" he shouted.

Wilson stopped and looked up. "Yes?" he said.

"I'm going to substitute for Billy," Dodd said.

"Are you sure you want to do that?" Wilson asked. "This is a three-month tour."

"Yes, sir. We done worked it out," Dodd answered, with Billy nodding beside him.

"All right, boys," Wilson replied. "Come on in and we'll do the paperwork," he said, before turning around and beginning to climb the stairs back to the courthouse.

Dodd and Billy dismounted, tied their horses to the hitching post, and followed Wilson into the building.

6

Lightfoot Farm
Maple Grove
Pittsylvania County, Virginia
January 8, 1781

Alice Lightfoot was incredulous. "What?" she said. "How can that be, son? Elisha just got back from Mr. Wrenn's not more than a half hour ago and he said the company filled its quota with volunteers."

"My number didn't get called," Dodd replied. "I substituted for Billy Lewis."

"You did what?!" she exclaimed.

"I made a smart bargain, Mama. Billy gave me his mare to take his place. She's good looking and spirited. I was fixing to volunteer anyway, so the way I see it, I got me a free horse out of the deal," Dodd said with a grin, stretching the truth.

"Dodd," Alice answered, her face flushed with anger, stamping her foot in frustration, "what you have done is foolish! Very foolish!"

Just as his mother's outburst ended, the door opened, and his father and his brother Elisha stepped into the house. As they were removing their coats and hanging them by the door, Elisha, eight years older than Dodd, laughed. "Oh, no. What has he done now?"

"This isn't a laughing matter, Elisha," Alice said angrily. Turning to her husband, she continued. "Laz, that Lewis boy somehow tricked Dodd into substituting for him."

As Dodd began to protest, his father raised a hand and silenced him.

"Did you substitute for him?" he asked.

"Yes, sir," Dodd answered.

"Why did you do it?"

"For two reasons," Dodd answered. "One is that he gave me a fine horse to take his place. The other is that I want to be there to help take Benedict Arnold's scalp."

Laz and Elisha both laughed, to the chagrin of Alice.

"Those aren't bad reasons, son," Laz said. "But you need to wait until your company is called. It will better if you and your brother are together." After a pause, he turned to Alice and said, "I'll go see Colonel Wilson about it. I'm sure I can get it undone."

"That ain't right, Pa!" Dodd protested. "I'm able to make my own decisions."

Laz turned to his son, face stern, and opened his mouth to speak, before being interrupted by Elisha.

"Who filled out the substitution paperwork?" Elisha asked Dodd.

"Colonel Wilson," Dodd answered.

Elisha turned to face his father. "I don't know, Pa. Maybe it isn't a good idea to tell Colonel Wilson that Dodd didn't know what he was doing, since Colonel Wilson is the man who signed him up."

"This is nonsense!" Alice interjected. "The Lewis boy took advantage of Dodd. It is as simple as that."

"That ain't what happened at all, Ma!" Dodd protested.

"It seems like to me," Elisha said, "that if it looks like Pa is trying to get Dodd out of his bargain, someone might say that his family don't regard Dodd as a man. Or someone might say Dodd got cold feet."

The room erupted in protests, with Dodd's the loudest. "No one will call me a coward!" he shouted.

After a few moments, Laz raised his hands and his voice. "Everyone quiet down. Now!"

They all fell silent in obedience.

Laz looked thoughtfully at Dodd, who was trembling with anger. "Son," he said, "I don't agree with what you done. You ought to have waited your turn."

Dodd started to speak, but Laz raised his hand, stopping him.

"A man must honor his contracts, his word. You made a deal and so, you must honor it." He turned to face his wife, "I've changed my mind. It ain't right for me to interfere in this, Alice. Dodd is old enough to make his own decisions on this."

Knowing she had been defeated, Alice didn't try to argue. Looking at her feet, she nodded her head slightly.

"I want to fight for my country, Pa. For our liberty," Dodd said.

Laz reached out and put his hand on Dodd's shoulder. "I know you do, son. I'm proud of you for it. When do you report?"

"Wednesday morning," Dodd answered.

"All right. Tomorrow we'll get you ready to go. You

and Elisha go do the milking now," Laz said.

They both mumbled yessirs, took down their coats and stepped outside. When the door closed behind them, Laz stepped over to his wife and wrapped her in a hug.

~~~

Three miles away, Jennie Lewis looked up at her brother Billy. "Aren't you going to need that horse?" she asked wearily, before looking back down at the sewing in her lap.

"I couldn't let them draft me," Billy answered. "Not now."

"Hmm…" Jennie said, not looking up.

"You need to go, Jennie," Billy said. "Go to Wilmington. You can stay with the Parkers. You know that. You need to go now."

Jennie shook her head. Without looking up, she said, "Not yet."

"When then?" Billy asked, impatiently.

Jennie shrugged her shoulders, continuing to sew. "When I have to," she said. Then looking up into her brother's concerned face she added, "But not yet."

Billy shook his head and sighed deeply. He stood facing his sister for a few moments, beating back the desire to argue with her.

"I've got to take Bella over to the Lightfoot place," he said at last.

Jennie continued sewing, making no response.

"Maybe Dodd will give me a ride home," he said, again drawing no response. "If not, I reckon I'll walk."

Jennie nodded slightly, continuing to sew.
~~~

7

Trabue's Tavern
Chesterfield County, Virginia
January 8, 1781

After securing a bed for the night, and fodder and a stall for his horse, Gus had settled onto a bench at a table in the back of the tavern. Although he would have preferred to be closer to the fire, he chose a place where he could eat alone, and from which he could see the door while he ate. He was spooning up beans from his plate when three men entered the tavern. Gus glanced up, briefly making eye contact with one of the men, then turned his eyes back down to his plate, sensing something troubling. The first of the three men to enter walked directly toward Gus's table, the other two following him. When they reached the table, the men stood silently for a few moments, staring down at Gus, who did not look up. Then the first man spoke.

"I haven't seen you here before," he said.

Gus glanced up, staring at the man. After a few moments he said, "I haven't been here before," then looked back down at this plate and resumed eating.

The man who had spoken to him remained standing, directly across from Gus, between him and the door. The other two men fanned out, flanking him on both sides.

"What's your name?" the man demanded.

Gus glanced up again, regarding the man for a few seconds. "Smith," he said. "Augustine Smith."

"Augustine?" the man replied loudly. "What kind of a name is that?"

Gus spooned another mouthful of beans, then picked up the slice of cornbread on his plate, took a bite, chewed for a few moments, then swallowed. As he began to spoon up another bite, he said, without looking up, "An august one."

The two men on his flanks glanced up at the man in the middle, who kept his eyes fixed on Gus.

"Which side are you on?" the man asked, demandingly.

Gus looked up at him calmly, while with his left hand, under the table, he carefully slid a knife out of his boot and laid it across his lap. "That depends," he answered. "Who's winning?"

The faces of the two men on the flanks turned fierce. One shot a glance at the man in the middle, as if seeking instructions.

"The man who owns this tavern is a Patriot," the man said.

Gus looked up indifferently. "Is he?" he said. Picking up his tankard and tilting it at the man, he said, "To his health," before taking a sip and setting the tankard back down on the table.

Gus resumed eating, appearing to have no further interest in the three men staring down at him. After a few moments the man in the middle laughed loudly and dropped onto the bench across the table from Gus. His comrades continued to stand, on either side of the table.

"So, where are you heading, Mr. August Smith?" he asked, putting sarcastic emphasis on "Smith."

"Richmond," Gus answered, without looking up, his left hand tightening its grip on the knife in his lap.

"Why are you going to Richmond?" the man asked.

Gus looked up at him, chewed his food for a second, swallowed, then said, "Why do you ask so many questions?"

The man leaned forward, bringing his face close to Gus's. "Well, Mr. August Smith, for one reason there's three of us and only one of you. For another, you have to be careful with strangers in times like these."

Gus kept eye contact with the man for a few seconds, then dropped his gaze to his plate and continued eating. "Nothing to do at home," he said, while chewing. "Going to Richmond to look for some seasonal work."

"Ha!" the man laughed. "I reckon you ain't heard about Richmond."

Gus looked up, then shook his head slightly.

"I don't know if this is good news or bad news for a man seeking 'seasonal work,'" the man said, "but Benedict Arnold burned Richmond down two days ago."

Gus looked at him for a few moments, then shrugged and continued eating.

The man contemplated Gus a few more seconds then laughed loudly again. Looking back over his shoulder toward the bar he shouted, "Rum!" Then he turned to the other two men and with a nod signaled that they should sit. They dropped onto the bench on either side of Gus.

"I like your style, Mr. August Smith," the man said, with a chuckle. "Let's have some rum and maybe we can help you locate some 'seasonal work.'"

By the time they were on their second pail of rum, Gus having surreptitiously poured most of his out on the floor, the man who was obviously the leader had become even more boisterous. "All right, Mr. August Smith, I have a proposition for you," he announced. "A business proposition."

Gus arched his eyebrows. "What?" he asked.

The man lowered his voice. "We could use another man to assist us in some commercial matters. Matters that will require discretion. Some flexibility in political allegiances would also be of benefit."

After a few silent moments, Gus asked, "What's in it for me?"

"Coin!" the man exclaimed, grinning. "The profits from our enterprise can be substantial. Just the thing for a man in need of 'seasonal work.'"

"All right," Gus said. "I'll consider it."

"Good!" the man said, slapping the table.

"We'll collect you here tomorrow evening," the man said, before standing and extending his hand to Gus.

Gus took his hand and shook it. "Your name, sir?" he asked.

The man laughed. "My name? Let's see… I reckon I'll have to think on that. I would say 'Smith,' but that one is already being used," he said, with a gleam in his eyes. "Come on, boys. Let's leave Mr. Smith alone so he can get some rest." As the other two men stood up, the man put his palms on the table and leaned forward, looking directly at Gus. "We will see you tomorrow,

Mr. Smith," he said, before laughing and marching away with the other two.

Gus waited a few minutes, then climbed the stairs to the sleeping quarters. Seeing that the other traveler with whom he was to share a bed was already asleep, and snoring loudly, Gus slipped off his boots then settled onto the straw mattress, disturbing the other man enough to interrupt the snoring. He stared up into the darkness of the rafters and pondered his options. If what the man said was true, if Richmond had been burned, then going there would be too dangerous, he reasoned. Better to try to slip in behind the lines, and better to be long gone by the time his three new acquaintances come calling for him tomorrow. Gus closed his eyes and tried to relax, knowing that a little rest would help him through the long, cold night awaiting him. He eventually drifted off to sleep, only to be jolted awake when the snoring resumed.

Gus sighed softly, then sat up and eased out of the bed. He slipped on his boots and coat and crept quietly down the stairs by the light of the dying fire, then stepped out the door into the cold night, lit brightly by a nearly full moon.

He slid open the stable door wide enough to allow him to quickly step inside, then pulled it shut behind him. In the dark he stepped in the direction of the stall where he had put his horse earlier that evening, stumbling over something on the floor as he did.

The stableboy woke suddenly when Gus stepped on him, springing to his feet, expecting to be facing a robber, his hands clenched in fists. Gus could barely see the boy in the darkness of the stable, but he sensed his tension and the fear.

"Sorry about that," he said, trying to lighten the

moment. "Didn't see you there. Just coming to get my horse. I need to get an early start."

The stableboy relaxed a little but kept his eyes cautiously on Gus as he reached behind him and took a lantern down from the wall. He struck a match, lit the candle in the lantern and closed the glass door, as the glow illuminated the area. "An early start?" he said, dubiously. "It ain't even one o'clock yet."

"I've got a long ride ahead of me," Gus replied. "I need to get going."

The stableboy held the lantern up higher and looked Gus over carefully, until satisfied he was looking at the same man who had delivered the horse that evening. "All right. That's your hoss yonder," he said, nodding toward a stall.

"Has he been fed and watered?" Gus asked.

"Yes, sir," the boy replied. "I'll saddle him up for you."

When the boy was finished, Gus handed him a few bills, which the boy took without attempting to hide his disappointment at being given paper.

"Best be on my way," Gus said. "It's a long ride into Richmond."

The boy nodded, stuffing the bills into his coat pocket.

"How long do you reckon it will take me to get to Richmond from here?" Gus asked.

The boy shrugged. "Four hours, maybe. No more than five. Long as you keep a good moon."

"Good. All right then," Gus said as he led the horse outside, positioning it next to a mounting block. He stepped up onto the block, then swung a leg across his saddle and mounted the horse. The stableboy watched him ride away, heading north.

Gus was out of sight of the tavern when he came to the first crossroads. He looked around and seeing no one, veered his horse to the right, to the east, away from Richmond.

For four hours he plodded along the country road, rubbing his hands together every few minutes to keep them warm, the silence of the night interrupted only once, by a distant barking dog. When Gus finally reached the ferry at Bermuda Hundred, there was no one there, and it was still almost two hours till sunrise.

He dismounted and stretched his aching legs. Reaching into his saddlebag, he brought out an ear of corn and offered it to his horse, who took it eagerly. Looking around again and confirming that the landing was deserted, he was just about to sit down when a man suddenly appeared out of the edge of the woods, the moonlight revealing that he was carrying a musket, which was leveled at Gus.

"What's your business?" the man asked.

"Come to take the ferry across," Gus answered calmly.

"Ain't no ferry," the man replied, keeping his musket aimed at Gus.

"When is the next crossing?" Gus asked.

"Ain't no crossing," the man replied. "Ain't you heard? Colonel Goode's orders. No boats to cross."

"Nope. I'm just in from Buckingham. Hadn't heard anything about that," Gus replied. "Why no crossings?"

"Have you been living under a rock?" the man asked, testily. "The British army is on the other side of that river." After a pause he continued, "I'm wondering if maybe that's why you want to get over there."

"I'm on my way to see my sister. She lives in Charles City. She's sick and her family sent for me," Gus said.

The man didn't answer and in the dim moonlight Gus was unable to read his expression.

"I'll pay well for a ride across," he said.

The man remained silent for a few moments, then said, "Ain't no crossing."

"If I can't cross here, I'll have to go all the way to Richmond and come in from there," Gus said.

"'Spect so," the man answered.

Gus sighed. "All right," he said, taking a hold on his pommel, then swinging himself up onto his saddle. "Sorry to have bothered you," he said, touching the edge of his hat and then riding slowly away. He rode for about a minute, then looked back over his shoulder. The man was still standing there, in the distance, in the road, holding the musket. As his horse carried him around a bend, and out of sight of the man at the ferry, Gus turned back around, and was startled to discover a dark-faced boy standing in the middle of the road.

Gus stopped his horse, directly in front of the boy.

"You want to go across?" the boy asked. "I can take you."

"How?" Gus asked.

"I got a boat," the boy said.

Gus pondered the boy for a few seconds. "How much?" he asked.

"What you got?" the boy replied.

"I'll pay you a hundred dollars to take me across," Gus answered.

"Paper?" the boy asked.

Gus nodded.

"You got any silver?"

"I'll pay you silver to bring me back," Gus said.

The boy thought for a few moments, then said, "All right. This way." He turned and walked into the woods, toward the river.

Gus dismounted and followed the boy, leading the horse by the reins. After a few minutes they came to a swampy cove and the boy began pulling back a pile of brush, revealing a canoe.

"What about my horse?" Gus asked.

The boy looked back at him, amused. "Ain't got room for him in the boat," he said. "You can tie him up here. Cain't nobody see him here."

Gus tied the horse to a tree, then fed him another ear of corn from the saddlebag as the boy began pushing the canoe out into the water. "Come on," he said. "We best get over before the sun comes up. It's bad enough with the moon being so bright."

Gus climbed into the canoe and the boy used a paddle to push them away from the bank. "Stay real quiet, sir," the boy said. "You might want to get down as far as you can. Ain't nobody gonna mind me so much, long as it looks like I'm by myself."

The boy steered the canoe across the river, being careful not to make splashes with his paddle, as Gus tried to squat, even though he realized there was no way to conceal himself in the canoe. After a few uncomfortable minutes they glided to a spot on the opposite riverbank, overhung with vines and brambles. Pushing through, the boy sidled up to a large fallen oak and tied the canoe to it. He stepped carefully out onto the trunk of the tree, then walked down it a few feet to the shore. Gus stood up and followed the boy, gingerly making his way across the tree and onto land.

"I'll be back here at nightfall," Gus said. Reaching into his coat pocket, he brought out a purse, opened it and took out a silver coin. "I'll give you this when I come back. Is it a deal?"

The boy nodded. "Yes, sir."

"I expect you to be here, and I expect my horse to be where I left him when we get back," Gus said, sternly.

"That horse ain't going nowhere," the boy answered.

"There's some corn in the saddlebag. Give him some of it in a little while."

"All right," the boy answered.

Gus furrowed his brow. "If you're not here, or if anything happens to my horse, I'll come looking for you," he said. "And I'll need to tell about your little ferry business."

"I'll be here at dark," the boy said. "Long as you still got that money."

Gus nodded and the boy walked back onto the log, toward his canoe.

"Wait!" Gus called out, causing the boy to look back at him. "Where are the British?"

"They all over," the boy replied. "But most of 'em are down at Berkeley. Down the river."

"All right," Gus replied. "Don't forget to feed my horse."

Without answering, the boy turned and climbed into the canoe.

Realizing that he could no longer feel his fingers, Gus pulled off his gloves and blew on them, while vigorously rubbing his hands together. "What have you gotten yourself into?" he said aloud, looking around. After a few seconds he began walking inland, soon reaching a road and turning east. He had only walked a couple hundred yards when two men stepped out from behind trees on either side of the road. Both were wearing green jackets and black leather hats adorned with silver crescents. Both held bayonet-tipped muskets, leveled menacingly at him.

8

Berkeley Plantation
Charles City County, Virginia
January 9, 1781

"He was walking down the road, alone. Claims he's got a message for General Arnold."

Gus had been marched about a mile by one of the two men who apprehended him. The sun had risen by the time they reached what appeared to Gus to be a camp, beside the river and behind an imposing brick manor house. The place was buzzing with activity. Men were striking tents, harnessing teams, and loading wagons. Black men, women and children were hurriedly carrying furniture, paintings, and household items from inside the house, piling them out back to the shouted commands of red-coated officers. His captor pushed him along, into the camp, bringing him to a halt before the man he was now facing. The man wore the same green uniform as the man who had marched him there, except that this man wore a sword belt and had an epaulet on one of his shoulders. "A message for General Arnold?" the officer said, looking inquisitively at Gus.

"Yes, sir," Gus answered. "I am Captain Augustine Johnson of the King's Halifax Militia."

The officer regarded Gus for a few moments, dubiously, then extended his hand. "Good morning, sir. I am Lieutenant Colonel John Simcoe. Queen's Rangers."

Gus took his hand, shaking it with relief.

"I hope you will not think me discourteous, sir, if I tell you that your claim strikes me as improbable," Simcoe said, deflating Gus. "Has he been searched, Private?"

"Yes, sir," the private answered. "He was unarmed, except for this, which was in his boot," he said, showing the officer Gus's knife.

"Return it to him," Simcoe said.

The soldier handed the knife to Gus, who took it and slid it into his boot.

"You will understand our need for caution, sir," Simcoe said. "There are spies and rebels about. Thieves and smugglers as well."

Gus nodded.

"You say you have a message for the general? Give it to me and I will see that he gets it."

"The message is oral, sir."

"Well then," Simcoe answered, showing impatience. "Speak it to me."

Gus hesitated. Over Simcoe's shoulder he could see a tall officer in a red uniform, walking with a limp while barking out orders. He decided to take a chance.

"General Arnold, sir!" he shouted.

Taken aback momentarily, Simcoe quickly recovered. "Arrest him, Private," he said, angrily.

Quickly stepping between Gus and Simcoe, the private shoved Gus with the butt of his musket.

"March," he ordered.

Gus stood firmly as the private raised his gun for another blow, just as the general arrived.

"Who called me?" he demanded. "What do you want?"

Gus pushed past the private and blurted out, "General Arnold, I am Captain Augustine Johnson of the King's Halifax militia."

"Yes," Arnold said. "What is your business here?"

"Sir, our colonel has sent me to request instructions—your orders, sir. We are prepared to strike," Gus said.

"Good," Arnold said. "Do it."

"Sir, we need arms and ammunition," Gus said.

"Take them from the rebels. Then march here and join me," Arnold answered.

"We cannot reveal ourselves without assistance, sir," Gus said. "Respectfully, if you could send a force into our area, the people will rally to the King."

"Where are you from?" Arnold said, growing impatient.

"Halifax County, sir. South of here."

"Halifax County? I have no time for this," Arnold said, gruffly. Turning to Simcoe he said, "Colonel, when the house is emptied, see that all the contents are burned."

"Yes, sir," Simcoe answered.

"The contents only," Arnold said. "Not the home. I think I shall claim it as a residence once the rebellion is crushed."

"Yes, sir," Simcoe said.

As Arnold turned to leave, Gus called out. "I have intelligence as well, sir."

Arnold turned and faced him. "What intelligence?"

"Colonel William Washington's dragoons have joined with Daniel Morgan and are encamped on the Pacolet River in South Carolina, operating against local Loyalists," Gus said.

"South Carolina?" Arnold said, disdainfully. "South Carolina?? Well maybe I'll just hop down there and engage him."

"We realize the information may be of limited value now, but we share it to show the kind of information we can obtain," Gus said.

Arnold shook his head in disgust and turned to leave.

"Jefferson has retreated to Charlottesville," Gus said quickly.

Arnold turned back around and stepped closer, looking Gus directly in the face. "Sir," he said, speaking slowly, "Jefferson is back in Richmond and has been for days." He turned to Simcoe. "Colonel Simcoe, interrogate this man thoroughly. If he is a spy, hang him. If he is merely an idiot, expel him."

"Yes, sir," Simcoe said, as Arnold walked away.

Once Arnold was out of earshot, Simcoe spoke to Gus. "Well, Mr. Johnson, it seems that I am under orders both to burn Mr. Harrison's furniture and to interrogate and hang you. I find neither assignment particularly appealing. Which should I attend to first?"

Gus glared angrily at Simcoe and was about to speak when a familiar voice came from behind him. "Well, if it isn't my friend Mr. Smith." The man from the tavern stepped up to him. "Did you get lost on your way to Richmond?" the man asked with a laugh.

"Larkin, do you know this man?" Simcoe asked. "If he is a friend of yours, then I'm even more inclined to hang him."

"He was at the tavern in Chesterfield last night," Larkin answered. "Said his name was Smith."

"I chose not to reveal my name to men whose allegiances were unknown to me," Gus answered, defensively.

"He is under suspicion of being a rebel spy," Simcoe said.

Larkin shook his head. "He's not a rebel," he said. "At least he's not one from around here. He's traveling alone. Came from the south. I pegged him as a Tory."

"I am an officer in the King's militia," Gus said.

"Well, all you are to me right now is a nuisance," Simcoe said. "Private, escort this man out of camp. If you see him around here again, shoot him."

The soldier stepped toward Gus, preparing to shove him with his musket, when Gus spoke, testily, "Sir, I resent this. I have risked my life for my King and country and…"

Simcoe interrupted, raising his hand. "That may be, sir, and if that is the case then I wish you well. But we have been marching and fighting for nine straight days and I simply have no time to deal with men like you."

Gus furrowed his brow and opened his mouth to speak but was interrupted by Simcoe again. "I do not have authority to give you orders, Mr. Johnson, or Smith, or whoever you are. But I am not prevented from giving advice and expressing opinions. If you truly are with the loyal militia, then I recommend you gather your men and come join us here. If that is not possible, then prepare to cooperate with our army when we are nearer. In the meantime, disrupt the enemy any way you can. Godspeed, sir. Now, begone."

As Simcoe turned and walked away, the private shoved Gus with this musket. "Come on," he said.

"Let's go."

As Gus and the soldier marched away, Larkin shouted out with a laugh, "So long, Mr. Smith! Let's treat our appointment for this evening as canceled."

9

Pittsylvania Courthouse
Pittsylvania County, Virginia
January 10, 1781

From atop a gray stallion standing directly in front of the courthouse steps, a mounted adjutant by his side, Colonel Peter Perkins shouted out, "Assemble by companies! Fall in, men!"

Perkins and his adjutant were wearing tri-corner hats and blue uniform coats, with epaulets on their shoulders and swords hanging by their sides. But nearly all of the several hundred other men who had been gathering on the courthouse lawn for the past hour, were, like Dodd, wearing fringed hunting shirts, buckskin breeches, and slouch hats. Some were carrying shotguns, muskets, or rifles, with powder horns or cartridge boxes hanging over their shoulders. Most were, like Dodd, unarmed, save for knives or tomahawks tucked into their belts.

Dodd knew nearly all the men who had arrived that morning, gathering to chat in small clusters along the street and in front of the courthouse. A dozen or more times he had explained that, yes, he knew that his number had not been called, but that he had agreed to substitute for Billy Lewis. Invariably they had asked why Billy had gotten a substitute and each time he answered that Billy had said it wasn't a good time for him to leave his sister.

As the men began to assemble, Dodd walked toward where Captain Joseph Morton's company was gathering. Even though he had known Morton for many years, he did not know him well. He had long been a butt of jokes among Dodd and his friends due to his refusal to wear a wig and the way he combed his hair forward to cover the sides of his balding head.

Once the men were assembled, Morton called the roll. Nearly all were present. Several of the men, like Dodd, were substitutes.

Just as the roll call was concluded, Perkins shouted, "Form by companies!" With nothing that an observer would call military precision, the seven clumps of men arranged themselves side by side and shoulder to shoulder, with their captains standing in front of their crooked line.

Perkins rode slowly down the line, looking the men over. Dodd suppressed a smile. He knew that Perkins enjoyed theatrical flair.

When he reached the end of the line, Perkins wheeled his horse around and trotted back, stopping near the center of the line and drawing back a little. He turned his head and scanned the length of the line, then slowly pivoted his head back to the center. Then, suddenly, he drew his sword, thrust it in the air and exclaimed, "Liberty!"

Hundreds of voices answered him spontaneously. "Liberty!" they shouted back.

"Gentlemen," Perkins said, "Like heroes and

patriots, you have answered the call of your state and your community!"

A man behind Dodd muttered, "We was drafted," triggering a few chuckles.

Perkins continued, "In our old age we shall all look back with pride at the service we did for our country and for posterity." After pausing for dramatic effect, he lifted his sword again and shouted, "Liberty!"

"Liberty!" they all shouted back.

"Gentlemen, I know you have all come today expecting that we would march immediately for Petersburg, but we have just learned that those are not our orders. For now, we are to stand ready but stand by. Until further notice you are to report here for drilling each Monday. Your captains have been briefed and can answer whatever questions you have."

There was a rustling among the line as the men squirmed and exchanged puzzled looks.

"Stand ready, men!" Perkins exclaimed. "Our time will soon come. Now, you are dismissed to your captains. Assemble by company." When finished, Perkins sheathed his sword and wheeled his horse. As he rode slowly away, each of the seven captains raised his sword and called out for his company to follow him. They all walked a few dozen paces, trailed by their men, until the groups were all 20 to 30 yards apart.

Dodd walked with the cluster of men following Morton. Some were murmuring, but most walked quietly, processing the news. Once they were separated, Morton stopped walking and raised his hand.

"Gather 'round, men. Gather 'round," he said, indicating with his arms that they were to form a circle around him.

As the men began to pepper him with questions, Morton raised his hand to quiet them. "Here's what I know, men. It turns out that the governor's call up order did not include Pittsylvania. No arms or provisions have been assigned to us. So, we're not going to Petersburg."

"What about Benedict Arnold?" someone asked.

"Other counties have been mobilized and their militia is being sent," Morton replied. "For now, we are just to stand ready for further orders."

"Are we still drafted?" someone else asked.

"Yes," Morton replied. "Your term of duty is unchanged. Three months. You are enlisted until April 8. We are mobilized now and effectively on duty. We just don't have weapons, ammunition, or marching orders."

"So what good are we?" the man on Dodd's right asked.

"You heard Colonel Perkins," Morton replied. "Our time is coming. Until it does, we will drill and prepare ourselves. Our instructions are to be ready to move out on a moment's notice."

There was more murmuring. "I can tell you this, men," Morton said, quieting the men. "The officers are all in agreement. There is going to be a fight and we are going to be in it. I repeat, our time will come."

A silence fell over them for a few seconds.

"Lieutenant Robertson," Morton called out.

A sandy-haired young man wearing a tri-corner hat stepped forward. Walter Robertson, who Dodd grew up calling Wally, was the oldest son of the owner of one of the largest farms in the community adjacent to Maple Grove. He had enlisted in the Virginia Continental Line in 1776 and had served three years under General Washington, earning front line combat experience that was uncommon in the county militia. Dodd knew him to be someone the young men of the county respected and trusted.

"Yes, sir," Robertson said.

"Drill the men, Lieutenant," Morton said. "We will reassemble at noon for parade."

"Yes, sir," Robertson answered. "Fall in, men!" he shouted. "Fall in!"

~~~

When Dodd arrived back at home that evening, Billy Lewis was waiting by the barn for him.

"I heard you didn't get called out," Billy said as Dodd dismounted.

"News travels fast," Dodd replied.

"So, I've come to get my horse back," Billy said.

Dodd looked at him, squinting. "We made a deal," he said.

"Yeah, but the deal was based on the militia having to go to Petersburg. Since y'all ain't going nowhere, then it ain't right for you to keep my horse," Billy replied.

"There weren't no conditions like that. Besides, just because we ain't left yet, that don't mean we ain't gonna leave," Dodd answered.

"It ain't right for you to keep my horse, Dodd. If I knew I didn't have to leave home, then I wouldn't have needed a substitute," Billy said.

"Look here, Billy," Dodd said, growing irritated. "You traded me that horse to take your place and I did it. I'm the one who spent all morning in drills, not you. I'm the one who could be called to march off and fight
~~~

the British any day, not you."

"You know it ain't fair, Dodd," Billy said with a whine. "All you got to do is go drill once a week. That wasn't our deal."

"Yes, it was," Dodd said, firmly. "We made a deal. I took your place. We're going to go fight, just not yet. But even if we don't ever go, I substituted for you and I'm keeping that horse."

Billy took a deep breath, intending to continue the argument until the determined look on Dodd's face convinced him that doing so would be pointless. He was angry but decided not to show it.

After the boys stared at each other for a few seconds, Billy smiled and shrugged.

"Well, Dodd," he said, "you can't blame me for trying. Mind giving me a ride home?"

10

Camp of the 3rd Light Dragoons
Grindal Shoals, South Carolina
January 12, 1781

The dragoons were finishing their final drill when Colonel Washington ordered Collin to sound the signal to assemble. On hearing it, the men broke off by troop and formed in a line facing Washington, their horses standing shoulder to shoulder.

"Very good, men," Washington said, scanning the faces of the men. "Very good. Be sure to rub and brush your mounts carefully. Be particularly mindful of any sign of sore back. Captain Wiatt!"

Ransom nudged his horse forward, "Yes, sir."

"Your men will take picket duty," Washington said.

"Yes, sir," Ransom answered, with a nod.

"Before you are dismissed, there is some business we need to attend to," Washington said to the assembled men. "Collin!" he shouted.

Collin was a few paces behind and to the right of Washington, when the colonel suddenly called his name, startling him. Collecting himself, he edged his horse forward. "Yes, sir," he answered.

Washington gestured to a nearby orderly, who stepped forward and took his horse by the halter. He dismounted, looked at Collin and said, curtly, "Dismount, Collin."

Puzzled, Collin slid out of his saddle and dropped to the ground, pulling the horse's reins over its head as he did.

"Take his horse," Washington commanded the orderly, who reached out and took the reins from Collin, then led both horses away a few steps.

"Step forward, Collin," Washington said.

Collin advanced to within arm's length of the colonel, who stood a foot taller than him.

"Well, Collin, now that you're thirteen…"

Collin interrupted, "I'm fourteen."

Washington laughed. "You're probably twelve, but we'll call it thirteen. As I was saying…" He looked over at one of the camp followers standing nearby and motioned for her to approach. The woman stepped toward them, carrying a bundle. "Now that you're thirteen, you need a regimental and a weapon."

Washington took the bundle from the woman, opened it, and brought out a white jacket with blue facings, the uniform of the regiment, handing it to Collin who promptly shed his tattered coarse linen coat and slipped it on.

"A perfect fit," Washington said, with a nod to the woman, who bowed slightly and stepped away.

As Collin was buttoning his jacket, his eyes registering his delight, Washington stepped over to his horse, opened his saddle bag and pulled out a pistol. He handed it to Collin, who took it eagerly. "We don't have a holster for you yet, but we're working on it," Washington said. "Until then, you'll have to tuck it in your britches. Try not to shoot your prick off."

A ripple of laughter passed along the line of dragoons.

"I should have a brace of them," Collin said, passing the pistol from one hand to the other.

Washington chuckled. "One will do."

"What about a saber?" Collin asked.

"You're too small to carry one, Collin," Washington answered. "Keep growing as you have been, and you'll have one soon enough."

Washington turned and faced the line of dragoons. "Men, as you well know, in combat our very lives are often dependent upon our trumpeter. Collin serves an essential role in the success or failure of this command."

Ransom smiled. By giving him a uniform and a weapon, Washington was acknowledging that Collin was an official member of the regiment, which meant that, by law, Collin would be free at the completion of his service.

Turning back toward Collin, Washington continued, "You have performed your duties well, Collin. Continue to comport yourself as a dragoon. Bring honor to yourself and to this regiment."

Swelled with pride, Collin removed his hat and dipped his head, bowing slightly. Washington nodded, returning the salute.

"Now, men," Washington shouted, "Attend to your stables. Dismissed."

~~~

Three hundred fifty yards away, lying on his stomach and peering over the top of a little rise,
~~~

William Gillespie spoke softly to the man lying beside him in the grass. "Beyond the cavalry camp you can see the tents of the infantry."

Lieutenant Albert Pendleton of Tarleton's British Legion raised a spyglass to his eye and scanned the fields before him. Closest to him, he could see a body of dragoons, evidently in formation for some kind of ceremony. Beyond them, close to the river he could see more tents, campfires, and men milling about, confirming the information Gillespie had ridden into their camp to report yesterday. As Gillespie was unknown to them, Colonel Tarleton wanted independent confirmation of the report, so he had ordered Pendleton to accompany the man and see for himself if what he described was indeed Morgan's camp. Using a little-known path, Gillespie had slipped them past the pickets. Leaving their horses tied in the woods, they had crawled on their bellies to reach this spot, which offered a view of the entire rebel camp. It was exactly what Pendleton had been hoping to see.

"How many of them are there?" Pendleton asked.

"About eight hundred, I estimate," Gillespie answered.

Pendleton turned the glass toward the cavalry.

"How many dragoons?" he asked.

"Eighty-two," Gillespie said.

Pendleton gazed through the glass, sweeping across the camp, thinking ahead. After a few moments he snapped the spyglass shut and put it in his pocket.

"Let's go," he said. "I need to get this information to Colonel Tarleton immediately."

11

Sandy Creek Baptist Meetinghouse
Halifax County, Virginia
January 13, 1781

When Bayard went to the church building after supper, he saw that there were two small stones on the step rock at the door—the signal for a meeting. He went inside, closed the door behind him, waited a few minutes, then lit a candle. A few minutes later there was a soft knock on the door. Bayard walked to the door and softly knocked twice, answered quickly by two knocks from outside. "Psalms," he said. A voice outside replied, "Fifteen. No, five. Wait… Hell, Wynn. Just let me in."

Bayard opened the door enough to allow Gus to slip inside, then closed and barred it behind him.

"You are a blasphemous and profane man, brother Johnson," Bayard said.

"And a half-frozen one at that," Gus said, pulling off his gloves and blowing on his fingers.

"Learn the signs, Gus. They may save your life," Bayard said.

Gus nodded, putting his gloves back on. "Sorry,

Reverend. The countersign slipped my mind. I've had a very hard day."

"I am eager to hear your report," Bayard said, sitting down and motioning for Gus to do the same.

Gus shook his head as he sat down. "Other than just about getting myself killed, I accomplished nothing."

Bayard arched his eyebrows.

"I saw General Arnold," Gus continued. "Let's just say that he was unimpressed by our intelligence."

"Will he provide us any assistance?" Bayard asked.

"No," Gus said, shaking his head. "All he said was 'Come and join me here.'"

"That's impossible," Bayard said.

"Obviously," Gus said.

"Where is Arnold marching? Is he moving toward us?" Bayard asked.

"They were moving east. Back toward the coast. I think the attack on Richmond was nothing but a raid," Gus said.

"So, the reports about him sweeping across Virginia…" Bayard began.

"Probably just the ravings of panicked rebels," Gus said. "I don't see it."

Bayard looked down, disappointment etched on his face. "Then nothing has changed," he said wearily.

"I spoke to another officer, the man who was detailed to hang me," Gus said.

Bayard looked up, surprised.

"Hang you?"

"It's a long story," Gus said. "But he said something sensible: 'Prepare to cooperate with our army when we are closer and, in the meantime, disrupt the enemy any way you can.'"

Bayard nodded thoughtfully. "Very nearly the same message Lord Cornwallis sent last summer—stay quiet until the King's soldiers are near. Was this one of Arnold's officers?"

"A Colonel Simcoe of the Queen's Rangers," Gus answered.

Bayard straightened suddenly. "The Queen's Rangers?" he exclaimed.

Gus nodded.

"The Queen's Rangers," Bayard repeated, distantly. "In Virginia."

"Why is that meaningful to you, sir?" Gus asked.

Bayard sat silently for a few moments, then chuckled. "We called them Robert Rogers' Rangers. During the War of 1755."

"Did you serve with them?" Gus asked.

"No," Bayard answered, shaking his head. "They were further north. But we knew them by reputation. They fought like Indians—used the same tactics, the same savagery. If the Iroquois took a scalp, the Rangers would take two." Bayard paused, then continued, "But an old man's reminiscences are of no consequence now. What do we do with the information you have obtained?"

"Continue to wait. What else can we do?" Gus answered.

"I am thinking of what that colonel said. 'Disrupt the enemy.' I must think on that," Bayard said. "What would the Rangers do?"

"Reverend, there is something else I saw," Gus said.

Bayard looked at him inquisitively.

"I will tell you frankly, sir, that I saw behavior by General Arnold and his army that I would characterize as nothing more than plundering," Gus said.

"It is war, Gus. The rebels must be made to suffer for their treason," Bayard answered quickly.

"It is not the damage to the rebels that seems wrong to me, Reverend," Gus said. "It is Arnold stuffing his own pockets. The talk of everyone there, Loyalist and rebel, is that Arnold is seizing tobacco and merchandise to keep it for himself. Love of money seems to be his ruling passion."

"Don't let it trouble you, Gus," Bayard said. "You will see much worse before this is done." Seeing that the response wasn't satisfactory to Gus, Bayard continued.

"I know the rebels say that General Arnold sold his allegiance," he said. "That may be true. Maybe he has no core convictions. There are opportunists in this struggle, and not all of them are rebels.

"But my faith is not in Benedict Arnold. Thirty years ago, I swore an oath of allegiance to the King, and I regard that oath as irrevocable. The crown has never broken faith with us. God alone determines rulers and sets them upon their thrones. Scripture teaches that rebellion is as the sin of witchcraft. The people require the firm hand of a King above them, on earth as in heaven. Our loyalty is a debt we owe, and our obedience and submission to the King has been commanded by God almighty.

"The traitorous men who have initiated this rebellion are charlatans, out to enrich and empower themselves. They maintain control through fear and intimidation only, hiding behind appeals to 'liberty' even as they force oaths on those who object, taking from them everything they own if they refuse. Those who follow such men in their madness are dupes and fools. We, men like you and I, have a sacred obligation to remain true to the cause of God and to restore justice and honest government to this land."

Gus listened, growing amused as Bayard continued, sensing that the pastor was trying to convince him or to overcome some lingering doubt. When he finally stopped talking, Gus smiled and said, "Well said, preacher. But as for me, I just hate Peter Perkins and all men like him. The sooner we start 'disrupting' them, the better."

Bayard looked back at Gus, the flickering candlelight revealing his subtle smile and the laughter in his eyes. What awaits us all this year, he wondered briefly. After a few moments he returned the smile. "All right, Gus. Let's think on that. For now, we will continue as before. Remain vigilant. Remain prepared. Remain quiet. Remain hidden."

Gus nodded and stood up to leave. As he stepped toward the door, Bayard spoke.

"Five ten. That's the countersign. Commit it to memory," Bayard said.

Gus smiled. "Yes, sir," he answered as he turned to leave.

"Gus," Bayard said, stopping him.

He turned around to see Bayard's hand extending toward him. Taking it, the men shook hands firmly.

"I'm glad you made it back safely," Bayard said. "Remain careful."

Gus nodded, unbarred the door, and slipped out into the night.

12

Wofford's Ironworks
Lawson's Fork Creek
Spartan District, South Carolina
January 14, 1781

Ransom dismounted and tied his horse to the hitching post before the feeding trough, his troop having just returned from picket duty. The regiment had been at the ironworks since dawn, their horses receiving a long-overdue reshodding. Ransom's troop went first, and once their horses had their new shoes, he and his men had been sent out to relieve the pickets stationed among the scrub pines, to enable them to take their turn with the farriers. After six hours in the cold mist, Ransom's troop was in turn relieved by fresh pickets, and when they returned to the ironworks it was nearly midnight. They left their horses saddled, as ordered by Colonel Washington as a precaution against surprise, but would finally be able to rest. After seeing that his horse had hay and water, Ransom reached into his saddle bag, took out his writing kit, walked to a dry place under a shed, and sat down on the ground, beneath a lantern hanging on the wall. He was trimming his quill when Colonel Washington approached.

"Go and use the writing desk in my tent, Ransom," Washington said.

"Thank you, sir, but I have become adept at using my knee for a desk," Ransom answered.

"No doubt you have," Washington said. "Necessity has taught us all new skills. But give your knee a reprieve. The desk is already set up and I'm finished with my dispatches. I will be up for at least another two hours, so I insist you use it."

"Thank you, sir," Ransom said, coming to his feet. "I am grateful for the chance to write in comfort."

Washington nodded and turned to leave, then stopped, looked back and said, "Use my ink too. I have plenty."

"Thank you, sir," Ransom said.

Ransom walked over to the colonel's tent, pulled back the tent flap and stepped inside. The desk was open, next to the colonel's cot, and a candle was burning on the stand beside it. During their many years together in the field, Washington had often invited Ransom to use his little folding writing desk—a courtesy that reflected both their comradeship as well as Washington's sometimes casual regard for the rank of men he respected.

He settled himself on the stool before the table, took a sheet of paper out of his writing kit and dipped his quill into the inkwell. Over the years Ransom had learned that when writing letters such as the one he was about to begin, he could conserve paper by writing very small.

Dear Mother,

I am cold and wet to the bone. It has been weeks since we've had anything good to eat and even longer since I have bathed. We are a foul, tattered, hungry, and ill-tempered lot.

Oh, how I long to breathe the air of Halifax again, to delight in a hot cooked meal in the warmth of my home, to sleep in my bed. I vow that if I ever make it back home, I will never again leave.

I have thought often of your last letter. I am sorry to admit that you credit us with too much, dear Mother. The sad truth is that we rarely contemplate philosophy in the way you suggest. I am still devoted to the cause, and I would rather die than submit to being ruled by the British, but the truth is that I rarely have or take the time to think of such things. Instead, as I begin each day my goal is to keep myself and my men alive. Lately, I am almost ashamed to say, it is not so much a desire for liberty that keeps us in our saddles, as a desire for revenge, and a desire to avoid becoming the victims of someone else's desire for revenge.

The militia here seem to come and go as they please. They'll come, individually or in companies, stay a few days or maybe weeks, consume provisions, then go back to their homes, maybe to return, maybe not. But it's hard to blame them. They have to defend their farms and families from the bands of Tory marauders who are terrorizing the countryside. Or maybe they leave to go do some marauding of their own. The Tories and the Whigs here hate each other with an unbridled passion, and they fight like savages. And each murder and atrocity begats reprisals, so that the bloodshed intensifies with each passing day. The violence and passions of the people here are beyond every curb of religion and humanity. I pray it does not come to this in Virginia.

Yesterday while we were on patrol, some of the local Whigs came to us and reported that there were Tories nearby, driving cattle to the British army. We found the men and made prisoners of them all. We had not marched them a mile before one of our Whig informers came up to one of the prisoners, knocked him to the ground, and bashed his brains out with the butt of his musket. Colonel Washington had the man arrested, but nothing will happen to him. He says the man he killed came to his house last month with a band of Tories and that they stole everything he owned, burned down his house, and left his family destitute. I do not doubt the truth of what the man said. And from what I have seen here, I suspect the Tories were themselves avenging some atrocity committed on one of their own. That is the way it is here now. If we withdrew the guards, I believe every one of those Tories would be slaughtered at once.

Whether we defeat the British here, or whether they defeat us, that will not end it. These people here are in a bloody battle to the death, and it seems to me that it will not end until one has entirely exterminated the other. I pray that I am wrong about that.

We hanged one of our men last week. A deserter. Colonel Washington required the entire regiment to witness the hanging. The drop did not snap the man's neck. He twisted at the end of the rope for several minutes until the life was finally choked out of him. His name was Wright. We all stood there and watched him slowly strangle to death.

This land is being drenched in blood. Please pray for us, dear Mother.

Ransom looked at his letter, tiny scrawl on a scrap of paper, illegible to anyone but him. Over the past five years he had written many such letters, a hundred or more, never posting any of them. He had found it helpful to unburden himself by writing his thoughts this way—thoughts that he would never share with anyone else, least of all his mother. He sighed, crumpled the paper, and stuck it in his pocket. He took another sheet from the kit, dipped the quill into the inkwell, and started again.

Dearest Mother,

As I write this, our long-suffering horses are being reshod. I am blessed to be in good health and the men in the "Flying Army" are all in good spirits. Though most of us are far away, our thoughts are continually on our homes. We are constant in our devotion to our beloved families and to the liberty of our country.

I do not know when I shall be able to see you again, as there seems to be no end to the campaigning here. I want you to know that the memory of your sweet face and your loving embrace sustains me in the field, as do your prayers. Your son rises up, dear Mother, and calls you blessed. Please give my love to all.

Your most affectionate son,

Ransom

Ransom looked over the letter and smiled wistfully. He sprinkled pounce on the paper to dry the ink, then blew the dust away. After waiting a few seconds, he shook the paper, then folded it. He tilted the candleholder, allowing a few drops of melted wax to drip onto the letter's folds, sealing it. On the front he wrote "Mrs. Jno. Wiatt, Peytonsburg, Virginia." Leaving the letter on the desk, he stepped outside, just as Colonel Washington was approaching.

"There are a dozen horses yet to be shoed," Washington said. "We will finish in the morning. Give your men and your mounts six hours of rest, then see that the pickets are rotated."

"Yes, sir," Ransom answered. "I left a letter on your desk, sir."

"Very well," Washington said. "I'll put it in the next post."

"Thank you, sir," Ransom said.

As Ransom stepped away, a rider suddenly galloped up on a lathered horse, skidding to a stop just before Washington.

"Colonel Washington, sir!" the man said,

breathlessly, reaching out with a folded piece of paper in his hand. "Urgent dispatch from General Morgan, sir. He orders that your command rendezvous with him at Burr's Mill. Tarleton is coming!"

13

Burr's Mill
Thicketty Creek
Spartan District, South Carolina
January 15, 1781

Daniel Morgan winced, his hand clutching his left hip. His men had been marching all day, covering nearly eighteen miles in the bitter cold, over swampy, muddy roads to reach the rendezvous point, and he had been in agony most of that time. "Damned sciatica," he said. "Can't hardly walk and riding is even worse. Hurts like hell."

Washington nodded sympathetically as he regarded the general. Notwithstanding his complaint, Morgan was a robust, physically imposing man, standing over six feet tall and with an ever-present air of confidence about him. The exploits of Morgan and his Virginia riflemen had made him a hero, before his failing health and his disgust at army politics he led him to resign and retire to his home in Winchester, where he remained until the disaster at Camden. Then, at one of the darkest hours of the Revolution, Morgan had ridden to North Carolina and offered his services to what was left of the American army there. A month ago, General Greene had given him an independent command, the "Flying Army" they called it, a force of approximately 600 lightly equipped and fast-moving men, assigned to move into the South Carolina upcountry to support the Patriots there and to keep Cornwallis's full attention off the rest of Greene's army. Morgan had fulfilled his mission well, so well that Cornwallis had determined that Morgan and his army must be driven out of South Carolina, and he had dispatched Banastre Tarleton, "Bloody Ban" as he had come to be known, to do just that. And now the Flying Army was flying, with Tarleton in hot pursuit.

"Old age and too much time in the saddle are catching up with me, Billy. But there is no time to worry about that now," Morgan said. "What do we know about the enemy?"

No one called Washington "Billy," not even his own mother. But Morgan had presumed to do so from the day they met. While he would have resented such informality and presumption from anyone else, Washington never considered expressing any objection to Morgan. He just wrote it off as an eccentricity of a frontiersman and a living legend.

"We have multiple reports from our scouts, local Patriots as well as my own videttes, sir," Washington answered. "In addition to his British Legion, Tarleton has two pieces of artillery and two regiments of redcoat regulars. About twelve hundred men in all."

"My God," Morgan replied.

"The regulars are the Royal Fusiliers and a battalion of Fraser's Highlanders," Washington added.

Morgan shook his head. "Those are some of the very best men they have," he said.

Washington nodded. "He also has a troop of the 17th Lancers," he said.

"The Death or Glory Boys," Morgan said, absently. "Well, Colonel Washington, it seems we have their attention," he added, with a smile.

"Yes sir, it certainly does," Washington replied.

"It would seem we are a bit overmatched, Colonel. I have 520 Continentals fit for duty. Maybe 350 or so militia, but that changes daily and who knows if they will fight," Morgan said, pacing as he spoke, his hands behind the back of his fringed linen hunting shirt. He stopped and looked up at Washington. "And to oppose the British cavalry I have only your dragoons, and they outnumber you three to one."

"Yes, sir," Washington said. "That seems to be how it stands."

"Where are they now?" Morgan asked.

"At Grindal Shoals," Washington said. "They have stopped at our old campsite there."

"All right. So that means we have about 15 miles and the Pacolet River between us. As long as he is stuck on the south side of the river, we've got some time," Morgan said. "Watch the fords closely, Colonel. We will camp here tonight. After the men have breakfast, we'll continue north, toward the Broad River. We'll move out at sunup."

"Yes, sir," Washington answered, turning to leave.

"Billy, I need your dragoons to screen us," Morgan said.

Washington stopped and turned to face his commander.

"Keep me apprised of what Tarleton is doing," Morgan said. "Where he is, where he's going. No surprises."

"Yes, sir," Washington answered.

As Morgan stepped away, Washington scanned the area. In the bustle of soldiers and horses outside the general's tent, he recognized Ransom, who was preparing to saddle his horse. "Captain Wiatt," he called out.

Ransom came to attention as the colonel approached. "Yes, sir," he said.

"Make camp, Ransom," Washington said. "Get some sleep. I need your men and mounts to be fully rested. I'll deploy Captain Parsons' troop as tonight's scouts. Your men will relieve them in the morning."

"Yes, sir," Ransom answered.

"It's going to take hard marching tomorrow to get the army across the Broad ahead of Tarleton," Washington said. "I expect we may have to cover as rear guard. You know what that means."

Ransom nodded. "Yes, sir," he answered. He knew.

14

Grindal Shoals
Spartan District, South Carolina
January 15, 1781

Lieutenant Colonel Banastre Tarleton brought his horse to a halt and swiftly dismounted beside Major Archibald McArthur, who stood waiting for him. "Orderly!" Tarleton shouted. Moments later a young soldier appeared, taking the horse by the halter. "Tend to him, Private. Rub him down thoroughly and have a fresh mount saddled for me and ready to ride in two hours."

"Yes, sir," the private answered, leading the horse away.

"Colonel," McArthur said. "We are entirely out of rations, sir. The men are exhausted, and we have no bread or rum to offer them. We are going to have to send out foragers."

"Pointless," Tarleton answered, brusquely. "They couldn't find anything in the dark and, besides, the rebels have already stripped this area clean."

"Perhaps in the morning, sir…" McArthur began.

Tarleton interrupted him. "We won't be here in the

morning, Major. Rest the men a few hours. We resume marching at 2 a.m."

"Begging the colonel's pardon, sir, but…" McArthur began.

Tarleton lifted his hand, cutting him off.

"We will give the appearance of making camp here—for the benefit of the rebel eyes out there in the dark—but we will march at two," Tarleton said. "We are going to cross the Pacolet tonight, Major. By sunup we will be pressing General Morgan."

"The fords may be guarded, sir," McArthur said.

"We are going to cross at…" Tarleton paused and turned to an elderly civilian on a horse nearby. "What is the name of the ford?"

"Easterwood," the man said.

"Easterwood Ford," Tarleton said, turning back to McArthur. "We cross tonight."

"Where is…" McArthur began.

"Six miles from here," Tarleton said, casting a glance at the civilian, whose nod confirmed the distance. Tarleton pointed west. "Upstream."

"Upstream, sir?" McArthur asked.

"Yes, upstream. The rebels will not expect us to cross there. Not tonight." Tarleton smacked his right fist into his gloved left hand. "The men can rest, Major. But only until two. Then we march."

"On no rations, sir?" McArthur asked, hesitatingly.

"On no rations," Tarleton answered. "We must press them, sir. We must catch the rebels before they escape across the Broad River and before they are reinforced. If we catch them before they can cross, we can annihilate them. We will eat tomorrow."

"Yes, sir," McArthur replied, swallowing the words he wanted to say: eat what?

15

Burr's Mill
Thicketty Creek
Spartan District, South Carolina
January 16, 1781

Ransom warmed his hands over the fire one last time. All around him the camp was beginning to bustle with activity, as the men were rolling up their blankets and beginning to prepare their breakfasts. He had roused his troop earlier. In an hour the sun would be up and by then his men would have relieved Captain Parsons and his pickets. Ransom looked around until he spotted Sergeant Lawrence Everhart, who was tightening the saddle on his horse. "Sergeant!" he called out. "Prepare to move out!"

Everhart raised his hand, acknowledging the order.

Ransom stepped into his stirrup and threw his other leg over his horse's back, settling himself into the saddle. As he turned his horse, preparing to ride, there was a commotion ahead of him in the dark. Everhart and the other men moved their horses aside to let through a rider, who rushed toward Ransom. As he approached, Ransom saw that it was Captain Parsons.

"Wiatt," he said hurriedly, "Where is the colonel?"

Before Ransom could answer, Parsons suddenly spurred his horse and rode toward the campfire, where Ransom saw that General Morgan was standing, in conversation with Washington and Colonel John Eager Howard, the 28-year-old Marylander who was commander of the Continental regulars. The three men looked up curiously as Parsons rode to them, then hurriedly dismounted. Ransom rode up behind Parsons to hear the report.

"Tarleton is across the river," Parsons said.

"Across the river?" Morgan responded. "Now?"

"Yes, sir," Parsons answered. "A scout reported that he crossed upstream from the mill during the night. I have confirmed the report, sir. His entire force is across and marching this way."

"Upstream?" Morgan said, incredulous.

"His movement to the mill must have been a feint, sir," Parsons said. "They backtracked and crossed at a ford called Easterwood. They are all across."

"Do you mean to tell me that Tarleton forded the river in this weather, in the middle of the night?" Morgan asked.

"He did, sir," Parsons said. "He crossed around four o'clock."

"That tenacious son of a bitch," Morgan said. "He aims to have my hide."

And mine, Washington thought.

"How far away are they?"

"About 10 miles, sir," Parsons replied. "Maybe less."

Morgan turned suddenly to Colonel Howard. "Break camp immediately, Colonel. Get the army on the road north at once. No delay!"

"General," Howard answered, "the men are preparing their breakfasts."

"Leave it!" Morgan said, urgently. "There is no time. I want the entire army on the road within the half hour, Colonel. No delays and no excuses. Move, now!"

"Yes, sir," Howard answered, before turning and rushing away.

Morgan spun around and faced Washington. "Cover us, Billy. Make sure we are clear from any ambuscades in the front and keep the enemy's dragoons off our rear. No mistakes, Colonel."

"Yes, sir," Washington answered.

As Morgan stormed away, limping and holding his hip, Washington turned to Parsons. "Your men will be our rearguard," he said.

"Yes, sir," Parsons answered, preparing to leave.

"Take no risks, Captain. Observe from a safe distance," Washington added.

Parsons nodded, remounted, and rode away.

Washington then turned to Ransom. "Collect your men and take the van, Ransom. Spread out and patrol ahead about two miles."

Ransom nodded, then rode toward Everhart, who was waiting with the rest of the troop.

~~~

Tarleton rode into the camp a few hours after its hasty evacuation and saw that his famished men had fallen on the Americans' abandoned breakfasts like a pack of hungry wolves. "Captain Ogilvie!" he shouted, summoning a mounted officer to his side. "It appears that the rebels have provided us with rations. Detail a squad to gather all the provisions here and distribute
~~~

them among the men."

"Yes, sir," Ogilvie said before riding away.

Tarleton steered his horse toward McArthur, who had just ridden into the camp. "We will rest the men for an hour, Major."

McArthur nodded.

"I will dispatch a squad of dragoons to gather up any stragglers," Tarleton said. He pulled a watch from the pocket of his tight-fitting green jacket, flicked it open, looked at it, then returned it to his pocket. "Have the men ready to march in an hour, sir," he said, before wheeling his horse around and riding away.

16

The Cowpens
Spartan District, South Carolina
January 16, 1781

Hearing the sound of hooves approaching from behind, Ransom wheeled his horse around and was surprised to see General Morgan riding up, with a man who appeared to be a militiaman riding alongside him. As they drew closer, Ransom gave a slight bow.

"Captain," Morgan said as he drew alongside Ransom, "Remind me of your name."

"Wiatt, sir. Ransom Wiatt."

Morgan nodded. "Captain Wiatt, this is Captain Dennis Trammel, who I have conscripted to serve as my scout."

The two men nodded at each other.

"I need a couple of your men to ride ahead with us as an escort," Morgan said.

Ransom cast a quick glance at Everhart, who had pulled to the side of the road when Morgan arrived. "Sergeant Everhart and I will accompany you, sir," he said.

"Good," Morgan answered. "Let's go."

The road, which they had been plodding along all day was not much more than a muddy path, barely wide enough to accommodate a wagon. Everhart rode in front of Morgan and Trammell, who rode side by side with Ransom close behind them.

"How far is it from here?" Morgan asked Trammell.

"We're almost there, sir," Trammell answered.

"You understand the kind of place I'm looking for?" Morgan asked.

"I believe I do, sir. I believe this place fits your description neatly."

"What's it called?"

"We call it Hannah's cow pens," Trammel said. "Or just plain 'the Cowpens.' Everyone who lives around here knows about it."

"The cow pens?" Morgan asked.

"Yes, sir. It's where we bring our cows to corral them for marking. It's perfect for that. You'll see what I mean," Trammell said.

In a few minutes they emerged from a wooded area onto the crest of a rise that offered a clear view into the distance.

"This is the place," Trammell said. "A Tory owns it, but I don't expect he'll come and object," he added, with a smile.

Morgan rode a few steps forward and looked quietly out over the area for a while. There were thick, seemingly impenetrable growths of canebrake about 500 yards apart, hemming in a grassy and lightly wooded pasture that stretched into the distance, dotted by a scattering of grazing cattle.

After a minute or so Morgan asked, "What is beyond that hill?" gesturing toward a rise in the distance.

"It rolls," Trammell answered. "Just like this part. I can show you."

"How far is it from here to the river?" Morgan asked.

"About six miles," Trammell said.

Morgan went silent again, continuing to stare out over the landscape. It seemed to the others that he was doing calculations in his head. After a minute or two he spun suddenly around in the saddle.

"Captain Wiatt, send a fast rider back to the column to hurry them along. And get me the most recent report on Tarleton's location." He swept his arm toward the clearing. "Have your men scout this area carefully and see that it is secure."

"Yes, sir," Ransom said.

Morgan looked back across the clearing. "Here will be victory or Morgan's grave, Captain. On this ground I will beat Benny Tarleton," he said, "or on it I will lay my bones."

~~~

Within an hour the army began to arrive, exhausted and muddy. As Colonel Howard rode up, Morgan was on the ridge, looking out over the meadow. He turned to Howard and pointed in the distance. "Make camp just beyond that hill, Colonel."

Howard looked at the hill, then looked back at Morgan. "Camp, sir? We are only a few miles from the river."

Morgan smiled. "That's right. Men sell their lives more dearly, Colonel, when they know there's nowhere to run. This is where we'll fight."
~~~

One of the nearby militiamen overheard Morgan's remark. He whispered it to his comrades and soon the word was spreading across the Carolina countryside: General Morgan was making a stand at the Cowpens.

~~~

Despite the grinding pain in his hip, Morgan stayed in the saddle, overseeing, inspecting, and greeting the men as the column arrived, exuding confidence. "Come on in, boys," he said as the exhausted men marched in. "I've picked out a nice spot for us. This is the place where we're going to give Benny Tarleton a whipping."

Morgan's cheerfulness and confidence was contagious, and soon it seemed the entire Flying Army had caught it. The effect was especially dramatic among the South Carolina militiamen, who had been grumbling all day. They had come to fight Tarleton, they said, not to run from him. Many had resolved that if Morgan crossed the Broad River, they wouldn't cross with him. They would just go back to their farms and defend their homes as best they could.

But now they were seeing the Daniel Morgan they had expected. The Old Wagoner. The Virginia rifleman. The fearless frontiersman. The hero of Quebec and Saratoga. The Carolina men were ready to fight, and Old Dan Morgan was ready to lead them.

As the men filed in, Morgan directed their officers to different parts of the field, choreographing a battle plan that was unfolding in his mind. When the commissary wagons arrived, he rode over and shouted instructions to the sergeant, making sure the nearby soldiers overhead him, "Round up all the cattle here,
~~~

Sergeant. Butcher them and prepare us a feast of beef. Let every man eat his fill tonight and give him enough for tomorrow's breakfast as well!"

A cheer went up from the men and word of the order spread across the camp like wildfire.

Colonel Washington was riding into the camp, dead tired, when Morgan suddenly rode up beside him. "Come with me, Billy," he said. "I'm going to get you some help."

Washington followed as Morgan rode to a part of the field where a large body of militiamen were making camp. As Morgan reached the men, an officer stepped forward and removed his hat. "Colonel Pickens," Morgan said cheerfully, "I have come to borrow some of your men."

Morgan had been greatly relieved when Colonel Andrew Pickens had arrived on the field about a half hour earlier, at the head of a column of 240 South Carolina militiamen. Long-faced, dour, quiet, and humorless, Pickens was a devout Presbyterian, known by his men to be personally courageous, without being reckless with their lives. He had their full confidence and respect. The British had an entirely different opinion of Pickens—they regarded him as a renegade who had violated the terms of a parole, making him subject to summary execution if captured, a fact not lost on Pickens or his men.

Pickens nodded at Morgan and replied, "They are at your disposal, sir."

Morgan laughed and rode into the midst of the militia camp, with Washington following.

"Gentlemen!" Morgan shouted, getting the attention of the men. "As you know, we are expecting guests in the morning, and they have considerably more dragoons that we do. I think it best that we try to help even out the odds for Colonel Washington.

"If you have a rifle, stay where you are. But if you are carrying a musket, a fowler, or a squirrel gun, or no gun at all, and if you are a good rider and have a strong arm, then I need you. You won't get a pretty white uniform like Colonel Washington's," he said, gesturing to Washington and drawing some laughs, "but I'll let you impress any horse here that doesn't already belong to a dragoon or an officer. I need 50 good men. Who will volunteer?"

When the men who stepped forward were counted, there were 56 of them.

Morgan looked them over approvingly then turned to Washington. "Colonel Washington," he said, "do your best to return these men to Colonel Pickens in no worse condition than you took them," again drawing laughter from the men. "Now get them ready to have a go at the British Legion."

"All right, men," Washington said. "Come with me."

After leading the men across the meadow, to the place where the dragoons were making camp, Washington called out to the quartermaster, who was overseeing the unloading of the equipment wagon. "Sergeant Lunsford! I have 56 new recruits. Issue them pistols and sabers."

One of the new men yelled out, "I'll take a carbine, or a second pistol, and you can keep the sword." There was a scattering of laughter from the men.

Washington wheeled around to face the men, his face flushed. Rising up in his stirrups, he drew his saber from its scabbard and lifted it up over his head. "This is the weapon of a dragoon!" he shouted, quieting the men. Turning back to the quartermaster, he said, "Sergeant, set up the dummies."

Ransom, who had been watching from nearby, chuckled when Washington called for the dummies. He had seen the colonel use this demonstration for new recruits several times before and he always found it enjoyable.

"I gather that some of you would prefer to use pistols in the fight tomorrow," Washington said. "Am I correct about that?"

Some of the men nodded and a bold one shouted, "Yes, sir. You got that right."

Ransom noticed that a crowd of amused dragoons had now gathered to watch Washington.

"I forbid it!" Washington shouted. "And I will show you why."

The sun was setting but it was still light enough to see that a couple of the dragoons were hammering stakes into the ground in the distance, holding up straw dummies shaped like men, as Lunsford walked out to the colonel carrying a box of pistols.

"There are six dummies out there," Washington said, pointing his saber at them. "They represent the enemy. I need six of you, good shots only, to step forward."

The man who had joked about the swords stepped forward immediately, soon followed by five others.

"Take pistols, men," Washington said. Turning to the dragoons he said, "Six of you lend your horses to these men."

Ransom turned to his troop and called out the names of six men, who reluctantly dismounted and led their horses over to the new recruits.

"Load your pistols and mount up, men,"

Washington said. While the men were loading, he called out, "Collin!", bringing the trumpeter quickly to his side. He turned back to the militiamen, who were mounting the horses and said, "The infantry use drums to signal commands and you men have probably been trained to recognize them. But it has been the experience of cavalrymen that the carrying and beating of drums while on horseback is exceedingly uncomfortable. Accordingly, our commands are communicated by trumpet. You will need to learn the commands.

"After we are done here, report to Corporal Collin, our trumpeter, and he will instruct you in all the command signals," Washington said. The dragoons exchanged glances, amused by Collin's impromptu promotion.

"Now men, when Collin sounds the command, you will charge those dummies," Washington said, pointing at them with the tip of his sword. "Unlike the men you will face tomorrow, the dummies are stationary, and they will not fight back. You are to shoot them, then return here. I will time you."

Washington glared at the men. "Charge them at a gallop, men, as you would in combat. Do you understand?"

There were mumbled yessirs, as the men loaded and cocked their pistols.

Washington sheathed his saber and said, "Collin, sound a charge."

Collin leaned forward, speaking softly but loudly enough to be heard by the nearby dragoons. "I ought to be a sergeant," he said.

Amid snickers from some of the men, Washington suppressed a grin, feigned annoyance, and was about to speak when Collin suddenly raised the bugle to his lips and blew the command to charge. At the familiar sound, all the dragoons' horses, including the six carrying the new recruits, became restless and jumpy. After a few seemingly confused moments, the first of the volunteers kicked his horse in the side and shouted out, "Yah!" taking off in a rush toward the dummies with his pistol leveled and the other five men rushing along behind him.

As the man in front approached the first dummy, he aimed his pistol and fired, his horse galloping past the dummy as he did. The other five men broke toward the other dummies, two running past their targets before they could get their shots off and two more nearly colliding as they jockeyed for position. One wheeled his horse around, accidently firing his pistol into the air as he did. After some scrambling around, eventually all the men had fired. As they came riding back toward Washington, he shouted to Lunsford, "Check them!"

The volunteers gathered around Washington as Lunsford examined the dummies. After looking at them all, he turned to Washington and shouted, "Naught!"

"Naught, gentlemen," Washington said, looking at them sternly. "Congratulations. Six shots and zero hits. Had this been actual combat, while you were fumbling around with your pistols the enemy would have hacked you all to pieces before riding off to slaughter our infantry.

"Pistols are not accurate even under the best of conditions. From horseback, at moving targets, they are essentially useless." He turned in his saddle to face the dragoons. "Captain Wiatt, show them how it is done."

Ransom nodded, easing his horse forward as he drew his saber from the sheath and twisted the sword knot around his wrist. Progressing quickly from a trot to a canter to a gallop, he charged toward the first dummy, slashing it with his saber as he rode past. Using his left hand and his legs to steer his horse, Ransom raced past the second and third dummies, slashing them both, then wheeled suddenly and charged the last three. He slashed the fourth dummy, then raced at full speed to the fifth, plunging his saber into the straw as he sped by. As he approached the final target, Ransom extended his arm, swinging it as he rode by, lopping off the dummy's head.

As Ransom trotted back, Washington faced the volunteers, drew his saber, held it up in the air and shouted, "This is the weapon of a dragoon, men, and *that* is why! In a third of the time you spent accomplishing nothing, one dragoon with a saber has taken out all six of the enemy. Do you understand what you have seen?"

The men nodded and mumbled their acknowledgments.

"Any man who fires his pistol tomorrow instead of using his saber will answer to me personally," Washington said, "and I assure you he will regret it!

"Now dismount, return those horses to these dragoons, and go to the corral and choose your mounts. Return here and after Sergeant Lunsford has issued you your weapons, *Private* Collin will instruct you on the trumpet signals."

Collin shot a confused and hurt look at Washington, who grinned and rode away.

17

The Cowpens
Spartan District, South Carolina
January 16, 1781

It was nearly midnight when Ransom returned to his tent, cold, exhausted, and ready to get a little sleep. He dropped down onto a stool and was beginning to pull off a boot when he heard Colonel Washington call out, "All officers report."

He sighed, rose wearily, and stepped back outside, where he saw Washington, standing next to a dying fire. A few of the regiment's officers were standing with him and others were approaching. "Join us, Captain Wiatt," Washington said. "General Morgan has called a meeting of all officers."

"Every officer in the regiment?" Ransom asked.

Washington chuckled. "Every officer in the *army*," he replied.

"Now?" Ransom asked. "He wants to meet with every officer in the entire army? Now?"

"That's right," Washington said.

"Why?" one of the other officers asked.

Washington shrugged. "It's Morgan," he answered.

Once the regiment's officers had all gathered—a dozen men in all—Washington led them to a roaring campfire near the back of the camp. Ransom could see that dozens of other officers were already there, Continentals and militiamen alike. Pacing before the fire, his hands clasped behind his back, was General Morgan, wearing a fur coat over his hunting shirt. Noticing the dragoons as they approached, Morgan called out to Washington. "I trust your cavalry have us well screened tonight, Colonel Washington."

"Videttes and pickets are set, sir. We will not be surprised," Washington answered.

"Very good," Morgan said. He waved his arm, signaling the officers to draw closer. Raising his voice, he called out, "Gather 'round, gentlemen. It is important that everyone hear this."

Ransom looked at the men gathering around the fire. Most of them he knew, having fought alongside them for months or years. But among the militia officers, distinguishable by the absence of regulation uniforms, he saw new and unfamiliar faces. He was not surprised by that. Men from the surrounding countryside had been arriving at camp all evening, alone or in organized militia companies, carrying whatever weapons they owned. The Flying Army was growing.

As the crowd of officers drew closer to the fire, Ransom noticed three men approaching uncertainly, a tall lanky man wearing a homespun hunting shirt, buckskin moccasins, and a bearskin cap, trailed by two shorter younger men, all three of them carrying rifles. Seeing the men, Morgan stepped toward them. "Good evening, my good man," he said to the taller man. "What can I do for you?"

The man looked around cautiously, his grizzled face lit by the campfire. Turning back to Morgan, he said, "We heared old Dan Morgan is fixing to fight Bloody Ban Tarleton. Me and my boys, we come to hep."

Morgan laughed and extended his hand heartily. "You heard right, my good man!" he said as the man reluctantly took his hand and shook it firmly. "Yes, sir, you heard right. Dan Morgan aims to whip the pants off of Benny Tarleton, right here!"

The man released Morgan's hand and looked again at the officers around the fire. Nodding toward those wearing blue Continental uniforms, he asked, "Which one of them is General Morgan?"

Morgan spun around and looked at the officers, who were watching the scene with amusement. "Morgan? That old cuss?" he said. After a moment, he spun back around to face the man, thumped himself on the chest and said with a laugh, "*I* am Morgan! The Old Wagoner hisself. In the flesh, my good man!"

The man looked Morgan up and down, dubiously at first, then nodded in recognition. Extending his hand again, he said, "Name's Jones. Duncan Jones. These here are my boys—Tate and Joshua. Right honored to meet you, sir."

"Likewise, my good man! Likewise!" Morgan said, again shaking the man's hand.

Ransom leaned over and whispered to Washington, "I've never seen an officer appear so at ease among the men."

Washington chuckled. "He *is* at ease. He's more one of them than one of us."

Nodding at the man's weapon, Morgan said, "Those look like good Kentucky long rifles you and your sons are carrying. Are you good shots?"

After a pause, the man said, "I reckon so."

"Ha! I'll wager you are!" Morgan exclaimed. Turning around, he scanned the officers until he found who he was looking for. "Colonel Pickens, here are three more riflemen for you."

At Pickens' command, one of the junior militia officers came over quickly and led the three men away. After pointing them to the correct part of the camp, he hurried back over to the fire.

"Gentlemen," Morgan said, addressing them all, "Men like that have been pouring in all evening. They've come because this army is going to make a stand. And it is with men like them that we will prevail. By God, I will crack my whip over Benny Tarleton in the morning as sure as I live!"

The man's confidence is infectious, Ransom thought. Stout and square-shouldered, Morgan had the physique of a young man, but a face that made him appear older than his 44 years. In the flickering firelight, the jagged scar on the general's cheek was plainly visible—the consequence of having been shot in the face in an Indian ambush twenty-five years earlier. Like everyone else in camp, Ransom knew about Morgan's scars. They contributed to his mystique: the scar on his face, from a bullet that entered the back of his neck and carried out half of his teeth when it exited beside his nose, and the scars on his back, which Morgan proudly showed any soldier who asked to see them and many who didn't, the consequences of the 499 lashes he had received after striking a British officer during the retreat from Fort Duquesne in 1755. Morgan had been sentenced to 500 lashes, usually a death sentence, but he insisted that he had counted them as they were delivered and that, as he often said, "King George still owes me one." He's an easy man to admire, Ransom thought.

Morgan had resumed his pacing. "Colonel Tarleton is fearless, ruthless, and merciless. He relies on intimidation.

"Gentlemen," Morgan continued, "we will use those traits against him, and by God we will whip that son of a bitch!"

Washington leaned over and whispered to Ransom, "With a bunch of farmers armed with their hunting guns, no artillery, and outnumbered three to one in cavalry. Difficult odds."

Ransom smiled and shrugged.

"I wanted you all to be here," Morgan continued, "because it is essential that we all understand the battle plan. Please listen carefully.

"Tarleton will attack at first light. He will behave exactly as he did at Waxhaws against Colonel Buford."

Washington whispered, "That isn't comforting." Ransom smiled at the gallows humor, but kept his eyes fixed on Morgan, who had resumed his pacing, his limp now gone.

"He will charge right up the middle, right at the center of our line, counting on us to break.

"We will be ready for him, gentlemen. We will deploy in three parallel lines, each about 150 yards behind the other. The Continentals will be our third line. The first two lines will be militia."

There was a stirring among the officers as they exchanged puzzled glances.

"Colonel McDowell and Major Cunningham, you will command the first line of skirmishers—deployed on either side of the road. Take 120 picked men—the best marksmen you have. They will have cover in the trees and tall grass. Form them into squads of threes, so that one man will always be firing while the other two reload. As the enemy advances, you will keep up a steady fire, then withdraw, firing as you do. Tell your men that when picking their targets to prefer those wearing epaulets. Cut them up, gentlemen! Then pull back and join the second line.

"Colonel Pickens, you will deploy your militia as our second line, along the tree line on the back side of the hill. You will have the advantage of concealment. When the British crest the hill, they will come in sight of your men and you will be able to give them a very warm welcome. Do not allow the enemy to come close enough to charge with their bayonets. Have your men fire two or three times, then withdraw, firing as you do.

"Colonel Howard's Continentals will be our third line, with the Virginia riflemen on each wing. We will hold that line and there we will defeat them. When the British see our militia withdrawing, they will charge after them. Their pursuit will bring them right to you, Colonel Howard, and you will finish them.

"Colonel Washington's dragoons will be in reserve, behind the hill. When the infantry have weakened them, Billy will hit them on their flank or rear, as the situation allows."

Morgan turned and faced Pickens, "Colonel, the success of the plan depends upon your militia. Indeed, whether we win or lose depends upon them. I know I am asking a great deal of them, a very great deal. But sir, I am not asking them to do more than they can do. That is where we have failed before. That is where General Gates failed at Camden.

"Militiamen cannot be expected to stand up to a bayonet charge from British regulars, nor should we ask that of them. Most of our militiamen do not have bayonets and they are not trained to use them in any case. If we ask the militia to stand and fight the British hand to hand, we will lose. Our men will run away rather than risk being bayoneted. We know from experience this is true. So, I will not ask them to do that. In fact, Colonel Pickens, I positively order that your men are not to engage the British hand to hand. All I ask of them is that they give two good fires, then withdraw. After your first fire the British will charge your line. With rolling fire, you should be able to hold them back long enough to load and fire a second time. Then, Colonel Pickens, you will lead them in an orderly withdrawal and reform them as a reserve in the rear.

"All I am asking these men to do is what they do best, what they have learned to do from when they were old enough to walk—shoot accurately. Just like my Virginia men, they are deadly shots. If they stay composed and deliver at least two good well-aimed shots, we will thin the British line so much that they are bound to fail when they reach our third line."

Pickens spoke up. "It is a good plan, sir. It will be done."

"Very good, Colonel," Morgan said. Addressing them all, he continued, "I am giving the militia a mission they can perform honorably. After two good shots, there will be no shame in falling back. In fact, they will be obeying my orders when they do so. They will reform behind the Continental Line as a reserve, and they will be ready to deliver our *coup de grace*."

Ransom cast a quick glance around at the men facing Morgan. Like Ransom, they all knew the character of the enemy they were about to face—the best-trained, best-disciplined, and best-equipped soldiers in the word, led by an audacious commander who has always won his battles. If history holds true, Ransom thought, by this time tomorrow most of us will have British bayonets planted in our chests.

"Have your men cook their breakfasts tonight, gentlemen," Morgan said. "There will be no time for that in the morning. I expect the enemy will attack at first light."

As the officers began turning to leave, Morgan spoke up again. "Tarleton knows only one strategy, gentlemen—pursue relentlessly, overtake his enemy, then attack immediately. He has done it repeatedly and he has always won. This time he will learn his lesson."

Noticing another little cluster of rifle-carrying men in hunting shirts wandering uncertainly into the camp, Morgan hurried over toward them.

18

On the road between Burr's Mill and the Cowpens
Spartan District, South Carolina
January 16, 1781

The men in Tarleton's army were nearing a state of collapse—those on horseback barely able to stay in the saddle and those on foot even more depleted. They had been chasing Morgan's army all day and deep into the night, plodding along the narrow churned-up muddy road, slowed by swollen creeks, by the trees felled across their path by the retreating Americans, and by bitter cold, hunger pangs, and numbing exhaustion. McArthur groped his way along the crowded column, searching for Tarleton in the dark so he could renew his plea.

"Colonel," he said, once he had found the commander, "it is nearly midnight. We need to rest the men. Respectfully, sir, we are demanding too much of them. Marching them for so long, in this mud, with only four hours sleep in the last two days, we risk ruining them for combat."

"Nonsense, Major," Tarleton fired back. "This is not the first time we have had to run down a pack of fleeing rebels. My men have always done what is required of them and have fought like tigers when the chase is won. We are closing on Morgan. We cannot allow him to escape."

McArthur took a deep breath, preparing to continue his argument, when Tarleton interrupted him, "Where is the artillery? Is it keeping up?"

"I believe so, sir," McArthur replied. "The column has become somewhat confused in the dark, but I have had no report of any problems."

"Be certain, Major," Tarleton said, irritated. "See to the guns, sir."

"Yes, sir," McArthur answered, suppressing his anger as he wheeled his horse around.

Looking up and seeing one of his dragoons approaching rapidly from the north, Tarleton called back, "Hold up, Major!"

McArthur turned his horse back around and brought it alongside Tarleton's just as the dragoon arrived.

"Colonel, the rebels have stopped and have made camp," the dragoon said.

"Where?" Tarleton asked.

"They are about six miles from here, sir," he replied.

"Six miles? How far are they from the river?"

"Five or six miles, sir," the dragoon answered.

"Ha!" Tarleton exclaimed. "Then we have them!" He turned to McArthur. "Morgan will break for the river at dawn. By the time he does, we'll be on him.

"Order the men into camp, Major. I know they are hungry but tell them the rebels will feed us in the morning. We will rest a few hours. We march again at 3 o'clock."

19

The Cowpens
Spartan District, South Carolina
January 17, 1781
6:00 a.m.

An hour before dawn, Morgan's voice was booming through the camp. "Get up, men! Get up! Benny's coming!" he shouted cheerfully as he rode among the tents, rousing the men. "Eat quickly," he said. "We don't want to be late for our appointment."

Ransom stepped out of his tent, and saw Lieutenant James Simons standing by the smoldering campfire, stirring it back to life.

"General Morgan is quite a character," Ransom said.

"He's been up all night," Simons answered. "Didn't sleep a wink. He personally greeted every farmer who came to join us."

"Well, let's try not to disappoint him today," Ransom said. "Have the horses been fed and watered?"

"Yes, sir," Simons answered. "We're ready."

As they were talking, Washington joined them,

rubbing his hands together over the fire. "It's colder than a witch's teat this morning. I didn't know it got this cold in South Carolina."

"This feels balmy compared to Pennsylvania," Ransom said, drawing chuckles and nods from Washington and Simons.

"Our last scouting report has Tarleton about five miles away and coming fast," Washington said. "We will fight today, gentlemen, and soon."

"How reliable is that report, Colonel? Should we deploy now?" Ransom asked.

Washington shook his head. "Not yet. But we do need to know exactly how close they are."

"I'll go," Ransom answered.

"No. I need you here," Washington said. Looking at Simons he said, "You go, Lieutenant. Take your squadron, determine where Tarleton is, then report back here as quickly as you can."

"Yes, sir," Simons answered.

"Do not engage them, Lieutenant. Just locate them," Washington added.

Simons nodded and stepped quickly away.

Washington rubbed his hands together over the fire. He began speaking, as if to himself, "No more flying away. We will face about and give battle to the enemy—acquit ourselves like men in defense of our country." He turned to face Ransom and continued, "We will be outnumbered today and up against their best," he said. "But no matter what else happens, I will not be humiliated and disgraced by Banastre Tarleton. Not again. Not ever again. I will die first."

Ransom gazed pensively into the fire, thinking of the times Tarleton had scattered them in the past. After a few seconds he said, "As will I, sir."

20

On the road between Burr's Mill and the Cowpens
Spartan District, South Carolina
January 17, 1781
6:00 a.m.

Tarleton had his army back on the march at three a.m., pushing the men down the muddy narrow road in the cold night with no breakfast and little rest, leaving his wagons behind with orders for them to join the march at dawn. He was riding at the head of the column, when an elderly civilian on horseback, flanked by two dragoons, rode quickly up.

"What is the situation?" Tarleton snapped.

"The rebels are not marching, Colonel," one of the dragoons said. "They appear to be forming for battle."

"A rearguard. To delay us while Morgan makes a run for the river," Tarleton replied dismissively.

"Respectfully, sir," the dragoon said, "That does not seem to be the case."

While Tarleton was pondering that, the civilian spoke, in a thick rustic accent. "They're hunkering down, Colonel."

Tarleton addressed the civilian. "Where are they?"

"'Bout five miles shy of the Broad," he answered.

"Do you know the place?" Tarleton asked.

"Yep," the civilian answered. "Folks round here call it the cow pens."

Tarleton thought for a few seconds. "They will have chosen a place suited for defense and unsuitable for our cavalry," he said, seemingly to himself. Turning back to the old man, he said, "Is the place heavily wooded? Swampy?"

"Naw," the man said. "It's mainly cleared. We use it as a place for catching cattle."

Tarleton was incredulous. "It's open ground, you say? Easy to ride on?"

"Oh, yes sir, that's for sure," the man replied. "Pasture mainly. Ain't no problem moving across it. Hit's a far sight better than this here road."

Tarleton slapped his fist into his palm. "It seems I have been overestimating General Morgan. He will give battle on open ground and with his back to the river? He is as incompetent as Gates. I would not have guessed him capable of such blunders."

After a few silent seconds, seemingly deep in thought, Tarleton looked up suddenly and said, "Let us press on, men. This morning we will destroy the rebels."

21

On the road between Burr's Mill and the Cowpens
Spartan District, South Carolina
January 17, 1781
6:15 a.m.

Simons leaned forward in his saddle, his head tilted, listening carefully. "Do you hear it, Sergeant?" he said quietly to Lawrence Everhart, the dragoon at his side.

"I don't hear anything," Everhart whispered back.

They had ridden out about three miles from camp and still had made no contact with the enemy. Now, as the sky began to brighten, Simons thought he could hear the sounds of horses approaching in the distance, but he wasn't sure.

"Let's try to get a little closer," he said.

The two men cautiously eased their mounts down the road, straining to hear, unaware that a squad of British dragoons was quietly advancing toward them, doing likewise. At a bend in the road, the two groups of horsemen suddenly found themselves face to face, separated by only a few yards. They all froze for a split second, regarding each other with surprise in the dim light of dawn. Then, instantaneously, the British dragoons spurred their horses and reached for their weapons, as their American counterparts wheeled suddenly and broke into gallops.

Racing away, Everhart heard the crack of a pistol and he felt his horse lurch. As the animal fell, he leaped off to avoid being pinned beneath. He came quickly to his feet and as he did a British dragoon sabered him, the blade ripping through his coat and tearing deeply and painfully into his right shoulder. As Everhart staggered backward, fumbling for his saber with his left hand, the British dragoon slashed him again, this time across his face, blinding him and dropping him to his knees. As he struggled to his feet, the dragoon rode up to him and raised his saber above his head, preparing to strike.

"Stop!" Ogilvie shouted as he rode up suddenly. "We need that man as a prisoner."

The dragoon looked at Ogilvie for a moment, then nodded, sheathed his saber, and rode away, joining in the pursuit of Simons. "Ground your weapon," Ogilvie said, leveling his pistol at Everhart. With his right arm hanging uselessly at his side, and with blood streaming down his face from the deep cut across his cheek, Everhart slowly drew out his saber with his left hand, then dropped it at his feet. At that very moment, Tarleton rode up.

"We encountered rebel dragoons," Ogilvie said. "Captured this one."

Tarleton dismounted quickly and stood facing Everhart.

"Has Morgan crossed the river?" he barked.

Everhart stood erect, saying nothing.

"How many men does Morgan have on this side of

the river?" Tarleton demanded.

Everhart remained silent.

"Get a rope, Captain Ogilvie," Tarleton said impatiently. "We shall hang this voiceless man right here." Stepping closer to Everhart he said, menacingly, "You will answer me, sir, or you will forfeit your life."

With the back of his left hand, Everhart wiped the blood away from his mouth and said, "What do you want to know?"

"What is Morgan doing?" Tarleton asked, brusquely.

Everhart turned his head and spat out a stream of blood. Turning back to Tarleton, he said, "What he's doing now I cannot say. Yesterday he was trying to gather the militia on this side of the river."

"So, he will fight?" Tarleton asked.

Everhart answered, "Maybe. It depends upon whether he can keep together the 200 men he has left."

"He's lying," Ogilvie muttered.

"Yes, but Morgan wouldn't be sending out dragoons to locate us if all we are approaching is a rear guard," Tarleton said, excitedly. "We have him! It will be another Camden. It will be another Gates defeat."

"I hope to God it will be a Tarleton defeat," Everhart said.

Tarleton flared and stepped closer to Everhart. "*I* am Colonel Tarleton!" he exclaimed.

With his left hand, Everhart wiped the blood from his eyes. He looked carefully back at the man standing before him. "And *I* am Sergeant Everhart," he said.

Tarleton grabbed the grip of his sword, his eyes ablaze, then hesitated. He stood for a few moments facing Everhart, who remained before him, unblinking as blood continued to stream down his face. Then, suddenly, Tarleton turned away and mounted his horse. "Have this man's wounds dressed," he barked out, before riding away.

22

The Cowpens
Spartan District, South Carolina
January 17, 1781
6:30 a.m.

As dawn broke over the frosty Carolina countryside, the men in Morgan's "Flying Army" were hastily deploying, forming in three parallel lines in accordance with the instructions Morgan had given his officers the night before. The riflemen of the first line were taking their positions when one of them touched a comrade on the shoulder, nodded at an approaching horseman, and said, "Well, look yonder."

"Good morning, gentlemen!" Morgan boomed, from atop his mount. "I'm looking for an impertinent little peacock named Benny. Have any of you men seen him?"

Morgan was answered with a scattering of laughter, the men amused by both his audacity and his attire. They had never seen Morgan wearing anything other than the hunting clothes of a frontiersman, but this morning he was in the full uniform of a brigadier general of the Continental Army. "I got all dressed up,"

Morgan said, "and I want to make sure I don't miss him."

As Morgan had ordered, Colonel McDowell had deployed sixty of his most expert Carolina riflemen on the right of the road, and Major Cunningham had sixty crack-shot Georgians on the left. "Give them two good shots, men," Morgan shouted.

Stopping his horse directly among the Georgians, Morgan lowered his voice and said, "You good Georgia men aren't going to let those Carolina boys over there shoot more of them than you, are you?" Morgan laughed as the men hooted and hollered in response. Then his smile suddenly vanished, and he said, "Take cover, gentlemen, and let them close on you. Then give them a rolling well-aimed fire. After you have fired, quickly reload and fire again—another good shot. Aim for the officers if you can. Then, after your second shot, fall back to the next line."

The men nodded and murmured. Morgan turned to Cunningham and spoke loudly enough for them all to hear. "These are a fine-looking lot of men, Major. With men such as these we cannot fail."

Morgan lifted his hat in salute and rode across the road to McDowell's men. "Two good shots, gentlemen!" he shouted. "Aim for the officers. Let them get close enough that you cannot miss. Fire, then reload and fire again. After your second shot, you are to fall back to Colonel Pickens' line there," he said, pointing at the line of militia forming about 150 yards away.

Leaning forward in the saddle and lowering his voice, Morgan continued, "Those Georgia boys across the road say they're better shots than you Carolina men. Is that true?"

As the men shouted their protests, Morgan laughed and raised his hand. "Give them two good well-aimed shots, men. Two good fires and the victory will be ours!"

As he was turning to leave, Morgan noticed the man who had come in with his sons the night before. "I am glad to see you, Mr. Jones. With men like you and your sons on this line, we cannot fail."

The man nodded, a look of grim determination etched on his furrowed face, "They killed my brother, General Morgan. Burned out his wife and children. We aim to pay 'em back."

Morgan nodded understandingly, his face tightened with emotion. "God bless you, men," he answered. "Give them hell."

As Morgan trotted toward the second line, Colonel Pickens rode out to meet him. "How many men do you have, Colonel?" Morgan asked as Pickens arrived.

"About 400," Pickens answered.

"Tarleton has over a thousand," Morgan said, "and by God, we will whip him!"

As they reached the line of militiamen, Morgan pulled up his horse and rose in his stirrups. "Give them two good fires, gentlemen!" he shouted. "Well-aimed shots. Make every one count! Just two fires, my good men. Two fires and you are free."

Morgan scanned the faces of the men. "Think today of your homes and families. After you have done your duty today and we have won our victory, think of the reception you will get! The old folks will bless you and the pretty girls," Morgan paused, laughed, and winked, "the pretty girls will all want to kiss you!"

Some of the men laughed nervously, then Morgan raised his voice even louder.

"Hold your heads up, men!" he shouted. "Two good fires my brave boys and the victory will be ours! After you have fired your second shot, you will fall back to the hill behind the line of Continentals and re-form there. From there you will launch the assault that will break their backs!"

Morgan paused, making sure he had the full attention of the men. He slapped his fist into his palm and shouted, "Old Dan Morgan has never been beat and by God he won't be beat today!"

Pickens raised his hat and the men answered with a cheer, as Morgan trotted toward the third line.

About 150 yards behind Pickens' line of militia, Morgan had deployed his Continental regulars—blue-uniformed veterans from Delaware and Maryland, the best soldiers under his command, flanked by Virginia militiamen and state troops, many of them former Continental regulars. Colonel Howard rode out to meet Morgan as he approached the line, which was formed behind a swale, making it invisible from the second line. "Sir, there are no men in the world I'd rather have beside me in a fight than these," Morgan said to Howard when he arrived. "Have them gather close. I want to talk to them."

Howard nodded and dispatched an aide with orders to have the men assemble. In a few minutes they were in place. From his saddle, Morgan looked out at them, battling back emotion.

"My friends in arms," he said. "I am proud to have the honor to be your general today. My dear boys, this is a day we are never going to forget."

He drew his sword and pointed it toward the lines of militia. "I have ordered those militiamen to fire two good shots, then fall back behind this line. You are to leave a gap in your line, for those men to pass through. When you see them coming, know that they have not been whipped. They will be falling back under my orders and only after they have greatly thinned the British line. When they pass through, you will cheer them for their heroism."

Howard suppressed a smile, pondering what Morgan had done. Instead of making it shameful for militia to retreat, he had devised a plan that made it heroic.

"The outcome of today's fight will come down to you, my friends," Morgan continued, somberly, without any of the jocularity he had used with the militiamen. "Remember all the times we have fought together. Remember Saratoga. Remember Monmouth. Remember Paoli. Remember Brandywine. Remember our friends and comrades who have fallen. Let us fight well this day, for our honor and for our liberty. Remember what is at stake here, my friends. May our countrymen someday say of us, remember what they did at Cowpens."

At that moment Colonel Washington rode quickly up and interrupted. "General," he said gravely, "the enemy is arriving on the field."

Morgan nodded at him, then looked back at the assembled men. "God bless you my brave boys," he said. "Do your duty today."

Morgan turned his horse and trotted toward the militia lines, with Washington riding alongside him. "You know what is expected of your men today, Colonel," Morgan said.

"I do, sir," Washington answered.

Morgan stopped his horse and looked directly at Washington. "Billy, you are a fine officer," he said.

"You will know what to do. When the opportunity presents itself, hit them. If they are routed, pursue them. If they whip us, you must cover our retreat."

Washington nodded, "It will be done, sir."

From the distant wood line came a long drum roll and the faint sound of shouted commands.

Both officers turned and gazed quietly in the direction of the sounds. After a few moments, Morgan spoke. "Benny's here. I reckon I ought to go have a look at him. Return to your command, Colonel. God be with you."

"And you, General," Washington said, as the men parted.

As Washington trotted up to the dragoons' assembly point, Collin rode up and took his place just behind and to the side of the colonel. "Double check all your tack, men," Washington shouted. "Make sure everything is tied tight."

Ransom edged his horse forward and spoke softly to Washington. "Shall we bring out Miss Elliott's flag, Colonel? Some of the men have inquired about it."

Washington shook his head. "I can't spare a man to carry it. See to your troop, Captain. Prepare for action."

23

The Cowpens
Spartan District, South Carolina
January 17, 1781
6:45 a.m.

Banastre Tarleton trotted his horse out onto the open field, as a squadron of British dragoons fanned out in front of him. "There they are, Colonel," Ogilvie said, pointing down the road. A few hundred yards in the distance, Tarleton could see what appeared to be a thin scattering of soldiers. He reached into his saddlebag and withdrew a spyglass.

"It's a skirmish line. Militia," Tarleton said, scanning the horizon. He snapped the spyglass shut and returned it to his saddlebag. "Probably just a rear guard. Try them with your squadron and let's see if they hold or run."

Ogilvie nodded and dashed off. In a few moments he and his dragoons were galloping toward the enemy line, sabers drawn. When they were about 50 yards away, the riflemen stepped out from behind trees and rose up from below the tall grass. Shots rang out from along the line and Tarleton watched through his spyglass as several of the dragoons tumbled from their saddles and the rest spun around and raced rapidly back.

Ogilvie rode up to Tarleton, breathless. "They are strongly positioned, Captain," Tarleton said. "Cover our flanks. We will drive them out with infantry."

Ogilvie nodded and rode away, just as a cluster of British officers rode up for orders.

"Bring up the guns," Tarleton barked. "Place them on either side of the road, here," he said, pointing. "Form lines of battle. I want the Fusiliers on the left and the Legion Infantry on the right. The Highlanders will form behind the first line, as our reserve. We will attack immediately."

"Shall we reconnoiter their positions first, Colonel?" McArthur asked.

"No," Tarleton immediately replied. "I have seen all I need to see. Look for yourselves," he said, gesturing toward the field. "Morgan is a fool. I have been overestimating his ability. The rebels are hemmed in and they have the river at their backs. They have no way to escape."

"They have no artillery, Colonel," McArthur said. "We could bombard them with impunity. Doing so would enable the men to rest and catch their breaths. They have been marching all night."

"No!" Tarleton shouted. "There is nothing before us but militia. Morgan's Continentals may be racing for the river right now. We must not allow them to escape. My orders are to attack immediately. Form your lines!"

The officers nodded and began to turn away, McArthur making no effort to conceal his disagreement. I was an officer before that boy was even born, he thought contemptuously as he turned away.

"Wait!" Tarleton shouted.

They all stopped and turned back to Tarleton. "When we charge them, they will break and run. Then we will chase them down and cut them to pieces. This whole thing will be over in half an hour. There will be plenty of opportunity to rest once we have annihilated this rabble. This is exactly how I handled them at Waxhaws. Now have your men discard their packs and prepare to attack."

With a final series of nods and grunts, the officers broke away and rode off to their men. Tarleton edged his horse forward and brought the spyglass back to his eye, noticing a blue-coated officer riding fearlessly in front of the skirmish line. He spun around and shouted to an artillery crew, as they were positioning their cannon. "Kill that man!"

24

The Battle of Cowpens
January 17, 1781
7:00 a.m.

Morgan reached the front line just as the squad of British dragoons were retreating. "That's good shooting, gentlemen!" he shouted to the riflemen as he arrived. "Keep giving it to them that way."

He rode through the line of militia and out into the field before it, as the British infantry was emerging from the woods to the beat of drums, forming into battle lines and unfurling their flags, their resplendent uniforms contrasting sharply with the Patriots' homespun attire.

"Ain't they a pretty bunch?" Morgan said, playfully and loudly enough for the men to hear him. He turned and faced his men. "They're just men, my brave fellows. No better than us. Remember that old Dan Morgan has never been beaten! Give them two good fires, gentlemen. Two fires and the victory will be ours!"

Colonel McDowell stepped out of the line, toward Morgan. "General," he said. "This is no place for you."

Morgan chuckled and nodded, as the drums of the British infantry were beating out commands behind him. "You are right, sir," he said. "I shall leave things here in your capable hands." Morgan spurred his horse and trotted through the line of riflemen, shouting as he passed, "Two good fires men and the day will be ours!"

Moments later a cannonball plowed into the ground in front of the line, exactly where Morgan's horse had been standing.

The Patriots tightened their grips and leveled their rifles, as the red wave before them began to advance.

Tarleton led the attack, riding among his men and shouting encouragement, even as the militiamen's rifles began dropping officers from their saddles. "Forward, men! Forward!" he shouted, waving his sword, his eyes ablaze.

As the toll of the riflemen's fire began to increase, Tarleton saw that some of the Fusiliers, Irishmen seeing their first combat, had stopped and were taking aim to return fire. Furious, he sprinted into the line, screaming, "Advance, damn you!" He slapped one of the soldiers across the back on the head with the flat side of his sword, knocking the man off his feet. "Do not fire!" he shouted. "Close on them then charge them with the bayonet!"

A few of the men fired anyway, then resumed marching toward the rebels. Angered by the lapse in discipline, Tarleton galloped to his reserve, McArthur and his Highlanders, who were advancing in a line behind the Fusiliers. "Come up now, McArthur!" he shouted.

The Highlanders were seasoned veterans, the best men in Tarleton's army. A year earlier they had turned their kilts into plaid trousers and had reluctantly abandoned their bagpipes, but they still wore their Scottish bonnets and still retained the fierce Highland fighting spirit. Tarleton had intended to hold the Highlanders back until the rebels had broken, then send them rushing in to finish them off. But worried about losing the momentum of the attack, he decided to bring them into the fight immediately.

"Move up, now!" Tarleton repeated, pointing his sword to the front. "Swing to the left of the Fusiliers."

McArthur obeyed, leading his men forward in a hurried rush, and seeing as he did that the formations were becoming disordered as the lines intermingled. Meanwhile, all across the British lines, the crack of Patriot rifles was being followed by thuds as the balls found their targets.

~~~

Morgan pulled up alongside Pickens behind the second line of militia. He could see the riflemen in the distance as they pulled back, doing exactly as he had ordered: firing, then slowly withdrawing as they reloaded for their second shot. The British line advanced relentlessly, dozens of officers and men falling as they did.

"Steady, men!" Morgan shouted, as the retreating riflemen ran for the safety of the second line. "Hold your fire and let them through."

As the riflemen passed through the line, Morgan greeted them with appreciation. "Well done, my brave boys! Well done!" he exclaimed, as their officers formed the men into line with the rest of the militia.

~~~

Washington had maneuvered his dragoons to a place in the rear, behind a rise that kept them out of sight of the British and shielded them from the artillery fire. While his men awaited orders, he rode to the top of the hill, Collin by his side, to observe the action. He was watching the skirmish line of riflemen retreat when he suddenly heard shouts and cheering coming from behind him. He glanced back to see that one of the dragoons was riding along the column, carrying Miss Elliott's flag, affixed to a pole. The trooper stopped his horse, waved the flag dramatically, then drove the pole into the ground, drawing wild cheers from the dragoons. Washington caught the eye of Ransom, who just smiled and shrugged. The colonel shook his head with a little grin and turned back to observe the fighting.

~~~

Tarleton rode frantically among his men, pressing them to keep going. "Double quick, men! Give them the bayonet!" he shouted, and the men, dead-tired, obeyed.

As the Highlanders came up Tarleton rode up to McArthur. "Sweep them off this field, Major!"

McArthur, swallowing his disapproval of what he regarded a rash and impetuous attack, answered only with "Yes, sir."

~~~

Two hundred yards away, Jones had just finished reloading his rifle when, through a clearing in the smoke, he saw two mounted British officers in the distance. As he raised his rifle, he spoke a single word to his sons: "Yonder." Seeing the men his father was targeting, Joshua raised his rifle and took aim too, as his brother Tate continued hurriedly reloading his gun. Jones and Joshua squeezed their triggers, and their rifles cracked.

~~~

At the very moment they fired, a courier galloped up to deliver a message to Tarleton, coming directly into the line of fire. One of the rifle balls slammed into the back of the young man's head, and he pitched forward and tumbled off his horse, his blood and brains splattering onto Tarleton's face and coat. Tarleton's horse suddenly reeled and bucked; the other shot having struck it in the neck. As he fought to control the frightened and dying animal, the Highlanders' regimental surgeon galloped up. "Colonel, are you hit?" he asked.

"No," Tarleton barked, dismounting quickly as his horse stumbled, then fell over.

"Take my mount, sir," the surgeon said, dismounting and handing the reins to Tarleton.

Without responding, Tarleton stepped into the stirrup and swung up onto the horse's back. Turning to McArthur, enraged, he shouted, "Give them no quarter, sir! Spare none of them!"

McArthur nodded and rode away. "Highlanders, advance!" he shouted.

The Scots dutifully leveled their bayonet-tipped muskets and went forward at a trot, shouting huzzahs.
~~~

~~~

Sitting atop his horse, just behind the militia line, Morgan watched as the shouting British infantry jogged toward them, the early morning sunlight glistening off their bayonets. The Highlanders' yell was intended to unnerve their opponents and Morgan feared it was working. Glancing around, he could see the men becoming uneasy, fighting the urge to run. He spurred his horse and moved out in front of the line.

"Listen at that!" he shouted to his men. "That's a British holler and that's the best they can do! Let's give them the old Indian holler, boys! The war whoop!" And with that Morgan leaned back in the saddle, tilted his head up and screamed "Yihee! Yihee! Yihee!" All along the Patriot line the militiamen began joining him, until they were all shouting back at the charging Scotsmen.

"Now let's show them what we're made of my brave boys! For liberty!" Morgan shouted, before walking his horse back behind the line of men.

When the British were about 100 yards away Pickens shouted, "Make ready!" His command was immediately echoed by Patriot officers all down the line and 400 guns snapped into position. "By battalions, left to right! Take aim!"

The men aimed their guns as the red wave continued rolling toward them, screaming huzzahs, bayonets leveled.

"Wait till you can see the whites of their eyes!" Morgan yelled, racing up and down the line. "Aim for their belt buckles!"

When the British had closed to 50 yards the captain of the leftmost American battalion yelled "Fire!" Like
~~~

a thunderclap a hundred guns fired into the charging British line, followed almost immediately by another crash of fire from the second battalion, then the third, then the fourth.

As the wind cleared away the smoke from the volley, it revealed a strip of dead and wounded British stretching across the entire front of the American line, and all along the Patriot line officers were shouting, "Prime and load, men! Prime and load!"—the command to reload as quickly as possible.

The British who were still on their feet hesitated momentarily, staggered by the blast and the carnage. Most of their officers were down, but those who were not were shouting orders and the seasoned, disciplined veterans promptly obeyed, leveling their muskets and unleashing a withering volley into the American line, then immediately charging forward again, shouting huzzahs.

As the Patriots who had not been struck by the British volley fumbled with their cartridges and ramrods, they were keeping their eyes on their charging, screaming enemies and their 16-inch bayonets. Under the best of circumstances, performing the multiple separate motions and steps necessary to reload a musket is not an easy process. A typical militiaman could do it in about 20 seconds, which is approximately the same amount of time required for a charging British infantryman to cover 50 yards. To the Patriots the math was obvious immediately—if they remained where they were, many of them would be bayoneted before they could finish reloading. Although some men nevertheless stubbornly held their ground, loading as fast as they could in the face of the British charge, all along the American line many men began to turn and run.

As the line began to melt away, Morgan rode among the men, desperate to prevent the retreat from turning into a rout. "Steady, men! We are not beaten!" he shouted at them. "Give them one more fire and the day will be ours!"

~~~

As Morgan was trying to stem the tide, from a distance Tarleton watched the sudden American retreat. It was exactly what he had expected. He galloped to Lieutenant Henry Nettles, commander of the dragoons on the British right flank, men from the feared and storied 17th Lancers Regiment, wearing their bright red coats and black helmets adorned with death heads. "Charge them, Lieutenant!" Tarleton shouted, pointing his sword at the retreating Patriots.

Nettles nodded and shouted the command to charge. With sabers drawn, his fifty dragoons sprinted into the mass of fleeing militiamen, slashing left and right, cutting them down.

~~~

Duncan Jones was running for the rear, his sons on either side of him, when he heard the horses coming. Turning as he ran, he saw the British cavalrymen thundering toward them, sabers raised. In an instant he shoved his son Tate to the ground, then lifted his rifle just in time to deflect a saber blow that one of the dragoons had aimed at his head. As Jones parried a second slash, his son Joshua swung his rifle like a club, striking the dragoon in the back with such force that the blow nearly knocked him out of the saddle, unaware that at that moment another British dragoon was charging toward them from behind, his saber raised above his head.

~~~

From his post atop the hill behind which his men were stationed, Washington had watched as the line of militia broke into retreat. Soon afterwards he saw what he had been waiting for: a force of British dragoons charging toward the fleeing men. "Our turn," he muttered. He turned his horse and rushed down the hill, to within easy earshot of his men. "Sabers!" he shouted, the command quickly followed by the sound of over a hundred swords being drawn from their scabbards. As the men hurriedly wrapped their sword knots around their wrists, Washington turned to Collin. "Sound the charge," he said.

Collin lifted his trumpet to his lips and blew out the command, and when he did the American dragoons thundered over the hill and down into the flank and rear of the unsuspecting British horsemen, Washington leading the way with upraised saber and Collin racing along at his side.

~~~

After his father had pushed him down to save him from the charging dragoon, Tate Jones scrambled back to his feet. With swinging British sabers slicing and slashing at the Patriot militiamen all around him, he saw a dragoon bearing down directly on his brother from behind. "Look out!" he screamed, pointing.

Joshua turned quickly and saw the dragoon galloping toward him, sword lifted, about to strike. Defenseless, he froze, awaiting his fate.

The British dragoon never heard the approach of the charging American cavalry. Just as he was about to cut the young militiaman down, Washington galloped past, slashing the dragoon across his neck and dropping him from his saddle instantly. Jones and his sons looked on in astonishment as Washington raced away, having sabered the British trooper without even slowing his charge, and with his American cavalrymen following at a gallop immediately behind him.

All across the field the scene was repeated. The British dragoons, confidently chasing down and sabering the retreating militia, had been caught entirely by surprise. As Washington's men crashed into them and began striking them down, Nettles called a retreat and the British who had survived the sudden attack, galloped away.

The force of Washington's assault and the sudden precipitate retreat of the British dragoons seemed to immediately settle and invigorate the shaken militiamen. Morgan and Pickens were riding among them, shouting "Rally, men!" and hundreds of them, who just moments before had been demoralized and on the edge of panic, began reforming their lines and loading their guns.

As the British dragoons retreated, Jones turned to his son Joshua. "You all right?" he asked.

"I reckon," the boy answered, uncertainly. "I sure thought my hide was in the loft that time."

After detaching a squadron to pursue the retreating British dragoons, Washington turned to Collin, whose face was shining from the thrill of the attack. "Sound the recall," he said calmly. Collin blew out the command and Washington led the men at a trot back to their position behind the hill.

25

The Battle of Cowpens
January 17, 1781
7:30 a.m.

Tarleton watched, chagrined, as his dragoons fled the field under the weight of Washington's counterattack. The charge had surprised him as much as it had surprised his dragoons. He was even more surprised when he crested the top of the hill, following his infantry, and saw before him, rather than a herd of panicked militiamen racing for the river, a solid line of blue—Morgan's Continental regulars standing shoulder-to-shoulder holding bayonet-tipped muskets.

The British soldiers jogging in pursuit of the retreating militia froze momentarily at the sight. But being seasoned veterans who knew only victory, after a brief pause they leveled their muskets and pressed forward, shouting huzzahs.

Peppered with Patriot rifle fire as they advanced toward the Continentals, the Fusiliers pressed resolutely forward, even as their comrades were falling around them. When they came within musket range, the Continental line erupted with a devastating volley.

The Fusiliers who remained standing obeyed with cool discipline when their officers shouted, "Make ready! Present arms!" Many of the men on the Continental line winced as the British leveled their muskets. "Fire!"

The British volley tore into Howard's line, dropping many of the Continentals. "Steady men! Close ranks! Prime and load!" Howard shouted as he rode along the rear of the line. The Americans quickly reloaded. No one ran.

Meanwhile the Fusiliers were also reloading as quickly as possible and within 30 seconds of their first volley they fired another and were answered moments later by another rolling volley from the Continentals. It became a slugfest and a contest of wills, as the two lines of soldiers stood hurling deadly volleys at each other.

Seeing that the Continentals had checked the advance and were showing no inclination to withdraw, Tarleton galloped to McArthur, whose Highlanders were coming up on the left rear of the Fusiliers. "Take them in the flank, McArthur!" he shouted, pointing his sword at the right end of the American line. "Swing around them and roll them up!"

McArthur nodded, having already recognized the opportunity. "Highlanders! Double quick!" he shouted as he led them forward, waving his sword. The Scots responded with a "Huzzah!" and followed him at a jog.

Howard saw them coming and he knew his men were about to be overwhelmed. The line of advancing redcoats extended beyond the right of the Continentals and would be able to sweep around the end of the line and descend upon the American flank and rear. To meet the danger Howard saw at once he must refuse his flank, that is, bend the right side of his line backward so that the men kept their faces to the enemy and blocked them from coming around the rear.

He rushed over to the captain commanding the company of Virginians on the far right and shouted, "To the right about face! To the right wheel! March!," then galloped away to attend to the rest of the line. The captain dutifully repeated the command he thought he had just heard. "About face! March!" he yelled. And suddenly, with the shouting Highlanders bearing rapidly down on them, the Americans on the right turned around and began marching away.

As the Continentals down the line saw the men on their right suddenly withdrawing, they assumed the men were acting under orders and they followed suit. Within moments, the entire American line was retreating. By the time Howard realized what was happening, it was too late to stop it without risking throwing the entire line into confusion.

To the advancing British, the sight of the rebels' sudden withdrawal was like an electrifying jolt of adrenaline. They quickened their pace, stopping just along enough to fire a volley into the backs of the Americans, dropping several of them. A generation earlier the Highlanders would have thrown down their guns at that point, drawn their dirks and knives, and rushed wildly at their enemy. Although the weaponry of the legendary Highlanders' Charge had evolved, the élan remained. With a cheer, they leveled their bayonets and surged forward.

From his position behind the line, Morgan saw what was happening and he was mortified. He spurred his mount and raced toward Colonel Howard.

~~~
~~~

Tarleton had seen it too—the Americans running just as he had expected they would. His eyes flashed as he raced along his lines shouting, "Charge them! Finish them off!" As Ogilvie came riding forward with a troop of dragoons for orders, Tarleton pointed his sword toward Howard's retreating line and yelled, "Flank them, Ogilvie! Swing into their rear! Envelope them! Give them no quarter!"

Ogilvie drew his saber and spurred his mount, leading his men at a gallop toward the American rear.

~~~

The sudden and inexplicable American retreat had astonished William Washington, watching from atop the hill behind which his dragoons were waiting. And when he saw Ogilvie's dragoons racing around the end of the American line, he realized disaster was imminent. "Sound the charge!" he shouted.

Once again, in their zeal to cut down the American infantry, the British dragoons failed to see Washington's cavalry coming until it was too late. The American horsemen crashed into the flank and rear of Ogilvie's troop, slashing and hacking their way through the surprised dragoons. After riding completely through them, Washington wheeled his men around and charged again, this time completely scattering the enemy riders who had not been cut down on the first pass. In a matter of seconds it was over—Ogilvie's troop was shattered and he and the other survivors were racing back to the safety of the British rear.

As the remaining British dragoons retreated, Washington looked out at the scene to the south of him—the elated British breaking formation to chase
~~~

the retreating Continentals. He immediately recognized an opportunity. "Captain Wiatt!" he shouted. In an instant Ransom was beside him. "Tell Howard they are coming at him like a mob," Washington said, his face flushed. "Tell him to give them a fire and I will charge them!" Ransom nodded in acknowledgment, spurred his horse, and galloped toward Colonel Howard.

Morgan arrived first. Furious, he shouted at Howard, "What is the meaning of this? Why are your men retreating?!"

His eyes flashing in anger and irritation, Howard spun around and pointed at his line. "Sir!" he shouted. "Do these men look like they have been beaten?"

In an instant Morgan saw his meaning. Yes, the Continentals were retreating. But they were marching away, not running. And they were still in formation, loading as they marched. There was no sign that they were panicked or demoralized.

"Very well, Colonel," Morgan said. "Form your new line on me." With that he sprinted to the top of the hill, turned to face the enemy, and drew his sword. "Form here, my brave men!" he shouted, waving the sword above his head.

Just as Morgan galloped away, Ransom arrived. "Colonel!" he shouted to Howard. "Colonel Washington says the enemy is coming at you like a mob. They are disorganized, sir. Give them a fire and we will charge them!"

Howard shot a fierce glance at Ransom. "Sir!" he shouted. "That is exactly what I am about to do!"

Only about fifteen yards separated the retreating Continentals and the redcoats pursuing them when Howard suddenly stood in his stirrups and shouted commands in quick succession: "Halt! Straight about face! Take aim!" As if on parade, the disciplined Continentals stopped, spun around, and leveled their muskets.

The British froze in their tracks. They would have been no more astonished had the Americans suddenly sprouted wings and flown away. In an instant they had gone from being just moments away from plunging their bayonets into the backs of their routed enemies, to facing over 400 muskets pointed at their faces.

"Fire!" Howard shouted and a wall of flame erupted along the Continental line. The British were mowed down like ripe hay. Immediately after the roar of the volley, and with the smoke still hanging over the line, Howard shouted, "Charge bayonets!" and with a shout the entire Continental line surged forward into the mass of reeling redcoats.

It had all happened in mere seconds—what would be remembered as one of the most stunning reversals of fortune in American military history. As the Continentals rushed forward with their bayonets leveled, Ransom heard a trumpet blast and looked behind him. What he saw was one of the most thrilling sights of his life—Washington's dragoons thundering onto the field, sabers drawn, screaming "Liberty!", with Colonel Washington in front and Collin galloping alongside him, sounding the charge.

Meanwhile Pickens and his militiamen rushed back into the battle, advancing and firing into the flank of the dispirited Highlanders.

It was more than the British troops could stand. With Howard's Continentals charging them from the front, Washington's dragoons crashing down on their flank and rear, and Pickens' militiamen advancing on their other flank, every man still on his feet knew the situation was hopeless. Encircled and exhausted, with over half of their officers dead, with the bodies of their dead and groaning wounded comrades lying all around them, they began to turn and run. Some threw themselves down on the ground, unable to continue. Many began throwing down their weapons.

As the British broke, some the American shouts changed from "Liberty!" to "Tarleton's Quarter!" Hearing the cry, Morgan dashed suddenly with sword raised into the midst of the melee that was threatening to become a massacre. "All who lay down their arms are to be given quarter!" he shouted at his men. "Harm any of them and you will answer to me!"

Meanwhile McArthur rode among his fleeing men, desperately calling on them to rally and finally managing to form some of them into a tight square, for a fight to the finish. "Die bravely, my Highlanders!" he shouted.

Seeing that the Scots intended to continue the fight, Howard rode boldly up to McArthur and demanded his surrender. McArthur stared back at him, sword in hand. "Our orders were to give no quarter and so we expect none," he answered coolly.

Furious, Howard yelled over McArthur's head, "Ground your arms and you shall all have good quarter!" The Highlanders hesitated, but then one man threw down his gun, another followed suit, and soon they were all dropping their weapons. As Howard spurred his horse and galloped toward another cluster of British who had not yet surrendered, Pickens rode up to McArthur. The proud Scotsman cast a glance at his defeated men, in their red coats, blue bonnets, and tartan trousers, and then back at the Carolinians surrounding them, in their tattered and stained buckskins. With a sad sigh, he handed his sword to Colonel Pickens.

~~~

Meanwhile Washington's dragoons were dashing among the broken British lines, striking down any man who resisted or who had not yet dropped his weapon. While chasing a fleeing British dragoon, James Simons spotted Everhart in the distance, his hands tied. Simons wheeled his horse and rode toward his captured comrade. As he approached, Simons saw a British officer put his pistol to Everhart's head. Everhart lunged at the officer, shoving him with a shoulder enough to deflect his shot, so that it only grazed his head. Enraged, Simons screamed and spurred his horse to a gallop. The British officer, who had not before noticed him, turned toward the sound of the scream. The last thing he ever saw was Simons' saber swinging furiously toward his face.

Simons dismounted and quickly untied his friend's hands. With blood streaming down his face from his lacerated scalp, onto a uniform already caked with blood from his earlier wounds, Everhart said, "I'm mighty glad to see you, Lieutenant."

"Are you hurt badly, Everhart?" Simons asked.

"I've been chopped up a lot today," Everhart answered. "But I seem to still be in one piece."

"I'll send the surgeon," Simons said, remounting.

"I'll find him, sir," Everhart answered. "You've got other business to finish."

Simons nodded and dashed away.
~~~

~~~

From his position behind the main line, Tarleton had seen it all unfold—his sweeping victory turned inexplicably into a sudden and colossal defeat, nearly his entire command dead, wounded, or surrendering. He raced around, calling in vain for the infantry to rally and searching frantically for his dragoons, most of whom had abandoned the field.

He was riding alongside Nettles and another officer when, from across the field, William Washington noticed the three men—two wearing the red coats and death-head helmets of the 17th Regiment and the third the green coat and black helmet of Tarleton's British Legion. Washington knew immediately that the man in the middle was Tarleton himself. Without hesitation, he spurred his horse and charged.

Knowing his colonel's tendency to take risk, Ransom had grown accustomed to keeping a watchful eye on Washington during battle. He was fifty yards behind Washington, chasing down a fleeing British soldier, when he saw the colonel suddenly wheel his horse and charge alone toward three mounted British officers. Ransom instantly gave up his chase, turned his horse, and galloped after Washington.

Having taken no notice of the lone American officer rushing toward him, Tarleton and the other officers turned to ride away. When Washington saw them turn, he rose in his stirrups, seething with anger. "Where is the boasting Tarleton now?" he shouted.

Stung by the taunt, Tarleton spun around, drew his sword, and charged toward Washington, the other two British officers racing to keep up with him.

The two colonels collided at full gallop, yelling as
~~~

their sabers clanged together. The force of the impact broke Washington's saber off at the hilt and with his eyes aflame Tarleton drew back his arm to slash again.

As he raced toward the dueling men, Ransom saw in a flash that Washington was about to be struck down—his saber broken and surrounded by three British officers with raised swords, preparing to strike. Screaming as he approached, Ransom drove his horse directly at Nettles, the man closest to him, reaching out and slashing his sword arm just as he was about to saber Washington. Meanwhile Tarleton swung his saber fiercely toward Washington's face, but with the hilt of his broken sword, Washington managed to deflect the blow. In the melee, the third British officer had circled behind Washington and was just about to plunge his saber into Washington's back, when he was unsaddled by a pistol shot.

At that, Tarleton wheeled and spurred his horse. Racing away, he drew his pistol, turned in his saddle and fired at Washington. The shot dug into the neck of Washington's horse and the animal suddenly staggered, spilling the colonel to the ground. Ransom dismounted hurriedly and ran to his side.

"All you hurt, Colonel?" he asked.

Washington scrambled to his feet, his blood still up. "Who fired that shot?" he yelled.

"It was Colonel Tarleton, sir," Ransom answered.

Washington looked fiercely at Ransom. "No!" he shouted, angrily. "Not that one. The one before it. Who fired it? My orders were no pistols!"

"That shot saved your life, Colonel," Ransom answered calmly. "That's who fired it," he said, pointing over Washington's shoulder.

Washington spun around to see who Ransom was

pointing to. It was Collin, seated on his horse with the smoking pistol still in his hand.

"Well, you wouldn't let me have a saber," the boy said.

Washington stood staring at him for a few moments, dumbfounded. After he regained his composure he said, "Well done, Collin." Turning back to Ransom the fire suddenly returned to his eyes. "To horse, Captain!" he shouted. "I will have him yet!"

"Colonel," Ransom replied calmly.

"What?" Washington barked, glaring back.

"Look," Ransom answered, turning, and sweeping his arm in the direction of the battlefield.

Washington turned quickly to see, then a look of wonder slowly spread across his face. The British army, which was on the verge of overwhelming them just minutes earlier, was surrendering *en masse*, their weapons at their feet, with scores of their dead and wounded lying about them.

"My God," he said quietly.

26

Gilbert Town
Rutherford County, North Carolina
January 18, 1781

A cold drizzle was falling as Washington and his bedraggled troopers rode wearily into the American camp at dusk. Morgan emerged from a little house where he had set up his headquarters and strode toward the front of the column, limping badly but beaming nonetheless.

Washington dismounted and handed the reins to an orderly, who led his horse away.

"I'm very glad to see you, Billy," Morgan said, grasping Washington's hand warmly.

Washington nodded in response. "I have brought you another hundred prisoners, sir, but I regret to report that Tarleton escaped. We pursued him for 24 miles, but a local woman sent us down the wrong road, and we lost him."

"A Tory?" Morgan asked.

Washington shook his head. "Patriot. We did not know it, but Tarleton had taken her husband as a hostage. She feared he would be killed if we caught them. She confessed it all later. By then it was too late."

Morgan nodded and stood silently for a few moments, then waved his hand and smiled. "It is no matter," he said. He threw his arm across Washington's shoulders and turned toward his headquarters. "Well, Billy, we gave that rascal Tarleton a devil of a whipping, didn't we?"

"That you did, sir," Washington answered as they walked.

As they entered the house, Morgan said, "Your duel with Benny is the talk of the camp, my friend. You should not take such chances."

"I would like to have that moment back, sir. I wanted that scoundrel to taste my steel," Washington said, sternly.

Morgan laughed, then lowered himself slowly onto a stool, grimacing as he sat. He motioned toward another stool and Washington took a seat.

"The men can't seem to get enough of talking about your young trumpeter either," Morgan said with a smile.

"He's a fine young dragoon," Washington answered.

Morgan's smile vanished as he continued. "Lord Cornwallis is not going to let us just stroll casually away with all these prisoners. He will press us hard to get them back. That's why we've been marching like hell. While you were pursuing Tarleton, we were moving out. I left Colonel Pickens behind to bury the dead and by noon the rest of us were across the Broad, with all the prisoners. We must keep moving, Billy. We've got to put distance and rivers between us and his Lordship.

"Now that you have returned, I am going to detach Colonel Pickens with the prisoners and have him march them north and west. The rest of us will stay to the south and move east. If Cornwallis is near he will assume that we have the prisoners and he will pursue us, allowing Pickens to move them out of danger. We will all regroup at Sherrill's Ford.

"I know your men and horses are fatigued, Billy, but I will need you to keep us screened and protected as we move. We must reach General Greene. We cannot afford to fight Cornwallis alone."

"Understood, sir. It will be done," Washington answered.

Morgan grimaced as he lifted himself from the stool. "Damn, I'm proud of how the men march in this rain and mud. I've been pressing them hard, and they have borne it without complaint. I only wish I was holding up as well as they are."

Morgan had somehow willed his infirmity away during the battle, but now it had returned with a vengeance.

"It's getting so I can barely walk or ride," he said, distantly.

Washington rose too, but stayed silent, uncertain of how to respond.

After a few moments Morgan stepped forward and clapped Washington on the back, his confident and cheerful demeanor having returned. "Well, my friend, let's get this army out of danger and then we can all rest."

"Yes, sir," Washington said. "I will dispatch videttes immediately. If Cornwallis is coming, he will not surprise us."

~~~
~~~

Across camp, Ransom was checking to see that his tent stakes were secure when he noticed Collin walking past, carrying his saddle. A few feet away some of the men were trying to start a fire.

"The wood is too wet, boys," one of them said. "We need some dry kindling." Noticing Collin passing by, he called out, "Collin!"

Collin stopped, turned, and looked toward the men, impassively.

The dragoon smiled and motioned with his arm. "Come on over and eat with us," he said.

Collin smiled slightly and stepped toward them.

27

Camp at Hillhouse Plantation
Turkey Creek, South Carolina
January 18, 1781

A cold drizzle was falling as Tarleton and his bedraggled troopers rode wearily into the British camp at dusk. Charles, Earl Cornwallis, emerged from the house he had appropriated for his headquarters. Short and stocky, 42 years-old, and wearing the uniform of a British lieutenant general, he strode purposefully toward the column, toward the handsome, muscular 26-year-old colonel at its head.

Tarleton dismounted and handed the reins to an orderly, who led his horse away.

"I'm very glad to see you Colonel, but the reports I have received are most distressing," Cornwallis said, gravely.

Tarleton sighed as he pulled off his gloves. "My lord…," he began.

Cornwallis interrupted him. "Come inside, Colonel," he said, turning and leading the way into the house and into the room he was using as an office. After both men were inside, Cornwallis said, "What has happened, sir?"

"The men were defeated, my lord," Tarleton answered, standing at attention.

"What are your losses?" Cornwallis asked.

"The artillery and the infantry," Tarleton replied.

"The artillery and the..." Cornwallis repeated softly, staggered by the news. He walked slowly to a small table in the center of the room, against which a sword was resting. Cornwallis gripped the sword by the hilt and pressed the tip into the floor, leaning on it like a cane. "What has become of your infantry, Colonel?"

"Captured, sir. Or slain on the field," Tarleton answered, remaining erect and staring straight ahead.

"The Fusilers? The Legion Infantry?" Cornwallis said.

"Captured or killed, sir," Tarleton answered.

"The Highlanders?" Cornwallis asked, with disbelief.

"Lost, sir. At the critical moment of the battle, they refused to obey my orders. They refused to fight," Tarleton said.

Leaning on his sword and shaking his head, Cornwallis said, "Refused to fight? The Highlanders? What of Major McArthur?"

"Presumably taken with the men, sir," Tarleton answered.

After a few silent moments, Cornwallis continued. "This information is most astonishing, Colonel. Did you not have superior numbers?"

"The enemy was in much greater force than we had anticipated, my lord," Tarleton replied, stung by the question.

Looking down, leaning on his sword, Cornwallis shook his head. "What have you left, Colonel?" he asked, without looking up.

"The dragoons, my lord. And the infantry that had been assigned to guard the wagons," Tarleton answered.

Cornwallis lifted his eyes, meeting Tarleton's. "Are you telling me, sir, that you have lost ninety percent of the troops under your command?"

"I overtook General Morgan on ground that was perfectly suited for battle, my lord," Tarleton said, hurriedly. "With his back to the river. We had every favorable circumstance to crush the rebels. At first light I formed the men for battle. The Fusiliers and the Legion infantry drove the rebels and forced them to retreat. The Highlanders were my reserve. I brought them up to oppose Morgan's regulars, but I regret they did not display their usual alacrity and valor. When the rebels launched a countercharge, the men threw down their arms. An entirely unaccountable panic, my lord. Had they done their duty, sir, the victory would have been ours."

Cornwallis let Tarleton's words sink in, making no immediate response. As incredible as he found the accusation against McArthur and his Highlanders, he knew he would have to depend heavily on Tarleton in the coming campaign and that he could not afford to bruise the young dragoon's ego. A swirl of emotions clouding his mind, Cornwallis leaned so heavily on the sword that it suddenly snapped in two, causing him to stagger forward. With a fit of anger, he slung the hilt into the corner of the room.

Tarleton had never seen such emotion from the usually stoical aristocrat.

"General, sir," he said, deferentially, "If I no longer have Your Lordship's confidence, then..."

Cornwallis lifted his hand and turned suddenly to face Tarleton, silencing him. His face was flushed, but he had regained his composure. "Lieutenant Colonel Tarleton," he said, measuredly, "the means you used to bring the enemy to action were able and masterly. The total misbehavior of the troops alone is to blame and has deprived you of the glory which you were due."

Tarleton nodded, in appreciation.

Cornwallis continued, "I need you now more than ever, Colonel. I will not rest until those prisoners are freed. However long it takes and however far we must go, I will not rest until the rebels are brought to heel. If need be, I will follow them to the end of the world." After a pause he said, "See to your men, Colonel."

Tarleton nodded, stiffly and formally, then turned and marched out of the room.

28

Peytonsburg
Pittsylvania County, Virginia
January 22, 1781

Miles before the town came into view, Bayard began hearing them—faintly at first, but more clearly as he drew closer. By the time he reached the outskirts of town it was not only the church bells in Peytonsburg that were clanging incessantly, but dinner bells on farms across the countryside were joining in as well. Noticing a chaise approaching from town, Bayard gave his horse a little kick and rode to meet it. The chaise halted as he pulled alongside it and Bayard saw that its driver was Tabitha Wiatt. She was weeping.

"What is the matter, Mrs. Wiatt?" he asked with concern. "What has happened?"

"Have you not heard the news, sir?" she answered, with tears streaming down her face. "Such glorious news! Praise be to God!"

"I have not," Bayard answered, feeling his stomach tighten.

"Oh, sir, our prayers have been answered!" she exclaimed. "General Morgan has utterly defeated the devil Tarleton!"

Bayard fought to stay composed, his face betraying nothing. "Remarkable!" he answered. "Are you certain of that, Mrs. Wiatt?"

"Yes, of course!" she answered cheerfully, wiping the tears from her face. "An express arrived with the news this morning. Major Giles himself! Oh, sir, it is the most wonderful news! I can hardly contain my joy!"

His head swimming, and fighting to suppress his distress, Bayard said, "And your son, ma'am?"

Tabitha nodded, wiping her eyes again. "I have no specific confirmation of that, but I trust that the Lord has safely delivered Ransom. I feel in my heart that he is safe."

Bayard nodded. "Pray that it is so, ma'am."

Her tears flowing again, Tabitha reached out and took Bayard's hand. "Mr. Bayard, I am sure that your prayers have contributed to this victory and to Ransom's safety. Our God is merciful and just."

Squeezing her hand, Bayard answered, "We must trust him to show us his will, as he shall do in the fullness of time."

"Thank you kindly for your concern, sir," Tabitha said, smiling warmly as she released his hand. "Now I must hurry home to share this wonderful news. God bless you, sir."

"And you, ma'am," Bayard replied, touching the brim of his hat, as the chaise pulled away.

The streets were thronged with people, wild with excitement, as Bayard rode into town—bells ringing, guns being fired in the air. Seeing John Wilson standing outside Martin's Tavern, Bayard rode to him, dismounted and tied his horse to the post.

"Quite the tumult, Colonel Wilson," he said as he

approached and shook Wilson's hand.

"A spontaneous celebration, my friend," Wilson said with a broad smile. "A *feu de joie*! It's quieter in the tavern than in the street. Come inside and have an ale."

Bayard followed Wilson into the tavern, and they settled at a table in the back, as far from the door as possible. By the time they were being seated, the server was already putting two tankards on the table before them. Wilson lifted one of them, tilted it toward Bayard and said, "To our great victory!"

Bayard took up the other tankard, bumped it against Wilson's and replied, "To victory."

The men took deep draughts, then set the mugs down.

"What exactly is the news, Colonel, and how reliable is it?" Bayard asked.

"General Morgan has won a signal victory. That is certain. I have that directly from General Morgan's aide de camp Major Giles, who is on his way to Philadelphia to inform Congress," Wilson answered.

"What are the details?" Bayard asked.

"Sir, they are magnificent," Wilson answered. "Tarleton's command was nearly annihilated. Somewhere in South Carolina at a place called Cowpens. Over 100 killed, at least 10 of them officers. Over 700 taken prisoner, 200 of them wounded. We captured their artillery, their colors, their wagons, at least 100 horses, and most of their baggage. Less reliable camp talk says Tarleton was wounded, perhaps seriously, by Colonel Washington himself no less."

"Simply astonishing," Bayard said, shaking his head and taking another drink. "General Morgan's losses?" he asked.

"Trifling," Wilson answered. "Twelve killed. Sixty

wounded."

Bayard took another drink, letting Wilson's remarks sink in.

"And mind you, Reverend," Wilson added, "these were not Tory militia that General Morgan defeated. They were British regulars."

"Then this is their worst defeat since Saratoga," Bayard said. "How did it happen?'

Wilson laughed and shrugged. "Dan Morgan," he said. Remembering Bayard's profession, he quickly added, "Well, Providence, that is."

Bayard smiled, then drained his tankard.

"Prayers are still needed, sir," Wilson said. "No doubt Cornwallis will be pursuing General Morgan now like a nest of angry hornets to try to reclaim the prisoners."

"To that chase, Colonel Wilson, I shall devote fervent prayers," Bayard replied.

29

Soblett Farm
Bedford County, Virginia
January 22, 1781

"Mama," Lucy Soblett cried out from the front porch of her home. "May I walk with Will down to the creek?"

"As long as you stay where I can see you," a woman's voice answered from within the house. After a pause the voice added, "You behave yourself, Will Lawton."

"Yes ma'am," the young couple answered in unison, Lucy blushing and Will grinning.

Hand in hand, they strolled down the path that led from the porch to the creek. Lucy leaned her head against Will's shoulder.

"I don't want to wait any longer, Lucy," Will said softly. "I want us to get married."

Lucy sighed deeply, then shook her head. "No, Will," she answered. "As I've told you at least a dozen times, Pa says we can get married when I'm twenty."

"But that's three years from now," Will protested with a whine.

"It's twenty-six months," Lucy said. "You heard what he said. Anything worth having is worth waiting for."

"I heard him. But doggone it, I don't want to wait that long," Will said. "How old was your mother when she got married?"

Lucy shook her head again. "It doesn't matter, Will."

"Don't you want to, Lucy?" Will asked, plaintively. "Don't you want us to get married?"

Lucy turned and faced Will, her brown eyes moistened with emotion. "Of course I do, Will. But we must be patient."

Will nodded, biting his lip. Then a mischievous sparkle appeared in his eyes. "You know, there is another way."

"What other way?" Lucy asked, looking at him skeptically.

"Well," Will began, feigning seriousness before suddenly playfully grabbing Lucy around her waist. "I could just come over one night, steal you, and carry you off."

"Oh, you stop it!" Lucy exclaimed, giggling as she struggled to escape his grasp.

"I could carry you off and scandalize the county," Will said with a laugh, continuing to hold onto Lucy as she giggled and squirmed.

"Lucy!" a woman's voice boomed from the house. "Y'all come on back now!"

Will released her with a chuckle. Lucy, straightening her dress, said, "Now you've done it."

As they were walking back to the house, they saw Lucy's father approaching on horseback. Will had known Abraham Soblett all his life and had long wondered at his composure and practicality. He could not recall ever having seen Mr. Soblett reveal an emotion. And Will had long since grown accustomed to the challenges attendant to any conversation with him.

They waited as he rode toward them, Mrs. Soblett having stepped out onto the porch to await him too.

"The town is astir," Soblett said, upon reaching the house.

Will stepped forward and took the horse by the bridle, as Soblett carefully dismounted.

"The town is astir," he repeated, "with news of a most astounding victory."

At once, questions and exclamations burst from Lucy, Will, and Mrs. Soblett.

"Victory?!"

"Whose victory?!"

"What victory?"

Soblett stood serenely, slowly removing his gloves while being battered with their questions.

"Tell us the news, Father!" Lucy exclaimed, reaching out and grabbing him by the hand.

Soblett looked back at her, his eyebrow cocked. "That is a rather demanding tone for a girl to use with her father," he said.

Frustrated, Lucy stamped her foot.

"Well, I shall use one more demanding than that if you continue to tease us, Abe," Mrs. Soblett said from the porch. "What is the 'astounding' news you have heard?"

Soblett looked at his wife for a few moments, expressionless. She met his gaze, unblinking.

"As you know, my good wife," Soblett said, removing his hat, "I traveled to Peytonsburg in the hope that some coffee might have miraculously appeared there for sale and in the even more forlorn hope that the script that we are advised is now money might have suddenly attained some value. I was ultimately disappointed on both counts. There is neither coffee nor any expectation that we may expect to have any for the foreseeable future. And if it did exist, it would require a wagon load of paper continentals to purchase any. The price of a half bushel of potatoes is now one hundred dollars. Well, I should be more precise. The price of the potatoes when I left Peytonsburg was one hundred dollars. By now the price may be two hundred dollars. Likewise, I was advised that a pint of whiskey may also be had for one hundred dollars. Not that I inquired as to the price of such an item as that, mind you. I believe that information must have been volunteered."

"Father," Lucy whined, "what is the news of the victory you mentioned?"

"Oh, yes," Soblett said, turning to his daughter. "That news came from Edward Giles, who, I was informed by multiple sources, came through town this morning in a rush. This is not one of our Giles', of course. I am referring instead to Major Edward Giles of the Maryland Line, who has evidently been dispatched as some sort of courier. He traded horses at the livery and took his breakfast, I was told, at Mr. Wimbish's, which was of course a poor choice as the fare at Martin's is superior."

"Father!" Lucy said, stamping her foot.

"Yes?" he replied.

"Tell us the news!" She exclaimed. "We are not interested in the major's breakfast."

"My dear," her father began condescendingly, "do

you not think it important that an officer on such an important mission be well nourished? Suppose such indifference and neglect had been shown to feeding his horse? And it was not, mind you. Even in these difficult times the fodder at Mr. Terry's livery is excellent. I am confident that the major's horse was better fed than the major was. That reflects poorly on our community, of course. How easily someone might have directed Major Giles to Mr. Martin's rather than Mr. Wimbish's. Please understand, of course, that I do not know with certainty that the meal he took at Mr. Wimbish's was unsatisfactory. I merely observe that one may expect a higher quality at Mr. Martin's."

"Excuse me, sir," Will said, deciding to try a different tactic. "Is it true that our army has been defeated?"

"Defeated?" Soblett said, puzzled. "Defeated, you say? To the contrary, young man. General Morgan has won a great victory in South Carolina. Haven't you been listening to what I've been saying?"

Lucy let out a little gasp and grabbed Will's arm.

"Over what force did General Morgan attain the victory?" Will asked.

"Tarleton," Soblett answered. "Bloody Ban Tarleton. General Morgan has thoroughly and positively thrashed the fiend and is even now marching north with over 700 prisoners, all of them British regulars."

"It's King's Mountain all over again," Will said softly.

"Except that Ferguson's men at King's Mountain were all Tory militia," Soblett answered. "General Morgan has defeated a large force of British redcoat regulars, among them an entire battalion of

Highlanders."

Soblett stepped up onto the porch, giving his wife a quick kiss on the cheek, then motioning to Will. "Come and have a seat, Will, and I will explain to you the tactics and personnel at the Battle of King's Mountain."

"Thank you, sir," Will said, "But as much as I would enjoy that, I must get home for evening chores. And I want to give the good news to my family."

"Yes, yes, of course," Soblett said, settling down into a chair on the porch. "You see, there were no regular troops at King's Mountain. Well, other than Major Ferguson himself, of course. But his command was…"

Will smiled and nodded and began backing away, giving Mrs. Soblett a little wave and being answered with a knowing and sympathetic smile.

As he walked toward the post where Caesar was tied, the sound of Soblett's voice fading in the background, Lucy hurried up to him.

"Will!" she said, excitedly. "Maybe this means you won't have to go! Maybe now y'all won't be called up!"

"Maybe," he answered. "But I'm not so sure of that. I'll see what I can find out."

Will sensed Lucy's disappointment. "It's great news for the cause, Lucy. Desperately needed."

She answered with an unenthusiastic nod.

Will leaned over and quickly kissed her on the cheek. After swinging up onto the horse's back, he turned to her and said, "Be careful tonight, Miss Soblett. There is a love-struck young man about who may come to get you and carry you away!"

Lucy blushed and Will answered with a broad smile. She blew a kiss at him as he trotted away.

30

Sherrill's Ford
Rowan County, North Carolina
January 25, 1781

Washington announced himself outside Morgan's tent and was answered quickly with, "Come in, Billy. Come in."

Washington pulled back the tent flap and stepped inside. He had to fight to suppress his surprise upon seeing that Morgan was lying down, propped up on a straw mat, in obvious pain. "Colonel Howard tells me that we're all across now," the general said.

"Yes, sir," Washington answered. "We are."

"Where is Cornwallis?" Morgan asked.

"No closer than 20 miles west of us," Washington replied.

"That's dangerously close, Billy," Morgan said.

"But we have the Catawba River between us now," Washington said. "It's up and still rising. He will not be able to easily cross it."

"Yes," Morgan said, grimacing as he tried to sit up. "We have been fortunate. So far."

"May I help you, sir?" Washington asked, unsure of

how to behave in the face of the proud but debilitated man.

Morgan shook his head, still grimacing. "I'm a damned cripple, Billy," he said as he managed to pull himself up straight. "It's getting worse by the hour."

"This horrendous weather is a factor, no doubt," Washington said. The men had been marching in a continuous cold rain for the past five days—over a hundred miles, with Morgan insisting on sharing their discomfort.

Morgan chuckled. "No doubt it is," he said. "But I've been rode hard and put up wet nearly every day for over 40 years. Maybe I'm just wore out."

Uncomfortable, Washington made no response.

"Help me up, Colonel," Morgan said, after a pause, reaching out his hand. Washington took his hand and elbow, steadying Morgan as he rose. Once on his feet, Morgan drew himself up to his full height and looked Washington in the eye.

"Billy, I've sent General Greene a letter announcing my resignation," he said.

The shock and dismay that flashed across Washington's face was involuntary.

"But sir…" he began, haltingly.

Morgan raised his hand and shook his head, interrupting.

"I can't go on, Billy," Morgan said. "I can neither walk nor ride. I'm a liability to this army now."

"Respectfully, sir," Washington began, intending to protest. Morgan again interrupted him.

"Major Triplett's Virginians are leaving," Morgan said. "Their enlistments have expired, and they can't be convinced to stay on. So, I've ordered Triplett to take the prisoners with him when he goes. Might as well get some use out of their march home. I just hope they're strong enough to hold them. I would hate to lose what we so dearly earned."

"Should I detach some dragoons to go with them?" Washington asked.

Morgan shook his head. "No, Billy. We're going to need every one of them here." He hobbled over to a stool and leaned on it.

"It is imperative that we reach the rest of the army," Greene said. "I will need you to slow his Lordship down while we make that happen."

"He is near Ramsour's Mill, General," Washington said. "We believe is heading for Beattie's Ford."

"Yes, I concur," Morgan said, the pain having returned to his face. "General Davidson is gathering the militia from the counties around here. We have to hold the fords until he arrives."

"Yes, sir," Washington said. "It will be done."

"We will march to Beattie's in the morning," Morgan said. "The ford here, and any others, must be blocked or guarded."

Washington nodded.

"Colonel, we are nearly out of provisions," Morgan continued. "The men and the horses are beginning to go hungry. I need you to scout the countryside. Find us food and fodder."

"This area has been picked pretty clean already," Washington answered.

"Yes," Morgan said. "I want Cornwallis to find it picked even cleaner."

"Understood, sir," Washington answered.

"Do your best to take what we need from the Tories, Colonel," Morgan said. "If we take from our friends, we have nothing to pay them with."

Washington nodded. Both officers knew that the men detailed to gather the provisions would bring in whatever they found, regardless of the allegiances of the local farmers, who, in any event, could not be trusted to declare those allegiances honestly.

"I will remain with the army and in command until General Greene appoints a successor," Morgan said. He stuck out his hand and Washington took it firmly.

"You are a fine horseman, Colonel," Morgan said, as the men shook hands. "I've never seen better. It has been a great honor to serve with you."

"The honor is entirely mine, General," Washington answered, feeling a tightening in his chest at the prospect of losing Morgan. "Forgive me, sir, but I hope that you will reconsider your decision."

Morgan shook his head. "I don't give up easily. If there was any way for me to stay with the army while in this condition, I would do it. But my time is up." He laughed, then added, "For now."

31

Near Ramsour's Mill
Lincoln County, North Carolina
January 27, 1781

Peering down the road, a steady cold drizzle slapping him in the face and soaking him to the bone, Cornwallis spotted the man he had been looking for. He spurred his horse and the animal slogged forward slowly, each step a struggle through the foot-deep sticky red mud. "What is delaying the column?" Cornwallis asked brusquely as he pulled alongside the other rider.

Lieutenant Colonel James Webster turned in the saddle to face his commanding general. "The wagons, m'lord," he answered in his thick Scottish accent. "Stuck up to the axles in this clay. The teams can barely pull them through. We've had men pushing them all day but it's slow going, sir."

"We will never catch the rebels this way, Colonel," Cornwallis said, trying to suppress his irritation.

"Aye, General," Webster answered. "Foul weather. Bad roads. Makes for slow marching."

Cornwallis slapped his thigh in frustration but gave

no other reply.

"It doesn't help that the rebels dropped so many trees into the road," Webster added. "But the lads can clear those quickly enough. It's bringing the wagons through this muck that is holding us back."

Cornwallis watched as a squad of red-coated soldiers stood in the cold rain, using poles to try to pry loose a stuck wagon. As he was watching, one of the poles snapped in two and a soldier cursed.

Webster turned toward the sound of the curse, "Mind your language, soldier," he snapped. After a pause, he added, "Put your shoulders to it, lads."

As the men tossed aside their poles and pushed up against the back of the wagon, their feet sinking deeply into the mud, Cornwallis turned away in disgust.

"Carry on, Colonel," he said. "Bring your column up to the mill and we will camp there."

Webster turned to Cornwallis and nodded. "Aye, m'lord."

Cornwallis nodded, turned, and rode away. This will not do, he thought.

32

Ramsour's Mill
Lincoln County, North Carolina
January 27, 1781
Dusk

As Cornwallis had ordered, the entire army was drawn up in formation, save only Tarleton's cavalry, which was deployed as pickets and guards. In a field before the men were nearly all the army's wagons, assembled and unhitched, as Cornwallis had ordered.

Brigadier General Charles O'Hara rode up and took a place in the line alongside Colonels James Stuart and Francis Hall. "Gentlemen," he said as he arrived.

"General," they answered simultaneously.

After a few moments, Cornwallis rode up, halting his horse a few yards in front of the assembled army, where all could see and hear him. "Soldiers of His Majesty," he said loudly in the accent of a high-bred aristocrat, his hair powdered and pulled back from his forehead as always, even in the rain. "This army is overburdened, and that is impeding our marches. To enable us to travel more rapidly, we shall forthwith strip ourselves down to only our necessities. We shall keep a wagon for the surgeons, one for salt and ammunition, and four for the sick and wounded." Cornwallis stopped, remaining silent for a few moments as he surveyed the men, standing before him at attention in the cold rain.

"All other wagons and baggage will be burned," he said. "Surplus provisions wagons, hospital stores, and all regimental baggage, including my own, shall all be burned.

"I have ordered the quartermaster to issue a double ration of rum," he said. "Enjoy it men, for it shall be your last for quite some time." With satisfaction, Cornwallis noticed no reaction from the men, grim determination etched on their faces.

"Henceforth, our supply of meal shall likewise be uncertain," he added, continuing to scan the faces of the soldiers.

"I have not the smallest doubt that the officers and soldiers will most cheerfully submit to the ill conveniences which must naturally attend a war so remote from our bases of supply," Cornwallis said, every eye in the army focused on him.

"Our foe is near. At this very moment he is just beyond our grasp," he said, gesturing to the east. Looking sternly up and down the lines of soldiers, he continued. "We shall pursue him. We shall catch him. And we shall destroy him."

At that some of the officers lifted their hats and a cheer broke out. "Huzzah!" the men shouted. "Huzzah!"

Cornwallis turned in the saddle to face a man standing near the wagons, holding an unlit torch. When Cornwallis pointed to the wagons, the man fired the torch. Walking down the line of wagons, he ignited the piles of straw that had been placed in their beds. As the flames grew into a roaring blaze, the men began another round of cheers and Cornwallis turned and rode away.

33

Lightfoot Farm
Maple Grove
Pittsylvania County, Virginia
January 29, 1781

After he finished saddling his horse, Dodd led it out of the barn and to the front of the house. He tied it to the post, then walked up the steps to the porch, pushed the door open and stepped inside, taking his seat at the table just as his mother was bringing over the family's breakfast—a plate of hoecakes, a jug of molasses, and a pitcher of milk. Once she had taken her seat, they all bowed their heads. "We are thankful for this food and all our blessings," Laz said. "Amen."

"Amen," the others replied.

As the plate was being passed around the table, Dodd spoke. "I'm not looking forward to another wasted day at the courthouse. Sorry I can't stay here and help."

"You are doing your duty, son," Alice said.

"Well Ma, all our 'duty' seems to be right now is marching around in circles all day while Colonel Perkins struts around on his racehorse watching us,"

Dodd said as he poured molasses over his hoecake.

"It's a question of preparedness, Dodd," Laz said, as he chewed. "Someday when you report, you'll find that you have orders to march immediately. Could be today. You have to stay ready."

"I don't see it, Pa," Dodd answered. "They can't provision us. There's no muskets, no bayonets, no flints, and no powder. They can't send us off unarmed."

"Don't be so sure of that," his brother Elisha replied. "I've heard of companies being ordered to march before being provisioned."

"Great," Dodd said, sarcastically. "We'll fight 'em with our knives and tomahawks."

"They won't send y'all off until they've provisioned you," Laz said, confidently.

Dodd turned to face his father, "Let me take the firelock, Pa. I feel foolish drilling without one."

Laz shook his head. "We need it here," he said. "Besides that, it's risky. They're required to provide you with a weapon. If you show up with that old shotgun, they might not issue you a musket. They might also impress it and give you a handful of worthless paper in exchange. Just be patient."

"Plenty of the boys bring their own guns and they ain't had 'em impressed," Dodd protested.

"Not yet," Laz answered as he took the last bite of his breakfast. "And do you really want to risk being sent into battle with that old gun? It doesn't have the range or power you need. It can't take a bayonet. You'd be just as well off using your knife."

Alice shuddered, stood abruptly, and walked away. Laz instantly realized his mistake.

"If your company gets orders to march, I'll see that

you're suitably armed," Laz said, looking supportively at his son. "But until then, just keep waiting. I'm certain they won't send you off until your company is properly provisioned."

Dodd nodded, disappointed but unsurprised.

"Well," he said, pushing back his chair and rising. "I'm off. Gonna be a long, cold ride this morning."

His father stood, stepped toward him, and took his hand, shaking it firmly. "God be with you, son. We'll see you tonight."

Dodd nodded in response, released his father's hand, and walked over to his mother, who still had her back turned, as she composed herself.

"Ma," he said.

Alice wiped her eyes with her apron, the turned around, straining to smile. She put her hands on her son's shoulders and said, "Be careful, Dodd. Godspeed."

Dodd wrapped her in a hug, which his mother eagerly accepted, squeezing him tightly. When she released him, her eyes were moist. Dodd kissed her on the cheek, turned and took down his hat and coat from a peg on the wall by the door. When he stepped out onto the porch, Elisha followed him.

On the eastern horizon the faint glow of dawn was beginning to appear, greeted by the crowing of the family's rooster. Dodd pulled on his coat and buttoned it to the neck.

"You ain't got nothing to worry about today, brother," Elisha said.

"I ain't worried," Dodd quickly answered.

"What I mean is that there ain't no chance y'all are going to march today," Elisha said. "Silas Rowlett told me yesterday that he heard directly from Colonel

Wilson himself that all the militia will be sent at the same time. We'll all be mustered in before any of us leave. They're just waiting on provisions from Richmond. He says General Greene can't even outfit the men he has now. It's going to be a while."

Dodd nodded. "Let's just hope Cornwallis gives us time to wait," he said.

34

Beatties Ford
Lincoln County, North Carolina
January 30, 1781

Morgan was waiting, standing at the edge of the camp and leaning on a cane, watching as three riders approached, wearing the uniforms of Continental regulars. When they reached Morgan, the officer in the middle dismounted and an orderly rushed forward, took the reins, and led the horse away.

"General Greene, I am delighted to see you, sir," Morgan said amiably, reaching out his hand.

Greene took his hand and shook it warmly.

"You are the toast of America, General Morgan," Greene answered. "Please accept my congratulations on your splendid victory."

"Thank you, sir," Morgan said. "Our success must be attributed entirely to the justice of our cause and the bravery of our troops. The men were magnificent." As the two generals released their handshake, Morgan continued, "But now I must chide you, my friend. Over a hundred miles through hostile and unfamiliar territory with such a small escort? You take too much risk, Nathanael."

Greene laughed. "When did Dan Morgan develop an aversion to risk?" he asked.

"My concern is for the commanding general of the army," Morgan answered, with a twinkle in his eyes. With a smile he threw an arm across Greene's shoulders. "Come inside, sir," he said, leading Greene toward his tent. "Let's get out of this infernal rain."

Five foot ten with bright blue eyes, Greene, the soft-spoken former Quaker, was in many ways unlike Morgan, the barrel-chested brawling frontiersman. In the same year that a teenaged Morgan had shown up in Winchester, Virginia, emerging penniless and illiterate from a mysterious childhood somewhere in New Jersey, the details of which he never revealed, ten-year-old Greene was already working in his family's business in Rhode Island, already beginning to acquire books while cultivating his insatiable thirst for knowledge. While Morgan had literally fought his way to prominence, teaching himself to read and write along the way, it was with his logistical brilliance that Greene had climbed the military ladder, earning the respect and favor of George Washington along the way. After Horatio Gates' disastrous defeat at the Battle of Camden, Congress had given command of the southern army to Greene, reluctantly accepting Washington's recommendation. And Greene had in turn given command of a wing of the army to his trusted old comrade Morgan. Even the limps the two men shared as they made their way to the tent sprang from entirely different causes, Morgan's having arrived recently with his sciatica and Greene having been lame from birth.

"I cannot adequately express how much joy your

victory over Tarleton has given the army," Greene said as they entered Morgan's tent and took seats. "Your battle plan was simply brilliant, sir. You have given us all a much-needed boost to morale."

"But you should see my brave men now, General," Morgan said somberly. "Half-starved and half-naked. It is disgraceful, sir."

Greene nodded, furrowing his brow. "I regret to say that the rest of the army is in no better condition."

"Congress cannot expect us to defeat the British without powder and lead, and on empty stomachs and bare feet," Morgan said.

"I harangue Congress and the governors of North Carolina and Virginia for provisions daily," Greene said with exasperation. "All they do is make excuses." After he pause, he changed the subject. "While riding here I received an express saying that Cornwallis has burned his wagons."

"It is true," Morgan said, nodding. "We have confirmed it. Burned them all at Ramsour's before marching."

"A bold move," Greene said.

"A foolish move," Morgan replied. "All this rain has swollen the Catawba. He can't cross it now. And the countryside has been stripped bare. He will soon wish he had those supplies back."

"Then he is ours," Greene said quietly, gazing into the distance. "We will fight him, General."

"Good," Morgan answered.

After a few silent moments, Greene looked directly at Morgan. "Now sir, let us come to the principal purpose of my visit. I am deeply distressed by your letter, General Morgan. The army needs you. Your country needs you."

"I'm a cripple, Nathanael," Morgan quickly answered. "Most days I can neither walk nor ride. The men have to haul me around in a damned chair like a pitiful old woman. A man who can no longer fight must step aside in favor of men who can."

Greene sighed, his hands on his knees. "I am not yet ready to accept your resignation, sir."

Morgan waved his hand dismissively. "You are stuck with me until this army is safe, General. Even crippled, I cannot leave now. But as soon as the immediate danger is gone, so will I be."

Greene smiled and nodded slightly. He knew Daniel Morgan well enough to know that once he had his mind made up, there was nothing that he or anyone else could say to change it. He would just have to be patient and hope for a change of heart, or a sudden improvement in Morgan's health. "Well, General Morgan, let us speak no more of it now."

"You must be exhausted, Nathanael. Go and rest and I'll have some food and drink brought to you," Morgan said.

"Not yet, sir. I want to see the river," Greene answered. "Have Colonel Washington and General Davidson join us."

"Yes, sir," Morgan answered. He began to rise from his stool, but then winced in pain and lowered himself back down, his legs refusing his command to stand. After muttering an oath, he shouted, "Orderly!"

A young soldier quickly stuck his head in through the tent flap, accustomed to being called this way.

"Fetch Colonel Washington and General Davidson," Morgan growled.

"Yes, sir," the young man said before hurrying away.

"Are you all right, General?" Greene asked with concern. "Should we delay the conference?"

"No and no," Morgan said. "Just give me a few seconds." After a pause he added, "Hand me that damned cane."

Greene stood up, retrieved the cane, and passed it to Morgan, who leaned into it and slowly rose to his feet. "It was Quebec that did this to me, Nathanael."

"You have endured much, my friend," Greene said sympathetically.

Morgan looked back at him, scarred and bent, with laughter in his eyes. "It's been a hell of a ride, sir. And God willing, I ain't done yet."

Twenty minutes later, it had stopped raining and Greene, Morgan, and Washington were seated on logs outside of camp, on a rise overlooking the swirling muddy Catawba River, when a tall thin man wearing a blue Continental officer's uniform came striding toward them. "Gentlemen," he called out, "Pardon me for being late."

"General Davidson," Greene said, extending his hand, as he and Washington stood to greet him. "It is good to see you again."

Davidson grasped Greene's hand and shook it warmly. Although 35-year-old William Lee Davidson was now a brigadier general of North Carolina militia, for four years he had served as an officer in the Continental Line and he continued proudly wearing his blue uniform coat, even though it made him a conspicuous target in battle. All four men were longtime comrades, Davidson and Morgan having become particularly close during the brutal winter at Valley Forge. Grievously wounded by a gunshot to the stomach the previous July, Davidson had recovered and now commanded the militia in ten western counties of North Carolina.

"The pleasure is mine, General Greene," Davidson replied.

"Come," Greene said, "Sit down and let's talk."

Davidson took a seat on a log, next to Morgan, who slapped him on the back with a grin.

"Everything is unfolding rapidly, gentlemen," Greene began, pacing before the other three men. "It seems a miracle to me that General Morgan got across this river. We are fortunate to now have it between us and Lord Cornwallis.

"It is imperative that we reunite the wings of the army. I left General Huger in charge of the main force, and he is marching it toward Salisbury now. General Morgan, your men must link up with him there. Once we have the army together, we will fight Cornwallis.

"Colonel Washington," Greene continued. "I need your dragoons to screen the army's flank and rear as we march."

Washington nodded.

"General Davidson," Greene said, turning to face him. "How many militiamen do you have?"

"About 800," Davidson answered.

"I need them to hold the fords here while we unite the army. It is essential that we keep Cornwallis on the other side of the river until the army is united and ready to fight him. Can you do that?"

Davidson chuckled. "Easily," he answered. Gesturing toward the river raging below them he said, "It will be several days, at least, before the river is fordable. If Cornwallis is foolish enough to try to cross it while it's up like this, his army won't survive the attempt."

"Good," Greene answered. "We need a few days." After a pause he continued, "Cornwallis will cross eventually. When he does, punish him all you can, then fall back and join the rest of the army." He scanned the faces of the three officers.

"In his zeal to reach General Morgan, Lord Cornwallis has pushed too far from his base," Greene said. "His army is poorly provisioned, and it will suffer in this miserable weather. I believe he is ours now. But first we must unite the army. We will assemble at Salisbury, and then we will fight him."

The other men nodded. "It's a good plan, General," Davidson said.

"In the meantime," Greene continued, "I have instructed Colonel Carrington to begin assembling all the boats he can find on the Dan River, in case of a reversal that would require us to retreat that far."

"The Dan River?" Morgan asked, puzzled.

"We must be prepared for all contingencies, General," Greene replied.

~~~

Across the river, Cornwallis stood on the edge of a clump of trees with three other officers, scanning the opposite shore through a spyglass. He stopped the glass suddenly when he spotted a Continental officer on the opposite ridge, pacing before three other men seated on logs. Cornwallis squinted, trying to bring the men into clearer focus. After a few moments he snapped the spyglass shut in frustration and stared down at the swollen muddy river below him.
~~~

35

Cowan's Ford
Lincoln County, North Carolina
February 1, 1781
4 a.m.

Cornwallis dismounted, his boots splashing down into ankle deep mud as an orderly took his horse's reins. The army had been marching since one a.m., trudging through the bitterly cold night, under strict orders requiring absolute silence and forbidding fires. He approached an officer who stood awaiting him, barely visible in the nearly pitch darkness.

"My lord," the officer said quietly.

"Good morning, Colonel Hall," Cornwallis replied softly. "I trust you are ready for today's affair."

A poised combat veteran, 45-year-old Lieutenant Colonel Francis Hall commanded the elite 3rd Regiment of Guards. "Most assuredly, my lord," Hall replied. He turned and gestured, and another man stepped forward, wearing civilian's clothes. "My lord, this is Mr. Frederick Hager, a friend of the King. He is the man who identified this ford for us. Mr. Hager is from this area and has volunteered to take us across."

Cornwallis removed a glove, reached out, and shook the man's hand. "Good morning, Mr. Hager. Describe the ford."

"Well sir," Hager said. "It's a long one. Four to five hundred yards all the way across, I reckon. There's two channels. One is deeper than the other. The deep one goes straight across but is too deep to wade. We call that one the 'wagon ford.' I'll be leading you across the shallower one. It branches off about halfway over, goes over a little island, and comes out about a quarter of a mile below where the wagon ford does. We call that one the 'horse ford.'"

"How deep is it?" Cornwallis asked.

"It's passable," Hager answered. "A man can walk across it. Even when the river is up like this."

Cornwallis nodded. "Is the water swift?" he asked.

"It's passable. You're just going to need to step carefully," Hager answered.

Cornwallis turned to Hall. "What do we know about the enemy on the other side?" he asked. "I had not expected to see so many campfires over there."

"Again, sir," Hall answered. "We are relying on Loyalist intelligence."

"I'll tell ya who's over there," Hager interjected. "There's about 250 rebels on the other side. Militia. Detached from their main force. I know most of them. I expect they're asleep right now. They ain't expecting you to cross until the river is down, and when it is, they ain't expecting you to cross here. The main force is up at Beatties Ford. That's where they're expecting you."

Cornwallis looked at Hager for a few seconds, considering what he had said. "Well then," he replied, "let's see if we can take them by surprise." Turning to Hall he said, "I have ordered Colonel Webster to make a convincing demonstration in front of Beatties Ford once we're underway here. The rebels will think he is crossing and that should delay them from sending any reinforcements here. But it is essential that we get across quickly."

"Yes, my lord," Hall answered.

"Your regiment shall have the honor of being in the van, Colonel Hall. Instruct your men to carry their guns over their heads, unloaded, to prevent any temptation to fire," Cornwallis said. "They are to cross in absolute silence, four abreast. The rest of the army will follow. We will move across quickly. Once on the other bank, we will form up, give them a volley, then charge them with the bayonet."

"Yes, my lord," Hall replied. "It will be done, sir."

"We must move out at first light, Colonel," Cornwallis said. "As soon as a man can see in front of him. The darkness and this fog will help conceal our crossing."

Cornwallis turned to Hager and continued. "We are relying on you to guide us across safely, Mr. Hager. A great deal depends upon your doing that."

Hager smiled. "Yes, my lord," he said. "It will be done, sir."

36

The Battle of Cowan's Ford
February 1, 1781
6:30 a.m.

Colonel Hall eased his horse out of the woods and down the steep embankment to the river, Hager riding alongside him. At the water's edge, the horse paused. Hall made a clicking sound and gently spurred the animal and it stepped obediently, but reluctantly, into the water.

In the mist and dim light of daybreak, Hall and Hager gingerly and quietly walked their horses further into the muddy swirling river. After they had gone about a hundred yards, Hall turned in his saddle and saw that his men were coming along silently behind him, treading cautiously, four abreast in the cold waist-deep water, with their muskets held up over their heads. Some of the men were bracing themselves with poles as they waded across; others were holding onto the man beside him. As they moved slowly forward, Hager squinted, peering out into the fog in search of the spot where the so-called "horse ford" bent to the right.

Once all of Hall's men had waded into the water, Cornwallis gently eased his horse in behind them, followed by General Charles O'Hara and the rest of the brigade of Guards. By the time Hall had reached the middle of the river, Cornwallis' entire force of over 1200 British and Hessian regulars was in the water.

On the opposite shore a militiaman walked sleepily down to the river's edge, unbuttoned his trousers, and began relieving himself into the water. Some flicker of movement in the distance caught his eye and he looked up, into the fog rising off the river. A sudden rush of adrenaline jolted him awake. For a few moments he couldn't definitely make out the shapes coming slowly through the mist. Then suddenly he recognized a horse and rider, and the gleam of bayonets. He hurriedly stuffed himself back into his trousers, turned and began running back toward the Patriot camp. "The British!" he shouted. "The British!"

Hager heard the shouting, and his heart began to race. A few moments later he heard the crack of a musket, followed quickly by more, and by the sound of bullets whizzing past him. To his left he heard a sickening thud. He turned in his saddle and saw Hall staring down at a dark red stain spreading rapidly across his chest. The colonel looked up, his eyes rolled back in his head, and he slid off his horse and into the river. Several of the soldiers behind him threw down their guns and dived into the rushing water after him. In a few moments they had pulled him up and were staggering back toward the shore, carrying his lifeless body.

Instantly the quiet and cautious crossing turned into a frantic tumultuous rush, as the rest of the Patriot militia awakened, rushed into position, and began firing. Once under fire, the British soldiers quickened their pace, plunging ahead and pressing Hager from behind. In the confusion he overshot the turnoff to the shallower ford and led the men directly into the chest-deep water of the "wagon ford" instead.

Cornwallis saw Hall drop from the saddle and saw that when he did, some of the Guards began to hesitate and waver, as shots from the Patriot militia began to find their targets. Sensing that disaster was imminent, he spurred his horse, drew his sword, and pushed his way through the river to the front of the column and into the deep rushing water. "Forward, men!" he shouted. "Forward, Guards!"

Hager soon realized that he had missed the turnoff and that was leading the men into the deeper ford, but he also realized it was too late to turn back. With Patriot musket balls whistling around him, he drove his horse on, deeper into the river, with Cornwallis soon coming up alongside him.

By then some of the soldiers trailing behind them were being swept off their feet and carried away by the rushing water, screaming for help. As O'Hara was riding alongside the column, urging his men forward, his horse suddenly slipped and rolled over, spilling the general into the swirling, murky, ice-cold river. At nearly that same moment, a few yards away, General Alexander Leslie was swept off his horse and into the water. In both cases, nearby Guards tossed aside their weapons and pulled the two generals from beneath the rushing water.

Amid the confusion, Cornwallis pressed forward at the head of the struggling column, urging the men on, as balls whistled past him. He was about fifty yards from the shore when a shot from a Patriot musket slammed into his horse's shoulder. The animal bucked and let out a frightened whinny before Cornwallis could wrestle it back under control. Spurring again, Cornwallis urged the horse toward the shore. The terrified animal took a few cautious steps before another bullet struck it in the throat. With that the horse bolted wildly, swinging its head from side to side and thrashing through the water toward the shore in a panicked rush. Just as the horse climbed up onto the riverbank, it collapsed, with Cornwallis barely managing to dismount before being pinned beneath it. As the general rose to his feet, musket balls thick in the air around him, the Guards behind him began pulling themselves up onto the shore. "Form up, men!" Cornwallis shouted. "Form up here! Make ready!" he yelled, waving his sword over his head, as more of the British soldiers began climbing out of the river and up onto the bank. In the distance he could hear the sound of Webster's diversionary cannonading at Beatties Ford, four miles away.

~~~

As soon as the firing at Cowan's Ford had begun, Davidson had quickly assembled and positioned his men, ready to gun down the British when they reached the river's edge. But Davidson had deployed the men at the shallower horse ford exit, a quarter mile down river from where the wagon ford emerged, not imagining that the British would attempt to cross the deeper ford, where he had stationed only twenty-five militiamen. Once Davidson realized that the entire British force was crossing at the wagon ford, he ordered his men to move there as quickly as possible
~~~

and he galloped off ahead of them.

~~~

Hager dismounted and raced to the cover of a nearby tree as soon as his horse was on the shore, distancing himself from the British troops drawing the Patriot fire. He watched, impressed, as the soaked redcoats emerged from the river and formed into a battle line, both the men and the officers commanding them seemingly oblivious to the musket balls that were raining down on them. In the distance he could see the American militiamen, firing from behind trees and logs, the smoke from their muskets revealing their locations but obscuring their faces. Glancing back and forth between the British and the rebels, something caught his eye—an officer in a blue Continental uniform galloping into the midst of the militiamen and shouting commands. "Davidson," he muttered contemptuously.

Hidden behind the tree, Hager took the powder horn from around his neck, unstopped it and poured a little down the barrel of his rifle. He then removed a greased patch from his patch box, and a ball from a pouch slung around his neck. He laid the patch across the barrel, placed the ball atop it, then pulled out his ramrod and drove the patch and ball firmly down into the barrel. After pouring a little powder in the pan, he stepped out from behind the tree and leveled the gun, searching in the distance for his target. In a moment he found what he was looking for—Davidson, on horseback, riding among the militiamen, shouting orders. Hager cocked his gun, centered his front sight on the general's chest, then lightly pressed the trigger.
~~~

The gun erupted, kicking out a spurt of flame along with the ball. Through the smoke he saw Davidson lurch backward, then fall from his saddle.

~~~

As the British continued wading ashore, they formed by companies and began firing volleys at the rebel militiamen, who had begun slowly falling back. Within a few minutes Cornwallis had enough men ashore to begin his attack. "Bayonets, charge!" he shouted, leading the men up the ridge on foot.

The sight of over a thousand British and Hessian regulars coming across the river had already unsettled the Patriots. When Davidson was killed, many began to retreat, ignoring the pleas of officers trying to rally them. The British bayonet charge sent those few who remained scurrying away.

By the time the British reached the top of the ridge the Americans were gone.

Cornwallis, still on foot, was directing the men, ordering them into position when Tarleton rode up. Glancing up at him, Cornwallis said, "Colonel, take your dragoons and find Morgan's army. Do not engage him, Colonel. Just find out where they are. Do not bother with the militia. Find Morgan."

"Yes, my lord," Tarleton answered, before turning and riding away.

At that moment, O'Hara walked up, soaking wet in his resplendent red uniform.

"See to your brigade, general," Cornwallis said. "Prepare for a counterattack."

O'Hara nodded. "Yes, my lord," he said.

"There ain't no need to worry about that," Hager
~~~

said with a smile, having rejoined the troops once the shooting stopped. "There ain't gonna be no counterattack, my lord. You've seen the last of them."

Cornwallis ignored him. "Prepare a defensive perimeter, General. Get the men dry and warm. We will march on Beatties in an hour."

O'Hara nodded and stepped away.

Hager shook his head and walked away, over to where he had seen Davidson fall. Looking down at the lifeless body he grinned. "Good morning, General," he said with a chuckle, while pulling a knife from his belt. "I reckon you won't be needing this anymore," he said, as he leaned down and sliced the epaulet off the shoulder of the dead man's coat.

~~~

About ten hours later Tarleton returned, riding into the British camp as the sun was going down. Cornwallis met him as he rode in.

"We have scouted as far as Salisbury, my lord," Tarleton said, as he dismounted. "There is no sign of Morgan or Greene. They must have marched out yesterday."

His brow furrowed, Cornwallis said, "Sir, I have been receiving reports all day of disgraceful atrocities attributed to your command. Homes burned, civilians murdered."

Tarleton showed no emotion and gave no answer.

"Of course, I do not attribute this misconduct to you personally, Colonel," Cornwallis said, haltingly. "But you must be diligent in preventing this disgraceful licentiousness by your men."

"Yes, my lord," Tarleton said stoically.
~~~

Cornwallis continued. "I am highly displeased at the burning of houses, sir, and henceforth will punish with the utmost severity any person found guilty of committing so disgraceful an outrage," he said, flushed.

"Respectfully, sir," Tarleton said, "the rebels must be pacified. Should they not be made to suffer for their disloyalty? Perhaps severity alone can reestablish royal authority here."

"Remember yourself, Colonel," Cornwallis said sharply. "Plunder and mayhem of this kind will harden the hearts of the civilians against us and are self-defeating."

After a few silent moments, Tarleton said, "Yes, my lord," his insincerity obvious to Cornwallis.

"See to your men, sir," Cornwallis said, testily. "We will march in the morning. We must find Morgan and destroy him before he reaches the rest of General Greene's army."

Tarleton nodded, remounted his horse, and walked slowly away. Cornwallis slapped his hand against his sword belt, turned and walked stormily away.

37

Trading Ford
Rowan County, North Carolina
February 3, 1781

Ransom dropped his saddle bag onto the hard-packed red clay barn floor and plopped down onto a little mound of old straw, too exhausted to remove his muddy boots. He leaned back against the barn wall and closed his eyes. After a few minutes he knew it was hopeless. Despite aching with fatigue, he couldn't sleep. Not yet. He reached out, threw back the flap on the saddle bag, and brought out his writing kit. He laid a little slate tablet in his lap, placed a piece of paper on it, and began to write. It was pitch dark in the barn and there was no ink in his quill.

My dearest Jennie,

This night I am quartered in a corner of a poor farmer's barn on the east side of the Yadkin River. You would think the abode rather mean, but it seems a palace to me. However humble the place, I regard myself as blessed to have shelter tonight from the wind and rain.

All day long I have been eagerly anticipating a chance to sleep. But now that I finally have that chance, I find that I cannot. I am kept awake by thoughts of you, my dear Jennie.

I suppose that when I do fall asleep, I will be too tired to dream. But if I do dream, I wonder if you will visit me again? As I have written so many times before, you are often in my dreams, my dear. In my most vivid dream, the one I cherish and yearn for, we are married, and we are living on a bountiful farm. In my dream I am holding you, and we are surrounded by our precious children. You are smiling at me, and we are happy. That dream warms my heart and when I wake from it my eyes are filled with tears. But it is a cruel dream, isn't it Jennie? When I shake away the sleep and understand that it was only a dream—when I remember instead the reality of our relationship—then my old familiar heartbreak returns. What are your dreams, Jennie? If only I knew.

As I suppose you have no interest in my dreams or desires, perhaps you would care to have an account of the latest adventures of General Morgan's Flying Army?

We marched from Beatties Ford two days ago, intending to link up with the remainder of the army, then prepare to fight Cornwallis. General Davidson and his militia were left behind to guard the fords, which we assumed would not be passable for several days. But it seems that Lord Cornwallis did not agree with our assessment of the situation. On Thursday morning at first light, he forded the river with his army. General Davidson was killed and Cornwallis unleashed Lieutenant Colonel Tarleton, who proceeded to do what he does best. He came upon the scattered and demoralized remains of Davidson's militia at a place called Torrence's Tavern. Bloody Ban charged them, killed many of them (along with any unfortunate civilians who happened to be there) and scattered the rest to the wind. Then he put everything to the torch. It is reported that Tarleton's dragoons were shouting "Remember the Cowpens!" as they were cutting down the militiamen and refugees. Oh how I wish we had been there, Jennie! Had we been, my dear, I assure you they would have remembered Cowpens indeed.

With Cornwallis over the Catawba before General Huger's wing of the army could join us, our plan to unite and fight him here was dashed. So instead we slogged through the mud and cold hard rain to the river here and then ferried the army across in small boats while our dragoons kept guard. Once all the men were across, we swam our horses over. The boats are all on our side of the river now, so Cornwallis cannot cross. We are, it seems, safe for now.

Once we were all across, the rain resumed and the river rose considerably, an event the faithful here are attributing to Providence. Presumably, for securing all the boats, General Greene should also get some of the credit for our escape.

The general has now ordered us to march to Guilford Courthouse, where General Huger has also been directed. General Greene has issued a call for the state militia to all rise up and meet us there. Will they answer the call? We shall see.

Do you remember how old Miss Jinsey Taylor had to be carried about in a chair after she could no longer walk? Well, that is how the great General Morgan must sometimes be transported now. He is no longer able to walk or ride. I have heard that his pride is much wounded by his condition, and it pains the men to consider it.

We have been subsisting for weeks on little more than water, cornmeal ash cakes, and an occasional tough piece of some skinny unfortunate pine barren cow.

The farmer who owns this place seems a good man, a loyal Patriot. He and his family are kindly sharing what little they have with us. But I am sorry to say that I expect he will hate us by the time we leave, as our army by sad necessity leaves little food and forage in its wake.

I will stop now, my dear. I continue to pray for your safety and your happiness, even as I recall with heart-rending affection our past happiness together, and even as I grieve with fading hope any such happiness in the future. I confess another prayer as well, my dear. I pray to be happily by your side tonight, in my dreams. Now to sleep, perchance to dream...

Your ever devoted,

Ransom

Ransom sat silently for a few minutes, staring out into the darkness, shedding a tear that no one would see. Then he put the slate and quill back into the bag, and carefully returned the writing paper to the kit. There was nothing written on it.

38

Dix's Ferry
Pittsylvania County, Virginia
February 8, 1781

Bayard tied his horse to the hitching post and walked down to the river's edge, where a handful of vendors had set up a market, their goods displayed on blankets spread out before them. From a distance he saw the woman he was looking for, her charcoal-colored skin contrasting sharply with her crisp white bonnet and shawl. He called out as he approached her, "Good day, Rebecca. I'm pleased to see you here."

"Good day, Reverend," the woman answered pleasantly.

Bayard picked a sweet potato up off the blanket spread out before the woman and held it out before him, regarding it. "Please don't tell my neighbors I said so, Rebecca, but the sweet potatoes you all grow in North Carolina are far superior to any we can grow here." He put the potato back down and said, "They make the finest pies I've ever had."

"Thank you, sir," Rebecca answered.

"How are things at home? I trust you and your

family have been well," Bayard said.

"Very well, sir, thank you," Rebecca replied. "We been right busy though. We have lots of friends coming to see us soon and we have to get ready for them. They comin' up from South Carolina."

Bayard felt his pulse quicken, and he glanced around to see if anyone was within earshot.

"Wonderful," he said. "I'm sure you'll be very happy to see them."

"Yes sir, we will," Rebecca answered. "We been waiting on them a long time."

"Where are your friends now?" Bayard asked.

"They was around Bethania, last I heard," she answered.

After a pause, Bayard said, "It's a lovely day, isn't it? I so enjoy coming down to the river this time of year."

"The Dan's been up mighty high with all this rain, ain't it, sir?" Rebecca asked.

"Mighty high, indeed," Bayard answered. "That's good for the ferryman's business, I suppose. It'll be a good long while before the river can be forded anywhere east of here."

Rebecca nodded, as she continued taking potatoes from a basket and arranging them on the blanket, not looking up.

"I 'spect anybody that wants to cross without having to pay a ferryman will have to stick to the upper fords," she said.

"I expect so," Bayard replied, nonchalantly. "But if they don't like getting wet and want to ferry across, they'll have to cross here, at Irvine's, or at Boyd's."

"Ain't but one boat here at Dix's," Rebecca said.

"And there's only one small boat at the other two, as well. I just rode past them yesterday," Bayard said.

Rebecca looked up. She and Bayard made brief eye contact and she gave an almost imperceptible nod.

"I'll take a peck of them," Bayard said, more loudly.

Rebecca gathered up the potatoes and handed them to Bayard in a cloth sack.

"Much obliged, Rebecca," he said, giving her a few bills.

"Good day, Reverend," she said, taking the money. "Please tell Mizz Bayard I asked about her."

"I will do that," Bayard replied. "And when you see your friends, please give them my best regards. Tell them I hope they'll come see us soon."

Rebecca nodded and Bayard turned and walked away.

39

Guilford Courthouse
Guilford County, North Carolina
February 9, 1781

Greene glanced around at the three men who had gathered at his command in the crude one-story frame building that served as a courthouse in sparsely populated Guilford County. Even though he detested councils such as this one, a decision had to be made—a decision of vital importance—and Greene did not want history to remember it as a decision he made alone.

"Gentlemen," he began, "I have convened this Council of War because I desire your opinions as to what measures should now be pursued in the interest of the army."

The two wings of the American army were finally united. Morgan and his men had reached Guilford two days earlier, after a 47-mile march in deep mud and in a driving cold rain. At nearly the same time, Huger had arrived with the other wing, tattered and poorly equipped. The next day, Lee's Legion had arrived, 180 light infantry and 100 green-jacketed dragoons under the command of Colonel Henry Lee, (widely known as "Light Horse Harry") a 25-year-old Virginian with a reputation for stellar horsemanship, courage, and (some would say) vanity. But the Virginia militia Greene had been promised had not arrived. And with Davidson's death and the twin defeats at Cowan's Ford and Torrance's Tavern, most of the North Carolina militia had seemingly vanished—only about 200 had answered the desperate call he sent out after Cornwallis crossed the Catawba.

The decision that Greene had to make now could well determine the outcome of the war. So, he called his senior officers together. The decision would be made by all of them.

"According to intelligence received this morning, Lord Cornwallis has crossed the Yadkin near the Moravian villages and is now about twenty miles away," Greene said. "He seems intent on bringing on a battle. We must decide whether to fight him here, or whether to retreat to Virginia.

"Here is the state of affairs, gentlemen," Greene continued. "According to field returns prepared today, we have at present 1,426 infantry, many of them badly armed and badly clothed. Several hundred of them are barefoot and few have tents or blankets. We also have about 600 militia, also badly armed and provisioned, who seem to come and to as they please. The force of the enemy, from the best intelligence that we can obtain, amounts to twenty-five hundred or three thousand men."

Greene paused and looked away, as if collecting his thoughts. After a few seconds he turned back and continued.

"Here is my opinion, gentlemen. If we risk a general

action in our present situation, we stand a ten to one chance of being defeated. If we are defeated, all of the southern states will fall—not just the Carolinas, but Virginia as well. As much as I hate the idea of abandoning North Carolina to the enemy, I am of the opinion that we must take this army across the Dan River into Virginia, to rest, reprovision, and receive reinforcements. I am also of the opinion that we must begin that movement immediately or we will risk being forced into battle, the consequence of which will likely be a disastrous defeat.

"But I do not want to commence any retreat to Virginia without having your advice. I ask each of you therefore to state your opinion and cast your vote. Shall we retreat, or shall we stand and fight here?"

Greene looked into the faces of the three men sitting before him. He knew them all to be fighters, men who were not inclined to run from danger. "Colonel Williams, what is your opinion?"

Thirty-one years old and six feet tall, Lieutenant Colonel Otho Holland Williams rose from his chair and looked grimly back at Greene. Orphaned at age 12, Williams had worked his way up from clerk to successful merchant in his hometown of Frederick, Maryland before volunteering for the Continental Army and being commissioned a junior officer in a company of riflemen at the very beginning of the war. Wounded and captured at Fort Washington, New York in November 1776, Williams had spent 15 brutal months as a prisoner of war, contracting the tuberculosis that would permanently weaken him and eventually claim his life. He had served in the Southern Theater under Gates, and after Greene replaced him Williams quickly won the respect and trust of his new commanding general.

"At present the army is in no condition to fight," Williams said. "I vote that we withdraw into Virginia."

Greene nodded, as Williams sat back down.

"General Huger, what say you?"

A 38-year-old descendant of South Carolina Huguenots, Brigadier General Isaac Huger had, like Williams, joined the cause at the very beginning. Severely wounded at the Battle of Stono Ferry near Charleston in June 1779, Huger had rejoined the army after recovering and had been assigned to command one of its wings. Like Williams, he had the respect and trust of General Greene.

"General," Huger said as he rose to his feet. "Nothing would give me greater pleasure than to fight the British. But we are not ready. The army is too worn down and we cannot risk another defeat like Camden. I also vote for withdrawal to Virginia."

Greene nodded. "General Morgan?" he said.

The instant that Greene spoke his name, Morgan banged his cane down loudly on the floor. The tension in the air was palpable. The other men all knew that it was Morgan's opinion that mattered most, and they also knew that if there was any man in the army who would insist on standing and fighting, it was Daniel Morgan.

"Nathanael," Morgan said loudly, making no effort to stand, "we'd be damned fools to fight him now. We need the militia. We need the Virginians. Get this ragged army into Virginia and get them fed, clothed, armed, and rested. Get fresh horses for the dragoons. Most of all, gather all the militia you can get. Then, when that is done, come back here and whip the pants off of Lord Cornwallis." He thumped his cane on the floor again for emphasis.

"So, then," Greene said, trying to conceal his relief, "we are in unanimous agreement." He turned to a young officer in the back of the room. "Write a summary of our proceedings and we will all sign it," he said. Turning back to his senior officers he said, "I will have copies sent to General Washington and to Congress."

"Now, gentlemen," Greene continued. "There is no time to lose. If we are to make this march successfully, it must commence immediately.

"Lord Cornwallis will expect us to head for the upper fords, as they are the only ones passable now. But for the last month Colonel Carrington has been gathering boats at the lower fords—at Irvine's and at Boyd's. So, we will march for those fords. The British do not know we have boats there and we must not allow them to discover our true destination until we have gained enough time to make it across before they can reach us. If the plan is to succeed, it is necessary that we deceive Cornwallis into believing we are marching for the upper fords.

"I am again separating the army into two wings. I will march with the bulk of the army for the lower fords, leaving immediately. The other wing will be a light corps, 700 men, consisting of Colonel Howard's Continentals, the Virginia riflemen, Colonel Lee's Legion, and Colonel Washington's dragoons. This force will screen the retreat of the main army and will draw off Lord Cornwallis. It is a very dangerous and grueling assignment. The light corps shall be commanded, of course, by General Morgan."

"No," Morgan boomed, interrupting Greene. As the other men all turned to face him, Morgan was looking down at the floor, shaking his head. "Nathanael, I cannot do it."

"Your country desperately needs you, sir," Greene said.

"I am not able, General Greene," Morgan said, looking up. "In my condition I risk slowing the army. I cannot fight. Hell, I can't even walk. My service here is over, sir."

A silence settled over the room. Greene knew it would be pointless to press the matter any further. "I am very sorry of that, sir," he said. "History will never forget what you have done." After a pause, he continued. "The command of the light corps shall fall then to Colonel Williams."

"I will depart immediately," Greene continued. "Within the hour. Colonel Williams, you will march in the morning. You will intercept Lord Cornwallis, deceive him into believing you are our entire army, then draw him away toward the upper fords. You will be the fox and he the hounds."

Morgan nodded knowingly, wearing a wry grin.

"I will send word when we are safely across the river," Greene continued, addressing Williams. "Then you will turn and come quickly to us."

"It will be done, sir," Williams said, gravely.

"You must get him to take the bait, Colonel," Greene said. "Stay close enough to keep him chasing you but not so close as to be caught in a general engagement. It will be very tricky and very risky work."

Williams nodded.

"Gentlemen," Greene said, "if we make it across the Dan safely ahead of Cornwallis, we can reprovision the army, gather reinforcements, rest the men, then cross back over and give him battle on our terms. If we do not make it across, then he will likely destroy us in detail.

"The stakes are high. Whether our cause will prevail or be lost depends upon us winning this race."

Greene allowed his words to hang in the air for a few moments before he continued. "Now see to your commands, gentlemen."

Williams and Huger stood and left the room. When they were gone, Morgan spoke.

"Hardly any of us have any formal military training," he said. "I don't. You don't."

Greene chuckled. "That is certainly true, General."

"Once again you divide your army in the face of a superior enemy," Morgan said. "Now I'm just an old waggoneer, but I'm pretty sure that isn't something a general is supposed to do."

"I do what I think is best," Greene answered.

"And I think it is brilliant, sir," Morgan said. "Audacious. Risky as hell. But brilliant. If you are able to give Cornwallis the slip and pull this off, you'll be adding a new chapter to some future military manual, Nathanael." After a pause he added, "And I believe you *will* pull it off."

"Pray that you are right about that, sir," Greene said quietly, answered by a nod from Morgan. "Cornwallis is desperate to fight us before we are reinforced. I have sent word for the Virginia militia to gather on the north side of the Dan. If they will not come to us, we will go to them."

"It's a very good plan, Nathanael. An excellent plan, sir. Now, my friend," Morgan said, "may I offer you some parting advice?"

"Of course, sir," Greene answered. "I greatly desire it."

"When you fight Cornwallis, fight him the way we fought Tarleton at Cowpens," Morgan said. "Put riflemen on your flanks and force him to cut through two lines of militia before he reaches your Continentals. Rely on the militia to give him two good fires before they withdraw but expect nothing more from them than that."

"The militia," Greene said wearily. "May the good Lord deliver us from them."

"Respectfully, my friend," Morgan said gently, "you are wrong in your assessment of the militia. They must be used correctly, sir. They must be inspired. They must know that they are respected. Hell, shoot some of them if they do not do their duty. But, sir, do not underestimate them and do not neglect them. The key to success is the militia. If they fight, you will beat Cornwallis. If not, he will beat you and likely cut your regulars to pieces."

Greene answered only with a nod.

After a few moments, Morgan leaned on his cane and lifted himself to his feet, grimacing as he stood.

"It is time for this worn-out sack of bones to go home," he said. "I may die trying, but I am determined to get myself back to Winchester."

"Be careful, General," Greene said, extending his hand. "I shall pray for your full and rapid recovery."

Morgan shook his hand warmly. "Thank you, Nathanael. I need all the help I can get. Best wishes to you, my friend. Give my regards to his Lordship when you see him."

As Morgan hobbled out the door, the adjutant approached. "I have the minutes of the Council, General."

Greene took the paper from him and walked over

to a nearby table. After reading through it, he pulled a quill out of a stand, dipped it in an ink bottle, then signed his name. "Get the other signatures, then send it out on the next express," he said, handing it back.

"Yes, sir," the young man replied.

Watching Morgan through the window as he limped away, Greene said distantly, "Great generals are scarce, Lieutenant. There are few Morgans to be found."

40

Bruce's Crossroads
Guilford County, North Carolina
February 12, 1781

Cornwallis took the bait, furiously driving his men in pursuit of Williams' detached light corps, which Cornwallis believed to be the entire American army. As Greene's main force slogged through the mud and biting cold rain toward the boats waiting at the Dan River, many of them on bloody bare feet, Williams led Cornwallis away from them, skirmishing constantly.

To stay ahead of Cornwallis, and to deny him any chance to rest, Williams set a demanding schedule. The army would march until 9 p.m., then make camp. Half the men were allowed to sleep while the other half were posted on guard or patrol duty. There were only a few tents, and they were used to keep the ammunition covered and dry. So the men slept as they marched, in the open rainy winter air. At 3 a.m. the army would resume marching, with a detail sent ahead to find a place to cook a quick breakfast—cornmeal and lean beef—the only meal of the day during the march. When the column reached the cook site, it would stop long enough for the men to eat quickly, the men who had been up all night on patrol being allowed to eat first. Then the march would resume. Each man slept only six out of every 48 hours.

The dragoons under Washington and Lee kept the same schedule but with the additional responsibility of staying in contact with the enemy, to lure Cornwallis on while preventing him from discovering that the army he was chasing was only a diversion. So, like two weary but determined fighters, Tarleton probed and jabbed, and the American cavalry screened and blocked, exchanging pistol fire and saber blows when they collided, as they did several times each day. It was grueling and exhausting work.

So, when a local farmer named Charles Bruce rode up to Washington and his weary and hungry troopers and invited them all to breakfast at his home, the colonel was pleased to accept, thrilled at the prospect of the first decent meal in weeks. He detailed a troop to remain on patrol, promising them a chance to eat next, and he and the rest of the dragoons followed Bruce as he led them down a narrow farm road. Bruce's home had just come into view when they heard a man calling out "Charles! Charles Bruce!" They turned to see a civilian riding toward them across a field, bareback atop a thin old gray nag, yelling and waving his arm over his head as he approached.

"Do you know that man?" Washington asked.

"It's Isaac Wright," Bruce answered. "He lives near here."

The column stopped, waiting for the man.

"The British," Wright said as he arrived, nearly out of breath, "They switched roads and are coming right at you. They just rode through my farm."

"Where is your farm?" Washington asked.

"Down the road yonder, about four miles," Wright answered, gesturing in the direction they had just come from.

Washington turned to Ransom, who shook his head.

"They could not have gotten past Captain Barrett's troop," Ransom said. "And if they were that close, he would have fired an alarm."

Washington turned back to Wright. "Describe the men you saw," he said.

"Green coats, black helmets with feathers sticking out of them. It's Tarleton's men. At least a hundred of them," Wright answered, plainly unnerved.

"Could it be Colonel Lee?" Ransom asked.

"The uniforms of Colonel Lee's dragoons are nearly identical to those of Tarleton," Washington said to Wright. "Are you certain the men you saw were British."

"Damn right I'm certain," Wright snapped. "It's Bloody Ban and he's coming up on you fast."

Washington glanced again at Ransom, who again shook his head skeptically.

"Mr. Wright, with all due respect, you must be mistaken," Washington said. "Tarleton's dragoons are not on this road, and they are not within five miles of here."

"I'm telling you I seen them, sir!" Wright exclaimed. "And I done rode all this way as hard as I could to warn you."

Captain Parsons eased his horse forward and spoke. "I'll take a couple of men and go check it out, Colonel," he said. After a pause he added with a smile, "Save us a few bites."

Washington hesitated, then said, "All right. Come quickly if you see anything. Signal to Captain Barrett if they somehow slipped past him. If Mr. Wright is mistaken," he added, "come on back as soon as you're satisfied."

Parsons nodded, then turned to the men. "Bradshaw. Evans," he said, and two of the dragoons peeled off to the side. Parsons then turned to Wright. "All right, Mr. Wright," he said. "Take us to them."

Wright looked at the three dragoons warily. "You want me to take just the three of you. I'm telling you the whole damned British army is out there."

"We'll be all right, Mr. Wright," Parsons answered calmly. "Lead us to where you saw them."

Wright looked carefully at the three men again. "I won't do it," he said.

The men in the column stirred restlessly. Washington and Bruce spoke simultaneously. "Look here, sir…," Washington began, angrily, as Bruce said, "Now, Isaac…"

Wright interrupted them. "I mean I won't do it on this horse," he said. "Y'all are riding good stout horses and I'm on this old nag. When Tarleton's men see us and come after us, y'all will ride off and I won't be able to keep up. That will be the end of me."

"There is no need to…" Parsons began.

Washington lifted his hand, silencing him. "Collin!" he said.

In an instant Collin was at his side. "Yes, sir," the boy said.

"Trade horses with Mr. Wright," Washington said.

Collin's eyes widened with incredulity. "Do what?" he said.

"You heard me," Washington said. "Trade horses

with Mr. Wright. When he and Captain Parsons return, you can have her back."

"My horse?" Collin said, pleading.

"Trade horses with him, Collin," Washington snapped, growing impatient. "Now!"

Collin sullenly dismounted and handed the reins to Wright, who took them and swung himself up onto the horse's back. "Follow me," he said, trotting off with Parsons and the other two dragoons trailing him.

"They'll be back shortly," Washington said to the pouting Collin. "There are no British dragoons out there. Come on," he said, turning his horse back toward Bruce's house.

"I'll wait here," Collin answered. "I want to make sure I get my horse back."

Washington answered with a laugh. "Suit yourself," he said. He signaled Bruce and said, "Let's go, Mr. Bruce."

Bruce nodded, prodded his horse, and led the column down the road. As they were riding away, Collin mounted Wright's old bareback nag, gave it a little kick in the side and began riding slowly back up the road.

He had been riding about twenty minutes, straining to see or hear Parsons' squad in the distance, when he heard the sound of horses rapidly approaching him from behind. Assuming it was Washington returning, he stopped the nag and began trying to turn it around. Suddenly six green-clad dragoons emerged from the bend in the road and rode quickly up to him, crowding their horses up against the nag. His heart racing wildly, Collin spun his head around quickly in both directions, and saw that he was trapped. The dragoons were laughing as they jostled him, reeking of liquor.

"Look here, mates," one of them said, circling around in front. "Somebody's pet monkey escaped."

The others hooted.

"And it's wearing a costume," the dragoon said, laughing.

Collin reached for the pistol in his saddle bag. His heart sank when he realized the saddle bag was still on his horse.

"Where did you steal that coat, monkey?" the drunken dragoon said.

"This is *my* coat," Collin answered.

The dragoon laughed loudly. "I declare! It's a talking monkey, mates! Probably worth a fortune!"

Collin tried to maneuver the nag past the dragoons, but they crowded up closer, penning him in.

The dragoon drew his saber and slapped the side of Collin's head with the blunt end. The boy groaned and threw his hand up to the throbbing spot on his head.

"Answer my question, boy!" the dragoon said, jeering. "Where did you steal that coat?"

Collin looked up at him, his hand still on his head. "This is *my* coat," he said, defiantly. "I am a trooper in Washington's Light Dragoons."

"Oh!" the dragoon said, mockingly. "A trooper in Washington's Light Dragoons!" The others were snorting and laughing.

"Well, in that case…" the dragoon said, swiftly and savagely swinging his saber, slashing through Collin's face, ripping to the bone across both cheeks and tearing off most of the boy's nose. Collin slid off the nag's back, in searing pain, groaning as he fell onto the muddy clay road.

The six dragoons had all drawn their sabers and were slashing and stabbing at Collin, laughing as he lay whimpering, drawn up in a tight ball on the road. Unable to reach the boy from horseback, the dragoon in front dismounted and stood over him, laughing, as he began raining saber blows down onto the boy's head and back, slicing him open deeply and repeatedly.

When Washington and Ransom rounded the bend in the road, at the head of the column returning from Bruce's, that is what they saw: Collin lying in the road, being hacked repeatedly by a British dragoon, while five more watched from horseback, laughing.

Ransom froze for the instant it took him to process what was happening, then everything before him turned red, as a wave of rage like none he had ever known before swept over him. Spurring his horse, he screamed, drew his saber, and charged furiously.

The mounted British dragoons looked up at the sound of the scream, their laughter suddenly vanishing as they saw Ransom and the other American horsemen racing toward them. They spurred their horses and galloped away.

The dismounted dragoon who had been sabering Collin reached frantically for his horse, his foot missing the stirrup as he tried to remount. He was still fumbling for the stirrup when Ransom, screaming wildly, galloped past him, swinging his saber violently as he rode by, decapitating the man with a single vicious blow, and continuing on furiously after the others.

Washington skidded his horse to a stop next to Collin and leaped off. He knelt down and gently rolled the boy over, seeing that his head and back had been hacked into a bloody pulp.

"Collin," he said softly, his voice cracking, as he looked down into the boy's bloody and mutilated face.

Noticing that his mouth was moving, Washington

wiped away some of the blood that was streaming down from Collin's head and oozing out of the wounds on his face. He turned his head and shouted, "Get the surgeon!"

Turning back to Collin, he resumed gently brushing away the blood around the boy's mouth, while cradling his head in his lap. "Hold on, Collin," he said. "The surgeon is coming."

A dragoon rode up beside him at that moment and Washington looked up at him, his eyes blazing. "Catch up to Ransom Wiatt," he said, his voice hot with anger. "Tell him my orders are to give them no quarter. Kill every damned one of them!"

The dragoon nodded his understanding, spurred his mount, and galloped away.

Collin sputtered, coughing out some blood, which Washington quickly wiped away.

"Hold on, Collin," he said.

"Colonel," the boy said weakly. "I'm sorry, sir. I didn't have my pistol."

Washington battled back the tears he felt rushing to his eyes.

"You are a brave soldier, Collin," he answered. "You are a gallant dragoon."

After a few minutes a horse skidded to a stop behind them. A young man dismounted quickly, removed a saddle bag, and knelt beside Washington and Collin. "I will attend to him, sir," the surgeon said.

Washington seemed reluctant to release the boy, who had lapsed into unconsciousness. "Sir," the surgeon said gently. "I will dress his wounds."

As if broken from a trance, Washington nodded slightly, tenderly lifting Collin's head out of his lap. The surgeon slid a bundle of fabric underneath the boy's head and laid it gently down, while Washington stood and straightened himself, his white uniform streaked with Collin's blood.

Washington walked to his horse, took the reins and was beginning to remount, when he paused, turned slowly around, and looked back at the surgeon. Their eyes met. With a shake of his head the doctor answered the question Washington's look was asking, then turned back to his work. The colonel bit his lower lip.

Washington looked up to see Ransom and several other troopers returning, leading a captured officer—one of Tarleton's dragoons. He flared with anger and stormed out into the road. "Why have you disobeyed my orders, Captain?" he shouted. "My orders were to give no quarter!"

"They are all dead, sir," Ransom answered calmly. "This man was not…"

Washington interrupted him, furious. "Silence!" he yelled. "My orders were clear! No quarter!" He turned around, trembling with anger. "Bring me a rope!"

Confused, none of the dragoons moved. "Bring me a rope, goddamn it! Now!" Washington shouted, sending a couple of the men scurrying away.

He stormed over to the captured officer, reached up, grabbed the man by his coat, pulled him off of his horse, and threw him down into the mud. "Say your prayers, sir, for you are about to die," Washington said, trembling with rage.

"Colonel…" Ransom began.

Washington spun around and pointed a finger at him. "Silence, Ransom! I don't want to hear another word from you!"

The captured officer had risen to his feet. He straightened his uniform coat and brushed away some of the mud.

Washington stood inches from his face, glaring at him. "You would murder an unarmed boy?" he spat at him, enraged. "An unarmed boy??"

The officer kept his composure, looking back at Washington, but not answering.

Washington lifted his hand, pointing at the man's face, his finger only inches from his nose. "You will answer for his murder with your life!" he said.

"Colonel," the captured man said calmly, "Those men had no orders to…"

"Silence, God damn you!" Washington shouted. He turned around. "Where is that rope? Damn it!"

From the direction of the house a dragoon rode up, carrying a thick rope, with Bruce riding alongside him.

Washington turned back to the officer. "Say your prayers, sir!" he exclaimed, before hurrying over to Bruce and the dragoon. Pointing to a tree he said, "Put it there!"

They were interrupted by a shout, coming from down the road. In a moment, Parsons and his squad came into view, galloping toward them, Wright riding alongside them on Collin's horse.

When he reached Washington, Parsons pulled his horse to a stop. "It's Tarleton, sir!" he said, breathlessly. "They're coming this way. Fast. Looks like all of them. They must have changed direction and gotten in behind Captain Barrett's patrol."

Washington seemed frozen for a few moments. The trooper with the rope had stopped, awaiting orders along with the rest of the regiment gathered there.

Ransom made eye contact with Parsons and signaled him with a slight nod. Then he turned in his saddle and shouted, "Troop assemble!" Parsons did the same, gathering his men.

The activity seemed to shake Washington back to his senses. He stamped the ground in anger, then turned to the man with the rope. "Take the prisoner to Mr. Bruce's house," he barked.

"Yes, sir," the man answered.

Washington glanced over at the crumpled bloody body by the road. The surgeon had covered the boy's face with a cloth and stepped away. He turned to Bruce. "Will you see that he is given a decent Christian burial, sir?"

"Yes, Colonel," Bruce said, gravely. "You have my word, sir. It will be done."

Washington nodded, pausing again after another quick glance at Collin's body. Then, after only a moment's hesitation, he turned quickly and reached for his horse, mounting in one swift movement.

"To horse!" he shouted. Turning to his right, out of habit, he said, "Sound the…" stopping when he realized Collin was not beside him, waiting for the command. He turned to face back up the road.

"Dragoons, advance!" he shouted. "Column of fours!"

The regiment formed up promptly and rode off to meet the enemy, Colonel Washington leading them.

41

The Race to the Dan
Caswell County, North Carolina
February 13, 1781

The game was over. Once Greene had a two-day head start, Williams began veering his men to the east, while ordering Washington to use his dragoons to keep Cornwallis' attention and keep luring him west. But Tarleton's probing cavalry discovered the shift and Cornwallis then realized that the Americans were heading for the lower fords. Determined to catch and destroy them, he pushed his army relentlessly, driving his hungry and fatigued men on, enticed by the belief that his prey was finally almost at hand.

It was nearly midnight, and Williams' light corps had been marching without rest since 2 a.m., pressed and dogged by their determined British pursuers. Using pine torches to light the narrow, rutted muddy road, the Patriot army staggered forward through the cold wet night, staying just beyond Cornwallis' reach. It was now a race. The survival of Williams' corps depended upon it being able to outrun Cornwallis to the Dan River.

Williams was riding alongside Washington, both on tired, hungry mounts, when a scout rode up. "The British haven't stopped, sir," the rider said. "They're still coming."

Williams sighed. "Carry the news to Colonel Howard and Colonel Lee," he said to the rider. "Tell them we must keep up the march. We cannot make camp unless the British do."

"Yes, sir," the scout said, before trotting away.

"It seems that his Lordship aims to have our hides," Williams said, distantly.

"His army must be as exhausted as ours," Washington answered. "The country has been stripped of all provisions, so his horses must have even less forage than ours. And he has to remove all the obstructions we are leaving on the road."

"And yet, he is still nipping at our heels, Colonel," Williams said. "We cannot seem to shake him."

The men rode on silently, adrift in weary thought, the only sounds in the quiet winter night being clanking canteens, and the thuds of boots, hooves, and bare feet plodding over the frozen red mud. After a few minutes, Ransom approached from the front of the column, pulling up alongside them.

"Colonel Williams, Colonel Washington," he said. "Y'all need to come and see this."

They followed him to the front of the column, past a long line of ragged and shivering men, trudging along in the dark. He led them to Lee, who was waiting atop a little rise in the road. "Look yonder," Lee said, pointing.

Williams and Washington stopped and peered into the distance. Across a hillside, about a mile away, they saw little twinkling dots of light, hundreds of them.

"My God," Williams said, gloomily.

"Do we know for sure what they are?" Washington asked.

"I've sent a rider ahead to confirm," Lee answered. "But those are campfires. What else could they be?"

"Then it's over, gentlemen," Williams said, sounding defeated. "I had hoped and prayed that by now General Greene would have gotten the army to safety. But if he is there, then we have no choice. We will have to turn this corps around and fight Cornwallis, to enable General Greene to escape. We will have to sacrifice this corps, to save the rest of the army."

There was no need for Lee or Washington to respond. They knew the truth of what Williams had said, before he spoke the words.

After a few silent minutes, Lee spoke. "Here comes my man now," he said, pointing to a rider approaching in the darkness.

As they watched the rider coming toward them, a second rider arrived suddenly from the rear of the column. "The British have stopped, Colonel," he said, breathlessly. "They are making camp, sir."

At that moment, Lee's rider came to within shouting distance. "They're not there!" he yelled, as he rode toward the colonels. "It's General Greene's campsite all right, but the army is long gone," he said, as he pulled up. Even in the darkness it was impossible to miss the man's smile. "There's a local farmer out there. He says General Greene passed through here 48 hours ago. The farmer and his family have kept the campfires burning to guide us." He paused to let it all sink in. "They're safe, sir. They're safe."

Williams let the man's report settle on him for a few

seconds, feeling relieved that in the darkness his tear-filled eyes would not be visible to other officers.

"Very good," he said at last, nodding. "Very good."

After a moment he added, "We will halt and rest here. Feed your men and horses if you have anything to give them. We will march again in two hours."

~~~

By 2 a.m. the men were forming up and preparing to resume the march, cold and wet, the one or two hours of rest having done little to relieve their exhaustion. Seeing Lee and Washington talking as they tightened the saddles on their horses, Williams walked over to them. He had not slept at all.

"Gentlemen," he said, "We have 40 miles to go. It's a sprint now. But even if we outrun him to the river, we won't be able to cross if Cornwallis is on us. We must gain some distance today.

"Spar with them. Harass them. Obstruct the road. Slow them at every opportunity."

"Sounds like a good day's work," Lee said, cheerfully.

"*Bon courage*, gentlemen," Williams said, reaching out and shaking their hands.

~~~

At that same instant, a few miles away, Cornwallis was mounting his horse. "The fox will be at bay today, General," he said to O'Hara, who was mounting beside him. "We have chased him to fords he cannot cross. Now the rebels will have no choice but to turn and fight, and then we shall destroy them."

"Are we certain those fords are impassable?" O'Hara replied.

"Absolutely certain," Cornwallis said. "I have it from all of our sources and have reconfirmed it multiple times. Those fords are too deep this time of year. The only way across is by boat and there are only one or two small boats there. It would be impossible for General Greene to ferry his entire army across on them. The rebels are trapped, sir."

"Then let us close the hunt, my lord," O'Hara answered.

"I know your men are fatigued, General," Cornwallis replied, "but we must continue to press them. Have them leave behind everything but their arms and their canteens. We must exert ourselves today. The discipline, endurance, and stamina the army has shown on this march has been nothing less than heroic. But we must finish it today, sir. We *will* finish it today. Then we shall rest on our laurels."

42

The Race to the Dan
February 14, 1781

Trudging forward at the head of a column of ragged, sleepwalking scarecrows, Greene's aching body was near a state of collapse. Other than a few brief naps, he had been four days without sleep. But as the road emerged from the woods, he was instantly invigorated by the sight before him: the wide, muddy, swirling waters of the Dan River, and alongside its southern shore, a dozen vessels—bateaux, flatboats, and canoes, eager ferrymen waiting by them all.

Carrington rode forward. Smiling, he extended his hand. "Welcome to Irvine's Ferry," he said. "I am very pleased to see you, sir."

An artillery officer before Greene had appointed him quartermaster, 33-year-old Edward Carrington possessed the kind of sober attention to detail that Greene admired. "And I you, Colonel," Greene answered, shaking his hand warmly. He scanned the river's edge and smiled with satisfaction. "This is quite a motley fleet you have assembled, sir."

Carrington turned in the saddle, took in the scene,

then turned back to Greene. "There is another one, equally impressive, waiting at Boyd's. Shall we put them to work, General?"

~~~

Bayard and his wife were just finishing their breakfast when they heard a horse approaching. Bayard stood up quickly, walked to the window and saw Gus Johnson coming at a gallop. "Stay here," he said to his wife as he stepped out the door, closing it behind him. He hurriedly crossed the porch and was waiting in front of the house when Gus arrived.

"Greene's army is crossing at Irvine's Ferry and at Boyd's Ferry," Gus said, speaking rapidly. "At this very moment."

"Are they being pursued?" Bayard asked.

"I don't know. I just got the news," Gus answered.

Bayard bowed his head and squeezed his temples. After a few seconds he said, "I expect the citizenry will rush out to greet the general and his army." He stepped closer to Gus and spoke quietly, "Any who do not offer assistance to them will attract suspicion. And there will be an opportunity to gain valuable information."

Gus nodded. "Understood and agreed," he said.

"Spread the word, Gus," Bayard said. "And do not discriminate. Let it be seen that you encouraged the entire community to welcome and offer aid to General Greene and his men."

"Yes, sir," Gus answered, turning to leave.

"Gus," Bayard called after him.

Gus turned to face him. "The hour will soon be upon us. At long last."
~~~

Gus nodded, spurred his horse, and rode away.

~~~

Like a wildfire, the word of the army's arrival raced across the countryside. Bells were ringing at every farmstead along Bayard's fifteen-mile ride to Irvine's Ferry, and by the time he arrived he had heard the story at least a dozen times—how General Greene had outfoxed and outrun Lord Cornwallis, how the British army was now stuck deep in hostile territory without provisions, and how Greene would surely now smite and utterly destroy them.

What he saw when he arrived at the ferry was simply astonishing. Not the sight of hundreds of soldiers, collapsed in tattered clusters alongside the road, sleeping where they fell. He had expected that. What surprised him was what he saw on the river—a flotilla of boats ferrying the men across in a steady stream.

As he looked out in amazement, a rider came alongside him. "It's a glorious day, Mr. Bayard," the man said.

Bayard turned to him and answered with an insincere smile. "I certainly would never have expected to see such a thing as this, Mr. Terry," he answered. "Where did all those boats come from?"

Terry laughed. "I was surprised myself when they started showing up here a couple of days ago. Turns out that Colonel Carrington had them hidden all up and down the river—where Tory spies wouldn't see them. He's had them stashed away for months, just waiting to unveil them when needed. You should see what's happening up at Boyd's. He's got more of them there. It's slow going, but with all these boats he'll have
~~~

the entire army across by dark. Looks like Lord Cornwallis is going to be stuck on the other side," he said, laughing loudly.

"Remarkable," Bayard said softly. "A very clever move by Colonel Carrington."

"He has saved our army, it seems to me," Terry said cheerfully. "We'll get these men fed and rested, we'll add our militia to the ranks, and then we'll be ready to give his Lordship a long overdue whipping."

Bayard just stared out at the river, shaking his head in disbelief. "Remarkable," he repeated.

Terry laughed again and rode away, leaving Bayard to reflect on what he was witnessing. How could I have missed this? he wondered. How did I allow this to happen?

~~~

As the last of the men were scrambling aboard the boats, Greene took out his watch and checked the time. Five o'clock. It would be dark soon.

He walked over to his horse, removed a quill and some paper from his saddlebag, stretched the paper across his saddle, and wrote a note. "Courier!" he called out, and a boy on horseback appeared quickly at his side.

"You must get this message to Colonel Williams as rapidly as possible," Greene said, handing the message to him. "Do not tarry. Do not spare your horse. Do you understand?"

"Yes, sir," the boy answered, taking the paper and sliding it into his saddlebag.

"Take this road," Greene said, gesturing. "Colonel Williams is following our trail. Reach him as quickly as
~~~

you can."

The boy nodded, spun his horse around, and left at a gallop.

~~~

At about seven o'clock a courier raced up to the head of Williams' column on a lathered mount. "Message from General Greene, sir," he said breathlessly, handing the paper to Williams.

"Bring me a light," Williams said, as he opened the paper. An adjutant approached, carrying a torch. As Williams read the message, Howard rode up alongside him.

After he read the message, Williams passed it to Howard, who tilted it to catch the torchlight.

After a few moments, Howard looked up and made eye contact with Williams. "Pass the word along to the men, Colonel," Williams said. "It will lift their spirits."

Howard nodded, "Aye, sir. It will indeed." He looked back down at the message and read it again:

Irvine's Ferry, 12 past 5 o'clock. All our troops are over and the stage is clear. I am ready to receive you and give you a hearty welcome. N. Greene, Maj. Gen.

~~~

At the head of his column, Cornwallis craned his neck and listened carefully, trying to make out an odd noise in the distance.

"What the devil is that?" he asked O'Hara, who was riding alongside him.

O'Hara stopped his horse and turned his head, listening.

After a few moments he said, "It sounds like cheering, sir."

"Cheering?" Cornwallis said, puzzled.

"I believe so, m'lord," O'Hara replied. "It's the rebels. They are cheering."

~~~

Williams sent for Lee and Washington. They arrived together.

"This is it, gentlemen," he told them, gravely. "Whether this corps makes it across or not will depend upon you. I will take the infantry to Irvine's, as fast as is humanly possible. You must strike the head of Cornwallis's column. Throw him on his heels. Obstruct and delay him any way you can. When you get word that we are across, you are to make a dash for Boyd's."

"Sounds like good sport," Lee said.

"Be cautious, gentlemen," Williams said, "but you must keep his full attention while we make our escape."

"It will be done, sir," Washington said. "We'll see you in Virginia."

"Very well," Williams said. "God be with you."

~~~

When Williams and his infantry reached the river, Greene was there waiting for them, a flotilla of boats at the ready. In less than two hours, the last of the men were boarding to cross.

"Well, Colonel Williams," Greene said, gesturing toward a canoe on the riverbank. "Shall we cross, sir?"

~~~

O'Hara cursed the darkness and the cold as his men stumbled along the road, which the fleeing Americans had churned into a deep muddy quagmire. "Press on lads, press on," he said as he rode along the column.

"We canna see a thing, sir," one of the men muttered. "It's as black out as the Earl of Hell's waistcoat."

"Just follow the man in front of you," O'Hara answered. "If the rebels can see, then so can we."

"Bloody hell!" someone exclaimed from the front of the column.

O'Hara rode toward the voice to investigate. "What is the matter?"

"There's more trees in the road, sir," a soldier answered.

"Axe men!" O'Hara yelled out. "Clear the road!"

The men in the front of the column dropped to the ground, taking advantage of a few moments rest, as a squad of soldiers carrying axes hurried past them. They had only been chopping away the branches a few minutes when pistol shots suddenly erupted from both sides of the road, sending them diving for cover. A few seconds later came the sound of horses, rushing off through the trees.

"They're bloody devils, they are," one of the soldiers said, as he came out from behind his cover.

Cornwallis pushed his way to the front of the column until he found O'Hara. "General, why have we stopped?" he demanded.

"More obstructions in the road, m'lord. Another ambuscade," O'Hara answered, testily.

"The enemy is slipping away, General," Cornwallis
~~~

said. "We must make better time."

"Sir," O'Hara said, edging closer and lowering his voice, "the men are spent. Perhaps we should allow them some rest."

Cornwallis shook his head. "Not yet, General. Press your men, sir. At midnight we will stop. For two hours."

"Yes, sir," O'Hara replied. He turned his horse back into the road. "Hurry up, lads," he said. "Let's get this cleared out."

~~~

Washington was helping a squad of his dragoons drag a fallen tree into the road when Lee rode up. "Colonel Williams and the infantry are across," he said cheerfully.

Washington straightened and peered up at Lee. "This road leads directly to the ferry at Boyd's?" he asked.

"It does. It's about twelve miles, I reckon," Lee answered.

"All right, gentlemen," Washington said, turning to his men. "Mount up. It's our turn."

Lee laughed. "I'll race you there," he said, turning and riding away.

Washington looked around in the dark. "Ransom?" he said.

"Here, sir," Ransom answered, drawing closer.

"You will be our rear guard. Stay here with your troop for one hour, then dash for the ferry," Washington said.

"Yes, sir," Ransom answered.

"I believe you have been eager to see Halifax
~~~

County again," Washington said.

"Indeed, I have, sir," Ransom said. "But my home is on the other side of the river."

"Keep your head down and we'll all make it there," Washington replied. "I'll see you at the ferry."

~~~

The cavalry began arriving around eleven p.m. and Carrington was there to greet them, sending the men over on boats, a few at a time, guided by torches on both sides of the river. Once Lee's dragoons were all across, Washington's men began crossing.

On the southern bank, Carrington, Lee, and Washington watched, warming themselves by a fire as the boats were being poled or paddled across. "Colonel Carrington, this will go down as one of the most magnificent feats of the war," Lee said. "Congratulations, sir."

"I won't relax until everyone is across," Carrington replied. "When the last man is safely over, I intend to sleep for a week."

"When that boat there is loaded," Lee replied, gesturing to a flat boat that was being pulled to the shore, "that will be the last of them. Then we three shall triumphantly close the event."

"No," Washington said. "My rear guard isn't in yet."

"It's after midnight, sir," Carrington replied. "Shouldn't your men be here by now?"

Washington sighed. "Yes," he said. "I am becoming concerned."

The men stood silently for a few awkward moments, until Washington stepped away. "You go ahead," he said as he walked to his horse. "I'll go see
~~~

about them."

"Hold on, Colonel," Lee exclaimed. "Not alone. Let's call back a squad to go with you."

"Not necessary," Washington replied as he mounted. "If they have been taken there is nothing to be done about it tonight."

At that moment, a rider appeared on the road, emerging from the woods, followed closely by a dozen more.

"Boyd's Ferry, I presume?" Ransom asked, playfully.

Carrington hurried over. "Get your men aboard boats, sir," he said. "Is this everyone?"

Ransom glanced over his shoulder. "Yes," he said. "We're a sorry lot, but we're all there is."

"I am pleased to see you, Captain Wiatt," Washington said, relief evident in his voice. "Where is Lord Cornwallis?"

"Miles away, sir," Ransom answered. "I would say he has had a most disagreeable day."

"Well done, men," Washington called out to the bedraggled and mud-splattered troopers. "Well done! Now get aboard those boats. Swim the horses across."

Halfway across the river one of the horses panicked, turned, and swam back to the southern bank—the rest of them mechanically turning and following. Grumbling and swearing, a squad of exhausted dragoons came back over the river, collected the horses, and got them safely over.

It was past one a.m. when Carrington, Lee, and Washington climbed aboard a flatboat and floated slowly across the river.

Five hours later Banastre Tarleton rode up to the river's edge and gazed across. Through the morning fog he saw a half dozen boats secured on the opposite shore, where a handful of rebel sentries stood jeering at him.

43

Halifax Courthouse
Halifax County, Virginia
February 15, 1781

Even though he was less than twenty miles from home, Ransom's request for a brief furlough was denied. "I can't do it, Ransom," Washington had told him. "As much as I'd like to, I cannot allow you to leave. General Greene remains concerned that Cornwallis may cross the river and if he does it will be our job to screen the army's retreat." Ransom ached for home and for his mother's embrace—his pain and disappointment obvious to Washington. "As soon as we are out of danger," Washington said, sympathetically, "I promise you a lengthy and leisurely visit."

Ransom understood. He thanked the colonel and returned to his duties. But by that afternoon, it seemed as if everyone in the county was pouring into the camps at the courthouse village, bringing food and spirits and giving the men heroes' welcomes. In mid-afternoon Captain Parsons approached him and said, "There's someone in camp asking for you, Ransom. An elegant and distinguished lady. I think you'll be pleased to see her."

Moments later Tabitha Wiatt was hugging her son as if afraid to let him go, her head pressed against his chest and her tears soaking into his shirt. "Oh, Ransom," she said, between sobs, "I have been so worried about you. This is an answer to my prayers."

"Why don't you find a quiet place to visit your mother, Ransom," Parsons said. "I'll cover for you here."

Ransom nodded appreciatively, battling back tears of his own. He wrapped his arm around his mother's tiny shoulders and led her away, toward the village.

Normally a quiet place, nothing more than a few shops and a tavern clustered around the log courthouse, today the village was crowded and buzzing with activity. In addition to the hastily established camps created by Greene's army, militiamen from Halifax and the surrounding counties were streaming in, armed with whatever they had, and hundreds of local citizens had turned out to greet and feed the army. Some, like Tabita Wiatt, searched out sons, brothers, and husbands, and were rewarded with tearful reunions. Others came just to offer whatever aid and support they could. Many came only to sightsee. And among the throngs were some who came for nefarious purposes.

"I will have to get back to the regiment soon," Ransom said.

Tabitha leaned her head onto his shoulder as they walked. "I know," she answered sadly.

"I expect to be able to come home soon, Mother," he said. "And when I do, I will allow you to pamper me for at least a week."

Tabitha stopped walking, stepped back, and looked her son over. "You need a new shirt," she said. "And stockings. I will bring them to you as soon as I can."

"Don't go to any trouble, Mother. I am well provisioned," Ransom said.

"You most certainly are not," Tabitha replied, sternly. "Nor are you being properly fed. I shall attempt to remedy that as well."

Ransom laughed. "Yes, ma'am," he said playfully.

Tabitha took his arm and they resumed strolling along the road.

"I pray for your safety every day, Ransom," she said. "You must do likewise, son."

"I am grateful for your prayers," he answered. "And I am grateful that the Lord has seen fit to answer them."

"Oh, Ransom," Tabitha said, pulling close to him. "I am so proud of you, son. How I wish your father could have lived to see the man that you have become. He would be the proudest man in Virginia."

They were interrupted by the shouts of a young boy. "Ransom! Ransom!" he cried, as he raced toward them, wrapping his arms joyfully around Ransom's legs when he arrived.

Ransom laughed and picked the boy up, recognizing him immediately. "My goodness!" he exclaimed playfully. "Can this be Tip Dodson? Look how much you've grown!"

"Hey Ransom, can I wear your helmet?" the boy said, excitedly.

"Of course," Ransom answered, taking it off. He sat the plumed leather helmet down on the boys' head and it was swallowed by it. "It seems to be a might large for you," Ransom said with a laugh.

The boy tilted the helmet back, so he could see, then looked up at Ransom's face. "I'm going to be a dragoon too when I grow up," he said.

"Splendid!" Ransom replied. "I hope to be retired by then."

"Hey Ransom," the boy said, eagerly. "How many redcoats have you killed?"

"Tip!" Tabita exclaimed. "For shame!"

Ransom just chuckled and set the boy down.

"Hey Ransom, is it true that Colonel Washington fought Bloody Ban in single combat?" the boy asked, his face glowing with excitement.

Ransom smiled and nodded. "Yes. He sure did."

Thrilled, the boy said, "Is it true that a negro trumpet boy saved Colonel Washington's life?"

A flash of pain swept briefly across Ransom's face. The boy didn't notice, but Tabitha felt a stab in her heart when she saw it.

Ransom nodded, with only a hint of a smile remaining. "It is true that Collin, our regimental trumpeter, saved the colonel's life."

The boy's eyes widened.

"Collin has since given his own life," Ransom said. "For the cause."

Tabitha reached out and took her son's arm. "I can only imagine the pain you have experienced, Ransom," she said sadly, her eyes filling with tears. "The suffering. Oh, my heart aches for you."

Ransom nodded, biting his lip, and struggling to preserve his smile.

"I'd better take that back, Tip," he said, removing the helmet from the boy's head and returning it to his own. "It's about time for me to return to my duties."

"Thanks, Ransom," the boy said, still beaming. "I

can't wait to tell the others I saw you!"

"Run along now, Tip," Tabitha said. "Your mama is probably wondering where you are."

"Yes, ma'am," the boy said with a nod before dashing away.

"I'm sorry, Mother, but I really do need to go back now," Ransom said.

Tabitha wrapped her arms around him, hugging him tightly as she answered, "I know you do."

As she released him, a voice called out, "Captain Wiatt!"

They turned to see Bayard approaching, his hand extended. "Welcome home, young man," he said.

Ransom shook his hand. "Thank you, sir. I'm happy to be back."

"I do not want to intrude on your time with Mrs. Wiatt, so I will come right to the point," Bayard said. "The county will want to know how to help. What are your regiment's principal needs?"

"Horses," Ransom answered immediately. "We desperately need new mounts, sir. The ones we have now are broken down and many are unshod. Without fresh strong horses, I do not believe the regiment is capable of successful combat."

"Understood," Bayard replied. "I will see what we can do about that."

"Thank you, sir," Ransom answered. "May I request an additional favor?"

"Of course," Bayard answered.

"Will you please see my mother to her chaise?" Ransom asked. "I must return to camp right away."

"I would be delighted, Captain," Bayard said, extending his arm to Tabitha.

Before taking it, she hugged Ransom again, then

stood on her toes to kiss his cheek.

"God bless you, son," she said, tearfully.

"I'll see you soon, Mother," he answered. "I promise."

Tabitha nodded, wiped a tear from her face, then took Bayard's arm and walked away.

His heart was full as Ransom turned and began walking back toward the camp. But as he turned a corner, he felt it rise suddenly into his throat. He found himself standing face to face with Jennie Lewis.

44

Jennie gasped, dropping her eyes to her feet, as Ransom quickly snatched the helmet from his head. They stood awkwardly for a few moments, as Ransom struggled to find words.

"Good day, Jennie," he said at last, painfully.

Jennie mumbled a greeting, fumbling with the basket she was carrying, and keeping her gaze lowered.

"I have so missed you, Jennie," Ransom said softly.

Jennie did not look up and she gave no response.

After a few moments, he said, "Jennie?"

She kept her eyes locked on her feet, giving no answer while fighting a powerful desire to flee.

Ransom became suddenly aware of his appearance—his whitened eye and the scars on his face. "I've had the pox," he said. "I never was much to look at it, but I know I'm a lot worse now."

Seemingly involuntarily, Jennie lifted her eyes, just for a moment—just long enough to catch a glimpse of Ransom's face. What she saw in that instant was what she had always remembered, a memory that had haunted her every day for five long years—the handsome face of the only man she had ever loved. For a split second she felt herself almost overcome by a powerful urge to throw her arms around him, but instead she dropped her eyes back to the ground, feeling them filling with tears.

In that fleeting glance, Ransom could not read her thoughts. "Jennie. Why?" he asked, painfully.

Becoming suddenly aware that her hands were trembling, and feeling as if her heart were about to burst, Jennie couldn't restrain herself any longer. She let out a pained sob, turned, and ran away, leaving Ransom standing there, bewildered and heartbroken.

He had not moved when, minutes later, Parsons came rushing up to him.

"Ransom, thank God I've found you," he said, nearly out of breath. "Come on, man. The colonel is looking for you. We've got to go."

The roar in Ransom's head began to abate, and he turned to face Parsons. "What?" he asked, distantly.

"We've been ordered to saddle up immediately," Parsons answered. "We're moving out. Come on."

Ransom shook his head, trying to clear away the confusion. "What?" he repeated. "I don't understand."

"We've been ordered to guard the fords. We're leaving now," Parsons replied.

"What?" Ransom said. "Leaving?"

"That's right," Parsons answered. "Come on. There's no peace for the wicked."

45

Lewis Farm
Maple Grove
Pittsylvania County, Virginia
February 15, 1781

When Billy came in from his evening chores, Jennie was sitting on the floor, packing her trunk. "Is there something you want to tell me?" he asked.

"I'm leaving in the morning, first thing," she said, not looking up.

Billy watched her silently for a few moments. "Wilmington?" he asked.

Jennie looked up, the paths of now-dried tears etched upon her face. "Haven't you been trying to get me to go for the past two years?" she said.

"Seems kind of abrupt to me," he answered. "How are you getting there?"

"I'm going with Nancy. Mr. Shelby is going to take us," she said, resuming her packing.

"It's dangerous," Billy said. "It's going to look suspicious."

"No, it isn't!" Jennie shot back, anger in her voice. "And I know what you mean, Billy. Dangerous for you, not for me."

"Dangerous for both of us, Jennie. For all of us," Billy replied, staying calm.

Jennie threw something into the trunk, then looked up fiercely at her brother.

"Nancy goes to see her family often. You know that. I'm going with her to help take care of the baby. There is nothing suspicious about it at all," she said, firmly.

"Maybe not," Billy said. "But it sure looks like y'all are leaving in a hurry. When did she decide to go?"

"Just this afternoon," Jennie answered. "They're going now because I asked them to. Nancy would do anything in the world for me. You know that."

"And y'all are not coming back?" Billy asked.

Jennie looked up, her eyes filling with tears. "Not until it's over," she said.

Billy looked at her for a few seconds, his face betraying no emotion. Then he turned away, walked across the room and stood before the window, looking out. Jennie stood up and walked to him, putting her hand on his shoulder.

"Come with us, Billy," she said.

He turned and looked his sister in the face. "I can't leave now, Jennie. Not with Lord Cornwallis practically on our doorstep."

"It's time for us to leave," Jennie answered softly.

Billy turned away, shaking his head. "You leave. I'm not going," he answered.

She stood behind him a few seconds, trying and failing to find the right words. She sighed, walked back to the trunk, then dropped to the floor. "There's some bacon and cornbread on the table," she said, resuming her work.

Billy didn't respond. He was still staring out the window, pondering the future, when he noticed a rider in the distance approaching at a gallop. He stepped away quickly and reached for the musket hanging over the door. "Someone's coming," he said, answering Jennie's questioning gaze.

She stood and walked to the window, looking out with Billy as the rider drew nearer. After a few moments she said, softly, "Oh, criminy. It's Gus."

When Billy saw that the rider was indeed Gus Johnson, he returned the gun to its pegs, opened the door, and stepped out onto the porch. Gus pulled his horse up at the bottom step.

"I've come to see Jennie," Gus said.

"She's busy," Billy answered, flatly.

Gus dismounted and tied his horse to the post. "I just heard from Armistead Shelby that they're leaving for Wilmington in the morning, and they're taking Jennie with them," he said.

"You heard right," Billy answered.

"I want to talk to Jennie, Billy," Gus said.

"Leave her alone, Gus," Billy replied.

"Dammit, Billy," Gus fired back. "I'm gonna talk to Jennie whether you…"

Gus stopped when Jennie stepped out onto the porch and stood next to Billy. He pulled his hat off his head and looked pleadingly at her.

"Jennie, I need to…" he began.

She interrupted him. "It's all right, Billy. Go inside and have supper."

Billy didn't move, continuing to stare at Gus.

"I'm all right, Billy," she said, putting her hand on his shoulder. "Go on inside."

Billy turned slowly and looked her in the face, seeing

the determined look he had expected. He nodded, gave Gus one more harsh look, then turned and walked back inside, closing the door behind him.

Jennie walked down the porch stairs. When she reached the bottom stair Gus reached for her hand, but she pulled it back quickly. He sighed, looked down and kicked the ground in frustration. After a moment he composed himself and looked back up. Jennie looked back at him, resolutely. They stared at each other a few moments, then Gus spoke.

"I don't mind that you're going, Jennie," he said, battling back his anxiety and feigning calm. "I think you ought to."

She stayed locked on his gaze, not answering him, and showing no emotion.

"I'd go with you if you would have me. You know that," Gus said. He paused, but she remained silent.

"Will you wait for me, Jennie?" he asked, a tone of pleading in his voice even though he had tried to suppress it.

Jennie closed her eyes and shook her head. "Gus," she said softly.

"Doggone it, Jennie," he said, hurriedly. "I love you. Marry me, Jennie. I'll be a good husband."

She continued shaking her head, her eyes closed. After a few moments she opened them and looked back at Gus, his face pitifully contorted.

"I do not want to have this conversation again, Gus," she said. "Just forget about it."

He opened his mouth, about to plead his case. Jennie interrupted him.

"I am not going to marry you," she said firmly, feeling a tinge of sympathy as she saw the pain on his face. "I am fond of you, Gus," she said, reaching out and gently touching his hand. "But I do not love you."

Gus looked down, nodding, and biting his lip. After a few moments, he untied his reins, stepped into his stirrup, and swung himself up onto his horse's back. "Have a safe journey, Jennie," he said, struggling to smile. "I will pray for you all."

"As will I for you," she answered.

As he turned to leave, she stepped back inside. When she did, Billy quickly stepped out onto the porch. "Gus!" he called out as he went down the steps.

Gus turned his horse around and waited as Billy walked to him. When he was close, Billy spoke quietly. "I'm leaving too," he said. "But I ain't going to Wilmington."

46

Halifax Courthouse
Halifax County, Virginia
February 16, 1781

Sitting behind a desk in the part of the courthouse in which he had established his temporary headquarters, General Green was composing a letter to Governor Jefferson, writing testily, even as he fought back the desire to be even more confrontational. He warned Jefferson that Cornwallis may march across Virginia to link up with Benedict Arnold, then struck that out of the letter, concerned that fear of Arnold may continue to divert supplies he needed to fight Cornwallis. Instead, he repeated his urgent requests for arms, provisions, reinforcements, and horses for the cavalry, advised the governor that without them there was a risk Cornwallis may march unimpeded across Virginia, and concluded with, "The country is inevitably lost unless decided measures are taken. You will consider the necessity and act accordingly." Stamping and sealing the letter he called out to a nearby orderly, "Place this in the express to Richmond."

"Yes, sir," the young man said, taking the letter and

turning to the door.

"And send in Colonel Boyd," Greene ordered as the young man exited.

"You sent for me, sir?" Colonel George Boyd asked as he entered the room, moments later.

Greene stood up and extended his hand. "Yes. Thank you for coming so quickly, Colonel," Greene answered, as Boyd shook his hand. "May I offer my belated gratitude for allowing us the use of your ferry."

"Of course," Boyd answered, with a smile. "How can I be of service, General?"

"Please be seated, Colonel" Greene said, gesturing to a chair.

As the men sat down, Greene took a deep breath. As county lieutenant, 46-year-old Boyd commanded the county's militia and was the highest-ranking authority in the local government. Greene knew that he needed to maintain good relations with men like him, but his disdain for militia sometimes made that challenging.

"As you have no doubt seen, Colonel, the army is ragged and nearly worn out. These men have been marching twenty miles a day in the heart of winter and hundreds of them are barefoot and nearly naked," Greene said.

Boyd nodded. "They are heroes, sir," he said.

"Heroes, yes," Greene replied, "but I fear they are in no condition to give battle."

"How can I help, General?" Boyd asked.

"We do not have the luxury of going into winter quarters," Greene said. "We must prepare to fight the enemy. Here in Virginia, if he comes to us. If not, we must go back to North Carolina and fight him there."

"The Virginia militia will be with you, sir," Boyd

said.

Heaven help us, Greene thought.

"I need your assistance, sir," he said. "The casks that we are using to carry our meal are inefficient and are slowing the army. We need cloth bags. At least 300 of them. Can you requisition them immediately from the citizenry here?"

Boyd suppressed a smile. He had been in the Continental Line when Greene was the army's quartermaster general, and he knew the man's reputation for logistical brilliance—no detail was too small for him. "I will see what we can do," he answered.

"We need them immediately, sir. It is of the utmost importance," Greene said.

"Understood, General," Boyd answered.

"You may issue receipts for them, Colonel, but I regret to say that the army doesn't have a penny to offer in payment," Greene said.

"Understood, sir," Boyd replied.

"On another matter," Greene continued, "the cavalry are in desperate need of mounts. I want you to know that I have issued orders today authorizing Colonel Washington to impress horses from the local citizens," Greene said.

Boyd's face clouded. "There are no surplus horses here, General. Those that our people have are necessary for their farms," he said.

"I regret the necessity of the order, Colonel, but the urgency of the situation requires it. We will give a receipt for the fair value of any horse taken," Greene replied.

"Receipts won't plow their fields, General," Boyd answered.

Greene's eyes flashed and Boyd braced himself, knowing he had spoken too hastily. After a testy pause, Greene swallowed his anger and said, "It's more than they'll get from the British if we are forced to withdraw."

"Begging the general's pardon," Boyd said, "but has this order been authorized by the governor?"

"I have requested his approval, but the exigencies do not permit me to await his answer," Green said. "I will assume all responsibility."

Boyd nodded but did not reply.

"You will no doubt receive complaints," Greene continued. "I request that you do your best to explain the country's need and the expediency of this measure. Surely their horses cannot be dearer to them than their liberty. I assure you that we will treat the inhabitants who are affected by this as tenderly as we can."

"I will do my best, sir," Boyd answered. "The people of Halifax are patriots, General."

"Thank you, Colonel," Greene replied. "Now to the final matter I need to address with you." He cleared his throat and adjusted himself in his chair, searching for a way to soften what he was about to say. "I am most dissatisfied with the militia that has turned out," he said.

"Well, General, we got the call out as soon as you issued it. The men are still arriving, sir, and I expect there will be another thousand by tomorrow," Boyd said.

"You misunderstand me, Colonel," Greene answered. "My concern is not that there are too few militiamen, but rather that there may be too many."

"Too many, sir?" Boyd replied, puzzled.

"Yes, Colonel, too many." Greene got up and paced

to the window. "How many have arrived? Fifteen hundred? Two thousand?"

"In that range, sir," Boyd answered. "According to my estimates."

"Look at them, sir," Greene said, gesturing out the window. "Lounging around, fraternizing with the civilians who have turned out as if this is a carnival. There is a complete absence of any military discipline out there."

Stung by the criticism, Boyd replied defensively. "I will see that appropriate military discipline is imposed, sir."

"I will be blunt with you, Colonel," Greene continued, turning to face Boyd. "Most of them are like teats on a boar. It's not just their absence of discipline, they're also poorly armed if armed at all. Most of the militiamen I've seen here can do nothing more for us than consume our meager provisions."

"General Greene, sir," Boyd said, tentatively, "those men have answered a call to defend the country. Your call, sir."

"Yes, Colonel, and I commend them for that," Greene replied. "But provisioned as they are, they are of little use to me."

"Sir, for months we have been doing everything in our power to obtain arms for the men. I have been assured that the arms will be arriving forthwith," Boyd answered.

Greene returned to his chair and sat down. "I will grant them this—they are mounted better than my cavalry. And their horses are eating up the fodder here. For God's sake, Colonel, they are infantry. Send the horses away."

Boyd reddened. He stood up and said stiffly,

"Thank you for sharing your concerns, sir."

"Colonel, none of what I have said is intended as criticism of you, sir," Greene said. "I asked you to gather the militia here quickly and you have done so. It's just that I was not aware that so many would come unfit for service."

"It has been a struggle, sir," Boyd answered.

"I am going to need the militiamen of this area, Colonel," Greene said, looking squarely into Boyd's eyes. "Without them, I do not believe we will be able to defeat Lord Cornwallis."

He stood up and stepped from behind the desk, coming face to face with Boyd.

"Make a careful review of the militia companies that have arrived. Have them set up camps and adhere to proper military discipline. Determine what is needed to outfit and arm them. Dismiss for now those who are not equipped for service," Greene said.

"Yes, General," Boyd answered.

"And let us both renew our entreaties to Governor Jefferson," Greene said. "Let us get those men the arms and provisions they deserve."

Boyd nodded and Greene reached out to shake his hand.

~~~

When word spread across the countryside that Cornwallis was about to cross the Dan and that General Greene was desperately in need of reinforcements, the local militia companies rushed to Halifax Courthouse, with whatever arms they had. Captain Morton's company of Pittsylvania militia was one of the companies that responded to the call,
~~~

among them Private Dodd Lightfoot, who arrived carrying the family's gun, his father having reluctantly surrendered it to him, even though doing so meant that Elisha had to march unarmed to the courthouse with his company.

When Dodd and his company set out for Halifax, the men believed that a battle with the British was imminent. At first Dodd wondered whether he was the only man in the company with shaking hands, sweaty palms, and a knotted stomach. But the nervous chattering jokes from some, and the stony silence from others, betrayed them all. He realized they were all afraid. And for the first time since he made the substitution deal with Billy Lewis, Dodd regretted it. As his tried to calm his fluttering stomach, he wished he was with his brother, as he would have been had he not signed on as Billy's substitute.

Lieutenant Robertson sensed the men's unease. He well remembered when he, as a frightened young private, had marched toward his first battle, and in the years since then he had seen and commanded many green soldiers nervously awaiting their first taste of combat. He knew that the jitters would go away in time, but he also knew that they were dangerous while they remained. The best treatment, he had learned, was to keep the men occupied.

So, when the company rode into Halifax Courthouse that morning, Robertson had immediately ordered them to fall in, and then he had proceeded to drill them relentlessly for hours. Meanwhile, Captain Morton had wandered off in search of information and orders.

By afternoon, the atmosphere around the courthouse village had become relaxed, festive even, and the tension began to recede as imminent battle with the British seemed less likely. The buzzing in Dodd's ears had quieted, the quivers in his stomach were gone, and it seemed to him that his comrades had settled down as well. Once Robertson saw that the fear had dissipated, he stopped the drills and ordered the men to make camp.

It was nearly dark when Dodd saw Captain Morton striding toward the camp, calling Robertson to him as he came. Dodd watched as the two officers spoke quietly for a few minutes, before turning toward the camp. "Form up, men," Robertson shouted, and the company hastily and clumsily gathered in a two-rank line.

Morton drew closer, then spoke. "Cornwallis isn't coming, boys," he said with a grin. "He has turned and is heading back south, into Carolina."

Most of the men cheered spontaneously, a wave of relief sweeping over them.

"Y'all are dismissed," Morton said. "Go on home."

As the men began laughing and chattering, he raised his voice, "Report on Monday, as usual."

Dodd led his horse over to Captain Wrenn's camp, in time to see that company also being dismissed. He and Elisha rode back home together, and there Alice Lightfoot tearfully welcomed them back.

47

Thomas Farm
Bedford County, Virginia
February 16, 1781

Henry Lawton kept Caesar at a trot for the full ride to Jacob Thomas's farm. "Sorry to work you so hard, old boy," he said as he arrived. He dismounted and tied the horse to the post, then patted him on the forehead. "It's important business."

Jacob stepped out onto his porch. "Come on in and have a cup of cider, Henry."

"Jake," Henry said. "I'm going to have to chain my boys down to keep them from going to Halifax. What are we waiting on?"

"We don't have any orders," Jacob replied.

"Word is that all the militia in Pittsylvania and Halifax are assembling at the courthouse for a big fight with Cornwallis," Henry said. "Shouldn't we be there?"

"Colonel Lynch will be back from Richmond any time now," Jacob answered. "He will have our orders."

"But Jake," Henry replied. "General Greene needs us now."

Jacob descended the porch steps and walked closer

to Henry. He lowered his voice and said, "There won't be a fight in Halifax."

"How can you know that?" Henry replied. "The river is dropping and there's going to be plenty of places the British can cross."

"You're right," Jacob said. "I didn't say Cornwallis isn't coming to Halifax. I said there won't be a fight there."

"I'm not following you, Jake," Henry said.

"Why don't you ride over to Coles' Ferry and have a look," Jacob said. "I just got back."

"Coles' Ferry?" Henry said, puzzled.

"Keep what I'm about to tell you to yourself, Henry," Jake said. "Don't tell anybody. Even your family."

Henry nodded.

"Colonel Carrington is at the ferry," Jacob said. "He's bringing boats there from all up and down the river." He paused to allow his words to sink in. "If the British cross the Dan, General Greene is not going to fight him in Halifax. He's planning to retreat across the Staunton. That's what all the boats are for."

"Retreat across the Staunton?" Henry said, shaking his head and staring at his feet. He looked up at Jacob, concern clouding his face. "Then the British are coming here? To Bedford?"

"Very possibly," Jacob said. "If they march on General Greene, it is clear that he intends to pull his army into Bedford County."

Henry closed his eyes, shaking his head slowly. After a few moments he looked back at Jacob. "When will he make a stand, Jake? He's got to stop and fight sometime, doesn't he? I know what Dan Morgan would do."

"General Greene knows what he's doing," Jacob answered. "We just need to wait for our orders, Henry. I expect we'll have them soon. Probably tomorrow."

Henry shook his head again, then looked away for a few moments. When he turned back, Jacob could see that he was shaken.

"Damn, Jake," he said. "We could have redcoats on our farms soon."

"Maybe so," Jacob replied. After a pause he added, "Look, Henry. There's going to be a fight and we're going to be in it. We just don't know when and where yet. Send one of the boys over around dinner time tomorrow. We should have our orders by then."

"All right, Jake," Henry said, reaching out and shaking his hand absently. "I've got a lot to tend to," he said, as he untied and mounted the horse.

Just as they turned to leave, he heard a woman's voice calling him. Henry spun the horse around and saw that Jacob's wife Ann was stepping down the porch steps toward him, carrying a little cloth bag, tied at the top with a cord.

"Take this to Martha for me, Henry," Ann said with a smile, handing the bag up to him.

As Henry took it, returning her smile, he said, "May I ask what I am delivering?"

"Just a little coffee," Ann replied. "I know how scarce it is now and I suppose you all could use a little."

"Now, Ann," Henry said, handing the bag back to her, "There's no telling when we'll be able to get coffee again. You should keep it."

Ann shook her head. "We have enough," she replied. "I want you all to have this."

"Mrs. Thomas, you are an angel of mercy," Henry answered with a chuckle, as he put the little sack into his saddle bag. "I've almost forgotten the taste of coffee. This will be a great treat."

"Now don't you go drinking it all up yourself, Henry Lawton," Ann replied teasingly. "I provide it on the condition that you share it with Martha and the boys."

"Yes, ma'am," Henry replied, tipping his hat. "I will assuredly do so."

"We are living in troubled times, Henry," Ann said, her smile having disappeared.

"That we are," Henry replied.

"Let us pray they improve," Ann said.

"Amen," Henry said. "Thanks again, Ann. Martha will be thrilled."

"Give her and the boys our love," she said.

"I will," Henry answered, as he turned the horse and rode away.

~~~

On the ride back, Henry felt his mind swimming, troubled at the thought that he might be forced to leave his home to the mercy of Cornwallis. And Tarleton. As the farm came into sight, he forced himself to quiet his anxiety. What I need most right now, he thought, is a clear head.

Seeing him approaching, Arthur ran out to meet him, Will following closely behind him. "All the militia are reporting to General Greene, Father," Arthur blurted out. "Cornwallis is advancing, and the battle could begin any minute! We need to leave now!"

"No," Henry said, continuing to walk the horse calmly toward the barn.

"But Pa," Arthur exclaimed, "We're gonna miss it!"
~~~

Henry didn't answer him. When they reached the barn, Will took the horse by the bridle, while his father dismounted. As he did, George came out of the barn, took the reins, and led the horse inside.

"What are we waiting for?" Arthur said loudly.

Walking toward the house, Henry answered without looking at his son. "We're not going to miss anything. We'll probably have our orders tomorrow."

"Tomorrow??" Arthur whined. "By then the..."

Henry spun around and interrupted him, his eyes blazing. "Hold your tongue, Arthur!"

His father's anger caught him by surprise and Arthur obediently fell silent.

Henry marched up the steps to the porch, then stepped inside the house, followed by his sons. When they entered, Martha turned from her cooking, her face showing her concern. Squire, who had been loading the wood box, stood up and faced them as well.

As Henry took off his hat and coat and hung them on pegs by the door, they all watched him anxiously, sensing his discomfort and awaiting the news. He closed his eyes, took a deep breath, then turned around to face them.

"We should have our orders by the end of day tomorrow," he said. "In the meantime, we need to prepare."

"That's already done, Father," Will answered. "Powder, flints, balls, victual bags—all done. And I've cleaned the rifles so many times I can see myself on the barrels."

"Right," Henry replied. "Well, we also need to begin making plans to put away some of the things we need."

"Put away?" Will asked. "What do you mean?"

"I mean that if the armies come though this area

they will be like a plague of locusts. They'll strip us clean," Henry answered.

"Coming here?" Martha asked, with concern. "Do you think that is possible?"

"Of course, it is possible," he answered, fighting back the urge to reveal just how possible it had become. "We need to be prepared."

When no one immediately responded, Henry continued. "We're in danger here even if the armies don't come through. In New London and Peytonsburg they're short of everything now. There aren't nearly enough provisions put up there to provide for the Continentals, much less to outfit the militia. I expect they're going to start impressing what they need. Soon."

"Impressing? Impressing what, Henry?" Martha asked.

"Our food, our livestock, our powder," he answered.

Henry turned and looked at Squire. Like Henry, Squire was husky and square-shouldered. He was approximately the same age as Henry, but his scraggly gray beard made him look much older.

"Squire, I want you to make a place in the woods where we can keep Caesar, the cow, and the sow, if need be," Henry said. "Don't tell us where it is and don't show it to anybody else. Just have it ready."

Squire nodded.

"If that day comes, after the stock is hidden, I want you to take down one of the hogs in the smokehouse and hide it too," Henry said, again being answered with a nod.

"But Henry," Martha said, "Is it right for us to hoard food? Couldn't we get in trouble for that?"

"Maybe," he answered, turning to her. "But I'm not talking about hoarding anything. We just need to keep the bare minimum necessary to keep us alive. They can take the rest."

"But surely they wouldn't take it all," Martha said.

"Surely they might," Henry replied. "It's prudent to plan for that."

"Henry, dear," Martha said with concern, "are you certain that things have suddenly become so dangerous and desperate."

Henry bit his lip, standing quietly for a few moments before answering. "No, I am not," he said, speaking softly. "But we must not allow ourselves to be caught unprepared."

When Squire stepped out onto the porch to leave, Henry followed him. Once they were out of earshot of the others, Henry leaned toward him and said softly, "You and George need to be prepared to hide too. Have a plan."

"Yes, sir," Squire answered, nodding slightly.

48

Halifax Courthouse
Halifax County, Virginia
February 16, 1781

"Have a seat, Colonel Lee," Greene said, gesturing to a chair.

Lee bowed slightly, removed his helmet, and sat down.

Handsome, fearless, and bold, an expert horseman and brilliant classical scholar, Lee had won the admiration of Greene years earlier, when they were serving together under General Washington in the north. With the trained eye of a quartermaster, Greene had long been amazed at Lee's ability to keep his troopers well-provisioned and well-attired. Indeed, Lee took great pride in his men's appearance, and it seemed that no matter how ragged the rest of the army became, he and the soldiers in his legion always looked as if they were on dress parade. Lee was particularly proud of the distinctive uniforms his dragoons wore, and he tolerated no deviation from it. Like Washington's dragoons, Lee's troopers wore leather breeches, top boots, and plumed leather helmets. But whereas

Washington's dragoons wore white uniform jackets with blue facing, Lee's men wore green. Facing his young meticulously uniformed cavalryman, it occurred to Greene how unkempt he must appear by comparison. It had been over a month since he had last changed clothes.

"There can now be no doubt, Colonel," Greene said as he sat down behind his desk. "Lord Cornwallis has marched away, to the south. We have reliable confirmation from several scouts."

Lee nodded. "We wore him out, sir," he said. "He burned his wagons, chased us all the way across North Carolina, and got nothing for it. He is hundreds of miles from any supply base. His army must be fatigued and desperate for provisions."

"Exactly, Colonel," Greene answered. "And we must keep them that way. While we are awaiting our reinforcements, we must try to prevent the British from resting and resupplying their army. Have you considered what the current state of affairs will mean for the people of North Carolina?"

Lee started. He had not considered it.

"The British will forage them naked, Colonel. We must not allow our friends there to think we have abandoned them," Greene continued.

Lee nodded. "What are my orders, General?"

"You are to take your legion across the river tomorrow morning," Greene answered. "I am detaching a company of Maryland Continentals and placing them under your command. General Pickens' South Carolina men will go with you as well."

"Where is General Pickens now?" Lee asked, grateful that he had been reminded of Pickens' promotion.

"He is somewhere in North Carolina, recruiting militia," Greene answered. "You must find him and combine with him, Colonel. I am quite concerned about him. You know what will happen to him if he is captured."

Lee nodded. He knew.

"Find General Pickens," Greene continued. "Join up with him. Then stay close to Cornwallis. Observe and monitor his movements. Harass him but avoid pitched battle. Await further instructions."

"Understood, sir," Lee answered.

"His Lordship will no doubt try to supplement his army with Tory militia," Greene continued. "Try to prevent this. Intercept them where possible."

"With pleasure, sir," Lee replied.

"I will follow you soon with the main army," Greene said. "Now that General Stevens has safely deposited the prisoners from Cowpens, I have instructed him to gather all the militia in this part of Virginia. As soon as they are assembled, I will cross. Sooner, if need be."

"Have we confirmed where Cornwallis is heading?" Lee asked.

"Hillsborough, it appears," Greene answered. "He will be easy to track, Colonel. Our scouts report he is leaving a trail of plunder and destruction in his wake."

49

Lawton Farm
Bedford County, Virginia
February 19, 1781

From the militiamen who had been steadily returning to the county over the past two days, the Lawtons had gotten the news that the crisis in Halifax had passed uneventfully—Cornwallis had turned away from Virginia. So, while still anxiously awaiting orders from Colonel Lynch, Henry and his sons had returned to their normal routines, knowing that the call to report for duty could come at any minute.

At dawn on Monday morning, impatient, Henry decided to ride over to Jacob's farm to see if he had heard anything new. As he was walking to the barn, Squire intercepted him. "Morning, Squire," Henry said, continuing to walk briskly.

"Morning, sir," Squire replied, falling in at Henry's side.

"What's on your mind?" Henry asked as he continued walking, sensing that Squire wanted to talk to him.

"You remember my cousin Sallie, that used to

belong to Mr. Watkins?" Squire asked, keeping pace alongside him.

"Sallie?"

"Yes, sir. Maggie's daughter," Squire answered.

"Oh, right," Henry replied, even though he had no idea who she was.

"Well, you know she got sold to Colonel Harrison 'bout five years ago. Back after Mr. Watkins passed," Squire said.

"Right. Have you heard from her? How's she getting along?" Henry asked, still unable to place the woman.

"Oh, she all right I reckon," Squire answered. "I ain't seen her since she left here, but after church last night her husband's cousin Moll told me something I think you gonna want to hear."

Henry stopped, fighting his impatience. "All right," he said. "What is it?"

"Well, sir," Squire said, "Moll said that her cousin Ernest that stay up near Richmond got sent with a load of corn out to the Harrison place and he saw Sallie when he was there."

Smuggling, Henry thought. "All right, Squire. I'm in a hurry. Come to the point."

"Well, sir," Squire said. "Sallie told him that last month she saw Mr. Gus Johnson up there at Colonel Harrison's place and he was talking to Benedict Arnold."

"What?" Henry said, incredulous. "Benedict Arnold?"

"Yes, sir," Squire answered, with a nod. "When General Arnold come through there he made the colored folks tote all of Colonel Harrison's furniture out the house so he could burn it up. Sallie told Ernest that when she was helping haul it all out, she saw Mr. Gus Johnson there and he was talking to General Arnold."

"Gus Johnson?" Henry said, still incredulous. "From out at Johnson's Mill?"

"Yes, sir," Squire answered confidently. "Sallie said he was standing out there talking to Benedict Arnold just as plain as day."

Henry shook his head. "Squire, that is very hard for me to believe. What would Gus Johnson be doing all the way up there and why would he be talking to Benedict Arnold?"

"I don't reckon I know about that, sir," Squire answered, although he knew full well what it meant.

"It seems nigh impossible to me," Henry said, shaking his head again. "It couldn't have been Gus Johnson she saw."

"Well, sir," Squire answered, defensively. "I reckon my cousin Sallie ought to know Mr. Gus Johnson when she sees him."

Henry could see that Squire had taken offense. He scratched his chin and nodded. "This is very interesting information, Squire," he said, feigning sincerity. "Very interesting indeed. You did the right thing bringing it to my attention."

Squire looked back at him and nodded.

"Thank you, Squire. I will look into this right away," Henry said. "If you hear anything else like that, bring it to me immediately."

"Yes, sir," Squire said, before turning and walking away.

Henry entered the barn and found Caesar already saddled and waiting. The horse lowered his head and nudged Henry's coat pocket—his way of asking for a treat. Henry laughed and pulled out a piece of dried fruit, which the horse took eagerly. He mounted the horse and steered him out the door and onto the road, toward Jacob's farm. Gus Johnson and Benedict Arnold, he thought, chuckling at such a preposterous claim. But when he reached the fork in the road, rather than continue toward Jacob's place, at the last moment he turned south instead. However ridiculous the allegation, he thought, I suppose I ought to pass it along.

50

Bayard Homestead
Halifax County, Virginia
February 19, 1781

Bayard was chopping wood when he noticed a horse and rider approaching. Even though it was so cold that he could see his every breath, he had worked up a sweat and had to wipe his eyes with his sleeve before he could recognize the visitor. When he could see clearly, he tossed the axe aside and called out, "Welcome, friend."

Henry walked his horse slowly to Bayard's woodpile, then dismounted, extending his hand. "Good morning, Reverend," he said with a smile. "A fine day for work such as that."

"It is indeed," Bayard answered. Taking Henry by the elbow, he turned toward his house and said, "Come on inside Henry and get out of the cold."

"Much obliged, Reverend, but I can't stay long," Henry replied, remaining where he was. "Important things are afoot at home."

Bayard turned back toward him. "Has your regiment been called up?"

"I'm expecting to get the word at any moment,"

Henry answered. "Colonel Lynch should be returning from Richmond soon and I expect he'll be bringing our orders with him." He paused and added with a smile, "It's been all I can do to keep Arthur tethered."

"These are troubled times, Henry," Bayard said. Playfully he added, "Have you come to have me baptize you into the true church before leaving?"

Henry laughed. "No," he said. "I intend to remain a Presbyterian. Disgruntled, but faithful."

Bayard smiled and nodded. "Well, hope springs eternal. I shall continue to pray that you see the light."

"Your prayers are appreciated, Reverend. I am sure I need all the help I can get," Henry replied.

"Well, what can I do for you, my friend?" Bayard asked.

Henry hesitated, glanced away for a moment, then looked back at Bayard. "Wynn," he said, "I don't know if I ought to be bothering you with this or not, but you told me that if I heard anything suspicious, I should come to you with it."

Bayard felt his pulse quicken. "Yes," he said. "Have you heard something?"

"It's the damnedest thing, pardon me Reverend, but my man Squire says one of his kinfolk saw Gus Johnson up in Charles City County last month," Henry said.

It was a struggle, but Bayard managed to show no reaction.

"I know it sounds mad," Henry continued, "but this gal says Gus was with Benedict Arnold."

"What?" Bayard said, his heart pounding. "Benedict Arnold??"

"That's what she said," Henry answered. "Well, at least that is what she is supposed to have said," he added quickly. "This is all second and third-hand through what my man calls 'the colored grapevine.'"

"Well, sir, it certainly is a strange claim," Bayard said.

Henry shook his head. "I don't know if I should have even bothered you with it," he said.

"Have you told anyone else?" Bayard asked.

"No," Henry answered. "I rode straight here after he told me. With Colonel Lynch not back from Richmond yet, and seeing how Gus lives in your county…"

Bayard interrupted him. "You did the right thing, Henry. It's probably foolishness, but I'll have my committee look into it. In the meantime, it's best not to say any more about it."

Henry chuckled. "Don't worry. I won't. But that won't keep it from getting out. You can be sure that every negro in both counties will have heard it by tomorrow, if they haven't already."

Bayard stood frozen, unable to answer.

Henry reached out his hand and Bayard took it, shaking it mechanically.

"I've got to get back home," Henry said, lifting himself back into his saddle. "My regards to Mrs. Bayard," he said, touching the brim of his hat.

"Yes, yes, thank you," Bayard replied absently.

As Henry rode away, Bayard dropped to a seat on the chopping block. He shut his eyes and squeezed his temples with his left hand, praying silently to clear his head. After a few minutes he stood up and strode purposefully toward his house.

51

Sandy Creek Baptist Meetinghouse
Halifax County, Virginia
February 19, 1781

Bayard was sitting quietly, deep in thought, when someone began to bang loudly and insistently on the door. Annoyed, he stepped across the room, unlatched, and opened the door, closing and barring it after Gus rushed inside.

"You should use the signals, Gus," Bayard said.

"What the devil is the meaning of all this, Reverend?" Gus said, his face flushed and angry. "I got the message to come here immediately and to come unseen. Do you know how difficult that is? It's broad daylight! Do you know how risky this is?"

"I do," Bayard answered calmly. "Settle down, Gus, and have a seat. We have a very serious problem."

Gus reluctantly sat down, and Bayard took a seat facing him.

"Henry Lawton came to see me this morning with a report to pass along to the committee. Seems that one of his negroes heard you were spotted with General Arnold last month," Bayard said.

Gus's eyes widened and he swallowed hard. After a pause he said, "Can we nip it in the bud?"

Bayard shook his head. "It's not possible. I've gone over every option we have. Too many people know. You've got to run. Tonight."

Gus dropped his head and stared at the floor, his hands on his hips. After a few moments he lifted his eyes and said, "Fine. I'm ready."

Bayard nodded. "Later today I'm going to go see a few of your neighbors. I will discreetly inquire about your loyalty and ask if anyone noticed you away overnight last month. Do you understand?"

Gus nodded grimly. "That will explain how I knew to run," he said.

"Yes," Bayard answered. "It will also be possible that the rumor circulating among the negroes got to you. Either way, that will provide some cover. I assume that you do not want to go to General Arnold."

"No," Gus answered quickly. "I'll go south. To Lord Cornwallis."

"As I assumed," Bayard answered. "I have made arrangements. Listen carefully, Gus. This is very important."

"I'm taking one of my men with me," Gus said, interrupting.

"What?" Bayard asked.

"One of my men is about to leave to go join Cornwallis. He and I will travel together," Gus said.

"Increases our risk," Bayard replied.

"There's no stopping him, Reverend," Gus said. "He's going."

"Who is it?" Bayard asked.

"Billy Lewis. From Maple Grove. We just refugeed his sister. I can't hold him here any longer," Gus said.

Bayard pondered it for a few seconds. "Our command will be in great danger because of all this. It will be a challenging time for us."

Gus looked back at him, unblinking. He made no reply.

"All right," Bayard continued. "I will count on you to pass along these instructions to him.

"Take Coles' ferry over the river tonight," Bayard began.

"Coles' ferry? I just told you I'm going south," Gus interrupted.

"Listen to me, Gus," Bayard said firmly. "These arrangements may save your life. You will cross the river on Coles' ferry, making sure you are seen. Then you're going to cross back over, using the horse ford at Hell Bend."

Gus furrowed his brow. "That's a tricky and dangerous ford," he said, skeptically.

"It is," Bayard answered. "Especially at night and in the middle of the winter. A man would have to be mad to try it. So, no one will expect it. Besides, why would you cross the river then turn around and come back? Everyone is going to assume you are heading north, to join up with your acquaintance General Arnold. You'll sneak back over the river at Hell Bend, while anyone pursuing you will be heading north."

"I don't know, Reverend," Gus said, dubious.

"Pay attention, Gus," Bayard said. "These are not suggestions." After a pause to make sure his meaning was understood, Bayard continued. "Do you know where the Pine Creek meetinghouse is?"

"The Presbyterian church?" Gus asked.

"Yes," Bayard replied. A man will meet you there. He will be waiting on the edge of the woods. He will take you to the ford and get you across."

"Who is he?" Gus asked.

"His name is of no concern," Bayard said. "He will know the signals and he will identify himself as 'Samuelson.'"

"A Presbyterian?" Gus said. "I've never heard of a Loyalist Presbyterian."

"I did not say he was a Presbyterian," Bayard replied. "After he has gotten you back across the river, he will report that he saw you heading north."

Gus nodded, squirming uncomfortably.

"Once you are back across the river, you must travel cautiously," Bayard continued. "Hide during the day. Move only at night. Stay away from the ferries. Cross the Dan at one of the upper fords. Meanwhile there will be several, reliable sightings of you heading north, toward General Arnold. I've made arrangements for that too."

Gus sat silently for a few seconds. "You worked all this out today?" he asked.

"I've got to get you safely out of here," Bayard answered.

"All right, Reverend," Gus said. "I can take it from there."

"I believe Lord Cornwallis is near Hillsborough," Bayard said. "The King has many friends in North Carolina, and they are not concealed as we are here. You should have no trouble finding them. They will be expecting you. But you will need to be cautious. That province is crawling with rebels too."

"Got it," Gus said, standing up. "Thank you, sir."

Bayard stood slowly. "The timing is very important, Gus," he said. "Take the ferry just before dark. Your contact will be expecting you at the church at about nine o'clock."

"Understood," Gus said.

Bayard reached out his hand and Gus took it. "I regret that this is necessary, Gus," he said as they shook hands.

"I don't," Gus answered quickly. "I've had enough of this hiding and waiting. I'm ready to be in the field. I believe our victory is certain, and it is near. I will see you again soon, Reverend."

Bayard nodded and gave a slight smile. "I will pray for you. For both of you. Be careful."

Gus turned to leave, then stopped and looked back at Bayard. "Before I go, Reverend, there is something I've always wanted to ask you. Do you have a single King's man in your congregation?"

Bayard laughed. "Who ever heard of a Loyalist Baptist?"

Gus shook his head in amusement. "Well, I reckon that gives you good cover," he said, turning to leave.

"May God be with you," Bayard said, as Gus cracked open the door and peeped outside.

"Thank you, sir," he said, slipping outside.

Bayard pulled the door closed and muttered, "God save the King."

52

Lightfoot Farm
Maple Grove
Pittsylvania County, Virginia
February 19, 1781

From his hiding place in the edge of the woods, Billy saw Elisha and Dodd Lightfoot come out of the barn, carrying buckets and walking toward the house. He knew their routine. When the evening milking was done, the family gathered for supper.

Once Billy saw the brothers go inside, he crept along the edge of the woods until he came to a place that allowed him to see into the pasture that stretched out behind the barn. He looked out across the meadow and gave a sigh of relief. She was still there.

Hidden from view by the barn, he slowly emerged from the woods. Walking toward the hobbled horse that stood grazing in the distance, he let out a soft whistle. The horse raised her head suddenly, ears perked, and she looked directly at Billy as he slowly approached, carrying a lead rope. He whistled again and the horse answered with a whinny.

"Hey, Bella," Billy whispered when he reached the

horse, reaching out and patting her on the neck. "Remember me, girl?"

The horse nudged him with her head. Billy laughed quietly and reached into his pocket, producing a dried apple that the horse took eagerly.

"Ain't that good?" he whispered, as he drew a knife from his belt and sliced through the bell strap around the horse's neck. After quietly placing the bell on the ground, he gently slipped the lead rope around the horse's neck. As the horse continued chewing the apple, he reached down and removed the hobble, then stuffed it into his pocket.

"Come on, girl," Billy said quietly. "We got a long ride ahead of us tonight." The horse followed obediently as he tugged the lead rope and led her into the woods.

53

Bayard Homestead
Halifax County, Virginia
February 19, 1781

Bayard put another stick of wood in the fire, then stirred the coals with the poker. He glanced out the window and saw that it was dark enough now.

"I'm going to the meetinghouse to pray," he said, distantly.

His wife looked up from her needlework.

"In an hour you will wonder why I haven't returned, and you will come to check on me," he continued, gazing out the window as he spoke.

After a few silent moments he turned to face his wife. "Don't ask me any questions, Ruth. I wish to prevent you from having to lie."

She answered with a sad but knowing nod, her eyes filling with tears.

Bayard stepped across the room, took his coat from the peg, and put it on. He walked to his wife, bent down, and kissed her head. "Everything is going to be all right," he said gently, as a single tear slid down her face.

He turned, stepped to the door, took down his hat and pressed it onto his head. With a sigh, he opened the door and stepped out into the frigid night air.

On the path to the church, he stopped and looked up admiringly at the clear winter sky, dotted with twinkling stars. We do not deserve the beauty of this world, he thought. He closed his eyes briefly and offered a prayer of gratitude.

As he resumed walking, he felt a familiar tightness in his chest—a feeling he had long attributed to weariness, a consequence of carrying the weight of years of lies, deception, and violence. I actually envy Gus Johnson tonight, he thought, as he came to the church door. He paused for a few moments, then exhaled deeply and stepped inside.

He walked to the front of the building and fell to his knees before the pulpit. He cleared his mind and said aloud, "Deliver me from mine enemies, O my God. Defend me from them that rise up against me." He fell silent but remained kneeling for a few minutes more, eyes closed and head bowed. After a while he sighed, stood up and walked behind the pulpit, taking up a coiled length of rope that was lying there, and looping it over his shoulder. He walked back outside with the rope, dropping it onto the ground beneath a nearby oak.

He stepped back toward the church, stopping and standing silently in the cold night air for several minutes, gazing at the starlit building. His heart swelled as he thought back on the day the Baptist evangelist Samuel Harris, his mentor, had preached the first sermon here, after helping cut and hew the logs the year before. He sighed deeply. God's word is permanent, but things like this building are not meant to last, he thought, as he reached into an opening beneath the meetinghouse and pulled out a pitch torch.

Bayard took a tinderbox from his pocket and sparked it, lighting the torch. He allowed the fire to catch, then stepped back and lofted the torch up onto the roof of the building, watching as the shingles ignited and the fire began to spread.

When the flames were dancing high into the night sky, he stepped a few paces away and picked up a fist-sized stone he had placed there earlier in the day. He took a deep breath, closed his eyes, tightened his grip on the stone, then bashed himself in the face with it.

54

Pine Creek Presbyterian Meetinghouse
Bedford County, Virginia
February 19, 1781

Gus eased his horse quietly off the road and toward the cleared area behind the church building, guiding his mount slowly toward a wood line about 50 yards away, with Billy following quietly behind him. He stopped when he thought he recognized movement at the edge of the woods, but in the darkness he couldn't be sure. After a few moments he eased his horse forward again, stopping suddenly when a man's voice came from the woods.

"That's close enough."

"Mr. Samuelson?" Gus replied.

After a few silent moments, the voice came again from the woods. "Psalms."

Gus' mind raced and his pulse quickened. "Damn," he muttered, immediately catching himself and adding, "No, wait."

From the woods came the sound of a gun being cocked and Billy, frightened, blurted out, "Five ten! It's five ten! Psalms five ten!"

A man emerged from the shadows of the tree line, carrying a musket and wearing a greatcoat and a tri-corner hat, his face not visible in the dark. He laughed. "It's all right, fellows. I was told you probably wouldn't remember it."

Neither Gus nor Billy was amused in the slightest.

"Have you been seen?" the man asked.

"At the ferry, yes," Gus answered. "But we haven't seen anyone in the last few miles."

"Good," the man answered. "Follow me. And for the rest of the ride, stay absolutely quiet. No talking at all. Understood?"

"Yes, sir," Gus and Billy answered simultaneously.

"Evidently you did not," the man said. "I said you are to remain absolutely silent. Do you understand?"

Gus and Billy nodded.

"Good," the man said. "Now follow me closely. We're going to be traveling mostly through the woods and I do not intend to speak to you again until we're at the ford."

The man stepped back into the shadows and emerged a few seconds later atop a horse. He gestured for them to follow, as he led them into the trees.

55

Bayard Homestead
Halifax, Virginia
February 20, 1781

Ruth Bayard opened the door and Colonel Boyd and the others removed their hats as they stepped inside. "I am so sorry about this, Mrs. Bayard," Boyd said, looking at her with concern. "We got here as quickly as we could."

"Thank you, Colonel," she answered. "We are grateful for the Lord's protection."

"How is he?" Boyd asked.

"Improving," she replied. "Praise God for his thick head."

Boyd smiled. "May we see him, ma'am?" he asked.

Ruth nodded. "Yes, of course. When I told him I saw you approaching, he seemed eager to speak to you. He's in here," she said, gesturing to a doorway that opened into the house's other room. Stepping in that direction, Boyd and the others followed her.

"I am glad to see you, Colonel Boyd," Bayard said as they entered the room. Sitting up on a bed, with his back leaning against the headboard, a bandage covered his forehead, one of his eyes, and the top of his head.

"I am sorry to see you in this condition, sir," Boyd said, reaching out and shaking his hand. "Are you hurt badly?"

"Ruth tells me that I have a deep cut over my eye and a lot of bruising and swelling," Bayard answered. "I am blessed to have such a fine nurse in attendance. I expect I'll be just fine."

Boyd nodded. "I will pray for your speedy and complete recovery, sir," he said. He turned and gestured toward the other men. "I couldn't round up the entire committee. But we got here as soon as we heard the news."

Bayard and the other men exchanged polite greetings.

"What happened, Reverend?" Boyd asked.

"Gus Johnson is a Tory," Bayard replied.

"We know," Boyd answered. "He was gone when our men arrived at his place this morning. We have reports that he was seen heading north. Likely he is on his way to Arnold's army." After a pause he added, "It is hard to believe."

Bayard shook his head sadly. "I agree. When Henry Lawton brought me the report yesterday, I took it to be utterly preposterous. Nevertheless, I made some inquiries about Johnson's behavior. Something must have gotten back to him. I'm afraid his escape may be my fault."

"Nonsense," Boyd said. "You were doing your duty. The fault lies with the Tory who alerted him."

"We must root out these traitors," Bayard said, sternly.

"We must and we shall," Boyd answered. "Tell us what happened, sir."

"After supper I had gone to the meetinghouse to pray, as is my practice," Bayard said. "When I came out, I thought I saw some movement around the side of the building. So, I stepped over there to see what it was. That's when he must have clubbed me on the head.

"Thanks be to God, when I fell to the ground I was lying right beside an opening under the foundation of the building—we keep it open as a crawl space. I managed to slide under before they could stop me," Bayard said. "Oh, I forgot to mention this. There was someone else with him, but I didn't see him."

"We believe it was Billy Lewis," Boyd replied.

"Lewis?" Bayard said.

"He lives in Maple Grove," Boyd said. "He was spotted with Johnson at the ferry last night. He and his sister are both gone. We think they're Tories. The Shelby's too."

Bayard shook his head. "Astonishing. We must do a better job of identifying these traitors."

"What happened next, sir?" Boyd asked.

"Well, I made it under the building in the nick of time," Bayard continued. "The blood on my face had blinded me and it was pitch black to boot, but I scooted far underneath, so they couldn't reach me without coming under themselves. Gus began calling for me to come out, but I didn't answer him. I could hear them talking but I couldn't make out what they were saying. I was in a great deal of pain and in fear that I might faint from loss of blood.

"After a minute or two, I heard Gus say, loud enough for me to hear, 'You'll be coming out directly.' Not long after that I smelled the smoke and realized they had set the meetinghouse on fire."

"Only a Tory dog would burn a church," one of the other men in the room said.

"Soon I was having trouble breathing and I could feel the heat," Bayard continued. "I resolved that I had no choice but to surrender to them. I reckon they aimed to take me prisoner."

"No, sir," Boyd replied. "They intended to hang you. They left the noose behind. We found it a few minutes ago."

Bayard shook his head. "I've known that Johnson boy his whole life."

"These Tories have no principles, sir," Boyd said.

"Well," Bayard continued, "I suppose I would have been hanged then, or cooked, if Ruth hadn't come along. Just as I resolved to come out, I heard her calling for me. Then she must have spotted the flames and started clanging the bell. I reckon that's when they must have run away. When I got out from under the building it was in full flame. I barely made it out and when I did, they were gone."

"They will be brought to justice," Boyd said. "They're traveling carelessly and have been spotted several times. It is clear they are heading to Portsmouth to join Arnold."

"What is the latest news on Arnold's movements?" Bayard asked.

"General von Steuben has him bottled up in Portsmouth," Boyd answered. "As long as Arnold has been in Virginia, the governor and legislature have been reluctant to commit our militia elsewhere. But it seems clear now that the greatest threat is from Cornwallis, not Arnold. All the militia is being mobilized now to join General Greene."

"With our militia gone," Bayard said, "the Tories

will be emboldened."

"You are right, sir," Boyd said. "We must be more vigilant than ever now."

"Colonel Boyd," Bayard said. "Johnson and this Lewis boy could not have been acting alone. They must have had accomplices. I would like to be put in charge of the investigation to find them."

Boyd nodded his head in agreement. "You are the perfect man for the job, sir."

56

Wiley's Tavern
Halifax County, Virginia
February 22, 1781

General Greene settled at a table in the single room tavern that he had appropriated as his headquarters, the same tavern that had been Cornwallis' headquarters a few days earlier. Reinforced, reprovisioned, and rested, his army had been ferrying across the river since the previous evening, continuing all night and into the morning. Back on the south side of the Dan now, Greene continued to fret over shortages of supplies and men.

As an aide placed his writing table before him, Greene took out a sheet of paper and began composing a dispatch, interrupted when Colonel Williams entered the room. "Pardon me, General," Williams said. "I have the honor to report that the army is now all across."

"Good," Greene said, looking up. "What is your best estimate of our strength?"

"Including the Virginia militia General Stevens has assembled, about 2,000, sir," Williams answered, as he dropped down in a chair facing Greene's desk.

Greene shook his head. "Not enough to fight Cornwallis. Not enough to defeat him."

"More Virginians are coming, sir," Williams said. "The local militias are only awaiting arms, which they are expecting to arrive from the Petersburg arsenal any day now."

Greene shook his head. "The governor is being timid. He is paralyzed by fear of General Arnold."

"Credible reports say the guns have been sent," Williams answered. "Enough to arm the Virginians."

"When they join us, *if* they join us, then we will be able to strike," Green replied. "I am especially desirous of Colonel Campbell's riflemen from the west. I have been told he will bring a thousand or more. With them, we will be able to defeat the British."

"There will be more Carolinians too," Williams said.

Greene snorted. "Their conduct has been shameful," he said, bitterly. "How many of them are with us? A few dozen? If there is not enough public spirit in these people to defend their liberties, they well deserve to be slaves."

"I believe you have misread them, sir," Williams answered. "They have returned to defend their homes. When we are back in North Carolina, they will come to us. I am certain of it."

"Well, Colonel, I pray you are right about that," Greene said. "As for me, I am decidedly *not* certain of it."

Williams nodded. "Shall we remain here in Virginia then?" he asked.

Greene shook his head. "No, Colonel," he said. "The situation requires that we take risks. If we permit the enemy to roam around North Carolina unmolested, I fear it will embolden the Tories there and send them flocking to Lord Cornwallis. The people who are now wavering in their commitments may turn against us. We must not allow our friends in the state to believe they have been conquered. We must protect their property to keep their loyalty and friendship." He shook his head. "We cannot afford a decisive engagement, but neither can we afford to appear to be running from one. We will be playing a dangerous game."

Williams chuckled. "That will be nothing new for us," he said.

"Scouts are reporting that the British are plundering the countryside," Greene said.

"Cornwallis is out of provisions," Williams said. "He will have no choice but to bleed the Carolinians white."

"As much as I feel for his victims," Greene replied, "that behavior will help keep the citizenry on our side." He stood up abruptly and began pacing, hands behind his back. "The enemy is at Hillsborough, refreshing themselves," he said, looking at the floor. Then he lifted his eyes and looked at Williams. "We will move the army toward them as if we plan to attack. Let us see how Lord Cornwallis responds."

57

Near Hillsborough
Orange County, North Carolina
February 22, 1781

As Tarleton's men searched the premises, a woman stood boldly in front of the windowless one-room log house, staring at him defiantly, as two little girls clung to her skirt, their eyes wide with fright. The woman's clothes were patched, and some of her disheveled hair was spilling from beneath her bonnet. Behind her stood an older girl, nine- or ten-years old Tarleton guessed, looking back at him not in terror like her sisters, but rather with a fierce, hate-filled glare. From the ages of the children, Tarleton guessed the woman must be in her early thirties, though her worn and weathered face made her look twice as old.

Two troopers emerged from behind the house, driving a pair of oxen. When the woman saw them, she exclaimed, "Them's draft oxen."

Tarleton looked down at her disdainfully, from atop his horse. "Tonight, they shall be a meager meal for His Majesty's army," he answered with an aristocratic lilt.

"The redcoats that come by here before said y'all don't take folks' draft animals," the woman replied.

"The policy has changed," Tarleton replied. "And besides, these don't look like draft animals to me."

"This ain't right," the woman said, angrily. "We need them to farm."

Tarleton turned away, ignoring her. "Mount up!" he shouted.

"Curse you, boy!" the woman shouted angrily.

When Tarleton turned to face her, the woman held up her left hand, then made a chopping motion across it with her right.

"I have noticed that the farms around here seem to be occupied exclusively by women," Tarleton said, disdainfully. "A curious thing, madam."

"Lucky for you," she answered with a sneer.

Tarleton sighed. "I am impressing these animals in the name of King George. As property of rebels, they are forfeited to the crown."

"We ain't rebels," the woman spat back.

Tarleton lifted his eyebrows. "So, you are friends of the King?"

The woman didn't answer.

"When your husband returns, he may come to our camp and lodge a protest. If he can prove his loyalty, you will be paid for the oxen," Tarleton said. "While there, he will be expected to join us. Lord Cornwallis is raising the Royal Standard. All good men must come with their arms and rally to the defense of the realm," he said mockingly.

Tarleton turned his horse away from the woman and shook the reins. As he was riding away, Captain Ogilvie pulled in alongside him.

The woman ran along behind them. "A pox on you, boy!" she yelled. "The devil swallow you sideways!"

"An appalling lack of respect for the King's officers," Tarleton said calmly as they rode, not looking back. After a few seconds he added, "Fire the house."

Ogilvie looked at him, inquisitively. Tarleton met his look impassively, then turned away.

Ogilvie wheeled his horse around and rode back toward the house. A few minutes later, from behind him, Tarleton heard the woman beginning to wail.

58

Courtney's Tavern
British Army Headquarters
Hillsborough, North Carolina
February 22, 1781

Tarleton walked his horse toward the small crowd gathering in front of the tavern. Even though he considered the ceremony farcical, he was pleased that he had not missed it.

Cornwallis had composed his proclamation two days earlier, shortly after the army had marched into Hillsborough, and he had ordered that news of it be spread throughout the surrounding countryside. But he insisted on the formalities and those required a Royal Standard and a suitable pole upon which to hoist it.

Tarleton watched from behind the crowd as Cornwallis strode out onto the porch of the tavern, resplendent in his scarlet coat. Beside him stood a young officer in full dress uniform. The crowd quieted, the officer lifted a piece of paper and began to read, his voice carrying easily.

"By the Right Honorable Charles Earl Cornwallis, Lieutenant General of His Majesty's Forces.

Whereas it has pleased the Divine Providence to prosper the operations of His Majesty's arms in drawing the rebel army out of this province and whereas it is His Majesty's most gracious wish to rescue his faithful and loyal subjects from the cruel tyranny under which they have groaned of several years, I have thought proper to issue this Proclamation to invite all such loyal and faithful subjects to repair without loss of time with their arms and ten days provisions to the royal headquarters now erected at Hillsborough, where they will meet with the most friendly reception, and I do hereby assure them that I am ready to concur with them in effectual measures for suppressing the remains of rebellion in this province and for the establishment of good order and constitutional government. Given under my hand at headquarters at Hillsborough, this 20th day of February in the year of our Lord one thousand seven hundred and eighty-one, and in the twenty-first year of His Majesty's reign. Cornwallis. God save the King!"

"God save the King!" the crowd shouted back.

Preposterous, naïve, and absurd, Tarleton thought. It was an ancient tradition—the raising of the Royal Standard in times of public emergency, the call for the King's able-bodied male subjects to come with their arms and rally to the banner. Tarleton snorted. Inappropriate, he thought. Demeaning in this rebellious place. We should not be inviting them, he thought. We should be compelling them.

The young officer folded the paper, then stepped snappily down to the pole that had been erected before the tavern. A soldier marched up to him and presented him with a folded bundle of cloth. The officer took it, affixed it to the rope on the pole, then ran it up to the top. Caught by the wind, the crowd cheered as the banner unfurled in the breeze—red and gold and blue, emblazoned with the royal arms of England, Ireland, Scotland, and Hanover. A squad of seven soldiers stepped forward, an officer shouted commands to them, and they discharged a volley into the air. They loaded, then fired again, and then a third time.

Tarleton grinned cynically and shook his head. A twenty-one-gun salute. This is theater, he thought.

He gazed across the cheering crowd. Sycophants, he thought. Not one among them who will shoulder a musket.

Soon bored by the spectacle, Tarleton turned his horse to leave. He was beginning to ride away when he heard a voice cry out from behind him. "Lieutenant Colonel Tarleton, sir!'

Tarleton wheeled his horse around and saw an orderly approaching on foot. "Sir," the man said, "Lord Cornwallis has sent for you. His orders are that you report to headquarters at once."

Tarleton nodded in acknowledgment, then walked his horse slowly toward the tavern, the crowd parting as he passed, some whispering his name. When he reached the porch, a soldier stepped forward, taking his horse by the bridle. Tarleton dismounted, climbed the porch steps, and stepped through the doorway, removing his helmet as he entered.

"Ah, Colonel Tarleton!" Cornwallis said, rising to his feet. "Come. Sit down," he said, gesturing to a chair.

Tarleton sat down, amused that Cornwallis was still obviously enthused by the ceremony.

"I have important work for you, sir," Cornwallis said, taking his seat.

"Very good, my lord," Tarleton answered.

"I expect I shall have to remain in this town for some time, busily employed in arming and training the loyal men who come to join us," Cornwallis said. "I am trying to open a supply line to the coast, to obtain shoes and other necessaries for the men. There are few provisions here. You must take your legion into the western part of the county and secure the mills there."

"Very good, sir," Tarleton replied.

"Seize the mills and see that they are kept in operation. The milled corn must be sent here immediately," Cornwallis said.

"It will be done, my lord," Tarleton answered.

Cornwallis paused before continuing. "I regret the necessity of returning to this subject, Colonel, but I continue to receive too many complaints of depredations by our men. We must put an end to it, sir. I am this day informing the officers that if their duty to their King and their country and their feelings for humanity are not sufficient to cause their obedience to my orders in this regard, I must reluctantly turn to the powers I have under military law."

Tarleton nodded, unconcerned with the threat.

"Likewise, this abominable marauding in search for liquor," Cornwallis added. "It must end. It is up to us as officers and gentlemen to enforce discipline among the men and to protect the citizens here."

Again, Tarleton responded only with a nod.

"Have you any questions, Colonel?" Cornwallis asked.

"Yes, m'lord," Tarleton said. "Regarding my orders…." He paused.

"Go ahead," Cornwallis said. "Speak freely, sir."

"What if General Greene moves on us, sir?" Tarleton asked.

"I pray he does," Cornwallis exclaimed. "Nothing would please me more."

"There are reports, sir, that he has increased the size of his force," Tarleton began.

"Yes, I know," Cornwallis interrupted. "My estimates are that he now has over 7,000 men."

"We have 2,000," Tarleton said.

"Yes, Colonel Tarleton," Cornwallis said confidently, "but we have 2,000 trained and disciplined regulars. General Greene is in command of a rabble, mostly militia who will run away at the first sight of us. Besides, sir, we will soon have a sizeable body of militia as well."

"What if we do not?" Tarleton asked.

"I beg your pardon, Colonel," Cornwallis said. "What do you mean?"

"I mean, my lord," Tarleton said, "what if the citizens here do not rally to us? What if they do not come?"

"But they shall, sir!" Cornwallis said. "The people of North Carolina are overwhelmingly loyal. We have been assured so by our friends here. I expect we shall gather thousands of them here over the next few days."

"I pray you are correct, sir," Tarleton said, his skepticism obvious.

"They are already coming, Colonel," Cornwallis said. "I have just received a dispatch that a man named Pyle, a doctor I believe, has gathered a body of armed Loyalists, hundreds of them. They are assembled somewhere in the area of Alamance. You are to find him and escort the men here."

"Very well, sir," Tarleton said.

Cornwallis stood, prompting Tarleton to do likewise.

"Keep me apprised of your progress, sir," Cornwallis said. "Once we have a strong force of loyal militia, armed and organized, we shall move against the rebel army."

59

Near Rainey's Mill
Orange County, North Carolina
February 23, 1781

Riding slowly down the road at the head of the column, Ransom heard Colonel Washington call out to him from behind. "Captain Wiatt!" he called. "Hold up."

Ransom stopped his horse and waited for Washington to catch up. When he arrived, Ransom saw that a civilian was riding alongside him.

"This is Mr. Lytle," Washington said.

Ransom and the man exchanged nods.

"Mr. Lytle's home is in this area. He advises that he knows the location of Tarleton's force," Washington said.

Ransom could easily imagine the man's anxiety. They had passed several homes that day that Tarleton's men had reduced to ashes.

"Colonel Lee is to our west, hunting Colonel Tarleton," Washington continued. "I need you to take two of your troopers and escort Mr. Lytle to him. Pass along this intelligence and my recommendation that we coordinate an attack on Tarleton's camp. Colonel Lee should approach from the west as we advance from the east."

"Very good sir," Ransom answered. "How will I find Colonel Lee?"

"Mr. Lytle believes he knows Colonel Lee's location," Washington said.

"I do, sir," Lytle answered. "He is following Tarleton's trail."

"Understood," Ransom answered. "Let us go at once." He signaled to two of his men, who immediately peeled out of the column and rode up alongside him.

"How far away is Colonel Lee?" Ransom asked Lytle, shooting a glance at the setting sun.

"About 15 miles," Lytle answered. "But he is moving away from us."

"We'll catch up to him," Ransom replied.

"I am going to continue toward Hillsborough," Washington said. "Send back confirmation once you have found Colonel Lee."

"Yes, sir," Ransom said.

"This is a splendid opportunity, Ransom," Washington said, his eyes gleaming. "If we are able to catch Tarleton in a vise, we can annihilate him."

"I find that prospect most agreeable, sir," Ransom answered. He turned to Lytle and said, "Lead on, Mr. Lytle."

60

American campsite near Stony Creek
Orange County, North Carolina
February 24, 1781
Dawn

The cold gray sky was just beginning to lighten and Lee's troopers were saddling their horses when Ransom and the others rode into the camp, after a hard ride through the night. From the sentinel who had led them in, Ransom learned that General Pickens had arrived the day before with about 700 militiamen, that Tarleton was believed to be nearby, and that a fight today was likely. They dismounted and passed their weary horses off to a young soldier who led them away. Ransom looked up and saw Lee striding toward them, smiling broadly and looking, as he always did, as if his uniform had just been delivered from his tailor. In his hand he was carrying Washington's message, which the sentinel had delivered to him.

"Captain Wiatt," he said, extending his hand, "How are you?"

"I am well sir," Ransom answered, shaking his hand. "But I admit to being a bit worn out from running you down."

Lee laughed and turned to Lytle, extending his hand. "Mr. Lytle, I presume?"

"Yes, sir," Lytle answered, taking his hand.

"Gentlemen," Lee said, addressing them all, "it seems your efforts were unnecessary. I already know where Tarleton is. He is just beyond us," he said, gesturing. "A few miles at most. We shall have him by noon."

"Colonel Washington suggests we cooperate," Ransom said, nodding toward the dispatch in Lee's hand.

"I agree entirely!" Lee exclaimed. He turned to Lytle, "Mr. Lytle, Tarleton is just up the road, a few miles from here. If he flees toward Hillsborough, what road will he take?"

"The Salisbury Great Road," Lytle answered.

"Very good," Lee said. Turning back to Ransom he said, "Give my compliments to Colonel Washington. Tell him I recommend he position his force on the Salisbury Great Road, so that he can intercept any of Tarleton's men who manage to escape our attack."

"Very well, sir," Ransom replied. "If you expect to give battle this morning, we must get back to Colonel Washington quickly. We will need fresh horses."

Lee wrinkled his brow. "That may be difficult, Captain. We will be in battle today. I don't know that I have any to spare."

"I don't need one," Lytle said. "I can make it home from here."

"It is important that we get your message to Colonel Washington," Ransom said. "Can you allow us two?"

Lee stared back, silently, for a few moments. Then he turned suddenly and called out to a nearby trooper,

"Lieutenant!"

The man walked over. "Yes, sir," he said.

"This is Captain Wiatt of Colonel Washington's regiment," he said. "Issue him two good horses."

"Yes, sir," the lieutenant said, turning and walking away briskly.

Lee reached for Ransom's hand. "Give my regards to Colonel Washington," he said. "He can run a fox like no man in Virginia but tell him I said he must also remember to cultivate his mind," he added, finishing with a laugh. "Tell him I asked if he has read the book I recommended."

"Thank you, sir," Ransom replied, "but the horses are for my men. They will rush the message to Colonel Washington. I will stay behind until my mount is refreshed."

Lee nodded. "Very good, Captain. But if you are going to stay and fight with us, I am sure we can find a horse for you." He paused, then added, "And thus you will have the privilege of witnessing the destruction of Tarleton's British Legion."

Ransom answered Lee's confident smile with a nod.

"Find some breakfast quickly, Captain," Lee said. "We will be departing forthwith."

61

On the Hillsborough Road, near the Haw Fields
Orange County, North Carolina
February 24, 1781
11:00 a.m.

Colonel Lee had insisted that Ransom ride alongside him and Ransom had dutifully complied, though nearly 30 straight hours in the saddle had left him with little energy for conversation. Tracking Tarleton that morning had been easy—the pillaged and plundered farms and homes along the way marked his path. "This will be that scoundrel's last day of depredation," Lee remarked grimly, as the column rode past the smoking ruins of a barn, beside which stood a distressed woman with a child in her arms, sobbing as one of Lee's officers interviewed her. May it be so, Ransom though.

Seeing a scout galloping toward them, Lee halted. The man pulled his horse to a stop just in front of them and said, "Tarleton is still on this road, Colonel. It's clear for the next two miles, but he's been through. Making frequent stops, as you have noticed."

"We're closing on him," Lee answered. "Keep watch for his pickets, Lieutenant. Tell your men to be careful to stay unobserved."

"Yes, sir," he replied. "There is a good spring just up that path," he added, gesturing to a side road.

"Excellent," Lee answered. "We will fill our canteens there."

The scout nodded, wheeled his horse, and galloped away, as Lee turned the column onto the path.

As the spring came in sight, Lee gestured toward a nearby little farmhouse. "Do you see anything unusual about that place?" he asked.

What Ransom saw was a one room log house, with a corral out back—likely a pig pen. "Looks typical of the houses in this area," he answered.

"Does the place look as if it has been disturbed?" Lee asked.

Ransom looked again and saw Lee's meaning. Unlike the other farmsteads they had passed that morning, this one showed no evidence of a visit from Tarleton.

Lee called one of his troopers over and tossed him his canteen. "Fill this for me," he said. Turning to one of his officers he said, "Captain Eggleston," then pointed at the house. Eggleston nodded, barked a command, and a squad of dragoons pulled out of the column and followed as Lee rode toward the house, Ransom riding alongside him.

As they approached the house a woman stepped out of the door and into the yard. Wearing a gray bonnet and a grimy apron over a patched dress, Ransom guessed that she was in her fifties.

Lee touched his helmet and said cheerfully, "Good morning, ma'am. What provisions can you spare for hungry and weary men and horses?"

"We ain't got no more," she replied, with a taut face.

"We done already gave you all we had."

"Us?" Lee asked, with a smile. "You gave provisions to us?"

"We sure did," she said. "Not more than a few hours ago when y'all..." She suddenly stopped, a concerned and suspicious expression sweeping across her face as she looked carefully at Lee and his men.

"I see," Lee said, shooting a glance at Eggleston, who in turn began to fan out his men. "You mean that this morning you provisioned horsemen wearing green jackets, like these?" He patted his chest as he finished.

The woman stood still, not answering.

"I trust you were well paid, madam?" Lee said. "It seems your neighbors have not been as fortunate."

Lee waited for a response, but the woman just stared silently back at him. After a few moments he said, "Captain Eggleston, search the premises."

As the troopers began to dismount, the woman spat out, "You ain't got no right."

"Oh, but indeed we do," Lee replied, pleasantly. "There are traitorous Tories about, and it is our duty to protect the good citizens from them."

As one of the dismounted troopers stepped toward the door of the house, the woman moved to block him. The trooper raised his hand to push her aside and as he did a grizzled old man clutching a musket burst suddenly through the door from inside the cabin, leveled his gun, and fired.

At the sound of the shot, Ransom instinctively flinched and ducked. Meanwhile, Lee sat calmly in his saddle as if nothing had happened, his expression unchanged, even though the ball had whizzed past his head, missing him by inches.

For a split second, Lee and the old man looked each

other in the eyes, then a trooper stepped suddenly forward, lifted his pistol, and fired it into the man's chest. He collapsed in a heap and the woman threw herself down on him with a piercing wail.

Lee looked down at them for a few moments, then said softly, "*Hektor egō dustēnos.*" Turning to Eggleston, he said, "See if there is anything here we can use," then wheeled his horse and began riding away. Ransom followed him.

They rode silently for a few minutes, then Lee spoke. "*Nun de su men Aidao domous hupo keuthesi gaiēs erkheai, autar eme stugerō eni penthei leipeis khērēn en megaroisi.* Do I have it right, Captain?"

Ransom closed his eyes for a moment, his mind clouded by fatigue and by the pathetic scene he had just witnessed. "Now Hector, thou art descended into Hades, leaving a bitter grieving woman in thy halls," he answered, the woman's cries fading in the distance behind them.

They rode on silently for another minute or so before Lee replied. "Yes, I think that's about right," he said. "'Unto the house of Hades, beneath the depths of the earth,' might be better, but you have it close enough I think."

My God, Ransom thought, what is becoming of us?

After another silent minute Lee spoke again. "*Quaeque ipsa miserrima vidi, et quorum pars magna fui.* 'So many terrible things I saw, and in so many of them I played a great part,'" he said. He paused and added, "It is good that war is so terrible, Captain. Otherwise, we should grow too fond of it."

Just then a scout galloped up, pulling his horse to a stop just in front of Lee. "Tarleton is over the Haw, sir," the man said. "He crossed at a ford called

Swepsonville."

"How far from here?" Lee asked.

"About four hours march, sir," the scout replied.

Lee looked away for a few moments, as if in thought, then turned back and said, "Very good, Lieutenant. Keep me apprised of his movements and continue to avoid contact."

The man nodded, turned, and rode away.

Lee looked at Ransom. "It appears our meeting with Colonel Tarleton will be later in the day than I had hoped." He paused then added, "He has crossed the river to make camp. We will follow him. We will have him before sundown."

62

Swepsonville Ford
Orange County, North Carolina
February 24, 1781
4:00 p.m.

Lee watched from the south bank of the river as the army splashed across the ford, the men doubling up on the horses to keep the infantry dry. Ransom, still beside him, was nearly numb with weariness, and so sleep-deprived that he was having trouble keeping his mind focused. His body was begging for rest, but with their goal so near, he had summoned the energy to keep going.

As the column was crossing, a scout had brought a civilian to Lee—a local farmer with information he was eager to share. "Are you certain, sir?" Lee asked the man.

"I am, Colonel," the man answered confidently. "I have no doubt. The British are making camp at Michael Holt's plantation. Their horses are unsaddled. They're waiting on Pyle's Tory militia, who are marching to meet them there."

"How far away is the camp?" Lee asked.

"About three and half miles," the man answered. "Right straight down this road."

Lee paused for a few moments, as if gathering his thoughts. Then he turned in his saddle and scanned a cluster of officers who had just crossed the river. Seeing the man he was looking for, he called out, "General Pickens!"

Wearing his customary dour expression, Pickens rode over.

"It seems Tarleton is just ahead, and we have a chance to take him by surprise," Lee said, speaking rapidly. "We have him now! The Legion infantry will take the middle. The dragoons will advance in column on the right. Position your men on the left. We will move off the road and advance through the woods until we are close enough for the dragoons to make a dash at him. The infantry and your militia will follow, to finish him off."

Ransom looked on, surprised to see Lee giving orders to Pickens. For his part, Pickens listened impassively, then nodded and said, "Very good," before riding away.

Lee, his eyes flashing, spun toward Ransom. "I must confess, Captain, that I have envied Colonel Washington's success at the Cowpens and his duel with Colonel Tarleton. It looks as if today I will have *my* chance!"

The men moved quickly but cautiously through the woods, staying as quiet as possible. In about an hour, a scout rode up and told Lee that the plantation was just ahead. Lee nodded and moved over to join the column of dragoons on the right. Ransom rode with him.

The expectation of imminent battle was nothing new to Ransom, but no matter how many times he fought, he was always accompanied by that familiar combination of thrill, dread, and anxiety that he was now feeling, and that was evident on the faces of all the men around him. "Form up, men," Lee said, as he rode along the line. "Charge on my signal. There will be no trumpet."

The men rode forward at a walk, Lee leading them, until the house was only a few hundred yards away. When he drew his saber, the other seventy-five dragoons did likewise. Ransom tightened the sword knot around his wrist and watched for Lee's command.

Through the trees Ransom could make out the house in the distance. There were a few horses hitched outside it, but otherwise he saw no evidence of a British camp. And it struck him as strange that they had not encountered any pickets.

Lee glanced around at his dragoons, their horses fidgeting nervously. He turned back toward the plantation house and raised his sword. After a few moments he spurred his horse to a trot, and Ransom and the others did likewise. Lee led them quickly to a canter, then, as they emerged from the woods, they all broke into a gallop, thundering down upon the house and fanning out as they approached.

As they charged past the house, anticipating swooping down onto an unsuspecting enemy camp, they came instead into an empty field. Squads peeled off into different directions to make sure, but it was clear to Ransom that Tarleton was not there.

A couple hundred yards past the house, Lee suddenly wheeled his horse around. "Establish a picket line!" he shouted to one of his captains, frustration and disappointment written on his face.

Ransom followed as Lee rode at a trot back to the

house. As they arrived, a couple of troopers were emerging from within, shoving ahead of them two disarmed officers who were wearing the green jackets of Tarleton's dragoons.

Lee halted his horse, just in front of the house, waiting impatiently for an explanation.

"These are the only two we found," one of his men said. "The Tory who lives here says they were 'settling accounts.'"

"Where is your camp?" Lee asked, looking down at the men contemptuously.

After neither answered him, Lee drew out his pistol and pointed it at one of the officers. "Answer me!" he demanded.

The man looked back at him a moment, then replied calmly, "We are your prisoners, sir."

Lee kept his pistol leveled at the man, their eyes locked unblinkingly on each other. After a few moments, Eggleston rode up suddenly.

"They're not here," he said, nearly out of breath. "A servant out back says they're making camp two miles from here. On the plantation of someone named O'Neal."

Lee, still staring at the officer, read a slight twitch in the man's face, revealing the truth of the intelligence. Smiling slightly, Lee re-holstered his pistol.

"Very good, Captain," he said, turning away. "We should be there in time to join Colonel Tarleton for supper."

Over his shoulder Lee saw that Pickens and the infantry were emerging from the woods, in a line of battle.

"Report the situation to General Pickens," he said to Eggleston. "Tell him we will maintain the same deployment—his militia on the left, Legion infantry in the center, dragoons on the right. Go and gather up any of the mounted militia who have sabers and have them fall in line behind the dragoons."

"Yes, sir," Eggleston answered, turning to leave.

"Wait," Lee said, stopping him. "Which way is this O'Neal's?" Lee asked.

"There," Eggleston replied, pointing to the south. "Down that race path."

"All right," Lee said, looking in that direction, "let's go." He turned to his trumpeter and said, "Column of fours. Guide on me. Forward march."

Lee rode forward a trot, Ransom following, as the boy blew the command. As the troopers formed up, Lee hurried up to the front of the column, leading them down the path. He had only ridden a few yards when a scout came galloping up, pulling to a halt just in front of Lee and Ransom.

"It's the damnedest thing, sir," the scout blurted out. He turned and looked behind him, at another scout approaching with two armed mounted men. "There's a large body of Tory militia just up ahead on this road." He paused. "They think we're Tarleton's men."

63

Pyle's Defeat
Holt's Race Path
Orange County, North Carolina
February 24, 1781
5:30 p.m.

Moments later the second scout arrived. Riding beside him were two men in civilian dress, each with a musket slung over his shoulder and a piece of red cloth pinned to his hat. "These men asked us to bring them to Colonel Tarleton," the scout said, addressing Lee.

"We're glad to finally find you, sir," one of the men said, with a smile. "We've been looking for y'all all day."

"And now you have found us," Lee answered pleasantly.

"Colonel Pyle is right up the road, sir," the man said. "We're ready to march with you."

"Very good," Lee answered. "How many men does Colonel Pyle have?"

"About 200," the man answered.

"More like 400," the man beside him said.

"All armed and mounted?" Lee asked.

"Yes, sir," the first man replied, grinning. "Ready for duty, sir."

Lee paused for a few moments, then asked, "Your name, sir?"

"Hargate, sir," the man answered. "Corporal Elijah Hargate."

"Very good, Corporal," Lee said, brightly. "Please return to Colonel Pyle with Colonel Tarleton's compliments. Ask him if he will be so good as to draw his men to the side of the road, to allow my much-fatigued troops to pass to the front."

"Yes, sir!" Hargate replied eagerly.

As the two men turned to leave, Lee called out. "Corporal, leave your comrade with us as an escort."

"Yes, sir," Hargate answered, before riding away with the scouts.

Lee gestured to one of his dragoons, who told the other man to follow him, then led him away.

Once they were gone, Lee began speaking rapidly. "We need to get by these damned Tories as quickly as we can," he said. He called over his adjutant. "Go at once to General Pickens. Tell him to proceed south along the road there," he said, gesturing, "but to keep his men concealed in the woods. Tell him to move parallel to the Tories, but out of their sight. I will bring the dragoons alongside them. Once we are in position, I will demand their surrender."

"Yes, sir," the man answered, then spurred his horse and rode quickly away.

"Captain Rudolph!" Lee said, calling over one of his troop commanders.

Rudolph rode up to him and Lee continued, speaking rapidly. "These rascals think I'm Tarleton, so we will make the most of it. We're going to ride through them. When I find this Pyle, I will inform him of the situation and receive his surrender. Pass the word to the officers and men. They are to ride peacefully by the Tories. Remember that they believe we are Tarleton's dragoons. Do nothing to disabuse them of that. Understood?"

"Yes, sir," Rudolph answered. After a pause he asked, "If we see that there are indeed hundreds of them, is this still the plan?"

"It is," Lee answered. "It makes no difference how many of them there are. We have the element of surprise."

"Yes, sir," Rudolph replied.

"If we are discovered, we will attack them immediately. But remember, it is Tarleton we are after," Lee said.

Rudolph nodded.

"Inform the men, Captain," Lee said. "We're marching immediately."

Rudolph nodded again then rode away, calling over officers and sergeants as he moved down the line.

Lee turned to Ransom and said with a smile, "Shall we proceed to the theater, Captain?"

"I will fall back a little in the line, Colonel," Ransom answered, his head swimming from fatigue and lack of sleep. "My uniform makes me a bit conspicuous."

Lee nodded, then turned to his wide-eyed trumpeter. "Single file, forward march," he barked, and the boy dutifully sounded the command.

The column had only gone about 50 yards when the Tories came into sight, lined up on horseback along the right side of the road, in double file, their firearms shouldered. They stretched along the road as far as Ransom could see, at least 250 yards.

Soon Lee's column, 75 dragoons in single file, reached them. It seemed to Ransom as though he was inside a crazy dream, as he and the others, outnumbered more than two to one, just walked calmly past the enemy, who sat at attention in their saddles, watching them go by, mere feet away. Then he noticed Lee.

Riding at the front of the column, about 40 yards ahead of Ransom, Lee was smiling and nodding at the Tories as he passed by them, occasionally offering a compliment or a greeting—and not displaying even the slightest hint of concern or discomfort. My God, Ransom thought, he's enjoying this.

It took about two minutes for the dragoons to travel the length of the Tory column—time that passed excruciatingly slowly as they filed silently by. At the end of the Tory line, Ransom saw Lee's scout and the Tory corporal Hargate, waiting alongside a mounted officer. Lee rode casually up to the officer, extended his hand and said with a smile, "Colonel Pyle, I presume?"

Pyle reached out and grasped his hand. "It's an honor to meet you, sir," he said, beaming.

~~~

At that very moment, Eggleston caught up to the rear of the column, riding at the head of the 70 mounted militiamen he had been sent to bring up. In the confusion and haste, no one had informed him of the situation and the plan

Seeing the Tories as he approached, he had assumed they were some of Pickens' men, standing aside to let the cavalry pass. But when he came nearer, he was puzzled to see that the men were freshly shaven and
~~~

wearing clean clothes. He also saw that they had pieces of red cloth pinned to their hats.

Captain Joseph Graham, commander of the mounted militia, was riding alongside Eggleston. He looked out with astonishment at the men lined along the road, turned to Eggleston and exclaimed, "These men are Tories! Why do they have their arms?"

Eggleston pulled out of line and rode over to one of the men, who appeared to be an officer. "Who do you belong to?" he snapped.

"I am a friend of His Majesty," the officer answered with a grin.

In a flash, Eggleston drew his saber and brought it down furiously, cleaving the man's skull. Taking that as their cue, the militiamen launched savagely into the unsuspecting Tories.

~~~

At that same moment, oblivious to what was happening at the end of the column, Ransom saw something out of the corner of his eye that sent a chill up his spine. His heart racing, he kept his eyes locked dead ahead, fighting back an urge to turn and look again. Then he heard it, unmistakably. From the Tory column, someone spoke his name.
~~~

64

Pyle's Defeat
Holt's Race Path
Orange County, North Carolina
February 24, 1781
5:35 p.m.

"They're rebels, Gus!" Billy said in a loud frantic whisper. "Rebels!"

Gus kept his eyes straight ahead. "Settle down," he whispered back. "They're Colonel Tarleton's dragoons."

"They are not!" Billy whispered, urgently. "Look at that one in the white uniform. That's Ransom Wiatt!"

~~~

Ransom glanced back, confirming in a moment what he had feared. Gus Johnson and Billy Lewis were in the Tory column. In that split second, he and Gus made eye contact, and in the moment of recognition, Gus's eyes flashed fierce hatred. He reached for his gun.

Ransom knew instantly that by being there he had
~~~

placed in jeopardy all of Lee's men, indeed the entire operation, perhaps even the cause itself. He also knew instantly what he had to do.

As Gus spun his musket around and was trying to bring it into firing position, Ransom drew his saber, wheeled, and spurred his horse. Gus's eyes were still burning with hatred when Ransom's sword slashed across his face, dropping him from his saddle.

When Ransom spun back around, he saw that Billy was fumbling with his musket, trying to ready it to fire. Ransom hesitated only an instant before slashing him across the arm, seeing the fear in Billy's eyes as the saber struck home.

The moment that Ransom drew his sword and attacked, the dragoons around him followed suit, setting off a chain reaction. As the confused Tories began shouting out, "Stop! We're King's friends!", the dragoons cut them down.

As the melee spread, the troopers hacking and slashing the Tories repeatedly, Ransom noticed Gus staggering to his feet, bleeding profusely but reaching for his gun. Ransom pressed his horse forward and swung his saber. Gus blocked the first blow with his hand, but with Ransom's second swing he felt the saber slice across Gus's face and dig deeply into the side of his head. Gus dropped to his knees, then pitched forward into the dirt.

Ransom spun his horse back around to face Billy, who had dropped his gun after Ransom sabered him. Their eyes met for an instant, just before a trooper's saber crashed into Billy's face, sending out a spray of blood and sending him staggering backwards. He threw his hands up to protect his head, but the trooper cut through them, raining down blows until Billy dropped to the ground.

~~~

At the front of the column Lee was still gripping Pyle's hand when he heard the commotion behind him. Glancing back and seeing that fighting had broken out down the line, he muttered, "Damn," then turned to his trumpeter and said, "Sound the attack."

As the bugle sounded the command, Lee turned to face Pyle, whose eyes had widened in alarm and confusion. Lee released his hand, swiftly drew his saber, then slashed Pyle across the face.

When the command to attack came, the dragoons who were not already fighting wheeled their horses and pitched into the befuddled Tories, hacking right and left, chopping them down and sabering them repeatedly, cutting down both those who were still on horseback and those already wounded who had managed to get on their feet.

It was a scene of uncontrolled carnage and chaos. Pickens' militia rushed through the woods to join in the attack as riderless panicked horses trampled the writhing bodies of the fallen Tories, many still screaming "We're on your side!", "We're friends of the King!", and "God save the King!"

In less than two minutes it was all over. A few of the Tories scrambled away and escaped in the confusion, but the rest lay in a long bloody heap, dead or wounded all along the edge of the road. Lee's only casualty was a militia officer's horse, killed by one of the few shots the Tories managed to get off.

~~~

In the thick of the melee, his uniform splashed with blood, Lee shouted to Captain Rudolph, "Get the men under control, Captain! Secure the prisoners. We must resume the march immediately!" He turned and saw a sergeant, then called him over. "Bring me one of these Tory farts!" he barked.

Dazed and blood-splattered, Ransom drew his horse near to Lee just as the sergeant returned, shoving a wounded man along, blood streaming down from a cut on the man's head. "I couldn't find one who ain't wounded," the sergeant said, "but this one ain't hurt bad."

Lee leaned over to face the man. "How far away is O'Neal's?" he snapped.

Wiping the blood from his eyes, the man looked up, stunned. "About two miles," he answered, confused.

"Is there any water to cross? Is the way clear or wooded?" Lee asked, speaking rapidly.

"It's uh…," the man hesitated, wiping his face again. "It's mostly clear. No streams to cross," he said.

Lee turned away from the man, looking into the distance as if in thought.

"Well God bless your soul, Mr. Tarleton," the wounded man said. "The men you have killed this day are subjects as good as His Majesty ever had."

Lee spun around to face him, his eyes flashing. "Call me Tarleton again you damned rascal and I will take off your head!" he shouted. "I am Lieutenant Colonel Henry Lee of the American Legion!" Lee paused, his temper fading, then added with a wry smile, while lifting his helmet, "At your service, sir."

The wounded man's jaw dropped.

"Take this man away," Lee said to the sergeant.

"Secure him with the prisoners."

Pickens rode up at that moment. Seeing him, Lee snapped, "General Pickens, this ridiculous band of Tories may have ruined our chances of taking Tarleton by surprise. Form up your men, sir! We must resume the advance at once."

Pickens nodded and rode away.

Wheeling his horse, Lee noticed Ransom. He paused, looking carefully at him. "Are you all right, Captain?" he asked.

Ransom tried to answer, but his mouth wouldn't obey. Then he saw something like a dark curtain descending in front of him and he tumbled unconscious from his saddle.

65

Camp of Andrew Pickens' Patriot Militia
On the Hillsborough to Guilford Great Road
Orange County, North Carolina
February 25, 1781
2:00 a.m.

Detailed to help guard a half-dozen of the Tory prisoners, Jones sat shivering by a small simmering campfire, the wounded prisoners huddled together a few yards away. It had taken a while to untangle the men after the attack on the Tories, and by the time they were ready to resume the move on Tarleton's camp, it was too dark to proceed. So, Lee and Pickens had pulled them back a couple of miles, with instructions to be ready to move out at dawn.

They had taken a few dozen prisoners, nearly all of them wounded, during what the men were already calling "Pyle's Hacking Match." Pickens had ordered the prisoners separated into small groups, to make them easier to guard. Jones and a few other men had been on guard duty a couple of hours, when the men arrived who were to relieve them. The men were carrying broadswords, and Jones didn't recognize them.

Jones stood up when the men approached, hoping there would be time for him to get a little sleep before the march resumed.

"Why in hell should we have to stay up in the middle of the night, in the freezing cold, looking after these sorry bastards?" one of the men said, speaking to no one.

One of the men looked at Jones. "Did you see what happened when the Injuns came up?" he asked.

Jones shook his head. He hadn't seen it, but by now all the men in camp had heard about what happened when the company of Catawbas had arrived at the scene of the battle.

"They was disappointed at having missed out on the hacking, so they took to spearing the wounded prisoners. Must have killed a dozen or so before the captain made 'em stop," the man said, ending with a chuckle.

Jones picked up his knapsack, choosing not to respond.

"They had the right idea if you ask me," another one of the new arrivals said with a sneer. "You can bet your arse them Tory bastards woulda kilt every single one of us if it had gone the other way. The way they done Buford's men."

Jones stood silently for a moment, his mind wandering back to a painful memory. "Tories killed my brother," he said softly. "Burned out his family and left them to starve."

"If you ask me, we ought to kill every damn one of them," the first man said, getting nods and grunts of approval from the others.

"Now we gotta haul their sorry arses around, feed

'em, tend to 'em," he said contemptuously. He hesitated, then looked around at his comrades, their faces lit by moonlight and the glow of the campfire. "How 'bout we give 'em Buford's play, boys?" he said, resting his hand on the hilt of his sword.

At that, a couple of the wounded prisoners glanced over at them. "What are you looking at, you Tory dogs?" the man snapped. "I reckon you think you can escape tonight?"

The Tories turned away.

"What's to stop them from murdering us in our sleep, boys?" the man hissed.

"They're under guard," Jones said, calmly.

"There ain't but one way to be safe from 'em," the man said, lifting his sword. "That's to send them to hell." He stood quietly for a few moments, then suddenly rushed at the prisoners, shouting "Remember Buford!"

As the Tories tried to scramble to their feet, the man rained down sword blows on their heads, hacking left and right, sending spurts of blood flying in all directions. Jones stood watching as the man's comrades rushed in and joined him, slashing and chopping the prisoners.

In a matter of seconds, none of the Tories were moving. The first man looked around, slashed one of the dead men again for good measure, then said, "Ain't nothing left for us to guard now." He spat on one of the bodies and walked away, his comrades following him, their swords dripping blood.

Jones stood facing the bloody heap of men for a few moments, then turned and walked away. Strangely, he had felt no emotion at all as he had watched the murder of the prisoners. But by the time he came to the campsite, where his sons were lying sleeping, a distressing gloom had settled over him. He unrolled his blanket and dropped down on it, exhausted, but unable to sleep, the brutal scene replaying over and over in his mind.

About twenty minutes later he heard an officer approaching. "Up, men!" he said, as he walked past the knots of sleeping militiamen. "We're moving out. No time to cook anything. Let's go."

Jones arose, sick of war.

As the men were breaking camp, Tate Jones spoke to his father, returning to a subject he and his brother had been suggesting for weeks. "Don't you think we ought to go home, Pa?"

Unable to look at his son, Jones just shook his head. "We signed on for two months," he answered. "We gave our word."

"Most of the others has done left and gone back to South Carolina," Tate replied. "Why can't we finish out our two months fighting the Tories there?"

Jones had forcefully rejected the suggestion every time his sons had brought it up before. But this morning, with the slaughter of the prisoners still haunting him, he felt no conviction as he repeated dully, "We gave our word."

An hour later, when the column reached Tarleton's campsite, they found the campfires still burning, but the camp was abandoned. The hungry militiamen stopped to scavenge, but Pickens soon rode up and broke them up. "Form back up, men!" he shouted. "We're going to run them down!"

The weary, ragged Patriots fell dutifully back into column and resumed the march.

About a hundred yards outside the camp, Tate

stepped out of line and into a clump of tall grass by the side of the road, to relieve himself. Startled, he called out, "Pa!"

Jones, his son Joshua, and a few other men hurried over, to find that Tate was standing over the body of a badly bleeding boy. Jones dropped to his knees and gently spoke, "Can you hear me?"

The boy, who appeared to be about twelve years old, opened his eyes and looked blankly back at Jones. After a few moments he gathered some composure. "Do you have a drink of water, sir?" the boy asked, his voice cracked and rasping.

All the men there suddenly thrust out their canteens. Jones gently lifted the boy's head as Joshua lowered his canteen to his lips, tipping it back and allowing the boy to take a swallow.

Carefully pulling back the boy's bloody shirt, Tate saw a deep jagged wound in his belly.

"Please tell my mama I'm sorry," the boy whispered, his eyes filled with tears.

"What happened, son?" Jones asked.

"I didn't do nothing, sir," the boy said. "I just wanted to see what the British soldiers looked like."

"Did they do this to you?" Jones asked.

"I was just trying to see them from here. I ain't no soldier," the boy said haltingly. "They must have seen me. Two of them run me down and one of them stuck me in the gut," the boy said.

"They bayoneted you?" Jones asked.

"Yes, sir," the boy answered.

"Were you armed?" Jones asked.

"No, sir," the boy answered. "I just wanted to see what they looked like." He hesitated as a tear rolled down his face. "Please tell my mama I'm sorry."

Jones turned to Tate. "Go find somebody who can tend to this boy," he said.

"Yes, sir," Tate said as he turned and ran back to the column.

"Just left him here to die, gut-stabbed," one of the other men muttered angrily.

Jones shot a fierce glance at the man, silencing him. He turned back to the boy. "We're getting someone to help you, son," he said.

The boy tried to speak, but what came out of his mouth instead was a cough, followed by a gush of blood. His eyes glazed over, and Jones felt the boy's body go limp.

Feeling a surge of rage and hatred sweeping away the doubt and gloom that had haunted him for the past few hours, Jones leaned down and whispered into the dead boy's ear, "Son, I promise you that I will kill every damned one of them I can."

66

On the Hillsborough to Guilford Great Road
Orange County, North Carolina
February 25, 1781
1:30 p.m.

Twelve-year-old Thomas Robinson noticed the buzzards before his father did—at least a dozen of them, silently circling overhead in the distance. "What might that be, Father?" the boy asked, gesturing toward them.

John Robinson glanced up. Maybe a large animal, he thought. But, he realized, in evil times like these, it could be something much worse. He just shook his head, said a quick silent prayer, and returned his eyes to the road, shaking the reins to keep the oxen moving. In the distance he noticed two figures on the road, walking toward them from the direction of the buzzards. As they drew closer Robinson saw that they were boys, dirty and ragged, carrying bundles.

"How are ye?" Robinson said, when the wagon reached the boys.

They answered his greeting with rough laughter. "If y'all are looking for the hacking match, it's down that path yonder," one of them said, pointing at a place where the road diverged. "Ain't nothing good left on 'em though," he added with a laugh. Then, as if seeming to notice for the first time how Robinson and his son were dressed, he added, "Not that I reckon y'all would care about that," ending with another loud, rude laugh.

"We thank thee," Robinson answered as he drove past the boys.

When they reached the path the boy had pointed out, Robinson turned the oxen onto it. His son looked up at him inquisitively. "It is our Christian duty to offer succor to these poor sinners," Robinson said.

A few hundred yards down the path they came upon a horrifying scene. Dozens of bloody dead bodies were lying along the road, some of them stripped naked, gruesomely stiff and contorted. "Regard this all well, Thomas," Robinson said to his nauseous son. "What thee sees before thee are the wages of sin."

Two black women were loading bodies onto a donkey cart. Robinson stopped his team and one of the women spoke to him. "Miz Holt told us to bring these here dead men up to the big house to keep 'em safe from the buzzards," she said. Casting an envious glance at Robinson's oxen and wagon she added, "All we got to carry 'em with is this here little cart and this po' old donkey."

"We will help thee move them," Robinson answered.

"Much obliged," the woman said. Taking the donkey by the bridle she said, "We'll be back directly. The house is just up this path a ways."

She led the donkey and the creaking cart away. The other woman followed.

Robinson climbed down from the wagon. He sensed his son's hesitation and detected the fear in his eyes. "Come down, Thomas," he said, and the boy obeyed.

Robinson walked to the closest body and gazed down at it. He saw that it was a young man, his mouth and eyes open, his face contorted and frozen. The young man's skull had been cleaved and his brains had spilled out in a putrid, congealed mass.

"Take his feet," Robinson told his horrified son.

The boy obeyed, lifting the dead man's legs as his father lifted him by the shoulders. They carried the body to the wagon and carefully lowered it into the bed. The boy glanced over at his father and saw that his shirt and coat were smeared with the dead man's blood. Feeling a rush of nausea, the boy turned his head and vomited.

"Can thee continue?" his father asked.

After a few moments, the boy wiped his eyes and nodded. "I'm sorry, Father," he muttered.

"Let this be a lesson to thee," Robinson said, walking to another body.

After a few minutes, the boy's nausea had settled enough to permit him to speak.

"I have heard it said, Father, that General Greene is a Friend," the boy said after they deposited another body into the wagon, his curiosity overpowering his fear of angering his father.

"Nathanael Greene was raised as a Child of the Light," Robinson answered calmly. "But he chose a path of sin—oath-taking and blood-shedding—and was therefore disowned and put out of the fellowship of Friends.

"We obey our Lord's commands, Thomas,"

Robinson continued. "The spirit of Christ, which leads us into all truth, will never move us to fight and war against any man with outward weapons. Let us pray that the Inner Light will yet guide Nathanael to repentance and deliver him from his sinful life. Until it does, he is not one of us."

The boy nodded somberly and glanced back at the bodies scattered along the road. He approached the nearest of them and stood waiting for his father. Then something, some slight movement, caught his eye. He edged closer to the body's blood-encrusted head and squatted down to look at it more closely. The man's face was so horribly mutilated and blood-covered that it was not even possible to distinguish its features—eyes, nose, mouth, all had dissolved into a bloody pulp. But as he stared at it, Thomas was startled by what he thought he saw. He pulled back reflexively, then slowly leaned in even closer. Then he saw it again, tiny bubbles forming and bursting in the center of the man's face. "Father!" he shouted. "This one is alive!"

After Robinson had gently wiped away the blood from around what was left of the man's nose, he and Thomas carefully placed him in the wagon and drove to the house at the end of the path. There, a middle-aged woman wearing a bonnet and a clean untattered dress stepped out to meet them.

"One of the men from the road is alive," Robinson said. "We have brought him."

Thomas hopped down from the wagon seat and scurried to the back.

"Show me," the woman said, coming to Thomas.

"This is the man," the boy answered, nearly out of breath.

The woman leaned over the wagon bed and looked

at the man for a few moments. She reached in and picked up his arm by the wrist, seeing immediately that it was not stiff. "Bring him up to the porch, please," she said, before turning and walking back toward the house.

Robinson and his son carried the man up the porch steps and gingerly put him down. The woman dipped a cloth into a bucket of water on the porch and began gently wiping away the blood on the man's face, her eyes bloodshot and swollen from many hours of weeping.

After a few silent minutes she spoke. "I do not recognize him," she said. "As no one has come to claim him, he must not be from around here."

Robinson remained silent, not knowing how to respond.

"The poor man," the woman said, quietly. "What kind of savages would do something like this?"

Robinson lowered his eyes and turned away.

"He cannot live much longer," the woman said. She looked up at Robinson and he turned to face her. "Thank you for bringing him here. We will bury him with the others."

"Perhaps it is God's will that he live," Robinson said.

The woman stood up, shaking her head. "His wounds are too severe, sir. It is a miracle that he has survived as long as he has."

"Perhaps the miracle is not yet complete," Robinson said.

The woman looked at him, her eyes sympathetic, but tired.

"I will see that he is kept comfortable, but no, he cannot possibly live," she said. She tossed her head in the direction of the house. "I have a dozen desperately wounded men inside who have a chance. I must devote myself to them."

"Will thee allow us to tend to him?" Robinson asked.

The woman looked at Robinson again, becoming aware for the first time that he had not removed his hat.

"Are you Quakers?" she asked.

Robinson nodded. "We are Friends," he answered. "We are returning home from visiting the Meeting at Lindley's."

"You are very kind, sir," she said with a weary sigh, shaking her head. "But this poor man will not be with us much longer."

"If the Lord has willed that the man is to die," Robinson said, "we will care for him until his time is up."

"Very well," the woman answered. "God bless you, sir. I will dress his wounds, then leave him to you." After a pause she added, "Should anyone come looking for him, who should I say has the body?"

"John Robinson," he answered. "Our home is at New Garden."

67

Ward's Ferry
Bedford County, Virginia
February 26, 1781

By the time the Lawtons arrived at the ferry dozens of other men from the regiment were already there, many of them, like the Lawtons, accompanied by their families. Martha had insisted on coming along to see Henry and the boys off. Henry had resisted at first, before reluctantly agreeing. And when he came out that morning to board the wagon that would take them there, he saw that it contained not only Martha, Will, and Arthur, but Stephen, Squire and George as well. Choosing not to risk spoiling the bittersweet occasion, he just climbed up onto the wagon, took the reins, released the brake, and drove off without comment.

The ride had been solemn and quiet, although from time to time, Martha had nervously checked and rechecked their haversacks, worried that something might have been left behind. They all rode silently, seemingly deep in thought, the occasion having silenced even the usually boisterous Arthur.

Martha's eyes misted when they came in sight of the

ferry and she saw the men gathering there. Known for their long Pennsylvania rifles and their skill as marksmen, the men of the regiment, Lynch's Riflemen they were called, took pride in their reputations, most have them having been training since they were old enough to shoot. Nearly all the men, including the Lawtons, were wearing their characteristic brown hunting shirts, buckskin breeches, and tricorne cocked hats.

After he stopped the wagon and the passengers began to climb down, Henry noticed Jacob hurrying over, wearing a sword.

"Good morning, Captain," Henry said, extending his hand.

"Good morning, Henry," Jacob answered, shaking his hand warmly, before stepping to Martha and giving her a hug.

"Take care of them, Jacob," she whispered.

"We'll all be fine," he answered softly.

"I hear that the British are running away," Henry said as Martha released her brother from the hug. "So, this will probably be a short deployment."

Jacob did not answer him, but Henry could read the disagreement on his face.

"The colonel wants everyone to assemble at the ferry in fifteen minutes," he said.

At that moment, Will recognized the Soblett family in the crowd. "Excuse me," he blurted out, before rushing toward them.

When Lucy saw him coming, she stepped in front of her parents, her hands extended. Will took them when he reached her. "I'm so glad you came," he said, gazing into her tear-filled eyes.

"Will," Mr. Soblett said loudly as he stepped toward

the couple, interrupting their tender moment, and grasping Will by the hand. "I have been reflecting on the life of Algernon Sidney. I would like to share some thoughts with you on that subject before you leave."

Lucy shot an angry and bewildered glance at her father, who was oblivious to it.

"A great martyr for liberty, he was. Sidney, I mean. But of course you know that, I suppose," Soblett said, as his daughter looked on, incredulous, while Will struggled to remain respectful. "I wonder if it wouldn't do your regiment good to ponder the man's words at times like these."

"Father!" Lucy said, frustrated.

Soblett continued, ignoring her. "Now don't get me wrong, young man. There can be no doubt of Colonel Lynch's military ability, but political philosophy is not his strong suit." Lowering his voice he added, "But please don't tell him I said that."

"Father!" Lucy repeated, stamping her foot, as Will looked back at Soblett trying to remain composed.

"I'm not saying that Colonel Lynch is unaware of Sidney's work, mind you," Soblett continued. "He may well know it. But obviously it would be unreasonable to expect a man to be thoroughly well-versed in all subjects, unless of course the man is a brilliant polymath—of whom there are few. I should add that I have had the great fortune of knowing…."

Mrs. Soblett suddenly took her husband's arm, interrupting him. "Look, Abe," she said, tugging his arm. "There is Tom and Nancy Helm. Let us go and say goodbye to Tom."

"What?" Soblett said, losing his train of thought.

"We must go and speak to Captain Helm," she answered, pulling him away.

"Oh, yes, right," Soblett answered. Turning back to Will he said, "Well, young man, God be with you," pumping his hand again.

"Thank you, sir," Will answered with a smile, as Mrs. Soblett led her husband away.

"Oooh, sometimes Daddy makes me so angry I could just spit," Lucy said.

Will laughed. Seeing that her parents had disappeared into the crowd, he grabbed Lucy playfully around the waist and pulled her toward him.

"Will!" she exclaimed, her eyes twinkling. "You behave!"

"How about a kiss goodbye?" Will said, teasingly.

"You are a scoundrel, Will Lawton," Lucy answered with a giggle, blushing.

When he pretended to be hurt by her remark, Lucy glanced around to confirm that no one was looking, then quickly pecked him on the cheek.

"Oh, be still my beating heart," Will said playfully, grasping at his chest and rolling back his eyes.

Lucy slapped him on the shoulder. "You are impossible," she said.

From a distance they heard Henry shout, "Will! Come on!"

Suddenly the playfulness was gone. Will reached out and took Lucy's hands again. "I will think of you constantly," he said.

Her eyes swelling with tears, she answered, "Will, I am afraid."

"I expect everything will be all right," he said, suppressing the "Me too," which had nearly escaped from his lips.

"Oh, Will," Lucy said, suddenly losing her reserve and throwing her arms around him, sobbing. "Please be careful."

Will returned the hug, battling back tears of his own. Once the lump in his throat had receded, he said, "I love you, Lucy."

"I love you, too," she answered, hugging him more tightly.

After a few moments, he said quietly, "I've got to go now."

Lucy reluctantly released him, wiped her eyes, and tried to compose herself. She nodded, biting her lip. As Will turned and walked away, she called out with a cracking voice, "God be with you."

By the time Will reached his family they could hear an officer shouting, "Gather 'round, men. Form by companies."

Colonel Lynch stepped up on a crate and shouted, "Never mind that. Just gather 'round."

When the men were all gathered and quieted, Lynch drew his sword, raised it above his head and exclaimed, "Liberty!"

"Liberty!" the men echoed immediately.

"Men," Lynch said loudly, scanning the group, "the governor has ordered us to report to General Greene. We are to assist him in repelling the British invaders. And with God's help it shall be done."

There was a murmur of assent among the men.

"Now," Lynch continued, "I see that many of you have brought your horses. I will not forbid you from bringing them, but General Greene has advised that the army will not provide forage for them. If you bring them, you are responsible for obtaining their feed. That will be very difficult to do. So, I strongly urge you to consider leaving them behind."

The pronouncement gave Henry some relief. The

family only owned one horse, and Caesar was needed on the farm. Bringing him along had not been an option.

Suddenly there was an excited stir in the crowd. They all turned in the direction of the commotion and saw a body of riders approaching. "It's Tom Watkins' cavalry," Henry said, recognizing the men.

But as the horsemen drew closer, the murmuring among the men intensified, and they began jostling for a view, voices asking, "Is it him?" and "Is that who I think it is?" It was more attention than the arrival of the company of Prince Edward County mounted militia would ordinarily garner.

The Lawtons spotted the rider who was causing the excitement just as Jacob walked up, wearing a smile. "Do you see him?" he asked, nodding in the man's direction.

"Is that Peter Francisco?!" Arthur exclaimed.

"Indeed, it is," Jacob replied.

Standing nearly seven feet tall and weighing almost 300 pounds, 20-year-old Francisco was one of the most instantly recognizable men in Virginia. Credited with amazing feats of strength and bravery while serving as a Continental regular at the Battles of Brandywine and Stony Point, he had become the most famous private in the American army. To save a cannon from capture during the retreat at Camden it was said that he had hoisted the twelve-hundred-pound gun up onto his massive shoulders and carried it off by himself. A quiet man, Peter Francisco could not avoid attracting attention wherever he went.

"How did Peter Francisco end up in Tom Watkins' cavalry?" Henry asked.

Jacob chuckled. "Seems he heard there was going

to be a fight and he didn't want to miss it. He just joined up with the first group he found on the way, and that turned out to be Captain Watkins' cavalry."

"I sure am glad he's on our side," Arthur said in admiring awe as Francisco rode past, seeming to dwarf his horse.

"I feel kind of sorry for that poor horse," Will said.

"All right men, settle down," Lynch shouted. "Say your goodbyes, gentlemen. We will depart in ten minutes."

Henry and his sons returned to the wagon, where the others were waiting for them. Martha stepped forward and wrapped Will and Arthur in a hug, shedding a few tears as she did.

Henry stepped over to Stephen. "I'm counting on you to look after things, son," he said.

The boy nodded, feeling the weight of the responsibility.

"Squire. George," Henry said, calling to them. When they drew closer, he said, "I'm depending on all of you. See that all the things that need doing get done."

"Yes, sir," Squire answered somberly, George nodding beside him.

"Now listen," he said to the three of them, turning so that Martha wouldn't hear him. "If anything should happen to us, it will be up to you all to protect Mrs. Lawton and the farm."

All three nodded, Stephen battling back a lump in his throat.

"Remember what I told you, Squire," Henry continued, looking directly at the man. "If things go badly for our side, I'm counting on you to hide and save what you can. I'm counting on you and Stephen to decide whether to stay or leave, if that day should come."

They all nodded and mumbled yessirs.

Henry shook their hands, then turned to his wife, who was still clinging to the boys.

"Martha," he said. "Have you saved a hug and kiss for me?"

She released her sons and they stepped aside, leaving her facing Henry.

After a few silent moments she spoke. "Henry Lawton," she said with a quivering jaw. "You had better come home to me."

He reached out and gathered her in a hug. "I intend to," he spoke softly into her ear. "You shall not be done with me for a good long while."

"Take care of the boys, Henry," she whispered, holding him tightly.

"They're not boys anymore, my dear," he answered with a laugh. "They may need to take care of me."

When Martha did not answer or relax her hug, he added, seriously, "I will do my best. We will look after each other."

She held on for a few more seconds, until Henry said, "We have to go now."

At that she released Henry from the hug, stepped back, wiped her eyes, and looked at all three of them.

"I am very proud of you," she said. "May God be with you."

68

Robinson Family Farm
New Garden Quaker Community
Guilford County, North Carolina
February 26, 1781

Sarah Robinson carefully wrapped clean bandages around the young man's head, assuring that they covered his wounds snugly, but not too tightly. Her father and brother had arrived with the man the night before and had placed him into her care. The man had seemed barely alive when he arrived, unconscious and with numerous deep and weeping cuts on his head, face, hands, and body. After making a straw pallet for him, she had, with difficulty, managed to get some cool water and warm milk down his throat. "Can he live, daughter?" her father had asked her. "If it be God's will," she replied.

In the 20 hours since the man's arrival he had made no movement nor shown any sign of consciousness. But it seemed to Sarah that his breathing had grown stronger. So, an hour earlier, she had removed his bandages and gently cleaned his wounds. When fresh bandages were in place, the man's face was completely covered, save for his mouth, his nostrils, and his one remaining eye. As she was inserting the final pin that would hold the new bandages in place, the man's eye suddenly popped open and in it Sarah saw an unmistakable look of panic and fear.

"Peace, good soul," she said gently. "Thou art with Friends."

The man's eye darted about, then she felt him trying to rise. She placed her hand lightly on his chest. "Peace," she said, with a comforting smile. "Thee must rest and remain quiet."

Sarah felt the man relax slightly. His eye turned to her, and he attempted to speak. But all that came out of his mangled mouth was a tortured gurgle. She saw intense pain reflected in his eye.

Sarah put her forefinger to her mouth and said gently, "Peace. Thy lips and thy tongue are too badly cut to permit thee to speak. Thee must rest them and allow them time to heal."

The man groaned and slumped back onto the pallet. After a few seconds he lifted his right arm and brought his bandaged hand into his line of sight.

Sarah lightly touched the arm and eased it back down. "Some of thy fingers are gone, but grieve them not, for the Lord has spared thy life."

The man responded by staring up at the ceiling, not attempting to look at her. She noticed a tear slide from his eye.

"I am Sarah," she said softly. "I will tend to thee until thou art well."

She waited a moment to see if the man would look back at her. When he did not, she rose and walked quietly away, sensing that he wanted to be alone.

69

Pittsylvania Courthouse
Pittsylvania County, Virginia
February 27, 1781

The militiamen were all assembled, hundreds of them, standing at attention in lines four deep, as Colonel Perkins rode slowly past them, inspecting the men. Two days earlier a shipment of muskets had arrived from the arsenal at Petersburg. Together with the arms deposited by the militiamen who had been discharged after safely delivering the Cowpens prisoners to Charlottesville, there were finally sufficient weapons to arm the county's militia and an order went out immediately, summoning them to assemble at the courthouse. As they arrived, those who did not have a suitable gun were issued one from the county arsenal.

The last few days had been tumultuous—the shock of discovering that Gus Johnson and Billy Lewis were Tories and that they had run away to join Benedict Arnold, news of the attempted murder of Wynn Bayard and the burning of his church, the suspicion that had descended upon other neighbors, and then the sudden call-up. Dodd cast a glance toward his mother, who was standing among the crowd of people who had gathered to see the men off, tears sliding down her face as she watched. She had tried desperately that morning to keep her composure, to send her sons off with dignity. But when the time came for them to leave, the strain of it broke her down, and she had wept piteously, hugging them, and praying aloud for their safe return. It pained Dodd to see her suffering.

Upon arriving at the courthouse, Elisha had fallen in with his company, while Dodd took his place in Captain Morton's company. Dodd had grown to feel a sense of camaraderie with the men he had been drilling with for nearly two months, but he could not help feeling a pang of regret. His father had tried to arrange for his transfer, but there was no time for the necessary paperwork and orders. Should the time come when he must stand in a line of battle and fight the British, he would not be standing beside his brother. Instead, he realized with grave disappointment, he would probably be standing beside George Dudley.

An otherwise amiable young man, Dudley grumbled incessantly during musters, to the annoyance of everyone else in the company. And unfortunately for Dodd, even when Dudley's mutterings were inaudible to the others, Dodd could still hear them, having the misfortune of being assigned a place right beside him. Dudley was at his worst today, complaining constantly. "Quiet down, George," Dodd whispered angrily, as Perkins trotted his horse back to the center of the line and began waving his sword above his head.

"Liberty!" the colonel shouted.

"Liberty!" the militiamen yelled back.

Perkins sheathed his sword, then pointed at the

crowd of onlookers. "Look at these people, men," he said. "Your families, your neighbors, your friends, your wives, your mothers, your sisters, your sweethearts. Remember their faces! Remember that they are trusting us to protect them, their homes, their lives, their liberty, and their honor. When the battle is raging, remember their faces," he said, sweeping his eyes across the ranks of men, "Think of the pride they will feel if we acquit yourselves with honor, and think of the shame we will bring on them if we do not."

Perkins paused, then wheeled his horse to face the crowd. "People of Pittsylvania!" he shouted. "Fellow Virginians! We leave you now to face a cruel foe, an enemy determined to subjugate and enslave us all! We go in defense of our homes and our families—in defense of you! We leave you now to meet the enemy and, with the blessings of Providence, to turn him back!"

Cheers erupted from the crowd. Dodd, both thrilled and nervous, sought and found his mother's face, seeing that tears were streaming down her cheeks.

"He's going to get us all killed," Dudley muttered.

Dodd shot an angry look at him, "Hold your tongue, George!" he hissed.

Perkins trotted away as the crowd continued to cheer. Captain Morton took a few steps forward, then turned and faced the line.

"Mount up, men. Let's go," he said.

As they were walking to the horses Dudley leaned toward Dodd and said, "I never would have agreed to be a substitute if I had known we were going to have to fight. I just did it for the money and it won't enough for this."

And I did it for Billy Lewis's horse, Dodd thought

to himself. And then Billy stole back the horse.

70

Near Hart's Mill
Orange County, North Carolina
February 28, 1781

Ransom sat up in the back of the small, abandoned cabin where he and several other troopers had spent the night. He leaned back against the wall, reached down beside the bed, opened his saddlebag, and took out his writing kit. The cabin had no windows, but through an unchinked gap in the logs the rising sun threw out a beam that landed on his lap, illuminating his writing tablet. Ransom lifted the ink bottle out of the bag and brought it into the sunbeam, seeing that there was enough ink left for a short letter. He tilted the bottle to pool the last of the ink, dipped his freshly trimmed quill into it, then began composing a letter on his last sheet of writing paper.

My dear Mother,

In case you have heard of my illness, I write to tell you that I am now fully recovered. I contracted a fever while briefly detached to Lt. Col. Lee's Legion, but I am now back with my regiment and the effects of the fever are gone.

We had a fight with some Tory militia a few days ago. Gus

Johnson and Billy Lewis were with the Tories and were killed in the contest. Please pass this information on to Col. Boyd and Rev. Bayard. Be cautious, Mother. The Tory presence there must be greater than we had feared.

Gen. Greene and Lord Cornwallis are like two wildcats, circling each other, snarling and growling. They will fight soon, and that fight will decide the fate of Virginia. If we are defeated and if the armies come into Virginia, you must leave at once. Make your plans now, Mother. I beg you. The horrors that accompany this war are unspeakable and you will not be safe.

Keep us in your prayers, dear Mother.

Your ever devoted son,

R

His abbreviated signature took the last drop of his ink. Ransom blew gently across the letter to dry it, then slid the paper into the saddlebag, wondering if there would be any opportunity to post it.

The sunbeam had vanished, returning the room to darkness. He sat silently for a minute, enveloped in sadness, then reached up and wiped away a tear. He squeezed his eyes shut, then, after a quick silent prayer, began scratching his empty quill across his writing tablet.

My dearest Jennie,

I finally understand the source of your coldness to me and why you have broken my heart. As I think back on your father's convictions, it is clear to me now that I should have understood yours. But Jennie, I did not.

I have now added a great burden of grief and pain to the weight of my heartbreak. If you have grown to hate me, now you will hate me infinitely more.

I remember when Billy got his first pony and how he insisted on racing me, even before he could sit safely in the saddle. I have many fond memories, Jennie, of his playfulness and I recall now, with wrenching pain, how he and I shared a deep devotion to you.

I did not kill Billy, but I saw him killed and he is dead because of me. The Tory militia had mistaken us for Tarleton's cavalry and Col. Lee used that mistake to surround them. Had I not been there, Billy and all the others would have been captured and paroled. But before that could be accomplished, he and Gus Johnson recognized me, and fighting began.

I killed Gus. I do not regret it, Jennie. Had I not done so, he would surely have killed me, and he would have enjoyed doing it.

Billy fought bravely. As he was preparing to fire his gun, I struck him, intending only to disable him, then watched helplessly as other troopers fell on him and all his comrades, killing nearly all of them. For your sake, Jennie, I would have saved Billy had I been able.

These are savage times. I grieve for Billy. I grieve when I imagine how you will suffer when you learn of his death. And, yes, I grieve knowing that our breach may now be irreparable.

Perhaps you will learn that although the Tory militia was defeated, our fight with them alerted Col. Tarleton of our presence and allowed him to escape the trap that Col. Lee had set for him. Perhaps this will afford you some small satisfaction as you mourn.

The political sentiments of your family are deeply distressing to me, Jennie. But my love for you endures, even in the knowledge that it must remain unrequited.

Your ever devoted,

Ransom

Ransom was staring into the distance when the cabin door was suddenly flung open.

"Captain Wiatt, sir," a young trooper said. "We are moving out."

Ransom nodded, rose from the bed, and buckled on his saber.

71

Dix's Ferry
Pittsylvania County, Virginia
February 28, 1781

As Bayard approached the ferry, he looked over to the market site and was pleased to see that Rebecca was there, alongside a couple of other vendors, a blanket spread out on the ground before her. He dismounted, hitched his horse to the post and walked toward the market. As he drew closer, he noticed that Rebecca seemed restless. He sensed that something was wrong.

When Bayard was a few dozen feet away, Rebecca stepped out from behind her blanket, picked up a basket and walked rapidly toward him. "I got them sweet potatoes you asked for, Reverend," she said, not making eye contact. "I'll carry 'em up to your horse for you."

"Thank you, Rebecca," he answered, falling in step alongside her as she walked away from the market.

"What is wrong?" he whispered, his pulse quickening. Rebecca made no answer, continuing to march toward the hitching post. It was obvious to Bayard that she wanted more privacy.

When they reached the horse, Rebecca glanced nervously around, to assure they were alone. For the first time, Bayard could plainly see the look of distress on her face.

"Rebecca," he said, quietly but firmly. "What has happened?"

She turned to face him, her eyes swollen and reddened. "Oh law, Reverend," she said. "Something terrible."

"Try to calm yourself," Bayard answered, glancing quickly around before returning his eyes to hers. "Tell me."

Rebecca put the basket down and began to wring her hands. "Them two young gentlemen you sent to us…," she began.

Bayard felt a sudden chill rush over him. "What?" he exclaimed, too loudly. "My friends?" He lowered his voice. "What has happened to them?"

Rebecca wrung her hands for a few moments, then looked up and into Bayard's face. "Lawd have mercy, Reverend. They got killed, sir."

Bayard felt his head swimming. He reached out and steadied himself on the post. "Killed?" he said, incredulous. "Killed? But how…?"

Rebecca released a rush of words. "We sent them young gentlemen on to Dr. Pyle. To the King's militia. But the rebels…" she paused, before continuing. "The rebels done butchered 'em like hogs, sir. Mi' near every one of them. Like hogs. Just chopped 'em up, without showing 'em no mercy a'tall."

Bayard felt his vision blur and he struggled for words. "I don't understand," he said softly and distantly. "How? I mean…"

Rebecca interrupted him, her voice cracking and

tears rolling down her face. "The rebels come on them poor men and pretended to be King's men. Then they just cut 'em all down with no mercy. Deceived them poor men and then kilt them all. Slaughtered 'em like hogs."

Bayard, shocked, was having trouble processing the report. "All of them, Rebecca? Were none spared?" he asked, pitifully.

"There was a few that got away, sir, but only a few," she answered.

"But my friends," he said, seizing on a glimmer of hope and looking her in the eyes, "Maybe they survived."

Rebecca dropped her gaze and shook her head sadly. "We ain't found no sign of 'em."

"Have you seen their bodies?" Bayard asked.

"Once it was safe, we went to get them," she answered. "But they had done already buried all the dead. Buried them all together."

Bayard stood silently for a few moments, then said, "This is shocking news."

Rebecca nodded. "It surely is, sir. The rebels are as thick as fleas down home now. The loyal folks are suffering mighty bad."

Bayard looked back into Rebecca's face. "Is there no hope for my friends?" he asked.

She looked down and shook her head. "I 'spect not. 'Twas hundreds of loyal men with Dr. Pyle and the rebels butchered mi' near every one of 'em. Even after they had done surrendered."

Bayard let the words sink in. After a few moments he asked tersely, "Who did it?"

"It was the devil Lee," she answered, hissing the name.

Bayard felt his grief being washed away by a surge of anger. After a few seconds he spoke, struggling to keep his composure. "Go back, Rebecca. This is dangerous."

She nodded and turned away, her head still drooping.

"Rebecca," he whispered urgently.

She wiped her face and turned to face him.

"We will avenge them," he said, squinting, his brow furrowed.

She answered with a slight nod, picked up the basket, then turned and walked away.

Bayard unhitched his horse, mounted, and rode away, seething with anger and consumed with a desire for revenge.

72

Robinson Family Farm
New Garden Quaker Community
Guilford County, North Carolina
March 1, 1781

"I have brought thee some porridge and some warm milk," Sarah said pleasantly to the bandaged man, who was sitting up in the bed, his back leaning against the wall. As she gently slowly lowered a cup to the man's mouth, he turned away and faced the wall.

"I know thou art in pain," she said calmly, "but thee must try to swallow some of this."

The man shook his head, still looking away from her.

Sarah sighed. "Wilt thee have nothing?"

The man shook his head again.

She stood looking down at him for a few moments, then stepped away and put the milk and porridge down on a table. She picked up a book and stepped back over to the man's bed.

"Would thee like for me to read to thee from the Bible?" she asked.

The man shook his head, still refusing to look at her.

She looked down at him for another few moments, patiently. "I would like to have a name to call thee by," she said, her voice soft and gentle. "Is thy name Jeremiah?"

The man shook his head again, still facing the wall.

"May I call thee by that name until thou art well enough to tell me thy true name?" she asked.

For a few seconds, the man made no response. Then, without turning his face, he nodded slightly.

"I thank thee," she said gently. "That pleases me. Dost thee want to know why I chose the name Jeremiah?"

The man gave no response.

After a few seconds, Sarah continued, "I think the name Jeremiah will suit thee until thee can speak, because thy condition reminds me of some scripture from the book of Jeremiah. May I tell it to thee?"

The man continued to look at the wall, giving no answer.

"'For I will restore health unto thee, and I will heal thee of thy wounds, saith the Lord,'" Sarah said. "It is from chapter 30. That is my prayer for thee, Jeremiah," she said pleasantly.

After a few silent moments, with the man still facing the wall and making no response, she carried the Bible back to the table and put it down. Returning to the bed, she said, "I will let thee rest, Jeremiah. I will return later to see if thee hast found an appetite." She bent over, picked up the man's chamber pot, and carried it away.

73

Pine Creek Community
Bedford County, Virginia
March 1, 1781

The man Bayard knew only as "Samuelson" stared back at him across a table in a one-room cabin near the Presbyterian meetinghouse. Looking incredulously at Bayard, the man said, "You want us to kill Squire?"

"He informed on my man, Gus Johnson," Bayard replied, with a clenched jaw. "Because of him, Gus and another good man are now dead. He must be punished for what he did."

Samuelson sat silently for a few seconds, keeping his eyes locked on Bayard's. Then he said, firmly, "No. I won't do it."

"What do you mean you won't do it?!" Bayard exclaimed. "We are at war, sir!"

Samuelson stared back at him, unblinking. "Yes, we are at war," he said. "But I've known Squire my whole life. He is not the enemy."

Bayard banged his fist down on the table. "He *is* our enemy!" he said, raising his voice. "Are you not listening to me? He informed on my man and got him and another one of my men killed."

Samuelson held his stare. Swallowing an urge to mention Bayard's own role in the events leading to the death of the two men, he said evenly, "Respectfully, sir, you are not thinking clearly on this. You are allowing yourself to be driven by passion. What you are asking us to do is not war, it is mere murder."

"I cannot believe what I'm hearing," Bayard said, trembling with anger. "If you refuse to do it, then I'll do it myself."

"You will not," Samuelson answered, his voice calm and level.

Bayard pushed his chair back and stood up suddenly.

"Reverend," Samuelson said evenly. "Please sit down."

Bayard leaned over the table toward Samuelson and looked him squarely in the eyes. "The negroes must be made to understand that they are to remain quiet, sir," he said. "They must see that if they aid the rebels, there will be consequences."

"Reverend," Samuelson repeated, gesturing to Bayard's chair, "Please sit down, sir."

Bayard remained standing.

Samuelson understood the importance of keeping good relations between the two camps. He could not afford to jeopardize their ability to cooperate, especially not now. He knew he needed to defuse the situation. "There are other ways to accomplish that," he said.

Staring back at him, Bayard reluctantly lowered himself back into the chair.

"It is not necessary that we take Squire's life,"

Samuelson said. "All we need to do is strike fear in him. Then we will plant the word in the negro community as to why Squire was targeted. They will get the message. It will silence the colored people just as effectively as killing him would—indeed, it will do it even better. Leave the details to us. We will handle it."

Bayard opened his mouth to protest, then thought better of it. He sat silently for a few seconds, then said, "All right. Perhaps you are right. I will leave the matter to you."

Samuelson nodded, rose from his chair, and extended his hand. Bayard stood, took Samuelson's hand, and shook it.

"You have taken a risk coming here this way," Samuelson said. "Respectfully, sir, we must remain cautious."

Bayard nodded, released his grip, and turned toward the door. Yes, we must remain cautious, he thought to himself as he left the house and walked to his horse. But we must also disrupt the enemy.

74

South side of Alamance Creek
Orange County, North Carolina
March 1, 1781

Ransom clasped his hands together and blew over his fingers, which were growing numb in the frigid night air. He and his troop had been on patrol all night, spread out across the Carolina countryside. He could not remember the last time he had felt warm.

General Greene had been playing a game of cat and mouse with Cornwallis for the past week, marching his men to a different camp every day, while anxiously awaiting the arrival of militia reinforcements. The constant marching, as much as 30 miles a day, baffled and frustrated the men, as they could detect no obvious purpose for it. Sometimes they would march away to a new camp, then return the very next day to the place they started from. Of course, if Greene's own men were confused by his movements, so were the British, who could not tell from one day to the next whether the enemy was advancing or withdrawing. And the constant movement of the American army kept the local Loyalists off balance and prevented them from organizing.

While Greene marched his army back and forth across central North Carolina, always staying within a dozen miles of Cornwallis, he dispatched Colonel Williams and his light corps to act as a screen between the British and the main American army. And, in turn, Williams dispatched Colonel Washington and his dragoons to act as a screen between the British and the light corps. If Cornwallis should launch an attack, it was the job of the dragoons to detect it and sound an alert. So, Ransom and his men rode wearily through the bitterly cold Carolina nights, keeping a watchful eye on the British army.

Ransom's horse jerked its head up and snorted, startled by a sound, the animal's breath visible in the moonlight. Within moments, Ransom heard it too. Movement in the woods behind him. He edged his mount around and gripped the hilt of his saber.

He relaxed when he heard a voice in the woods call out the sign. Ransom gave the countersign and two riders emerged. He saw that one of them was one of his troopers and the other appeared to be a militia officer. When they drew closer, he recognized Joseph Graham. The men exchanged nods.

"Captain Graham is asking to see the colonel," the trooper said.

"Thank you, Private," Ransom said to the trooper. "I'll take it from here. Return to your post."

The trooper nodded and rode away.

"Come with me," Ransom said to Graham, as he turned his horse and rode slowly away.

Graham pulled alongside him. "How far away are the British?" he asked.

"About a mile," Ransom said, gesturing to the south. "Maybe closer. We should ride quietly."

Graham nodded.

After a few minutes, a voice in the dark called out the sign. Ransom answered with the countersign, and they rode forward, soon coming into sight of several dragoons. Colonel Washington was one of them.

"What is it, Ransom?" he asked.

"This is Captain Graham, sir," Ransom answered. "He is with General Pickens' command. He says he has a message for you."

"Colonel Williams sent me, sir," Graham said. "I am to reconnoiter the enemy position in preparation for an attack."

"An attack?" Washington said. "I haven't been told anything about an attack."

"I have been instructed to advise you of it, sir," Graham said.

"That was thoughtful," Washington said, his tone betraying his annoyance and disapproval. "Does General Pickens approve of an attack?"

"Colonel Williams requested permission to attack and General Greene has authorized it, sir," Graham answered, evading the question. "The attack is to commence at two o'clock. It will be led by Colonel Lee."

"What?" Washington replied, incredulous. "Does Colonel Lee approve of an attack?"

Graham squirmed, not answering.

"How did Colonel Lee respond to the order, Captain? Please speak freely, sir," Washington said, insistently.

Graham hesitated, then replied, "Colonel Lee would prefer that we attack while the enemy is on the march."

"Of course he would," Washington said. "What did he say about us attacking now, while the enemy is encamped before us?"

Graham sighed. "Colonel Lee said an attack now would be rash and ruinous, sir," he answered.

Washington stared at him for a few moments then said, "Have you ever known Harry Lee to turn down an opportunity to attack?"

"General Greene overruled Colonel Lee's objection, sir and the attack is to commence at two o'clock," Graham replied.

Washington shook his head. "Four hours from now? General Greene has grown impatient."

"Colonel Williams advises that we must not lose an opportunity to strike at the British detachment at our front," Graham said. "We must hit them before they unite with the rest of their army."

"Detachment?" Washington replied, shaking his head again. "Come with me, Captain."

Graham and Ransom followed as Washington rode to a clearing on a rise about 50 yards away. When they reached it, he stopped and pointed to the south. "Look, Captain," he said. "There is a sky gale ahead yonder."

Graham looked to where Washington was pointing and saw his meaning at once. There were so many campfires in the distance that it looked as if the woods were on fire.

"That is no detachment, Captain," Washington said. "That is the entire British army. We are greatly outnumbered. An attack on them could only end in disaster."

Graham stared out at the campfires for a few seconds, then stammered, "But, Colonel, my orders, sir…"

Washington interrupted him. "Please return to Colonel Williams and tell him what I said. I strongly object to this proposed attack. Tell him we should strike the British once they are spread out and on the march, but not now."

Before Graham could reply, Washington called over one of the troopers. "Sergeant," he said when the man arrived, "Escort Captain Graham back to Colonel Williams. Go quickly." He turned to Graham and continued, "Tell Colonel Williams that if he remains inclined to make this attack, I must speak to him first." Turning back to the trooper he said, "In that case, return here at a gallop to get me, Sergeant." He then turned back to Graham, "Do you understand me, Captain?"

"Yes sir, I do," Graham answered, before turning and riding away with the sergeant at a trot.

When the men were out of sight, Washington looked at Ransom. "We cannot take such a foolish risk. If our army is shattered out in this wilderness, our next line of defense may be the Potomac."

Ransom heard the colonel but made no response.

After a few silent moments, Washington said, "You seem troubled, Ransom. Do you disagree with my assessment? Speak freely, Captain."

"What?" Ransom said, absently. "Oh, no sir. I do not disagree. Pardon me, sir. I had allowed my mind to wander."

"Are you all right, Ransom?" Washington asked.

"Yes. Excuse me, sir. I, uh…" Ransom began. Then he stopped, gazed off into the distance and sighed deeply. After a few silent moments he said, quietly, "Her name is Jennie Lewis."

"What?" Washington replied. "Whose name?"

"You once asked me if I had a girl at home," Ransom said. "I did not answer you honestly. I did have a girl there. Her name is Jennie. Jennie Lewis."

Sensing that the story was a painful one, Washington did not reply, instead just waiting silently to see if Ransom would choose to continue. After a few seconds, he did.

"When I left home for Williamsburg, we had an understanding between us," Ransom said. "Nothing announced formally, but an understanding nonetheless." Ransom paused, seeming in doubt as to whether to say more. After a few seconds he continued. "Not long after I joined the regiment, her letters stopped. On my few visits home over the years, she has avoided me. When I did manage to see her, she wouldn't even look at me."

Ransom fell silent for a while. Just when it seemed to Washington that he wasn't going to say any more, he continued. "For years I have racked my brain, wondering what had happened. Was there another man? That did not appear to be the case. Had I somehow offended her? If so, I could not imagine how."

He turned and looked into Washington's face. "Last week I finally discovered the answer. I discovered that she and her family are Tories. It makes perfect sense now. She broke off relations with me when I joined the regiment. Her love has turned to hate—because we have chosen different sides."

Ransom turned away, and the two men sat silently for several minutes.

Eventually, Washington said, "This war has brought so much pain," at a loss for anything better to say.

"I saw her brother with those Tories we fought last week," Ransom said, still looking away. "He was with another boy from home. They saw me, and that's how the fight started." After a long pause, he said, "I saw Billy get killed, her brother I mean." He fell silent again, before saying, "I've known him all my life. He should have been my brother-in-law. There can be no doubt now. I have lost Jennie forever."

Several minutes later, after another long uncomfortable pause, Ransom turned to Washington and said, "Pardon me, sir. I have had trouble clearing my mind." He then turned his horse, preparing to ride away.

"Ransom," Washington said, stopping him.

Ransom turned to face him. "I desperately need you here. That is the truth. But if you need a furlough, I will get it for you."

Ransom shook his head. "No, sir," he said. "Thank you, but I am all right. This too shall pass."

Washington nodded, then sighed. "When all of this is over," he said, "this killing, this destruction, then it will be a time to heal. We will have lots of work to do."

"To every thing there is a season," Ransom answered, with a slight smile. "Thank you, sir."

They were interrupted by a rider coming at a gallop. It was the sergeant who had left with Graham. "Colonel Williams wants to see you, sir," he said breathlessly.

Washington looked at Ransom, nodded, then turned and rode off with the sergeant.

75

Near Clapp's Mill
Orange County, North Carolina
March 2, 1781

One of the North Carolina militiamen, a man from Lincoln County who Jones knew only as Tom, plodded over to the campfire, his face streaked with gunpowder. He dropped wearily onto a log across from Jones and his sons. "You South Carolina boys was smart to sit that one out," he said, staring into the fire.

"We didn't sit nothin' out," Tate Jones fired back, stung by the suggestion.

Tom looked up at him. "Seems like General Pickens found something else for y'all to do today. Something that wouldn't get you kilt. He was looking out for y'all. I don't blame him."

After meeting with Washington, Williams had canceled the planned attack, at the last minute. Instead, he allowed Lee to look for an opportunity to catch the British on the move. Lee took his dragoons, some Continental regulars, a couple hundred militiamen,

Graham's cavalry, and a squad of Catawba Indians, and went off in search of the enemy.

"What happened?" Jones asked.

Tom spit into the fire, then answered. "When Colonel Lee found out Tarleton was marching toward us, he set up an ambush. We laid down behind some fences and along the side of the road. Before too long here come the British and we let 'em have it. I reckon we musta killed 20 or more of 'em. The Injuns smelt 'em coming," he added with a chuckle. "They snorted like deer to let us know."

"Then what?" Jones asked.

"Well," Tom answered, "then the British ran off, but you know how they are. They won't gone long. They formed up and came back and charged us and when they did them Catawba took off like a flock of wild turkeys. The rest of us held 'em off for a while but when it started to get real hot, Colonel Lee pulled the regulars out and left us militia out there to get kilt by ourselves." He spit into the fire again. "The ones with uniforms don't reckon that us militiamen count for much, I reckon."

"It's time for us to go home, Pa," Joshua Jones said.

"Most of the North Carolina boys has done already left," Tom said. "I don't mind doing my part, but I didn't sign up to get kilt while the Continentals run off. We ain't gonna stay no longer."

"Pa?" Joshua said, looking at this father.

Jones continued staring into the fire, showing no emotion. After a few seconds he said, softly but firmly, "We gave our word."

None of them had noticed Pickens. Standing in the shadows a few yards away, he had heard the conversation. Quietly, he turned around and paced back to his tent. Once inside, he lit a candle and wrote a letter to Greene, requesting permission to return with his men to South Carolina.

76

Camp of Nathanael Greene's American Army
Buffalo Creek
Guilford County, North Carolina
March 3, 1781

The sun was setting as General Edward Stevens arrived at the little house where General Greene had established his headquarters. He dismounted, handed the reins to an orderly, and stepped inside.

Greene rose when Stevens entered, stepping forward with his hand extended. "General Stevens, I am most pleased to see you, sir."

"And I you, General," Stevens answered, shaking his hand. "I came as soon as I received your message."

A corpulent man, weighing at least 250 pounds, Stevens was a veteran officer of the Continental Line, and now a brigadier general of Virginia militia. His otherwise distinguished record had been marred by the panicked retreat of his men at the Battle of Camden six months earlier—a disgraceful stigma that he was determined to erase.

"Good. Please sit down, General," Greene said,

motioning to a stool. "Colonel Perkins has just arrived today with a regiment of militia from Pittsylvania County. I am attaching them to your command."

Stevens nodded.

"As with the men you already have," Greene continued, "some are these new men are former Continentals, most are not. Some of them have combat experience, most do not."

"What of arms and provisions?" Stevens asked.

"Most of the men are armed adequately, but some are not," Greene answered. "Colonel Perkins says they still require about 50 more guns."

"Do we have them?" Stevens asked.

Greene shook his head. "We do not. I don't even have enough good guns to properly arm the regulars." He paused, clenching and unclenching his fist. "Colonel Lynch should arrive soon with his riflemen. I have just received a letter from him saying that of the 360 men with him, 60 lack guns and flints. I am expecting General Lawson soon as well. He reports that many of his men are armed with their shotguns and hunting pieces. Likewise, I have heard from Colonel Munford. He has four or five hundred men coming, but many of them lack powder, flints, and ammunition."

Stevens sighed. "It's the same old story," he said.

"Yes, it is," Greene answered. "But there is hope. Governor Jefferson has assured me that 750 good guns from the Petersburg arsenal are on their way here."

Stevens brightened. "They will be a godsend."

"Yes," Greene said. "As will Colonel Campbell, who is on his way with over a thousand of his mountain riflemen. When all the militia are up, General, we shall strike Lord Cornwallis, with or without those guns. I do not trust the militia to wait on them."

The comment stung Stevens. "My men will do their duty, sir," he said.

"I trust that you will keep them here and keep them disciplined, General," Greene said. "The Carolinians are melting away like snow on a warm day. They seem to just come and go as they please."

"I believe that when the time comes to fight, the Carolina militia will be here," Stevens said, more hopeful than confident.

"Let us hope so," Greene answered. "Place your men in the center of the camp, General. That makes it more difficult for them to desert."

Stevens cleared his throat. "These men have made a difficult march, sir, leaving behind their families and homes. They came to fight the British," Stevens said, testily.

"Very good, General," Greene said, rising from his chair. "They will soon have their chance. Have them ready, sir. When the rest of the Virginians are up, I intend to give battle to Cornwallis."

Stevens, who had risen with Greene, nodded, turned, and left the tent.

~~~

Once they had made camp and the horses had been put up, Dodd wandered over to where his brother's company was camped. Seeing him approach, Elisha shook his head. "You shouldn't be away from your company, Dodd."

"I'm not on duty," Dodd answered.

"Still, it's better to spend time with your own
~~~

company," Elisha replied.

"George Dudley stays on me like a flea, Eli, and all he does is carp," Dodd answered. "I feel like strangling him."

Elisha chuckled, then smiled sympathetically. "When the shooting starts, you'll need to look after each other."

"I don't think he looks after anything but his own self," Dodd replied bitterly.

"I sure do miss Mama's cooking," Elisha said, as he stirred the fire.

"Me and you both," Dodd said. He turned to his brother, "Eli, ain't there no way to get me transferred to this company? Maybe if you asked again…"

Elisha interrupted him, shaking his head. "No point in trying. I've asked a half dozen times already."

Dodd kicked the ground.

"There's a lot of good men in your company, Dodd," Elisha said. "Spend your time with them, not with George."

"It just ain't that easy," Dodd said, with a whine.

"Now what's that you were saying about carping?" Elisha asked playfully. Seeing that his brother was hurt by the remark, he added, "We need to keep our minds on more important things, Dodd. The British army is just over yonder," he said, tossing his head toward the south. "Let's stay focused on what we're here for."

Dodd looked away, bit his lip, and nodded.

77

Bayard Homestead
Halifax County, Virginia
March 4, 1781

"Company," Ruth Bayard said, without looking up from her sewing.

Bayard had already heard the horse and was stepping to the window when she spoke.

Recognizing the approaching rider, he said, "It's Colonel Boyd."

Ruth put down her sewing, stood up, and walked over to the hearth.

Bayard opened the door and greeted Boyd as he mounted the stairs to the porch. "Come on in and warm up, Colonel," he said, extending his hand.

Boyd shook his hand warmly and stepped inside.

"Good morning, Colonel," Ruth said with a smile, as she stirred a pot hanging above the fireplace.

"Good morning, Mrs. Bayard," he answered pleasantly.

"Hang up your coat and hat, George, and come sit by the fire," Bayard said.

Boyd hung his hat on the peg by the door. As he

was taking off his coat he said, "Thank you, sir. I don't mind if I do."

The men walked across the room and sat down in chairs by the fireplace. Ruth came over and handed them both cups.

"Thank you kindly," Boyd answered, taking the cup. "This is sure to warm me up."

He and Bayard sipped the cider as Ruth returned to her sewing.

"Reverend," Boyd said. "I expect you know why I'm here."

Bayard shook his head. "A social visit I presume."

"When I heard this morning that you are giving up your church I rode straight here," Boyd said.

"Well…," Bayard began.

Boyd interrupted him. "There is no need to do that, sir," Boyd protested. "We'll help you build it back. Every good man in both counties will lend a hand, Baptist or not. You ought to know that."

Bayard smiled knowingly. "I thank you, sir. But it isn't that."

Boyd lifted his eyebrows. "So, you're not giving up the church."

"I am," Bayard answered. "But not because the building is gone."

"I'm afraid I don't understand," Boyd said.

"We're going to rebuild the meetinghouse and we're going to go on trying to save your lost souls," Bayard said with a smile. "But I have resigned as pastor."

"But why?" Boyd asked.

Bayard took a sip of cider, then made a wave with his left hand. "Time to let a younger man take over," he said.

Boyd looked at him, puzzled. "A younger man?" he

asked, skeptically.

"Well, George, that is my official explanation," Bayard said. "But there is another reason."

"May I…" Boyd began, cautiously.

"The truth of the matter, sir, is that I want to give my undivided attention to rooting out the Tories," Bayard said.

"I see," Boyd answered, looking solemnly at Bayard. "You are a true Patriot, Reverend. Your selfless devotion to the cause is admirable, sir. Most admirable."

78

Camp of Nathanael Greene's American Army
Buffalo Creek
Guilford County, North Carolina
March 4, 1781

Stevens stormed into Greene's headquarters at dawn, holding a piece of paper in his right hand. Greene looked up at him and said, "See to your command, General. We march in a half hour."

"General Greene, sir," Stevens said, "I respectfully request that you reconsider this order. It will have a terrible effect on morale, sir."

Greene rose slowly to his feet, looking Stevens in the eyes. "Remember yourself, General Stevens," he said, sternly. "The commanding general's orders are not subjects for debate."

Stevens composed himself. "Begging the general's pardon, sir," he said, more calmly. "I only want to make sure that you are aware of all the circumstances, sir. These horses are the private property of the men, sir."

Greene nodded. "I know that, General. Our

dragoons are greatly in need of new mounts. I could easily have impressed horses belonging to your men to satisfy that need. Aware of the effect it might have on morale, I have chosen not to do so. Waiting on the new horses to arrive from Virginia puts us at some risk, but I am accepting that risk to avoid offending your men."

"Yes, General," Stevens began, "but…"

Greene cut him off. "There is no forage for their horses, sir. What little we have must be used to keep the horses needed by our cavalry and trains fit for duty. Besides, the militia are infantry. They aren't armed or trained for mounted duty. And having horses nearby increases the chance that they will run, or desert."

There is it again, Stevens thought. Distrust, contempt even. He reddened, not daring to reply.

"I have issued the order advisedly, General Stevens," Greene said. "I am mindful of your concerns, sir, but my order is to be obeyed."

~~~

Captain Morton stood facing his men, having called them into assembly. Their guns slung across their shoulders, most were holding saddlebags.

"Men," Morton said, scanning their faces, "General Greene has ordered that all horses belonging to the rank-and-file militiamen be returned to Virginia at once. Only officers will be permitted to keep their mounts."

A wave of indignation swept over the men and a dozen questions and objections were flung back at the captain.

"Men, men," Morton said, holding up his hand but having little effect on them.
~~~

After a few seconds of disorder, Lieutenant Robertson stepped up beside Morton, scowling. "Quiet down!" he shouted. "Attention!"

Robertson's firmness settled them down. Only a few scattered murmurs continued, and they too ceased when Robertson's fierce glare found the offenders.

"No one is happy with this order, men," Morton said. "But there is nothing here for the horses to eat."

"Not much for us to eat either," Dudley muttered.

"Two men from each company are to be detailed to take the horses back," Morton said.

"I'll do it!" Dudley exclaimed, answered by scowls from his comrades.

"The men will be chosen by lot," Morton said.

As the men began to become restless again, Robertson leaned over and whispered to Morton, "May I, sir."

"Yes, of course," he answered.

"Listen up, men!" Robertson shouted, getting their attention. "We're about to fight Cornwallis and you all know what is at stake. We are not going to fight him on horseback. The horses are a hindrance to us now. General Greene knows that. These men in General Greene's army," he swept his hand out toward the camp, "have marched hundreds of miles, many of them barefoot, to save our country. Are we so weak that we cry like babies if required to go a few days on foot? Now, show yourselves to be men and Patriots and quit this petulant fussing!"

"Listen to him," Dudley whispered. "He gets to keep *his* horse."

Never in his life had Dodd more wanted to punch someone in the face.

79

On the Salisbury Road
Near Low's Mill
Orange County, North Carolina
March 4, 1781
About 10 p.m.

A hundred horses, each carrying one of Tarleton's dragoons, plodded along the frozen road, dimly lit by the moonlight that occasionally shone through breaks in the clouds. The men and their horses were tired and hungry, but Tarleton was determined to find the mounted rebel militia that they had skirmished with earlier in the day. If they are still out here, Tarleton thought, they will be on this road, and if they are on this road, I will destroy them.

Captain Ogilvie trotted up alongside Tarleton and said, quietly, "Mounted militia approaching, Colonel. About 80 or so."

"Ours or theirs?" Tarleton asked.

"I don't know," Ogilvie answered. "Impossible to tell. They haven't seen us."

Tarleton's eyes flashed. "Deploy the men, Captain.

Prepare to attack."

"Yes, sir," Ogilvie replied.

As he turned to ride away, Tarleton added, "Do it quietly, Captain."

Ogilvie nodded and rode down the column, whispering commands. The dragoons began to fan out, wrapping their sword knots around their wrists.

Tarleton rode out a few yards ahead of the men and waited in the center of the road. A few minutes later the van of the militia column appeared.

Tarleton rose in his stirrups and shouted, "Identify yourselves!"

The shout startled Captain John Bryan, riding at the head of the column. "Halt!" he said, bringing the column to a stumbling stop.

The man riding beside him leaned over and whispered, "What should we say?"

Bryan and his men had been riding for three hours, coming from Rowan County in answer to Cornwallis' call and riding at night to reduce the chance of being intercepted.

"They might be rebels, John," the man said. "Remember what happened to Pyle."

The hesitation convinced Tarleton. "Sound the attack," he yelled, as he spurred his horse and charged into the column.

As the dragoons fell on them, chopping and slicing them from all sides, Bryan's men panicked. Those who could, galloped away. The rest were cut down.

Just as Tarleton ran down and sabered one of the men, who had been trying to escape on foot, Ogilvie rode up, blood-spattered and nearly out of breath. "They are Loyalists, Colonel," he said.

"What? Are you sure?" Tarleton spat back, casting

a glance at the sabered man, who had gotten to his feet and was stumbling toward the woods.

"Yes, sir," Ogilvie replied. "They're from Rowan County. King's men."

"Damn!" Tarleton muttered. "Fools."

He shot an angry look at Ogilvie. "Take your troop and go after them. Try to bring them back."

"Yes, Colonel," Ogilvie answered before rushing away.

But when the dragoons rode back into camp hours later, they brought along only a few of the militiamen, and most of those were wounded. The others ran all the way back home. And stayed there.

80

Lawton Farm
Bedford County, Virginia
March 4, 1781
Near midnight

A hooded man crept silently toward the little house, an unlit pitch torch in his hand. He dashed out to a walnut tree a few feet from the house, then bent over to light the torch. As he did, a powerful blow knocked him off his feet and sent him sprawling, the unlit torch falling by his side.

Something Squire had eaten at supper had disagreed with him and he had spent much of the night shivering in the privy. He had been just about to return home when he heard the muffled sounds of horses nearby in the woods. He eased quietly out of the privy and some movement nearby caught his eye. He edged closer and saw a man wearing a hood and carrying a pine torch, sneaking toward his house. Squire quietly approached the man from behind, and when the man bent down to light the torch, Squire landed a roundhouse punch that knocked him to the ground, senseless.

Squire stepped over the man and reached down to pull off the hood. Then suddenly he felt the sharp pain of a knife plunging into his side. He spun around to face his attacker, and as he did the blade tore through his body, opening a deep wound. He briefly saw the second man, also wearing a hood, and he drew back his right arm, but before he could swing it his knees buckled, and he dropped to the ground.

As Squire fell, the second man rushed over and helped the first man to his feet, murmuring something. As they hurried away, the second man picked up the torch, lit it, and tossed it into the barn's open hayloft door. The men disappeared into the woods, as the hay burst into flames.

Squire struggled to his feet, hearing the sound of horses running away. He staggered to the door of his house and fell against it. "George," he said, unable to raise his voice much above a rasping whisper.

In a second the boy was at the door, in his underclothes, his eyes wide with fright. "Daddy!" he exclaimed.

"Ring the bell," Squire rasped. "Wake up the white folks. The barn is on fire."

At that, George looked over to the barn and saw flames beginning to shoot out of the loft door. He scrambled over to the bell, clanged it twice, then continued on to the Lawtons' house, screaming.

Squire stumbled over to the barn door and staggered inside. Caesar, panicked, was banging against the walls and door of his stall as the heat from the fire intensified. With one hand pressed to his wound, Squire reached out with his other hand, threw up the latch, and pushed open the stall door. When the door opened, Caesar bolted through it, knocking Squire to the ground.

As the terrified horse raced out of the barn door a burning timber swung down and struck him on the rump. He whinnied, kicked wildly, then disappeared into the night.

Unable to get to his feet, Squire began crawling back toward the barn door, the thick smoke choking him. He only managed to move a few feet before he was overcome. Everything went dark and his head fell unconscious onto the barn floor.

Moments later, George and Stephen rushed into the burning, smoke-filled building, a wet blanket draped over their heads. They each grabbed one of Squire's arms and dragged him toward the door. Their eyes and throats burning, the boys managed to pull him through the door and into the night air just seconds before the barn collapsed behind them.

Martha Lawton rushed over and fell to her knees, wrapping her arms around the boys and exclaiming "Thank you, Jesus!" over and over. Then she released them and turned to Squire, gently rolling him over.

"We must move him farther away from the fire," she said urgently. The three of them lifted him and carried him a few yards closer to the house. "Sit him down here," she said, and they lowered him to the ground.

It was only then that she noticed that Squire was bleeding.

She turned to George, whose eyes were wide with fear. "Ring the bell, George!" she said. The boy rushed away and began vigorously clanging the bell.

"Bring me some rags and my kit," she said to Stephen, who turned and rushed toward the house. "And bring the lantern," she yelled after him, as he ran away.

She turned back to Squire, tears streaming down her face, and began gently pulling away his bloody shirt. In the distance she could hear the sound of neighbors hurrying toward them.

81

South of Swepsonville Ford
Orange County, North Carolina
March 5, 1781

Washington was peering through a spyglass when Parsons spoke. "There's two dozen of them."

Washington passed the spyglass to Ransom, who put it to his eye and gazed out at the herd of cattle a few hundred yards away. There were men scattered along the edges of the herd, driving the cattle, muskets slung over their shoulders. "No pickets, no guards," Ransom said. "It will be easy to take them."

"Idiots," Washington muttered.

"Thieves," Parsons said. "And now their time is up."

They had been on the trail of the men most of the day, after a local Patriot came into camp and reported that Tories were driving a herd of cattle to Cornwallis. Searching for them, they had passed three plundered homesteads, where distraught women told them the Tories were supplementing their herd by stealing the cattle off the farms of Patriots—milk cows and draft animals included. By the time the dragoons located the Tories and their herd, they were seething with anger.

"We'll swing around and block them from the front and flanks," Washington said, pocketing the spyglass. "We should be in place in ten minutes." He turned to Ransom. "Stay behind them with your troop, Captain. In ten minutes, charge them. Your attack will be our signal to close in."

Ransom nodded. "Yes, sir. With pleasure, sir."

Washington looked away for a moment, then said, absently, "What is the penalty for cattle theft?"

"Hanging," Parsons answered quickly.

"And yet," Washington continued, still looking off into the distance, "these thieves won't hang. If we take them as prisoners, we have no way to keep them. And we're soldiers. We can't try them. So, we'll have to parole them. Then they'll disappear and probably never answer for their crimes."

Washington fell silent, letting his words sink in. "Seems unjust," he added.

Ransom and Parsons exchanged a quick glance, confirmation that they understood the colonel's meaning.

Washington looked at Parsons. "Stay out of sight as you get into position, Captain. Let's go."

Washington and Parsons rode away in opposite directions and Ransom returned to his troop. As he came into sight of his men, he motioned for them to approach, and they gathered around him.

"The Tory thieves are ahead, about 400 yards over that ridge," he said, pointing. "We'll get as close as we can, without letting them see us. Then, on my signal, we will charge them. The rest of the regiment will take them from the front and flanks."

The men nodded. A few muttered their understanding.

"Let's try not to stampede the cattle, gentlemen. The army hasn't had a cooked meal in three days," Ransom said, answered by a few smiles.

"What about the Tories?" one of the men asked.

Ransom paused, looking up into the sky reflectively. After a few seconds, he drew his saber and wrapped the sword knot around his wrist. "No quarter," he said.

82

Lawton Farm
Bedford County, Virginia
March 5, 1781

Squire leaned on his son, as Martha led him to a waiting buckboard. "It don't seem right leaving you here, Miz Lawton," he said, wincing as he spoke.

"Enough of that, Squire," she replied. "There will be men staying here with us until the danger has passed. In the meantime, you should be with your wife. She can nurse you back to health better than anyone else."

Lucretia Thomas, Martha's widowed sister-in-law, stood by the wagon as they approached, her long gray hair descending from beneath a light blue bonnet. "I meant to ask you, Martha dear. Did y'all ever find that poor horse?"

As Martha held his hand, Squire gingerly eased himself up into the buckboard. "Stephen is out searching for him now," she answered. "I expect we'll have them both home by dark."

As Squire settled himself in, George appeared from

behind the house, carrying a large sack.

"What is this, Martha?" Lucretia asked, as George dropped the sack into the wagon.

"Just a little cornmeal, dear," Martha answered. "I'm hoping Squire's big appetite returns soon."

"I won't hear of it!" Lucretia said, stamping her foot. "Take it away," she said to George curtly.

The boy looked at Martha for instructions.

"Now Lucretia," Martha answered gently. "I will be offended if you do not allow me to send it. I know having to tend to Squire will keep Annie from her duties and it's only fair that we lighten your load."

"Martha, I won't take it," Lucretia replied. "After your loss," she gestured toward the remains of the barn, "you must be in need."

"But we are not, dear," Martha answered. "Other than a little hay, we lost nothing of value."

Squire raised his eyebrows, thinking of everything that had gone up in smoke inside that barn.

"We have plenty," Martha continued. "Thanks be to God."

"Very well, dear," Lucretia replied. "But you will please let us know if you need anything."

"Of course, I will," Martha answered. Then, as if suddenly remembering something, she said, "There is something else I need to send too. Can you come inside a moment?"

"Yes, of course," Lucretia answered, following Martha to the house.

Once the women were gone, George stepped up the wagon and spoke to his father. "I want to go and stay with Mama too," he said, plaintively.

Squire shook his head. "You just stay here and do like you're told. Look after Miz Lawton."

"But it ain't fair, Daddy," the boy said with moistening eyes. "How come we can't live together like a family, like other folks do. It ain't right."

Squire had taught his son to never "talk back." He furrowed his brow but just as he was about to rebuke the boy, he thought better of it. He reached out his hand and George took it.

"You're right, son," Squire said, looking into the boy's sad face. "It ain't fair and it ain't right. Ain't nothing in the world right about it. But, at least for now, that's just the way it is."

"But, Daddy, I…" George began.

His father interrupted him. "Do as I say, George. You stay here and help look after Miz Lawton."

George looked down, battling back tears. He nodded hesitantly.

"You're getting to be a man, son," Squire said. "You stay here like you ought to and you will make your mama proud." As soon as the words were out of his mouth, Squire began to wonder if they were true.

83

Camp of Nathanael Greene's American Army
Boyd's Mill
Reedy Fork
Guilford County, North Carolina
March 5, 1781

Greene stood facing William Campbell, the buckskin clad hero of the Battle of King's Mountain. "The word 'disappointed' is not strong enough, Colonel Campbell," he said. "I was informed that you were bringing at least a thousand riflemen and you have arrived with only sixty."

The towering redheaded Scotsman squinted and took a breath, taming his temper. "I have done my best, General. Most of the boys wouldn't leave their homes and families to the mercy of the Cherokees, as the brave men who came with me have."

The remark hit home. "Yes," Greene said, more calmly. "And we are glad to have them, sir. But I am forced to reconsider my plans, which depended heavily on a thousand of your crack shots."

Campbell shook his head slightly and lowered his

voice. "Our county lieutenant behaves like a puppy sometimes, General. It was him that got the boys so worked up over the Indians."

"We shall make do, sir," Greene said, holding out his hand. As Campbell shook it, Greene said, "I am attaching you to General Pickens' command, with the Light Corps. I expect your men will have plenty to do over the next few weeks."

~~~

A hundred yards away, Dodd, footsore and exhausted, was pulling off his shoes, noticing that the soles had begun to separate. "Another day like this one," he said, speaking to no one, "and I'll be marching barefoot."

He groaned when he looked up and saw George Dudley hurrying over. "Did you hear, Dodd? Them over the mountain boys was smart enough to stay home. Didn't but about a dozen of 'em come, and I don't expect they'll be sticking around too long either."

"Let me alone, George," Dodd said, refusing to look at him.

"Plenty of the Virginia boys have been slipping away lately," George said, drawing closer to Dodd. He lowered his voice, "Going back home. Going to get their horses back while they still can."

"Hold your tongue, George," Dodd said. "I don't want to hear it."

"They say it's easy," George continued. "Just wait till dark then wander off. General Greene can't spare nobody to go tracking 'em down."

Dodd suddenly turned and glared at George, startling him. "You don't give a fig about liberty, do
~~~

you George? You can't wait to start licking redcoat boots, can you?"

George stared back at Dodd, seemingly surprised.

"I just want to stay alive, Dodd Lightfoot," he said. "You should too."

84

Camp of Lord Cornwallis' British Army
Smith's Plantation
West of the Haw River
Orange County, North Carolina
March 5, 1781

Cornwallis rolled out a map onto a table in the house he had commandeered for his headquarters. He motioned for Tarleton and Webster to come nearer, and he moved a candle closer to illuminate the map as he spoke.

"The countryside is crawling with rebels and the King's friends in this part of the province have been too timid to venture out," he began, looking up at the officers. "Consequently, I have been totally destitute of information, and we have lost a very favorable opportunity of attacking the rebel army. But now, finally, we have reliable intelligence and another promising opportunity."

He pointed to the map and Tarleton and Webster leaned in to see. "General Greene has fallen back to this place called Boyd's, on the Reedy River." He looked up at the two officers. "There are thousands of Virginia militia on the march to join him. It is apparent that he will avoid risking an action until his reinforcements arrive.

"But he has made an error, perhaps a fatal one," Cornwallis continued. "Our informers report that the enemy's light troops and militia are still near us, posted carelessly at separate plantations, here and here," he said, pointing at the map. He looked up at the faces of the officers. "Notice that not only are those forces separated from the main rebel army, but they have the river at their backs."

Tarleton and Webster nodded, understanding. Tarleton was smiling.

"We must strike them," Cornwallis said, leaning toward them, with both palms on the table. "With a vigorous assault we can destroy their light troops and scatter their militia. If General Greene comes up to protect them, we have the opportunity to destroy his army too, before his reinforcements arrive."

"Splendid," Tarleton said, looking down at the map. "A fine opportunity, as you say, my lord. A fine opportunity indeed." He looked up at Cornwallis. "And a fine opportunity to carve up the rebel cavalry as well, sir."

"What are your orders, m'lord?" Webster asked.

"You two shall lead the attack," Cornwallis answered. "You will also have the Guards, the Fusiliers, the Jaegers, and the artillery. A formidable force."

"Aye, m'lord," Webster answered, nodding.

"Begin your march at 3 o'clock. Strike swiftly, gentlemen," Cornwallis said, his eyes flashing. "Punish them. Drive them into the river!"

85

The Battle of Weitzel's Mill
Reedy Fork
Guilford County, North Carolina
March 6, 1781

Ransom leaned forward in the saddle, peering out into pre-dawn fog, straining to hear. Something was out there. Then he heard it again—in the distance, the muffled sound of creaking wagon wheels, the clunking of canteens, a cough. The sound of an army on the move. He turned to the trooper beside him and said softly, "Fetch the colonel."

Washington rode up a minute later. "Listen," Ransom said, pointing ahead.

Washington turned his head and closed his eyes. After a few seconds they popped open. "My God," he said. He motioned for a trooper to approach. "Get to Colonel Williams immediately. Inform him that the British are marching on us in force. Go!"

The man turned, spurred his horse, and galloped away.

Washington called over another dragoon, "Find

Colonel Lee," he said. "To reach him, you will have to swing around the front of the enemy column," he said, pointing. "Tell him we must block the British attack."

"Yes, sir," the man answered, before sprinting away.

~~~

When Tarleton's dragoons came thundering out of the fog, Campbell's pickets were taken completely by surprise. One of them, stumbling away, managed to get off a warning shot before he was cut down.

The riflemen at the camp, all veterans of frontier warfare, were on their feet in a flash, priming their guns without awaiting orders. When the first British dragoon appeared out of the mist, he was immediately struck by three rifle balls.

"Fall back, men!" Campbell yelled, pulling on his boots. "Load as you withdraw!"

Tarleton rode out past the fallen dragoon and saw the Virginians hurrying away, abandoning their camp.

He called out to Ogilvie. "Form for the attack, Captain," he said, with a lilting aristocratic confidence. "Let's finish them off."

As Ogilvie shouted the commands, Tarleton turned back toward the fleeing rebels, about 300 yards away across an open field. Then he noticed some movement, coming from the direction of the rising sun. Trotting out onto the field, between him and the rebel militia, came a body of about 60 rebel dragoons. Moments later, from the opposite direction, sixty more rushed out into the field. When the two columns of cavalry met, they turned and faced Tarleton.

~~~

Washington and Lee were riding at the heads of their respective columns when they arrived on the field. "Colonel Lee," Washington said with a nod, as he reached his counterpart and wheeled his horse to face the enemy.

"Good morning, Colonel Washington," Lee replied, as he did likewise, the rest of the dragoons fanning out alongside them.

The two lines of cavalry faced each other, 300 yards apart across an open field. Men fidgeted, horses snorted and pawed the ground, but neither side advanced. After a few minutes, Washington spoke.

"Colonel Tarleton seems hesitant to attack," he said. "I wonder why. It is unlike him."

"The answer is obvious, Colonel Washington," Lee answered, nonchalantly. "He can see that he is facing a superior force."

Washington turned to Lee, an eyebrow cocked.

"Those men," Lee continued, gesturing dismissively toward Tarleton's line, "are inferior horsemen. You see," he said, looking at Washington, and speaking as if he were at a dinner party rather than facing the enemy on a battlefield, "no place in the world produces better riders than the southern United States. Our boys are riding by the time they are seven years old. And by the time they reach puberty, they are equal to the most expert horsemen in the world."

Washington smiled and shook his head.

"Of course, our horses are superior as well," Lee continued. "Ours are from Virginia or from Virginia stock. Superior in all respects to those from elsewhere. Those beasts Tarleton's men are riding are probably worn down. They can't match our mounts."

Washington cleared his throat. "Well, Harry," he said grimly, "I have always found Colonel Tarleton's troops to be competent. And his horses can't be any more worn down than ours are."

~~~

Tarleton stared out across the field at the American cavalry waiting in the distance. After a few uncomfortable minutes, Ogilvie edged his horse forward and said quietly, "Shall we charge them, Colonel?"

The question seemed to awaken Tarleton. "It could be a trap," he replied.

Ogilvie wondered if the colonel had Cowpens on his mind.

At that moment, Cornwallis rode up. He snatched a spyglass from his pocket and scanned the American line. Snapping it back together, he pushed it back into his pocket and turned to Tarleton. "What is the delay here, Colonel?"

Tarleton glanced at Cornwallis. "The flanks are not secure, my lord."

"Hang the flanks!" Cornwallis exclaimed, as Webster pulled up beside him.

Turning to Webster, Cornwallis barked, "Drive them away, Colonel, and resume the pursuit."

"Aye, m'lord," Webster answered before turning his horse and rushing out to his advancing infantry.

Without a word, Tarleton rode away, dispatching troops of his dragoons to probe each flank to assure there were no rebels waiting in ambush. Meanwhile Webster's 33rd Regiment of Foot hurried forward, spreading out into a battle line and unfurling their
~~~

colors, with drums beating out the commands.

Cornwallis, his face flushed, called out to the orderly by his side. "Order Lieutenant MacLeod to bring up his guns and give them grape!"

"Yes, sir," the man said as he turned and galloped away.

~~~

Washington and Lee watched as the scarlet-clad British soldiers fanned out into a line, with Tarleton's dragoons taking up places on the flanks. After a few moments they saw two six-horse teams arriving, pulling artillery pieces. They could sense the men around them starting to squirm.

"I think it's about time for us to move along, Colonel," Lee said calmly.

"Colonel Campbell has a good head start now," Washington answered. "Let's drop back out of sight of those guns and redeploy. We can keep feinting to slow them down."

"It's ten miles to the ford at the mill," Lee answered.

"We'll have to screen the rest of the army while they make for the ford," Washington said.

"Sounds like good sport," Lee replied. "Let's go."

Both colonels rode down their lines, issuing the command to withdraw as, in the distance, Webster's men started coming at the double quick, the British cannons unlimbering behind them.

As the British closed in, they saw the Americans ride off, vanishing into the fog.

~~~

The Patriot militia and the Continentals raced for the ford down parallel roads, while Lee and Washington threw out a screen, skirmishing with the British the entire way. The Americans stayed ahead of their pursuers, but never by more than a quarter mile.

The roads converged at the ford and both American columns arrived at the same time. Rather than cross immediately, with the British hot on their heels, Williams deployed the men in a line blocking the ford, while the cavalry fell in behind them.

The British came on recklessly, not expecting the Americans to turn and make a stand. As they advanced out of the mist and fog they were met by a devastating volley. Shattered, they fell back to regroup.

Then, to the dismay of the militiamen, Williams ordered Howard to take the Continentals across the river, leaving the militiamen to face the British without them. As the blue-coated American regulars were splashing across, the British resumed their advance. They were met by a rolling volley from the line of Patriot militia.

~~~

"They're leaving us out here to dry, Pa!" Tate Jones shouted, as he drove a ball down the barrel of his rifle.

"Pay attention to what you're doing, son," his father shouted back, aiming his rifle. He squeezed the trigger and as the smoke cleared, he saw that his target had crumpled and dropped to the ground.

All along the line, the militiamen were loading and firing as rapidly as they could, pouring shots into the British ranks as they rushed up and began forming into a line. Officers were shouting orders but in the roar of
~~~

gunfire it was impossible to hear them.

Jones glanced quickly to each side of him, to assure that his sons were still there and unharmed. Like the hundreds of other militiamen, he could see that the British line was beginning to overlap both Patriot flanks. As the British resumed their advance, they began to pour a withering enfilading fire into the militiamen.

"We need to get out of here, Pa!" Joshua Jones shouted, as he was reloading.

"Just pay attention to the redcoats! Load and fire!" his father yelled back.

~~~

Lee and Washington were conferring, fifty yards behind the Patriot line and with their backs to the river, when Williams rode up hurriedly. "Take your men across, Colonel Lee," he said.

Lee looked back at him for a moment, puzzled.

"Withdraw over the river," Williams repeated. He turned to Washington. "Once Colonel Lee is over, send your men across too. After your main body is over the river, bring the militia across. Leave behind a small rear guard until everyone is over. Colonel Howard's Continentals will provide a covering fire."

Williams wheeled his horse and rode toward the militia line, making his way to Campbell as musket balls whizzed around him

Lee looked at Washington, shrugged, then rode away. He summoned his trumpeter, who blew the order to withdraw, and Lee and his troopers splashed across the ford.
~~~

~~~

"Once the cavalry is over the river," Williams shouted to Campbell, "bring your militia across. The Continentals will cover you from the other side. Once across, form up on the rise on the left," he said, pointing. "If the British try to cross, give them hell."

Campbell cast an angry glare at Williams, answering only with a nod, before turning back to his beleaguered men. In the distance he saw the British advancing, bayonets gleaming, as Williams galloped away toward the ford.

~~~

Washington trotted over to Ransom. Pointing at the ford, he said, "Lead the men across, Ransom. Follow Colonel Lee. Once across, deploy on the heights. Strike the British if they cross and there is an opportunity." He gestured to a squad of dragoons. "Lend me these six men," he said. "I'll return them shortly."

"You?" Ransom asked.

"These men and I will be the rear guard. We'll screen the riflemen and militia as they're crossing," Washington answered.

Ransom looked back at the colonel, furrowing his brow.

"Get going, Captain," Washington barked, before signaling the squad to follow him forward toward the militia line.

~~~

The Patriot riflemen raked the British with deadly
~~~

accuracy, staggering them and breaking up the charge. As the men frantically began reloading, they could see green jacketed infantry advancing to the British front. Cornwallis was deploying his Jaegers, sharpshooting German riflemen.

Washington raced up to Campbell, who was on foot, pacing behind the line and shouting encouragement to his men. "Pull your men back, Colonel Campbell!" he shouted. "Hurry!"

As Campbell shouted the order to retreat, Washington spurred his horse and led the other six dragoons out in front, fanning out and facing the enemy. Moments later Ransom galloped up and took a place by his side.

"What are you doing here, Captain?" Washington demanded angrily.

"Just came to report that the men are on their way, sir," Ransom answered calmly. "Wondered if you could use a little help here."

Washington wanted to rebuke him, but there was no time. The Jaegers were preparing to fire and the British artillery was unlimbering behind them. He glanced back at the ford and saw that it was crowded with militiamen, wading across. He looked back at the British just as the Jaegers' rifles began to crack, followed by a booming blast from a cannon.

"Their cavalry isn't coming," Washington yelled. "There's nothing we can do here. Let's go."

~~~

Jones and his sons were struggling through the waist-deep water, crowded in among the other fleeing militiamen, trying to keep their footing on the slick
~~~

rocks, while holding their guns over their heads. Then suddenly the air was thick with Jaeger lead and all around them they could hear the whistling sound of near misses and the sickening thuds of bullets striking flesh. Men screamed and pitched into the rushing river, the wounded trying to keep their heads above water as they crawled or stumbled toward the shore. Looking across the swirling river, Jones could see Howard's Continentals atop the hill opposite the ford, positioned behind hasty field works and with their muskets leveled. But they were not firing. The Jaegers were not in range.

The fleeing Patriots were about two-thirds of the way across the river, their comrades continuing to drop around them, when Jones was startled by a sharp cracking noise just to his right—the sound of wood shattering. He spun his head toward the sound and saw Joshua's arms fly out as he fell face first into the river. Jones dropped his rifle, reached down, and pulled his son up out of the water.

"Can you walk?" he asked, anxiously.

Joshua sputtered, coughed, then said, "Yeah, I think so."

"Are you hit?" Jones asked.

Joshua hesitated, seemingly confused, then said, "I don't think so. The shot must have hit my rifle."

"Come on," Jones said, pulling the boy forward, through the hailstorm of lead. "We've got to get out of here."

Tate bent over and pulled his father's rifle out of the water, then scrambled after them.

As the militiamen pulled themselves up onto the riverbank, Campbell directed them to firing positions. When Jones splashed ashore, still holding Joshua by his arm, his son Tate handed him his rifle. They scrambled up the hillside and took their places in the newly formed line.

~~~

"Pursue them, Colonel," Cornwallis shouted.

"Aye, m'lord," Webster answered. Trotting his horse out into the ford he pulled his sword and waved it over his head. "Come on, lads! After them!"

The redcoats filed into the water, lifting their muskets over their heads, wading after the Patriot militiamen, who were emerging from the river on the opposite shore, trailed by Washington's small rear-guard detachment.

~~~

Howard's Continentals, wet and cold, leveled their muskets, waiting for the British to come in range. Meanwhile Campbell's riflemen, equally wet and cold, and angry to boot, were hurriedly loading and priming their guns.

When Webster's men were about halfway across the river, the order to fire rang down the American line, followed by a roar of gunfire and a sheet of flame.

~~~

The American volley dropped a dozen of the redcoats into the river and brought their advance to a sudden confused halt. Many of the men crouched in place. Some turned and began scrambling back toward the bank.
~~~

Cornwallis charged up to the edge of the river and shouted at Webster. “Force the crossing, sir! Advance!”

Without a word, Webster spurred his horse and plunged out to the middle of the river, ahead of all his men. “Forward my brave lads!” he shouted, waving his sword over his head.

~~~

Just as it appeared to the riflemen that they had driven the British back, an officer on a large black horse rode out into the middle of the ford, waving a sword over his head.

“Shoot him!” Campbell shouted, pointing at the officer.

A dozen marksmen took aim and fired.

~~~

Seeing their colonel alone in the middle of the river, waving his sword and shouting for them, with rifle balls whizzing past and splashing into the water around him, the men rallied quickly. “Huzzah!” one shouted, plunging forward toward the colonel. A few more took up the call and soon the entire regiment was chanting “Huzzah!” and storming across the river, seemingly unfazed by the American fire that continued to tear into their ranks.

Their nerves were further steadied when the artillery behind them suddenly erupted. They could see some of the Americans on the other side beginning to break and run.

“Huzzah!” Webster shouted, leading them across,

as shots continued to whistle harmlessly past him.

~~~

As the British drove relentlessly forward and solid shot from their cannons began to rain down on the American line, the Patriot militiamen began to peel off and run away. Seeing that there was nothing he could do to stop it, Campbell gave the order to retreat.

~~~

Across the river, Cornwallis snapped his spyglass shut and spun around, searching for Tarleton, and was surprised to discover that he was right beside him.

"They are running, Colonel!" Cornwallis exclaimed. "Pursue them, sir! Cut them up!"

"Gladly, my lord," Tarleton answered with a smile. He turned and signaled to his men, then rode toward the ford, with his dragoons following him.

~~~

Williams rushed up to Lee and shouted, "We will rally and reform at the Haw, Colonel. You must hold them off here."

Lee could see the British cavalry splashing across the river, behind Webster's now disorganized and depleted men. "*Avec plaisir*," he answered with a grin.

As Williams hurried away, Lee led his men a couple hundred yards to the rear, to a cleared area out of range of the British infantry. There he formed them into a line of battle and awaited Tarleton.

He didn't have to wait long. A few minutes later
~~~

Tarleton's column appeared, his eighty dragoons instantly fanning out into a battle line when they spotted Lee and his sixty troopers.

Almost simultaneously, both colonels rose in their stirrups and shouted "Charge!" and the rival horsemen thundered toward each other, sabers aloft, while trumpets blasted the orders.

The cavalrymen collided at full gallop, shouts and the clanging of sabers ringing in the frosty morning air. Lee was swinging his saber left and right, blocking and parrying blows while trying to locate Tarleton in the melee, while Tarleton, several yards away, was doing exactly the same thing.

A few minutes into the fight, neither side having gained an advantage, Lee heard a trumpet blaring behind him. He spun around to see Washington's sixty white-clad dragoons coming at a gallop, with Washington leading them, yelling "Liberty!" as he held his saber above his head. Lee smiled when he noticed that one of Washington's men was carrying the odd little red flag of which they were so fond.

~~~

Several of Tarleton's men were struck down immediately as Washington's dragoons crashed into them. The rest were unnerved, and many began to break away and retreat.

Tarleton saw that he could not hold. Nearby he noticed one of his dragoons dueling with one of Lee's men, both men blocking every thrust and swing. He muttered an oath, spurred his horse, and sabered the American rider in his back as he rode past him.

"Withdraw!" he shouted, his trumpeter immediately
~~~

echoing the order.

~~~

As Tarleton's men raced away, Lee rode up to Washington, both of them blood-splattered. "Shall we go after them?" Lee asked.

Washington shook his head. "Can't risk it, Harry. Our orders are only to screen the withdrawal and keep the enemy cavalry back."

"A pity," Lee replied, looking out at the retreating British.

~~~

Webster was waiting on the riverbank as Cornwallis emerged from the water. "Shall we pursue the rebels, m'lord?" he asked.

Cornwallis eased his horse up onto level ground, sighed deeply, then slapped his thigh in frustration. He shook his head. "No, Colonel. Once again they have managed to escape."

"Sir," Webster said, "I can have these men on the march instantly."

Cornwallis shook his head again. "And what will we feed them?" he asked.

For days his army had been subsisting on turnips, Indian corn, and an occasional bite of tough lean beef. And now even those meager rations were gone.

"We can't go deeper into this God-forsaken wilderness until we find some provisions," Cornwallis said. He turned to an aide by his side, "Find the commissary officer and tell him to locate a campsite near food and forage."

"Yes, sir," the man replied, before turning and riding away.

Cornwallis turned back to Webster. "You behaved gallantly, Colonel Webster," he said. "You seem to have been charmed today."

"Just a bit of good luck, m'lord," Webster answered.

Cornwallis snorted, then his face clouded over. "We must bring these rebels to battle soon, Colonel," Cornwallis said. "This country has been stripped clean. We cannot subsist here much longer."

86

Camp of Nathanael Greene's American Army
Boyd's Mill
Reedy Fork
Guilford County, North Carolina
March 6, 1781

Having spent the day meeting with South Carolina Governor John Rutledge at General Greene's headquarters, Pickens had not been present at the battle at Weitzel's Mill. But although he had not witnessed the events that cost the lives of over two dozen of his Patriot militiamen, he was seeing the consequences of those events now, with many of his men walking defiantly out of camp and the rest grumbling and threatening to leave.

Jones stood patiently nearby as Pickens conferred with several officers beside a campfire. When the meeting broke off and Pickens stepped away, Jones intercepted him.

"What can I do for you, Mr. Jones?" Pickens said, in his ordinary gruff manner.

"We got hung out there to dry today, General,"

Jones answered. "General Morgan wouldn't have done that to us."

Pickens took a close look at Jones. On his grizzled face he wore a three-day beard. His clothes were patched and threadbare. He was wearing one shoe. His other foot was wrapped in rags held in place by a strip of buckskin.

"Mr. Jones," Pickens answered, "I have always permitted you to speak freely, but let me remind you that you are addressing your commanding officer."

Jones stared back silently for a few seconds, his brow furrowed. "Begging the general's pardon," he said, "But I do not speak plainly because you gave me permission to. I speak plainly because it's the only way I know how to speak."

"It is our duty to follow the orders of our commanding officers, Mr. Jones," Pickens replied.

"I'm proud to serve under you, sir—to fight by your side," Jones answered. "But General Greene? He don't give a dog about us militia. It's time for me and my boys to go home."

Pickens' mind flashed back to the scene at the campfire the night Jones and his sons first arrived, the night before the Battle of Cowpens. "It is with men like them that we will prevail," Morgan had said.

"You and your sons have fought valiantly," Pickens said. "I implore you now. Stay with us. Your country needs you."

Jones stared back, gave a slight nod, then said, firmly, "General, my family needs me more. It's time for us to go home. Here we're just being used as bait." He looked down, shook his head and continued, "Strung us out to dry after all we've done. It's time for us to go home."

"The penalty for desertion is death, Mr. Jones," Pickens replied. "If you leave and are caught, you may be shot."

"I ain't never run from a fight, General, and I ain't fixing to start now," Jones answered, unblinking. "I'll fight them till it's over. But there's plenty of fighting to do back home and that's where I aim to do it."

"I forbid it," Pickens answered sternly. "You are to stay with this army until I order otherwise."

Jones stared back at him for a few seconds, then said, "I ain't asking your permission to leave, General. I'm just asking whether you're going to come with us."

Pickens fell silent, staring back for a few moments at Jones' determined face. "Are you speaking for all the South Carolina men?" Pickens asked.

"If there's any punishment to be had for what I said, it falls on me alone," Jones answered. "But I believe the men are all of one mind on this."

The men stared silently at each other for a few seconds, eyes locked, jaws clinched.

"I will carefully consider what you have said, Mr. Jones," Pickens said. "I can make no promises. Now return to your company."

Jones gave a slight nod, keeping his eyes fixed determinedly on Pickens, until turning and striding away.

Pickens waited a few seconds, then turned around and marched to Greene's headquarters, entering without waiting for permission.

Greene was hunched over a writing desk, scribbling out orders by candlelight. He glanced up at Pickens. "One moment, General," he said, returning to his writing. After a few moments he finished, put away his pen, sprinkled some pounce onto the paper and called out, "Orderly!"

A young soldier popped quickly into the room.

"Deliver this to Colonel Davie," Greene said.

"Yes, sir," the soldier said, taking the paper and hurrying away.

Greene stood up and stepped out from behind the desk. "What is it, General?" he asked.

"It is time for me to return to South Carolina with my men, sir," Pickens answered.

Greene sighed and shook his head. "As I have already told you, General Pickens, I have taken your request under advisement."

"Respectfully sir," Pickens said, "It is time to send me back."

Greene stared back at him silently and sternly for a few seconds. "Now, General?" he asked. "You would leave us now? On the eve of a crucial battle?"

"General Greene," Pickens replied, guardedly, "I would proudly serve my country anywhere. But sir, I am capable of doing more good for the country there than here. I am known there, General. I can do great damage to the enemy there."

"But we need you *here*, General," Greene said.

"The South Carolina militia are in a miserable, pitiful condition, sir," Pickens said. "Their clothes and shoes are coming to pieces. They simply cannot go on."

Greene shook his head. "They are no more ragged than the rest of the army."

Pickens stared back, hesitating before speaking. "I confess that I want to see what becomes of Cornwallis, but I repeat, sir, that it is best that I return now."

"After the fight, General," Greene said. "Then your men can…"

Pickens interrupted him. "General Greene," he said, "I am unable to keep them here, sir."

Greene fell silent. He could see how difficult it had been for Pickens to say those words.

"These militia," Greene said, with unconcealed disgust. "They just come and go as they please. They are entirely without discipline."

Pickens' eyes flared. He swallowed before answering. "Begging your pardon, General," he said, "but these men have fought hard and bravely. Many of them have died. Many will die yet. But they are not professional soldiers, sir. They have families and homes to defend."

Greene stared back at Pickens. After a few uncomfortable seconds he spoke, "Very well, General. I expect to receive substantial reinforcements of Virginia and North Carolina militia over the next few days. So, I will issue an order directing that you return to your district in South Carolina, with your South Carolina and Georgia men. There you will gather more militia and pursue and harass the enemy wherever you can."

Pickens nodded. "Thank you, sir."

"You will be missed, General," Greene said, extending his hand. As Pickens shook it, Greene added, "I wish you great success in South Carolina. I intend to bring the whole army and join you there, sir—once I have broken his Lordship's leg."

87

Lawton Farm
Bedford County, Virginia
March 6, 1781

George burst through the door and into the house, startling Martha Lawton, causing her to drop her spoon into the pot she had been stirring. She looked up and saw that there was a look of distress on the boy's face.

"There's men coming, Miz Lawton," he said, nearly out of breath. "I think it might be Cap'n McCraw."

Martha shuddered. "Where is Caesar?" she asked.

"He's tied up right outside," George answered, fear in his eyes. "They done seen him already."

Martha wiped her hands on her apron. "Go find Stephen," she said. "Hurry."

The boy dashed out the back door as Martha stepped out onto the front porch.

A man on horseback approached her. Two other men were riding behind him and a third was driving a wagon pulled by a two-horse team. "Good morning, Mrs. Lawton," the man in front said, pleasantly.

"Good morning, Captain McCraw," she answered, betraying no emotion.

William McCraw, the district quartermaster, had earned a reputation for the energetic and uncompromising performance of his duties. It had won him no friends among the civilian population. He halted his horse, dismounted, and wrapped the reins around the hitching post.

"I need to take a look at your horse, Mrs. Lawton," McCraw said, stepping toward Caesar.

"Our horse is not for sale, Captain," she answered.

One of the other men pointed to a burned patch of hair on the horse's rump, and McCraw drew close and looked carefully at it.

"As you can see, our horse is injured," Martha said.

McCraw looked at the spot for another few seconds. "Superficial," he replied, not looking at her as he walked back over to his saddlebag and pulled out a piece of paper. He stepped up to the porch steps and reached out toward Martha, handing her the paper.

"On the authority of Governor Jefferson and the Commonwealth of Virginia, I am impressing this horse for the Continental Army," he said, flatly.

"Captain," she answered without taking the paper, her voice cracking, "This is our only horse, sir. We need him here."

At that moment, Stephen rushed up from behind the house, trailed by George. He looked up searchingly at his mother.

"They are taking Caesar," she said.

Stephen spun around and faced McCraw. "You cannot take this horse!" he exclaimed.

McCraw laid the impressment order on the porch, then picked up a stone and set it down on it. He turned to Stephen.

"Son, if your father was here, he would gladly turn that horse over like the Patriot he is," McCraw said.

"He would not!" Stephen shot back, defiantly.

George stepped forward. "Suh, dis ole hoss heah, he cain't hardly pull nothin'. Naw suh, he ain't no good a'tall 'cept as a ridin' hoss."

Martha looked down at George, seeing that he was deliberately exaggerating his dialect, a tactic he had learned from his father. She stepped down off the porch toward the boys.

"Well, that's fine," McCraw answered, drawing another piece of paper from his saddle bag. "This horse is being impressed for service with the dragoons."

"Oh, he lame 'bout haf de time, suh," George said, speaking rapidly. "Cain't hardly walk nor run and you ain't neva seen a hoss dat eat so much."

"George," Martha said softly, laying her hand gently on the boy's shoulder, and shaking her head slightly.

McCraw extended his arm toward Martha, handing her the paper. "Here is your receipt, Mrs. Lawton. The horse is valued at $5,000 continentals or $50 specie."

"He's worth a lot more than that!" Stephen said angrily.

McCraw looked over at him. "Really? A lame old horse that can't pull, walk, or run?" he said sarcastically, answered by the boy's angry glare.

Martha not having taken the receipt, McCraw carried it over to the porch and placed it under the rock, atop the impressment order. "We have all been called upon to make sacrifices for the cause, Mrs. Lawton," he said.

"How much sacrifice must be demanded of my

family, sir?" Martha said, trembling, her eyes filling with tears. "We have been attacked by Tories. Our man Squire was nearly killed. Our barn was burned down. My husband and two of my sons are with General Greene now, risking their lives for our country. And you would rob us of our only horse?"

McCraw looked back at her sternly, his temper rising. "Mrs. Lawton, many of us have family with General Greene right now," he said, knowing that she knew his brother was there.

"So you're stealing our horse so you can give him to your brother!" Stephen said bitterly.

McCraw spun to face Stephen. "Hold your tongue, young man!" he shot back angrily. "I am stealing nothing. My orders are to procure twenty horses and get them to Colonel Washington urgently. I will obey that order in the service of my country!" He turned to the other men. "Take him," he said.

As they stepped over and began untying Caesar, Stephen was trembling with rage, trying desperately not to shed tears. His mother reached out and touched his arm.

Caesar whinnied as the men led him away and tied him to the back of the wagon. McCraw, having regained his composure, turned back to face Martha and the boys. "If you dispute the valuation of the horse, you may file an objection with the district office in Peytonsburg and it will be evaluated by a citizen's council," he said. There was no response.

"Our men, your husband and sons included, are about to fight Cornwallis," McCraw said. "Our cause—our liberty—depends upon us giving them everything they need to defeat him."

As McCraw remounted and led the men away, with

Caesar trailing behind the wagon, Martha put her arms across the shoulders of the boys.

88

Peytonsburg
Pittsylvania County, Virginia
March 7, 1781

"Fine work, Captain," Bayard said, looking out at the horses penned behind the district headquarters office. "These animals all look stout. I'm impressed that you were able to gather them so quickly."

"Thank you, sir," McCraw answered. "We're sending them off to Colonel Washington first thing in the morning."

"I'm sure he will be pleased to receive them," Bayard said. "When the army was in Halifax, Ransom Wiatt told me of the dragoons' great need for horses."

"Well, sir, it seems that they have already worn out the horses we obtained for them then," McCraw said. "Fresh hardy mounts such as these should give our men a material advantage over the enemy."

"No doubt," Bayard replied.

"If you will excuse me, sir," McCraw said, casting a glance at the setting sun, "I must attend to some other matters before dark."

"Of course," Bayard said, shaking McCraw's hand

and then watching him hurry away toward his office.

Bayard looked back out over the corral again. It was just large enough to contain the animals and there was a single feed trough. Part of his plan would be easy to accomplish. He looked over at the guard, a tall young man standing by the gate with a bayonet-tipped musket on his shoulder and a large knife in his belt. Bayard knew the boy—a diligent, serious, and athletic young man. He would be a difficult nut to crack.

While he was pondering the situation, Bayard noticed a man approaching the guard. After the two men exchanged words, the guard handed the musket to the new man and walked away. Bayard recognized the replacement guard. John Saunders. Bayard knew him well—an amiable man, but somewhat dim-witted and overly fond of liquor. Maybe this won't be so difficult after all, he thought.

He walked toward a tavern about a hundred yards away and bought a jug of whiskey, answering the keeper's ribbing by insisting his wife needed it to make medicines. Bayard put the jug in the bed of his wagon and, from a distance, watched Saunders pacing around the corral, as the evening grew darker. After watching him make a couple of circuits, Bayard edged as close as he could without being conspicuous, then, when Saunders turned his back to continue his looping circuit, he hurried over and set the jug down where Saunders wouldn't be able to miss it. He then walked back to his wagon and waited.

After a couple of hours, Bayard pulled back the tarp on the wagon and brought out a covered bucket—the contents of which he had mixed at home earlier that day: oats, molasses, and rat's bane. The molasses would make the concoction irresistible to the horses, and the arsenic would assure they would never reach Greene's army.

It was pitch dark by the time Bayard walked back to the corral, carrying the bucket. He crept forward quietly and as he neared the gate he saw what he had expected to find. Saunders was lying on the ground, asleep by the uncorked jug.

Bayard eased toward the gate and was about to open it when it suddenly occurred to him that the jug could incriminate him. He set the bucket down, walked back and quietly picked up the jug. After taking it to the wagon, he walked back toward the corral.

When he came near, Bayard felt as if his racing heart skipped a beat. Saunders was gone.

Bayard squinted his eyes in the darkness and scanned the area, feeling a wave of relief sweep over him when he noticed Saunders' body sprawled on ground a few dozen feet from where he had been before. As he felt his heartbeat slowing, Bayard quietly crept toward the gate. When he was nearly there, he felt the ground go soft beneath his feet. Looking down, he saw a trail of syrup and oats, leading to the overturned bucket at the bottom of a little hill. His heart sank as he realized what had happened. Saunders must have gotten up and stumbled over the bucket, spilling it before passing out again.

Bayard gritted his teeth. Suppressing a powerful urge to swear, he said a quick silent prayer instead. In moments he knew what he must do. Although his opportunity to poison the horses had been ruined, he could at least herd them out of the corral.

He lifted the latch on the gate and pushed it open. Just as he was about to step inside, he froze as a voice called out.

"Halt! What are you doing there?"

Bayard turned slowly around, to see a man with a lantern approaching, carrying a musket. He was frantically trying to formulate a plan when the man lifted the lantern, paused, then said, "Mr. Bayard?"

"Yes," Bayard answered calmly. "I came down to check on things here and discovered the gate to the pen open. We're fortunate these horses didn't escape."

"What?" the man said, lowering the lantern to illuminate the open gate.

At that moment, Saunders was rising unsteadily to his feet.

"I found this man asleep," Bayard said, gesturing to Saunders. "He appears to be drunk."

The man swung the lantern in that direction, glaring angrily at Saunders, who muttered something and took a stumbling step.

89

Peytonsburg
Pittsylvania County, Virginia
March 8, 1781

It was mid-morning when Bayard rode into town. During his ten-mile ride from home, as he pondered how best to resolve the situation with John Saunders, his mind wandered to the many difficult moral challenges this struggle had created, and to the frequent need for lies and deception.

The previous autumn suspicion had begun to fall on some of the local Loyalist leaders, but he had been able to orchestrate a plan to throw the rebels off their scents. Framing three innocent men to take the fall for them had not been difficult. The three men, Billings, Lawless, and Lay, had long been known to be indifferent to independence. Lawless was surly and irascible, Lay was friendless and anti-social, and Colonel Wilson had a long-standing grudge against Billings. So, acting on a supposed anonymous tip, Bayard had the three men arrested in their beds, and the counterfeit continentals and "seditious" pamphlets that Gus Johnson had planted in their barns were soon discovered. With those three in custody, and the Tory plot seemingly exposed and foiled, the suspicion that had fallen over the actual Loyalists disappeared.

Bayard felt a pang of guilt as he thought back on the episode. The three innocent men had been whipped, disgraced, imprisoned, their farms and homes forfeited to the state, and their families impoverished. But they had not been hanged—he had helped assure that. When this infernal rebellion is finally suppressed, he thought, there may be time to make right such things. In the meantime, this is war.

Things should go more easily with John Saunders, he thought, as he dismounted and tied his horse at the district headquarters. He would point out that Saunders is a simple-minded, inoffensive man, and that no harm had been done. He would recommend that the man be whipped and released, and he felt confident that his recommendation would be accepted.

"Good morning, Reverend!" McCraw said cheerfully, emerging from the building and stepping toward Bayard with his hand extended.

"Good morning, Captain," Bayard answered pleasantly, shaking his hand.

"You are the talk of the town, sir. Quite the hero," McCraw said.

"Nonsense," Bayard said, dismissively.

"But sir, had you not discovered that open gate, all those horses—which are now on their way to Colonel Washington, I'm pleased to say—might have escaped."

"Fortuitous at best, Captain," Bayard said. "Hardly heroic." After a pause he added, "I feel sorry for John Saunders. He's always been a little feeble-minded, you know."

McCraw's smile vanished, and he nodded

knowingly. "Yes, it's a shame about John. He denied opening the gate, but he admitted being drunk and asleep on duty. Colonel Wilson felt it was important to make an example of him."

"What?" Bayard said, his pulse quickening.

"His wife and mother were here this morning pleading for him. It was a pitiful sight to see John crying like a baby, begging for mercy," McCraw said.

"What has happened to Mr. Saunders?" Bayard asked, hesitantly.

McCraw looked surprised. "Oh," he said. "I assumed you knew. Colonel Wilson had him shot."

90

Robinson Family Farm
New Garden Quaker Community
Guilford County, North Carolina
March 8, 1781

Sarah was gently mopping the young man's mutilated face when she noticed his eye begin to quiver. She withdrew her hand and in a moment the eye opened. The man glanced around the room at first, seemingly confused, then she sensed him relaxing, recognizing his surroundings.

"It is a joy to see thee awake, Jeremiah," she said pleasantly. The man's gaze turned to her.

"Thou hast been asleep for some days now," she said, "overcome by infection and a vexing fever. But, praise God, thy fever has lifted. It appeared to us that the Lord was going to take thee, but in his mercy, he has again spared thy life."

The man looked over at his right arm, lifting it slowly and seemingly reluctantly. When he could see his hand, Sarah saw sadness sweep across his face.

"It is a blessing that I have been able to begin removing thy bandages. Thy hand is nearly healed," she said.

The man dropped his arm and rolled his head away from her.

"There is a man I know, his name is Richard Calvin, who is missing fingers, just as you are," Sarah said. "When Richard was a boy, he and his brother were chopping wood and his brother accidentally struck Richard's hand with the axe. It was a terrible accident."

She paused to see if the man would look at her, but he kept his head turned to the wall.

"Richard has learned to live without those fingers," she continued, "and there is no man's work that he is unable to do."

Again she waited for a response, and again the man kept his head turned away.

"I believe it will be the same with thee, Jeremiah," she said confidently. After a few silent moments she said, "I have something for thee. Look."

The man slowly rolled his head back toward her. Smiling at him, she was holding out a slate and piece of chalk. "I have become accustomed to calling thee Jeremiah, but I suppose I ought to learn thy real name. Will thee try to write it for me?"

The man looked at the slate for a few seconds, as if deep in thought. Then he nodded and sat up gingerly in the bed.

Sarah handed him the slate and he took it in his left hand and placed it on his lap. When she offered the piece of chalk, he reached for it with his mangled right hand.

His thumb and little finger were intact, uninjured. But his middle three fingers had all been cut off at the knuckles.

He grasped the chalk with his thumb and the nub

of his forefinger, wincing slightly as he did. He lowered the chalk to the slate and began making a mark. As he did, the chalk slipped out of his hand and rolled off the slate and onto the floor. In frustration he pushed the slate away.

Sarah reached down and picked up the chalk. "Will thee try with thy left hand?" she asked gently.

The man shook his head and turned to face the wall.

Sarah sighed and forced a smile. "Let this not trouble us," she said. Placing the slate and chalk under the bed she said, "Thou art healing. I shall learn thy name when thou art able to speak it to me."

The man rolled over suddenly and sat up again, surprising her. He lifted his left hand to his face, and he looked at his palm. He seemed to be gesturing, glancing at her anxiously as he did.

"Art thou asking for something?" she asked, puzzled.

The man nodded rapidly, then resumed looking at his palm, moving it around and following it with his stare.

After a few seconds, Sarah's face lit up with understanding. "Art thou asking for a looking glass?"

The man dropped his hand, nodding rapidly.

"Oh, Jeremiah," she said with a smile and a gentle little laugh. "We are Friends. Simple folk. We do not keep such vanities."

At first the man made no response. Then he nodded, understanding and disappointed.

91

Camp of Nathanael Greene's American Army
North of High Rock Ford
Guilford County, North Carolina
March 9, 1781

"Gentlemen," Greene said, rising as Colonels Williams, Lee, and Washington entered his headquarters, led in by the young officer who had been sent to fetch them. "Have a seat, please," he said, gesturing to three chairs arranged before his desk.

"A decisive moment is approaching, gentlemen," Greene said, exhibiting animation unusual for him. "A critical moment, indeed."

As the officers all took their seats, Greene continued. "Hundreds of troops have been added to our ranks in the past few days and more are expected imminently. General Caswell is on his way with a considerable force of Carolina militia, as are more Virginia regulars and General Lawson's brigade of Virginia militia.

"As you know, General Cornwallis has pulled his army back, to distance it from our own." Greene stood up and began pacing. "With the benefit of that distance, the British have intensified their outrages, plundering and destroying the farms and homes of Patriots. When the rest of our force arrives, I trust we shall be able to put an end to these depredations," Greene said, emphatically.

"We must strike Cornwallis, gentlemen, and we must do it soon. He has a large and disciplined force, but he is low on provisions and far from his base. Our militia are unreliable, and they come and go as they please. So, we must bring the enemy to battle soon, before they decide to return home.

"Hitherto I have been obliged to practice by finesse that which I dared not attempt by force. But now," he said, scanning the faces of the officers, "now it is time to strike a blow."

"Very good," Williams said, Lee and Washington nodding beside him. "What are your orders, sir?"

Greene sat back down.

"It is time to strengthen the main army for battle. I am dissolving the Light Corps," he answered. "Colonel Williams and his men shall return at once to the Continental Line."

Williams answered with a slight bow.

"In lieu of the Light Corps I am creating two parties of observation, to be commanded by Colonels Lee and Washington."

He turned to Lee. "Colonel Campbell's Virginia riflemen shall be attached to your legion," he said, being answered immediately with a nod.

"You shall also command a legion, Colonel Washington," Greene said, turning to Washington. "I am attaching Captain Kirkwood's Delaware Continentals to your command, as well as Colonel

Lynch's Virginia riflemen, who are with General Lawson and should arrive shortly.

"Until we have the opportunity to strike Lord Cornwallis with the entire army, you and Colonel Lee, either separately or conjunctively as you may agree, are to give the enemy all the annoyance in your power."

Greene stood again. He scanned their faces.

"Ready your commands, gentlemen," Greene said. "We shall bring the British to battle soon. I need not remind you what will be at stake."

92

Camp of Nathanael Greene's American Army
Speedwell Ironworks
Troublesome Creek
Guilford County, North Carolina
March 11, 1781

Sitting atop his horse, alongside Colonel Washington, Ransom marveled at the columns of men marching and riding into the camp. "They've been flocking in all day," he said. "How many do you reckon?"

"Thousands," Washington answered. "A sight for sore eyes, Captain."

Indeed, they had been arriving all day—hundreds of new Virginia Continentals, General Lawson with over twelve hundred Virginia militia, and at least a thousand more militiamen from North Carolina.

"I think it probable that our army and Lord Cornwallis' are about to become much closer neighbors," Washington said with a grin.

Ransom nodded in the direction of one of the riders passing by. "There's the man everyone in camp is talking about," he said.

Washington chuckled. "That horse looks like it

should be riding him, instead of the other way around," he said, as they watched Peter Francisco ride by, a six-foot-eight-inch, 270-pound giant of a man.

"The Virginia Hercules, they call him," Ransom said. "If half of what is said about that man is true, he is a singular and most extraordinary soldier."

"He refused a commission, you know," Washington said. "He said he would rather remain a private."

Ransom nodded. "I heard that during the retreat at Camden, when all the artillery horses were killed, he put a cannon on his shoulders and carried it out on his back."

"I heard that too," Washington replied. "But I'm skeptical. Those guns weigh well over a thousand pounds."

"I've heard that General Washington himself gave him that big sword he carries, after Francisco complained that a regulation saber was too small for him," Ransom said.

"Well, Ransom, I'm dubious of that claim too," Washington answered. "On the other hand, I've heard that he personally killed a dozen of the British at Stony Point, most of them after he had been bayoneted in the stomach. That one is probably true. I heard it from General Wayne himself. But I'll tell you what I know for certain. When Peter Francisco heard that General Greene was gathering militia to fight Cornwallis in North Carolina, he sold everything he owned and bought that horse," Washington said, nodding toward them. "He caught up with Captain Watkins somewhere in Bedford County and signed on."

"That is the spirit that will win our independence, sir," Ransom replied. After a pause he added, "Speaking of Captain Watkins, here he comes now."

A skilled horseman and the 19-year-old son of a prominent Patriot politician, Thomas Watkins was smartly dressed in an officer's uniform, contrasting with the rest of his thirty-man troop, who wore hunting shirts and buckskin.

"Good evening, gentlemen," Watkins said as he brought his horse to a halt in front of Washington and Ransom.

After they greeted him, Watkins continued, frustration ringing in his voice. "I have assembled an excellent troop, Colonel Washington, and we are eager to face the enemy," he said.

"Very good, Captain," Washington answered. "I am confident you and your men will soon have that opportunity."

"I have just returned from offering our services to Colonel Lee," Watkins said. "He refused us. He says we are not uniformed properly for dragoons."

Ransom turned away quickly, so neither man would see the look that had appeared involuntarily on his face.

"My men are wearing what they own, sir," Watkins continued. "I dare say there are no better riders in Virginia than these men. They are all armed with sabers and pistols and are skilled in using them. Might you have any use for such men, Colonel?"

"Captain Watkins," Washington answered without hesitation, "we would be honored to have your troop ride with us."

"Thank you, sir," Watkins said with a bow. "I regret that I did not come to see you first."

Washington turned to Ransom. "Captain Wiatt," he said, "Escort Captain Watkins and his men to our camp."

Ransom nodded. "This way, Captain," he said to

Watkins, gesturing as he turned his horse and began to ride away.

93

Camp of Nathanael Greene's American Army
Speedwell Ironworks
Troublesome Creek
Guilford County, North Carolina
March 11, 1781

Arthur Lawton punched his knapsack and laid his head in the depression left by his fist. He groaned, sat up, and punched it again. "I might as well just lay my head on a rock as try to get comfortable on this lumpy thing," he complained.

"Don't steal all the blanket again tonight," Will said, settling in beside him and anticipating their nightly competition for the little warmth provided by the thin tattered blanket they shared. He pulled it over him.

"This flimsy rag doesn't deserve to be called a blanket," Arthur said, as he tugged it in the other direction. "I'll tell you one thing I've learned for sure, brother. I ain't never again going to take for granted a roof over my head, a warm place to sleep, and a decent pillow."

The brothers laid quietly back-to-back for a few

minutes. Will broke the silence.

"Art, are you nervous?" he asked.

"Nah," Arthur replied.

After a few seconds Will said softly, "Well, I am."

For a minute or so, Arthur didn't reply. Then he said, "I reckon I am too. A little."

"I ain't so much afraid of getting hurt, or even getting killed," Will said. "What I'm most afraid of is losing my nerve. Of running. I can't quit thinking about it."

"That ain't gonna happen, Will," Arthur said confidently. "The Riflemen can't be beat and there ain't a single one of us who's gonna run."

"You're a good shot, Art," Will said, after a long silent pause.

"You're dang right I am," his brother answered quickly.

"But ain't neither one of us ever had to load, aim, and fire, while somebody was shooting back at us," Will said.

"I ain't worried about that," Arthur said, unconvincingly.

"And I keep thinking about trying to load while the redcoats are charging us with their bayonets," Will said.

"Forget about it, Will," Arthur said. "They'll never get close enough."

"I don't like telling you this," Will said, "but you need to hear it: if you see me fixing to run, stop me. Club me over the head if you have to. I couldn't live with the shame of that."

"Will, you are one odd duck," Arthur answered. "You think too dang much."

"Just remember what I said, Art," Will said. "I mean it."

"Go to sleep," Arthur replied.

~~~

Forty feet away, Jacob Thomas reached out and stirred the embers of the dying campfire. "I made my will today, Henry," he said quietly. "If I don't come out of this fight, it is in my knapsack."

Henry glanced over at him. "Have you got a bad feeling about this, Jake?"

Jacob shook his head. "No, not really," he answered. "Just being prudent. You ought to think about doing it too."

For a few moments, Henry stared into the fire silently. "I've got the boys," he said after the pause. "They'll know what to do."

Jacob nodded, grunted, and stirred the fire again.

"They're good boys," Henry said, after another long pause. "But you'll help too, won't you Jake? If something happens to me, you'll check in on things from time to time and give them good advice when they need it?"

Jacob nodded. "Of course," he said. "I don't expect it will come to that, but you know you can always count on me."

"Thank you, my friend," Henry said, as he stood. "I reckon we ought to try to get a little sleep. I'm sure General Greene will put us to work tomorrow."
~~~

94

Camp of Nathanael Greene's American Army
Speedwell Ironworks
Troublesome Creek
Guilford County, North Carolina
March 12, 1781

The eastern sky was just beginning to brighten, in anticipation of the sun, as Ransom tossed his saddle onto the back of a gray mare, who accepted it indifferently. As he reached underneath her to fix the strap, he heard a voice call out.

"Hold on, Captain!"

Ransom turned to see William Lunsford, the regimental quartermaster, approaching, leading a large chestnut horse.

"You can finally give that poor old nag a rest," Lunsford said. "Colonel McDowell arrived last night from Virginia with new mounts. This stallion has been issued to you."

As Lunsford arrived, Ransom began carefully inspecting the horse.

"He's shod and rested, Captain," Lunsford said.

"This looks like a good one."

"He's a big one, that's for sure," Ransom said, rubbing the horse as he paced around it. He stopped when he noticed something on its rump.

"Looks like his hide got singed somehow," Lunsford said. "Didn't break the skin."

Ransom rubbed the burned spot to confirm that the horse wasn't sensitive there. "All right, Sergeant," he said. "I'm obliged." After a pause he added, "Now I'll have to adjust all my tack."

Lunsford chuckled. "I think you'll be happy with him, sir," he said.

As Ransom turned and lifted the saddle off the mare, Lunsford said, "I'll need you to sign for him, sir. You know what a stickler General Greene is."

Ransom took the quill that Lunsford handed him and scribbled his initials onto a receipt.

"Thank you, sir. I'll send someone for the mare," Lunsford said, walking away as Colonel Washington arrived.

"Ransom," he said as he approached, "Colonel Lee's scouts say that his Lordship is marching north, towards us. Maybe we won't have to chase him down after all."

"Good," Ransom answered, as he pulled the saddle blanket off the mare and put it on the stallion.

"With these new mounts we're equipped to give Colonel Tarleton the whipping he deserves," Washington said. He paused and took a long look at the new horse. "This one is a bit large, isn't he, Captain?"

"That he is, sir," Ransom said, as he tossed the saddle up onto the horse's back. "He looks like he's better suited for jousting."

"Riding that high, you may need a longer saber," Washington said jokingly.

Ransom chuckled, then suddenly stopped adjusting the saddle, staring off into the distance as an idea settled into his mind.

95

Bayard Homestead
Halifax County, Virginia
March 13, 1781

Hearing a horse approaching, Bayard took down his coat and hat and stepped out into his yard. In a moment, the horse emerged from around a bend in the road, pulling a chaise, and he could see that its rider was Tabitha Wiatt. When the chaise drew up to him, he removed his hat and said pleasantly, "Good morning, Mrs. Wiatt. Come inside and warm yourself."

"Mr. Bayard," she answered, clearly flustered, "Please forgive me for being abrupt, but I have received an important letter from Ransom and have hurried straight to you with the news."

"I trust Ransom is safe and well," Bayard answered, his curiosity piqued.

"Yes, I suppose he is," Tabitha replied. "He has been ill but says he has recovered. But the news is not about him, sir. It is about those two Tories who tried to murder you."

Bayard's heart began to race. He struggled to stay composed.

"What of them, ma'am?"

"Well, they are dead, praise God," she began, unaware that her words pierced Bayard's heart. "The troubling bit is that they were in North Carolina. How could they have made it to the enemy there if they ran to Benedict Arnold? It makes no sense."

"Is Ransom sure they are dead?" Bayard asked. "How does he know?"

"Yes," Tabitha replied, taking the letter from her bag and opening it. "He says, 'We had a fight with some Tory militia a few days ago. Gus Johnson and Billy Lewis were with the Tories and were killed in the contest. Please pass this information on to Colonel Boyd and Reverend Bayard.'"

Bayard fell silent, pondering her words, which extinguished the little hope he had remaining.

"I doubt Ransom is aware of the attack on you," she continued. "He must have been surprised to see those boys with the Tories."

Bayard nodded. "Where did this fight happen? Where is Ransom's regiment now?"

"He doesn't say," Tabitha answered. "But I know he is in North Carolina. With General Greene."

"Does he say how many men General Greene has now?" Bayard asked. "Does he say where the army is headed?"

"No," Tabitha answered, puzzled by the questions. "You are welcome to read the letter, sir," she said, handing it to Bayard.

Bayard took it and read it through twice. "I had hoped his letter might give us a clue as to how Johnson and Lewis got there," he said, handing it back to her.

"If there is something you want me to ask Ransom, I can try to send him a letter," she replied.

Bayard shook his head. "There is no need for that now," he said. "Perhaps later I will ask for your assistance."

"I will help in any way I can," she said, as she returned the letter to her bag. Casting a troubled look at Bayard, she said, "Ransom says there must be a strong Tory presence here. I am concerned, sir. What must we do?"

"These Tories are clever, Mrs. Wiatt. Clever and devious," Bayard said. "Johnson and Lewis led us north, then somehow slipped away to the south. They must have had allies." He reached out and took Tabitha's hand. "We must be vigilant, madam. Watch carefully and report anything, even the slightest suspicion, to me."

Tabitha nodded. "I will, sir. I will." Pressing his hand, she added, "It is a great comfort to know that you are protecting us, Mr. Bayard. God bless you, sir."

96

Camp of Nathanael Greene's American Army
High Rock Ford
Guilford County, North Carolina
March 13, 1781

Ransom rode slowly along the makeshift road that coursed through the camp until he spotted the soldier he was looking for. He dismounted and approached the man.

As was his custom, Peter Francisco was sitting alone before a campfire. When Ransom drew near, he could see that Francisco was sharpening his saber.

"That's quite an impressive sword," Ransom said, awkwardly trying to initiate a conversation.

Francisco looked up at him, then returned to his work, saying nothing.

"A big man with a big saber ought to have a big horse," Ransom said. Francisco continued sharpening the sword, making no response.

Ransom cleared his throat. "I know that you are a man of few words, Mr. Francisco, so let me come right to the point. That mount of yours is too small for a man your size."

Francisco looked up, no expression on his face.

"I've just been issued this big stallion here," Ransom said. "I prefer a smaller mount. I find it easier to maneuver on a smaller animal. But this big horse here would be just right for a man your size."

Francisco continued to stare at him, still without showing any reaction.

"I'm willing to swap if you are," Ransom said.

Francisco looked back at him a few moments, then rose to his feet. He walked over to the horse and circled it, dragging his hand along its flank as he carefully looked it over, pausing for a second at the burnt patch. Stepping in front of the horse he pulled down its bottom lip and looked at its teeth. Then he stared directly into the horse's eyes for a few moments. Finally, he walked over to Ransom and extended his enormous hand.

Ransom shook his hand but did not immediately release it. "I worry about Colonel Washington," he said, maintaining eye contact with Francisco. "He can't resist getting right in the thick of things when we fight."

Francisco stared back at him, the two men firmly gripping each other's hand.

"In battle the colonel becomes mindless of danger," Ransom continued. "He's liable to get himself killed."

Francisco remained silent, showing no reaction.

"A man who wants to see a lot of action would do well to stay close to the colonel," Ransom said. "A man could have lots of close contact with the enemy that way."

Still gripping his hand, Francisco stared back at

Ransom, without a response.

"That would be good for the colonel too," Ransom said.

Francisco answered with a slight nod. Ransom slightly squeezed his hand, then released it.

"Well, I reckon we ought to get the tack switched," he said as he turned to the horse.

97

Headquarters of Lord Cornwallis
Deep River Quaker Meetinghouse
Guilford County, North Carolina
March 14, 1781

"I have called in all detachments and ordered the baggage removed to the rear," Cornwallis said, as he stepped into the Quaker meetinghouse he had appropriated for his headquarters, trailed by his senior officers O'Hara, Webster, and Leslie. An aide was lighting candles as the men entered.

"You are dismissed," Cornwallis said brusquely. The aide bowed slightly and quickly exited.

Cornwallis moved behind a desk that had been set up for him, gesturing for the other men to take seats.

"Prepare your men, gentlemen," he said. "Our scouts report that the rebel army is making camp at the courthouse. We will strike them there in the morning."

"My men have been issued no rations, General," O'Hara replied.

"There are none to issue," Cornwallis shot back. "There is nothing left in this country to forage. We will have to make do until after the battle."

"It's not just food the men lack, m'lord," Webster said. "But shoes as well. From here to the courthouse is twelve good miles, a long march for men without shoes, rum, or anythin' to eat."

"Our material deficiencies are well-known to me, gentlemen," Cornwallis replied, annoyed. "But we cannot resupply here, and neither can we withdraw in the face of the enemy. It seems that General Greene finally wants a battle. I intend to give him one."

"Begging your Lordship's pardon," Leslie said, "but the reason the rebels are willing to fight is because they have been heavily reinforced."

"We will be greatly outnumbered," Cornwallis said. "Just as we were at Camden. But discipline and the superiority of our men shall carry the day, gentlemen, just as it did there."

The officers looked back at him, without responding.

"We have not come this far and endured this much, to leave without a fight," Cornwallis continued. "I resolved from the beginning of this campaign to fight the rebel army if it approached me. General Greene now dares to do so, and so we must defeat him. The Loyalists of this province will not rise if they doubt the superiority of our arms. We must demonstrate the hopelessness of the rebellion."

"My men will do whatever is asked of them m'lord," O'Hara said.

"Aye," Webster quickly added. "As will my lads."

"Very good," Cornwallis replied. "General Leslie will be on the right, Colonel Webster on the left. General O'Hara, the Jaegers, and Colonel Tarleton will be our reserve. We march at five o'clock."

98

Guilford Courthouse
Guilford County, North Carolina
March 14, 1781

After a 14-mile march that began at six a.m., Greene and his senior officers gathered for a conference in the little courthouse building at the crossroads. A little more than a month earlier, in that same building, his council of war had determined to retreat. This time he announced a different decision. "We will fight them here," Greene said.

"Yesterday's field return reports the army's strength at 4,943," Greene said. "We are as strong as we are going to be. The time to give battle to the enemy has arrived.

"I had planned to attack Lord Cornwallis, but it appears he intends to spare us that trouble," he continued. "So, I have decided to take General Morgan's advice and fight a defensive battle."

There was a stir among the officers in the room—the commanders of the Continentals, Williams and Huger, of the cavalry, Lee and Washington, of the Virginia militia, Stevens and Lawson, and of the North

Carolina militia, John Butler and Thomas Eaton.

"I have examined this site thoroughly when we have been here before," Greene continued. "It is well-suited for the tactics General Morgan used at the Cowpens.

"We will deploy in three parallel lines. The North Carolina militia will occupy the first line. The second line will be composed of the Virginia militia. The third line will be the Continentals. Colonel Lee's legion will be on the army's left wing and Colonel Washington's will be on the right.

"The militia lines will inflict as much damage on the enemy as possible, before falling back behind the Continentals. Colonels Lee and Washington will protect the flanks and fall back as the militia does. The riflemen will rake the enemy as they advance. The dragoons will exploit any opportunity that presents itself.

"The Continentals will stand firm. When the time is right, we shall commence a general counterattack.

"If we all do our parts, gentlemen," Greene said, scanning their faces, "God willing, the British army will be destroyed.

"Questions?" he asked.

"Rations?" Stevens replied.

"Have your men cook their breakfasts tonight," Greene replied. "We will take up our positions at first light, but I do not anticipate that we will be rushed. I expect Colonel Lee and Colonel Washington to assure that we are not."

"Our orders, sir?" Lee asked.

"You will take your command two miles down the New Garden Road and make camp there," Greene answered. "Colonel Washington will do likewise down the Salisbury Road. You will both send out scouts to detect the approach of the enemy and report it to me immediately. When you encounter the British, damage and delay them as much as you reasonably can before returning to the main line and taking up your positions on the wings."

"Sounds like good sport," Lee said.

"Be careful with your men," Greene said sternly. "Take no foolish risks. The success of the general action will depend on you."

The cavalrymen nodded their understanding.

"Gentlemen," Greene said, "this fight will be the climax of much effort and sacrifice. It may determine the fate of our cause. There is nothing more I need say about that. See to your commands and see that they are ready."

99

Robinson Family Farm
New Garden Quaker Community
Guilford County, North Carolina
March 15, 1781
6:00 a.m.

It was a familiar nightmare—the pounding of hooves, shouting, sporadic firing, portents of suffering and death. Then the man sprang up in bed, suddenly wide awake. He cocked his head to listen carefully. He heard them coming. It was no dream.

His heart pounding against his chest, he threw himself from the bed. Staggering as his feet hit the floor, he stumbled toward the window, threw open the shutters, and looked out anxiously into the crisp dawn morning, the sky just beginning to brighten.

When the horsemen rushed suddenly into view, he felt a wave of rage rush over him. He recognized them immediately—Lee's partisans, the green-clad dragoons who had mutilated him and killed his comrades. And riding at their head was the man he knew must be Lee himself.

He looked around frantically for a weapon, then his

attention was whipped back outside by shouting and the clanging of sabers. The little Quaker village was suddenly swarming with cavalry, dueling in the road and among the homes. He knew at once that the cavalry that had charged into the rebels must be Tarleton's troops. They too were wearing green. An officer among them dashed forward and sabered a rebel, dropping him from his saddle, before turning and shouting commands to a company of redcoated infantrymen approaching at a trot. Tarleton! He saw the officer wheel his horse around, lift his saber in the air, then suddenly drop it and shout in pain, as a musket ball tore through his hand.

His heart racing, the man felt a hand on his shoulder and an urgent voice.

"Get thee back to bed," Sarah said, pulling him gently away from the window. "This is no place for thee. This is not thy fight."

He tried to speak, to object, but only a painful groan emerged from his mangled lips.

"Come, Jeremiah," she said, leading him back. "Thou art too weak yet to be on thy feet."

Feeling faint, he obediently allowed Sarah to lead him back to his bed. Just as he laid down, Robinson and his son Thomas rushed in from outside. "Get behind the table, Sarah!" Robinson said urgently, pushing his son in that direction as he spoke.

As Sarah and Thomas crouched down behind the table, Robinson turned to bar the door. But before he could insert the bar, the door flew open and two men carrying rifles and wearing linen hunting shirts burst into the house. They scrambled over to the window, one dropping to a knee and the other standing above him, both pointing their rifles out the window. The house roared and echoed as the men fired simultaneously.

After they fired, the men both spun away from the window and with their backs against the wall began hurriedly reloading their guns. As they did, a volley of shots crashed through the open window, striking the wall a few feet over the man's bed, showering him with splinters.

Robinson, standing serenely in front of the table that was shielding his children, his hands by his side, turned his palms outward, lifted them slightly, looked up, and began to speak. "The Lord is my shepherd; I shall not want." Sarah and Thomas joined in as he continued. "He maketh me to lie down in green pastures, he leadeth me beside the still waters."

The riflemen continued loading, casting hurried glances out the window.

"He restoreth my soul, he leadeth me in the paths of righteousness for his name's sake."

When they had finishing reloading, the men spun around, aimed their rifles out the window and fired again. After firing, the men again quickly ducked away from the window and again musket balls screamed back through the window in response, the bullets slamming into the opposite wall.

"Yea, though I walk through the valley of the shadow of death, I will fear no evil, for thou art with me, thy rod and thy staff they comfort me," the Robinson family continued.

One of the militiamen raised his head, peered quickly out the window, then dropped back behind the wall. "We're pulling out," he said to his comrade. "Time to go."

"Thou preparest a table before me in the presence

of mine enemies, thou anointest my head with oil, my cup runneth over."

Ducking to stay below the opening of the window, the men hurried back to the door. One cracked it slightly open and peeked outside. "We've got to make a run for it," he said. His comrade nodded. Both seemed to take deep breaths before throwing open the door and rushing outside.

The man on the bed looked on in amazement as Robinson raised his hands in the air.

"Surely goodness and mercy shall follow me all the days of my life, and I will dwell in the house of the Lord forever."

100

The Battle of Guilford Courthouse
March 15, 1781
Noon

General Greene rode along his first line of defense—a thousand North Carolina militiamen stretching out on either side of the Great Salisbury Road, deployed behind a rail fence and facing south across a muddy recently plowed field that extended 400 yards to a wood line. Two pieces of artillery were positioned in the center of the road. "This is the most advantageous position I have ever seen," Greene remarked to the aide riding beside him.

The North Carolina men watched as Greene and his entourage, one of them carrying a large flag, rode to the center of the line. Once there, Greene stepped out in front and turned to face the men. The soft-spoken general removed his hat and began addressing the troops.

Nathanael Greene was a brilliant general, but he was not an inspiring speaker. He spoke haltingly, and his voice did not carry.

A few dozen yards away one of the militiamen

turned to a comrade and asked, "What did he say?"

"He said you Carolina boys can kiss your arses goodbye," the man replied, before turning and spitting.

Further down the line a young militiaman turned around and peered into the distance. "Where is the next line?" he asked, nervously.

"Back yonder in the trees somewhere," the man beside him answered.

"We're sitting ducks out here," the young man said.

"Reckon so," the other man replied.

In a few minutes, Greene's speech was over. He put his hat back on and rode away. The militiamen all turned their eyes back to the road, fidgeting with their muskets.

After several anxious minutes a troop of cavalry wearing green tunics and plumed helmets suddenly burst out of the woods, trotting down the road toward them. Some of the militiamen lowered their muskets and began to take aim. "Hold, men!" an officer shouted. "It's Colonel Lee."

Lee's troopers dashed down the road, then veered right, riding off to take their position on the flank. Lee himself rode directly to the far end of the Patriot line. Once there he drew his saber and rode down the line, standing in his stirrups. "My brave boys!" he called out. "Your homes, your lives, and your country depend upon your conduct today!" Waving the bloody sword above his head he shouted, "I've already whipped the British three times this morning. And I will do it again!"

There was a scattering of cheers as he caused his mount to rear, then galloped away to catch up with his men.

Unimpressed, one of the militiamen turned to the

man beside him and said, "That's the last we'll see of him."

Within an hour the British army began emerging from the woods. In their brightly colored uniforms, with drums beating, they began filing into lines of battle, their bayonets gleaming, their flags unfurled and waving in the breeze, officers on prancing horses riding among them, shouting commands. The uneasiness among the Patriot militiamen was palpable as teams of horses pulling cannons appeared, and the British artillery began to unlimber. A militia officer walked behind the men, carrying a sword. "Steady, men," he said, calmly. "Let's give them two good shots."

On the far right of the line, Ransom sat atop his horse, watching as the British deployed. Washington's Legion—the dragoons, Kirkwood's Continentals, and Lynch's riflemen—secured the American right flank, the same role Lee's Legion was filling on the left.

As Ransom was watching the British filing into position, Washington rode up to him. "God be with you today, Captain," he said, gazing out at the British.

"And you as well, sir," Ransom answered.

"Well, Ransom," Washington said. "This is the fight we've been waiting for."

"It looks like Cowpens," Ransom answered.

"Much different," Washington replied quickly.

Puzzled, Ransom turned to face the colonel. "But it's General Morgan's battle plan," he said. "Entirely the same."

"It's different," Washington said, gesturing. "Look at the distances between our lines. The men can't see their supports behind them. And neither can they see what is happening at the line in front of them. It will be easier for them to become unnerved."

Ransom nodded, seeing his point. "But at Cowpens we were outnumbered," he said. "Here, we are not."

"But at Cowpens we had Daniel Morgan," Washington replied. "Here, we do not."

They were interrupted by the roar of cannons. The battle had begun.

101

The Battle of Guilford Courthouse
March 15, 1781
The First Line
1:00 p.m.

Once the British were in formation, the command echoed down the line. "Forward!" The men stepped out, Leslie's brigade of Highlanders and Hessians on the right side of the road, and Webster's brigade—the 33rd Regiment of Foot and the Royal Welsh Fusiliers, on the left.

The North Carolina militiamen were lying down behind the rail fence, their guns resting on the bottom rail. "Hold your fire, men!" their officers were shouting. "Wait 'till they're in range."

~~~

From their position on the right flank, in front of Washington's dragoons, Lynch's riflemen watched as the British attack began. Jacob Thomas was still standing in front of his company, mesmerized by the unfolding scene, when Arthur Lawton called out, "Get
~~~

out of the way Uncle Jake, so we can shoot!"

Jacob stepped through the line, amid a few nervous chuckles, and took his place behind the men. "Hold your fire, men," he said. "Let them get closer."

Arthur lowered his rifle, taking aim at a mounted British officer almost 300 yards away. "Our orders are to wait," Will whispered, tensely. "They're too far off."

"Oh, heck," Arthur replied. "I can hit a turkey at that distance." He squeezed his trigger, the rifle roared, and the officer tumbled from his horse.

"Good shot, Art," one of the men said.

At the sound of the shot Jacob rushed over. He slapped Arthur on the back with the blunt edge of his sword.

"The next man who fires without orders will answer to me!" he shouted, hotly. "And he will regret it!"

Will glared angrily at his brother, who was grinning as he reloaded.

Henry Lawton, who had been standing just behind the main line, pushed his way in between his sons and took a place on the firing line. "It won't happen again, Captain," he said, casting a stern glance at Arthur. "Will it, son?" he asked, testily and with a growl in his voice.

Chastened, Arthur answered, "No, sir," as he rammed a ball down his rifle's barrel.

~~~

As the British marched steadily across the field toward the first American line, a few scattered rifle shots from the flanks began to pepper them and men began to fall, mostly officers. The firing quickened the pace of their advance.

In a few minutes the British had come close enough
~~~

to clearly see the long line of Carolina militiamen awaiting them—their muskets aimed and resting on fence rails—an unnerving sight that caused the advance to hesitate. Seeing his men pause, Webster dashed out in front of the attacking line. "Come on my brave Fusiliers!" he shouted, waving his sword from atop his horse. He was answered with a "Huzzah!" and the line surged forward.

As the British resumed their advance, the Patriot line erupted, sending out a storm of lead.

~~~

Seeing the British marching resolutely forward, and seeing the Carolina militiamen opening fire, Colonel Lynch yelled from behind the line of riflemen, "All right, men! Pick your targets! Fire!"

Will's ears roared in protest as his and 150 other rifles suddenly exploded around him. As soon as he fired, he pulled his rifle down and began reloading. Having his father beside him helped steady him, but his heart was racing as he fumbled with the powder. Settle down, he told himself. He had taken careful aim at a British officer 150 yards away, but with a wall of smoke rising from the firing of the guns, he could not tell if he and the others were hitting their targets.

They were. The blast of rifle fire from the Virginians on their flank tore into Webster's men and dozens fell, dead or groaning with wounds. Riding up ahead of the line, Webster shouted, "Wheel left, lads! Charge them!" He pointed his sword at the Virginians and the men of the 33rd Regiment of Foot turned, leveled their muskets, and drove forward.

The Patriot rifles had a much greater range than
~~~

muskets, but they took twice as long to reload and could not be fitted with bayonets. As the Lawtons and the rest of Lynch's riflemen hurried through the laborious reloading process they could see the British rushing toward them, with bayonets fixed.

Will glanced rapidly back and forth between his gun and the British, who were coming with a shout. "Hold steady, boys," Henry said, as he continued to load.

When the British were about 60 yards away, while the riflemen were still hurriedly loading their guns, Kirkwood's Delaware Continentals suddenly rose, leveled their muskets, and fired a volley, carpeting the ground with dead and wounded redcoats and sending the survivors staggering back.

~~~

Cornwallis was furious. The 33rd was his old regiment and he still had a special affinity for it. Seeing the carnage being inflicted on it by the rebels on the flank enraged him. He turned to an aide. "Tell General O'Hara to move into the gap!" he shouted, pointing at the part of the line Webster had vacated to go after the riflemen. As the aide raced away to deliver the order, Cornwallis called over another courier. "Tell the Jaegers to come up!" he shouted.

He was committing all his reserves.

~~~

The volley from the North Carolina militia behind the rail fence had cut through the British like a scythe in a hay field. Scores of Highlanders, Fusiliers, and Hessians were down. But those who remained, after a volley of their own, leveled their bayonets and charged the Patriot line, shouting huzzahs.

Most of the militiamen had never seen combat before. The sight of the screaming enemy coming at a run with 16-inch bayonets was more than they could bear. Many continued frantically trying to reload, and some managed to fire a second time, but most turned and ran, many throwing down their guns as they did. The panic swept down the entire line and the retreat became a rout.

~~~

From his position atop a hill on the American right flank, Washington saw the militia line dissolving. The men under his command had held, but he knew that if they remained where they were they would be outflanked and possibly enveloped.

He spurred his horse and rode up to Lynch and Kirkwood. "Fall back," he told them. "Take up position on the flank of the next line. The cavalry will cover your withdrawal."
~~~

102

The Battle of Guilford Courthouse
March 15, 1781
The Second Line
1:15 p.m.

Shortly after the cannonading ended, the Virginians on the second line heard the crack of rifle fire in the distance, soon ascending to a general roar of musketry. "Check your flints, men. Get ready," Colonel Perkins said, riding slowly behind the line.

His heart racing and his stomach in a knot, Dodd confirmed, for at least the sixth time, that there was a new flint in his musket. He looked again in his cartridge box, confirmed that it was full, then peered nervously out into the trees, gripping his gun with sweaty palms, even though the air was crisp and cold.

General Greene had positioned his second line of defense in a heavily wooded area about 400 yards behind the first line. The Virginia militiamen who occupied the line straddled the Salisbury Road, General Lawson's brigade on the right side of the road and General Stevens' brigade on the left.

As the shooting in the distance intensified, Stevens

rode along the front of the line, repeating a variation of a speech he had been giving all morning. When he reached Perkins' regiment he stopped, turned in the saddle to face the men, and shouted over the sound of the gunfire.

"We will hold this line!" he yelled, his face flushed. "The stain on Virginia's honor from Camden will be erased today, men!"

Dodd swallowed hard. He could feel his hands trembling and hoped no one noticed.

"Any man who runs today is to be shot instantly!" Stevens shouted. "As for me, I will not leave this line unless I am carried off!"

"Ain't a man here strong enough to carry his fat arse," Dudley muttered.

Dodd turned to him and hissed angrily, "George, when this is over, I am going to punch you in your face."

As Stevens rode away, Perkins stepped out front and said loudly, "Never mind that, men. It's not going to come to that. I know we will all do our duty here. Make ready!"

The firing in the distance was dying down and Dodd spotted movement in the trees ahead of them. He could sense the unease all around him.

Suddenly a man burst into view, running toward them, wearing a hunting shirt and not carrying a gun, fear etched on his face.

"Hold steady, boys," Lieutenant Robertson said. "Let him through."

The panicked militiaman dashed by the Virginians without pausing. Within moments dozens more began to emerge from the woods, racing past them, some weaponless.

"No need to be concerned, men," Perkins said, pacing behind the line. "This is all part of the plan."

"The devil it is," Dudley said, glancing around nervously. "They're whipped."

Then, seemingly in an instant, there were hundreds of them, pouring through the line of Virginians and rushing toward the rear. As the North Carolina men were surging past, Dudley suddenly exclaimed, "Look at the captain! He's hiding behind a stump!"

Dodd turned to see that Captain Morton was sitting beside a tree stump, rebuckling his shoes.

"He ain't hiding, you blockhead," Dodd said. But as he was speaking, Dudley suddenly dropped his gun and leapt into the mob of retreating Carolinians.

"Halt!" Robertson shouted, swinging his sword at Dudley, who dodged it then broke into a run.

Dodd swung around angrily and leveled his musket, taking aim. Then he felt Robertson reach out and push the gun barrel gently to the side. "Don't waste the powder on him," the lieutenant said. Dodd glared at the fleeing men, unable to make out Dudley in their midst, then turned reluctantly back around.

A wounded Carolina militiaman, using his musket for a crutch, limped toward the line. As he passed through it, he called out, "Y'all's turn now. Give 'em hell, Virginia."

After the last of the Carolinians had passed through, an eerie unnerving silence fell over the area. The men squirmed and fidgeted, their unease palpable.

Sensing the danger, Robertson spoke, loudly enough to be heard by the entire company. "How we behave here today men is how we will be remembered for the rest of our lives," he said. "Think of the people who are depending upon us—our families, our neighbors, our sweethearts, our wives, our mothers. This battle may determine whether our country, our cause, our liberty, shall survive. That is on us at this moment. How we behave here today will be remembered for all time."

Morton walked up from behind and placed his hand on Robertson's shoulder. "Well said, Lieutenant," he said. "Now get ready, men! Find a good tree to stand behind. We're going to give it to them Indian style."

In the woods in the distance, Dodd began to see movement—flashes of red, the gleam of polished steel, then the unmistakable figures of soldiers advancing steadily in a line, shoulder to shoulder, wearing red coats, blue Scottish bonnets, and tartan trousers.

"Here they come, boys!" Perkins shouted, riding along the line. "Take aim!"

~~~

Henry Lawton and the rest of the riflemen had finished reloading by the time they reached their new position on the right flank of the second American line. Colonel Lynch and the other officers hurriedly assembled them into a line, with Kirkwood's Continentals on their right and Washington's cavalry behind them. "Steady, men!" Lynch shouted as he rode to a place behind the line. "Here they come!"

Henry glanced over each of his shoulders, to assure that his sons were still there and unharmed. "Careful, boys," he said, trying to appear calm. "This is fixing to get hot."

~~~

Cornwallis intercepted Captain Friedrich Wilhelm von Roeder as he was leading his company of green-jacketed Jaegers to the front. Still seething over the damage the Virginia riflemen had done to his beloved 33rd Regiment, he rode up to the young mustachioed Prussian officer and barked, "Target their officers, Captain. Do you understand me?"

Von Roeder looked back at him, impassively. "*Jawohl*," he replied, with a nod. "Of course, General."

Without another word, Cornwallis wheeled his horse and rushed back toward O'Hara, who was deploying his men to renew the attack.

~~~

Just as Stevens' militiamen leveled their muskets, the Highlanders suddenly stopped and did likewise, volleys erupting from both lines simultaneously.

As he fired, the British musket balls rushed past Dodd like an angry spring storm. As he hurriedly began to reload, the enemy obscured behind a wall of gun smoke, he heard screams and cries from wounded men on either side of him. "Prime and load!" Morton yelled. "Keep up the fire!"

In less than 30 seconds Dodd had again shouldered his musket. The smoke had lifted enough to reveal the British line, advancing steadily with bayonets lowered. He took aim and fired again, beginning the reloading steps as soon as the shot had left his musket.

The first Patriot volley had staggered the Highlanders, who were struggling to mount a charge through the heavy woods. They had not expected the militia to fire again. After a second round of shots tore into them, dropping many, they fell back to re-form.
~~~

At the sight of the redcoats withdrawing, Colonel Perkins raised his sword and shouted "Liberty!" Dodd felt a rush of exhilaration. "Liberty! Liberty! Liberty!" he and the rest of the men chanted, as the British pulled back beyond the range of their muskets.

~~~

Over on the flank, the Jaegers trotted toward Lynch's regiment. Once they were within range, they took up firing positions, aiming their feared short-barreled hunting rifles, targeting the officers among the rebel militia. As sporadic firing began to ring out from the Americans, the Jaegers opened fire.

Their first shots ripped into the riflemen with deadly accuracy. Captains Thomas Helm and William Jones fell instantly, both shot through the head. Ensign Henry Brown collapsed, shot painfully through the thigh. Struck by a Jaeger bullet, Captain James Dixon's horse threw him, then fell dead to the ground.

As the balls whizzed past him, Henry centered one of the Jaegers on his front sight and squeezed his trigger. Though the gun smoke temporarily blinded him, he knew he couldn't have missed. After firing, he quickly pulled his rifle down to reload, but was interrupted by a voice calling out painfully from behind him, "Henry!" He turned to see Jacob, holding his side, and staggering backward.

Henry dropped his rifle and ran to him, catching him just as he was collapsing. "I'm shot, Henry," Jacob groaned.

"I've got you, Jake," Henry answered, wrapping Jacob's arm around his neck. Another man hurried over and took Jacob's other arm, and together they
~~~

began carrying him toward the rear.

After a quick glance back to see his father rushing to Jacob's side, Will spun back around and continued reloading, biting his lip, fighting back tears, and silently praying.

~~~

Dodd went through the motions steadily—loading, aiming, and firing, pulling round after round of buck and ball from his cartridge box, trying to stay focused, his heart still racing, but his hands no longer trembling. When the British charged again, he and his fellow militiamen tore the redcoat line apart with another volley. For a second time, the British fell back to regroup.

A few minutes later, when the British once again returned, Dodd could see that they had been reinforced--their line was longer and stouter than before. The sight of the redcoats coming at a jog, yelling, with their bayonets leveled, sent a chill down his spine. He lowered his musket and pressed his trigger, as the line of American muskets again erupted and roared.

The woods were littered with dead and wounded redcoats, but this time they did not fall back. As Dodd hurriedly began to reload, he could hear their officers shouting the command to present arms. The British formed up in two ranks, leveled their guns, and unleashed a volley into the line of Virginians. Again Dodd felt the balls whistling past him and again he heard the now-familiar thuds as some of them slammed into his comrades.

He dropped the butt of his musket to the ground
~~~

and was beginning to reload, when a shot whisked past him and slammed into Morton's chest. The captain groaned and stumbled forward, knocking the musket from Dodd's hands, as Robertson reached out to grab him.

"Private!" Robertson yelled, summoning a man from the line. The man rushed over. "Get Captain Morton to the rear. Find a surgeon."

"Yes, sir," the man said, lifting Morton onto his shoulders and scurrying away, as Dodd retrieved his gun and cast a worried glance at the British, who he could see were swiftly reloading.

"Prime and load, men!" Robertson shouted, lifting his sword above his head. "Take aim, boys!"

~~~

Shot in the thigh during the attack on the Virginia line, O'Hara had been carried to the rear, where a surgeon was dressing his wound when Cornwallis suddenly rode up. "Are you hurt badly, General?" he asked, from atop his mount.

O'Hara looked up. "I don't think so, my lord," he answered, although the grimace on his face suggested otherwise.

"We must sweep this rebel militia aside, sir," Cornwallis said. "Our attack has been delayed too long. Who has taken command of your brigade?"

"Colonel Stuart, my lord," O'Hara replied.

"Very well," Cornwallis said. He turned his horse, preparing to leave, then stopped and turned back to O'Hara. "I pray your wound is not dangerous, sir."

"Thank you, my lord," O'Hara answered, as the surgeon was finishing wrapping the bandage.
~~~

Cornwallis trotted off toward the British line, reaching Stuart, a twenty-five-year veteran and son of a Scottish earl, just as he had given the order to advance. "Give them the bayonet, Colonel!" Cornwallis shouted.

"These infernal woods are making it difficult, m'lord," Stuart replied.

Cornwallis, frustrated and unaware of how close he was to the American line, spurred his mount and dashed out in front of the advancing redcoats. "Forward, men!" he shouted, lifting his sword.

"M'lord!" Stuart yelled with alarm as he rushed out toward Cornwallis.

A sudden blast of gunfire roared from behind the trees. Struck in the head by a musket ball, Cornwallis' horse squealed, stumbled, then fell to its side, spilling the general onto the ground. He quickly sprang to his feet, as Stuart and several of the Guards rushed to his side.

"Blast it!" Cornwallis exclaimed, furiously. An officer hurriedly dismounted and handed Cornwallis his reins. He took them, then turned to Stuart angrily. "Push through them, Stuart!"

"Aye, m'lord," Stuart answered, as the brigade rushed forward, presented arms, and prepared to fire.

~~~

As the Virginia militia battled the British, the attack on the American right flank had ground to a halt as the Jaegers and Lynch's riflemen dueled—some of Europe's finest marksmen trading shots with some of America's. Washington was watching anxiously from his position behind the line, waiting for an opportunity
~~~

to present itself, when a courier galloped up with an urgent message from General Greene.

"The general directs you to move your cavalry to the left flank of the Continental line," the courier said, nearly out of breath.

"The left flank?" Washington answered, puzzled.

"Yes, Colonel," the courier replied. "To the left of Colonel Williams."

"But what of Colonel Lee?" Washington asked.

"It seems that Colonel Lee is engaged some distance away. Our left is uncovered and General Greene orders that you move there at once."

"Understood," Washington replied. As the courier rode away, Washington rode quickly up to Kirkwood.

"General Greene has directed me to move to the other flank," he said. "Hold your line here as long as you can, Captain, but watch your flank." Pointing to the left he continued, "I am concerned about General Lawson's brigade. Your flank will be exposed when they retreat. Do not allow yourself to be trapped."

"Understood, Colonel," Kirkwood answered.

"You will have to cover the riflemen when they withdraw," Washington said.

"We will do so, sir," Kirkwood answered.

"God be with you," Washington said, as he wheeled his horse and rode hurriedly away, followed by his dragoons.

~~~

The British unleashed another volley, Dodd and the rest of his regiment firing simultaneously. Once again, a hailstorm of musket balls flew into both lines.

This time, at the moment he pulled his trigger,
~~~

Dodd felt his legs buckle. He dropped to his knees and a jolt of searing pain rushed up his body. When he tried to stand, he realized that he had no command over his left leg. He looked down to see a gaping bloody hole where his kneecap had been.

Using his musket as support, Dodd pushed himself to his feet, shifting his weight to his right leg. All around him the scene was roaring and chaotic. Officers were shouting orders, wounded men were calling out for help or screaming in pain.

Shot from his horse in the same volley that had wounded Dodd, Stevens tumbled to the ground. Three men immediately rushed forward, threw down their guns and lifted him back onto his horse. Once they had him back in the saddle, two of the men held him up, while the other led the horse away. "Retreat, my brave boys!" Stevens shouted, grimacing in pain. "Retreat!" On Stevens' command, all along the line the Virginians turned and began running to the rear.

Nearly blinded by pain, Dodd looked ahead, out into the woods. Fifty yards away he could see the British emerging from the smoke, yelling as they charged, their bayonets leveled. Unable to run and unable to reload, he closed his eyes in resignation, feeling a darkness descending, as an image of his family appeared in his mind.

~~~

When Stevens ordered the retreat Robertson turned to leave. But as he did, he noticed Dodd nearby, wounded and leaning against a tree. With the British only yards away, coming at a run, Robertson rushed forward, picked up Dudley's discarded musket and
~~~

fired it point blank into the face of a charging British soldier. Narrowly dodging a bayonet thrust at him by one of the other redcoats, Robertson clubbed the man with the musket, then dropped the gun, threw Dodd over his shoulder, turned, and hurried away, darting for cover in the trees and thickets.

~~~

"Retreat!" Colonel Lynch shouted, seeing the Virginia line collapsing on his left. "Retreat, men!" At the command, the riflemen turned and began rushing to the rear.

As Will turned to go he saw that Arthur was still loading. "Come on, Art!" he exclaimed. "We've got to go!"

"One more shot," Arthur said, ramming home his round, then lifting the gun.

"Now, Art!" Will shouted. "We're retreating!"

Ignoring him, Arthur was taking aim when a shot from one of the Jaegers tore into his left shoulder. Arthur's rifle fell to the ground, and he winced, grabbing the wound with his right hand, blood spurting out between his fingers. Without saying a word, he turned and began staggering away.

"Lean on me," Will said, pulling his brother's uninjured arm around his shoulders. "Let's get out of here."

Seeing the American riflemen beginning to break and run, a cheer went up from the British. They broke formation and surged forward in pursuit.

But Kirkwood and his Delaware Continentals had not retreated. With the British coming at a run, the Continentals leveled their muskets and fired a volley.
~~~

Kirkwood then stepped forward, pointed his sword at the enemy and shouted to his men, "Bayonet, charge!" With a yell, the Delaware men rushed forward, crashing into the astonished redcoats, and sending them reeling. As the British fell back, Kirkwood glanced behind him. Seeing that the retreating riflemen were now clear, he yelled to a wide-eyed drummer boy. "Beat the retreat!"

103

The Battle of Guilford Courthouse
March 15, 1781
The Third Line
2:30 p.m.

Watching as the Virginia militiamen began pouring through and beyond his third line, Greene turned to Williams, elated. "The Virginians behaved nobly," he exclaimed. "They have fought with great valor." He slapped his hand on his thigh. "The enemy is broken up, Colonel," he said. "We will stop them here, sir! We shall deal them a defeat!"

"My men are ready, General," Williams answered.

Greene nodded, then rode away to encourage the men on the other end of the line.

Deployed 500 yards behind the line of Virginia militia, Greene's third and final line was composed of Huger's two regiments of Virginia Continental regulars on the right of the line, and Williams' two regiments of Maryland Continentals on the left, all positioned along the edge of woods, with open fields in front of them. Lynch's riflemen and Kirkwood's Delaware Continentals took up position on the right flank of the

American line, while Washington's dragoons deployed on the far left. The American artillery was in the road, between the Marylanders and Washington's troopers. Greene's strategy, like Morgan's at Cowpens, was to hold and defeat the British at this line.

~~~

Webster emerged from the woods first, at the head of the 33rd Regiment of Foot. Quickly scanning the scene before him, the area appeared to be lightly defended, punctuated with clumps of retreating militiamen. Believing the Americans had been routed, the Scotsman stood in his stirrups, drew his saber, and shouted, "Forward, lads!" The redcoats answered with huzzahs and surged forward.

But Webster had failed to notice the Virginia Continentals, who were concealed behind the tree line. As he and his men rushed across the field, the Virginians leveled their muskets, took aim, then unleashed a devastating volley at nearly point-blank range.

A musket ball slammed painfully into Webster's leg, shattering his femur and kneecap, and knocking him off his mount. Around him, dozens of his men fell dead or wounded under the blistering American volley. The survivors turned and raced back toward the safety of the woods, two of them carrying their badly wounded commander.

Greene was thrilled. It was exactly what he had hoped would happen. Depleted and overconfident, the British had crashed into the Continental line, and they had been stopped cold. As Webster and his men retreated into the woods, Greene could see more
~~~

redcoats emerging along the road and forming up in the field opposite the Marylanders. He spurred his horse and galloped over to that end of the line, anticipating a repeat performance. Victory was at hand.

~~~

His wound dressed, O'Hara had returned to his men, and it was he who personally led them out of the woods and into the field opposite the Maryland Continentals and the rebel cannons positioned in the road. "Guards, advance!" he shouted, pointing his sword at the American line. At his command, the 2nd Battalion of Guards, one of the most elite and storied regiments in the British Empire, answered with a cheer and surged forward.

For most of the men in the 2nd Maryland Regiment of Continentals, this was their first battle. As the British veterans charged forward, bayonets fixed, some of the green Marylanders became unnerved and began to panic. At first only a few peeled off and ran away, but within moments more followed. Soon the entire regiment was disintegrating, abandoning the artillery, and fleeing in a frantic undisciplined retreat.

As the Marylanders ran away, the redcoats sprinted forward. Led by O'Hara, they overran the American line, and swarmed jubilantly around the captured cannons.

Looking on in shock, Greene was mortified. Without firing a shot, the Continental line upon which he had depended for victory, had inexplicably collapsed and his artillery was in enemy hands. Rushing into the midst of the retreating mob, he tried desperately to rally the panicked men—yelling,
~~~

demanding, pleading. But it was in vain. The Marylanders fled, seemingly oblivious to his entreaties. Realizing the hopelessness of his efforts and finding that he was a mere 30 yards away from the charging British, Greene spurred his horse and galloped away.

As he raced to safety amid the unfolding disaster, his flank collapsing and the British threatening to encircle the rest of the army, Greene recognized that he was in danger of losing the entire Continental Line—an unthinkable catastrophe. He saw that the battle had been lost and that he would have to issue an order for a general retreat.

~~~

But what William Washington saw was something entirely different. From his position on a rise to their left, he watched as the regiment of Marylanders dissolved and fled before O'Hara's attack. But when the British swarmed forward, flush with victory, Washington saw that in the zeal of their pursuit they had left themselves exposed. It was the opportunity he had been waiting for since the battle began. He drew his saber, wrapped the sword knot around his wrist, and shouted, "Liberty! Charge!"

At that, Washington and his 120 dragoons thundered across the field, leaped a ravine, and crashed into the flank and rear of the unsuspecting Guards, who never saw them coming. The horses barreled into the crowd of redcoats at 25 miles per hour, bowling them over as the American dragoons slashed and hacked their way through the British ranks.

Twisting in his saddle, holding the reins in his left hand, Ransom was cutting down any redcoat he could
~~~

reach when he spotted Peter Francisco nearby, storming through the now-scattering British, furiously swinging his sword and striking them down like Samson slaying Philistines, his big chestnut stallion knocking over and trampling any who evaded his saber.

After passing all the way through the British regiment and recapturing the cannons, Washington rose in his stirrups and gave the command to wheel and charge again. With another shout, he and the dragoons plowed back into the redcoats, cutting and slashing their way through them a second time.

Among the Guards who were not cut down, some threw themselves onto the ground in an effort to get out of reach of the American sabers. Others fought back with their bayonets, stabbing at the cavalrymen and their horses.

After running down and sabering a British officer, Ransom noticed two redcoat soldiers, twenty yards away, rushing toward Washington from behind, with their bayonets raised. Urgently, he turned and spurred his horse but before he could reach the colonel, Francisco suddenly appeared, striking down both redcoats with two mighty sweeps of his sword. For an instant, Ransom and Francisco made eye contact, then they both turned away and rushed back into the fight.

~~~

Colonel John Eager Howard of the 1st Maryland Regiment had seen it all unfold—the disastrous and inexplicable rout of the 2nd Maryland, followed by Washington's devastating charge into the unsuspecting British. Now the opportunity became his. His regiment
~~~

of veteran Marylanders wheeled left, aimed their muskets, and fired a deadly volley into the British flank. Then, with a shout, they leveled their bayonets and charged.

Already reeling from Washington's surprise attack, suddenly the Guards were also facing a bayonet charge from the finest and most elite regiment in Greene's army. As the British desperately struggled to defend themselves, Washington wheeled his troopers and charged, plunging into the redcoats for a third time.

It was a brutal, bloody, hand to hand melee—a chaotic sea of bayonets, sabers, clubbed muskets, fists, and scattered gunfire. The Guards were fighting for their lives, refusing to surrender, as Washington's troopers and Howard's Continentals were cutting them to pieces.

O'Hara was slashing about with his sword, yelling for his men to stand firm, when a musket ball struck him in the chest, nearly knocking him out of the saddle. With a groan he slumped forward on his horse, which broke and ran for safety.

Francisco was in the thickest part of the fighting, ferociously striking down the enemies closest to him, when a screaming redcoat suddenly lunged forward and drove a bayonet deep into his left hip. Francisco turned to face his attacker, who was trying desperately to pull the bayonet back out. Showing no emotion or evidence of pain, Francisco reached down with his left hand, grabbed the bayonet, and pulled it out of his hip like he was pulling a splinter out of his finger. As the British soldier looked up at him, frozen with astonishment, Francisco slammed his sword into the man's head, cleaving it to the shoulders. At that moment he felt a bayonet pierce his other thigh. He spun in the saddle, swinging his saber.

In the confusion of the fighting, Ransom had lost sight of Washington. He was searching for him, while chopping at the British around him, when he spotted Francisco a few yards away, just as he was being bayoneted. Moments after Francisco killed the redcoat who had bayoneted him, Ransom watched helplessly as a second British soldier surged forward and plunged his bayonet deep into Francisco's other hip. He saw Francisco spin suddenly in the saddle and swing his sword at the man, who ducked and avoided the blade. Ransom spurred his horse and rushed toward them, cutting the redcoat down from behind.

Seeing that Francisco was badly wounded in both thighs, Ransom dismounted hurriedly and helped him out of the saddle, while the fighting swirled chaotically around them. As he eased the giant of a man to the ground and began dragging him toward a nearby tree, the chestnut stallion bolted and raced away. As Ransom propped him up against the tree, Francisco turned and looked at him. The two men made eye contact. Unsure of what to say, Ransom just nodded. Francisco answered with a nod of his own, and Ransom turned away, quickly remounted, then rushed back into the fray.

~~~

Looking out at the bloody struggle, Cornwallis could see that the Guards were being cut to pieces, his victory evaporating before his eyes. He spurred his mount and rushed up to the two cannons deployed in the road and facing the melee, reaching them just as the twice-wounded O'Hara was being helped off his
~~~

horse, just behind the guns.

Cornwallis stared out at the mass of men for a moment, then looked down at Lieutenant John MacLeod, the officer in command of the artillery. “Grape,” he barked.

MacLeod looked back at him incredulously. “My lord?”

Cornwallis, pointed ahead and said, loudly and impatiently, “Give them a shot of grape, sir!”

“But my lord,” the officer replied, “the men are all mixed together.”

“Grape, Lieutenant! Now!” Cornwallis shouted.

MacLeod and the gun crews sprang into action, loading, priming, and aiming the cannons.

“My boys!” O’Hara groaned as MacLeod gave the command to fire.

With a roar, the cannons spewed grapeshot into the melee, tearing a wide bloody swath through the tangle of men and horses, cutting down British and Americans alike. Lacerated horses screamed, spilling their riders and rolling on the ground in pain amid the writhing bodies of bleeding men. Stunned by the sudden blasts, the combatants separated. Howard’s Continentals and Washington’s troopers fell back, away from the British artillery, while the surviving Guards staggered back toward the British rear, just as the Highlanders, the Fusiliers, and the 33rd Regiment of Foot began to arrive on the field.

~~~

Greene watched as the British grapeshot brought the attacks of Washington and Howard to a bloody and sudden halt, rescuing Cornwallis’s beleaguered Guards.
~~~

From his vantage he could see the Continentals and the dragoons withdrawing, and he could also see the rest of Cornwallis' army beginning to arrive on the field. Greene had a momentous decision to make. He recognized at once that a full-scale counterattack now might break the British lines and win the battle. But he also saw that failure could cost him his entire army. The risk was too great. Reluctantly, he gave the order for a general retreat.

~~~

Cornwallis pulled the spyglass away from his eye, snapped it shut, and dropped it into his pocket.

"The rebels are running, my lord," the aide at his side said.

Cornwallis turned and mounted his horse. "No, Lieutenant," he said, as he settled into the saddle. "They are leaving. But they are not running."
~~~

104

Headquarters of Lord Cornwallis
House of John Hoskins
Guilford Courthouse
March 15, 1781
5:00 p.m.

Cornwallis stepped into the small log farmhouse just as a hard cold rain began to fall. Trailed by his adjutant and aides, he dropped wearily into a chair and pulled off his gloves.

"Congratulations on your splendid victory, my lord," said one of the aides.

"Another such victory will be the ruin of this army," Cornwallis answered, quietly. He turned and gazed out the window. "I never saw such fighting since God made me," he said, distantly. "The Americans fought like demons."

The staff officers glanced around nervously. After a few seconds one of them said, "My lord, in addition to the rebel artillery, we have recovered over a thousand stand of small arms on the field."

Cornwallis looked at him. "Any provisions? Anything to eat?"

"No, my lord," the man answered, hesitantly.

Cornwallis straightened himself in his chair, recovering his composure and his dignity. "Are the casualty reports ready?" he asked.

"They are preliminary, my lord," one of the aides answered.

"Well, go ahead," Cornwallis said, brusquely.

The aide cleared his throat and began reading, "Lieutenant Colonel Stuart, killed. General O'Hara, wounded. Lieutenant Colonel Webster, wounded. Lieutenant Colonel Tarleton, wounded. Lieutenant O'Hara, killed. Lieutenant Robinson, killed. Lord Dunglass, wounded. Brigadier General Howard, wounded. Captain Goodricke, killed. Captain…"

"Enough," Cornwallis said, lifting his hand. "What of the rank and file?"

The aide flipped to another sheet of paper. "The Brigade of Guards, 37 killed, 157 wounded, 22 missing. The 33rd Foot, 11 killed, 65 wounded. The 23rd Foot, 13 killed…"

"What is the total number of casualties, Lieutenant?" Cornwallis barked impatiently, interrupting him again.

"We estimate about 510, my lord," the officer replied.

Cornwallis looked down at his desk. "More than a quarter of the army," he said, shaking his head.

The aides remained silent, squirming awkwardly. After a few moments Cornwallis spoke.

"Issue the last of the rations to the men," he said. "They haven't eaten all day. It is going to be a miserable night in this rain without tents."

"Yes, my lord," an aide answered.

"Have the wounded been collected?" Cornwallis

asked.

"Not all of them, sir," one of the aides replied. "The darkness and this rain will make the task very difficult."

"Attend to it, sir," Cornwallis said. "The wounded must be brought in. Find shelter for them."

"What of the rebel wounded, my lord?" the aide asked.

Cornwallis shook his head. "Bring in the officers if feasible. Leave the others. We have no way to feed or care for them."

"Yes, my lord."

Cornwallis turned to his adjutant. "Prepare a proclamation for me to issue for the benefit of our timid Loyalist friends, announcing our complete victory, etc. etc." he said.

"Yes, my lord," the adjutant replied

"We must get what remains of this army to a secure base, where we can provision the men and get care for the wounded," Cornwallis said.

"Wilmington, sir?" his adjutant asked.

"Yes," Cornwallis said. "Begin making preparations for our departure."

105

Camp of Nathanael Greene's American Army
Speedwell Ironworks
Troublesome Creek
Guilford County, North Carolina
March 16, 1781

Henry was beginning to nod off when the sight of Jacob's flickering eyelids suddenly jolted him awake.

Jacob opened his eyes, cautiously it seemed. He glanced around the interior of the ironworks factory, crowded with wounded men. After a few moments his eyes met Henry's and his vision came into focus.

"Where are we?" he asked, his voice rasping.

"We're at Speedwell, Jake," Henry said. "At the ironworks."

It was a good thing that Jacob had been unconscious all night, Henry thought. The thirteen-mile march from the battlefield to the ironworks, in the pitch dark and under a torrential unrelenting cold rain, had been torturous. But General Greene, ever the logistician, had prepared the place for just the contingency they faced. When the exhausted and shivering army finally arrived, provisions and shelter were waiting.

Jacob made an effort to sit up, then groaned in pain and gave up.

"The ball passed through you, Jake," Henry said. "You're going to be all right."

Jacob looked at him. "You know that isn't true, Henry," he said painfully. "I'm all tore up inside."

"Let me see if I can find the surgeon," Henry replied, looking around.

"How did it end?" Jacob asked.

Henry looked at him.

"The battle," Jacob said. "How did it end?"

"We withdrew," Henry answered.

Jacob sighed and closed his eyes. "We were defeated," he said.

"No," Henry said, shaking his head. "We withdrew but we were not defeated. We hurt the British badly, Jake. The men are saying General Greene is fixing to have another go at him. As soon as it stops raining."

Jacob's face brightened slightly. Henry could see that his words had had a good effect.

"How are the boys?"

Henry paused, trying to conceal his pain and concern. "Will is fine. Arthur was wounded."

"How badly?" Jacob asked.

"A ball went through his shoulder and came out by his backbone," Henry answered. "He's in a lot of pain. Will is tending to him."

Jacob winced. "Go to him, Henry," he said.

"I will," Henry answered with a nod. "I just wanted to check on you first."

"Henry," Jacob said, looking at him gravely.

"Yes, Jake."

"See that Annie is taken care of. Look after her."

Henry opened his mouth, intending to insist that Jacob was going to recover, then thought better of it.

"I will, Jake. If need be, I will. You can count on that," he said firmly.

"Thank you, my friend," Jacob said. "Now go look after that boy of yours," he said wearily. "Tell him I asked about him."

"Will do," Henry said, standing up. "Get some rest, Jake. I'll be back shortly to check on you."

Henry weaved his way through the wounded men stretched out over the factory floor. Working his way toward the door he was intercepted by Colonel Lynch.

"Henry," Lynch said, pulling him aside and speaking softly. "General Greene has ordered that the wounded men who can be moved are to be taken back to Virginia as soon as possible. I'm detailing you and Will as part of the escort."

"Thank you, sir," Henry answered, recognizing the kindness and sympathy that was behind the colonel's choice.

"You will leave in the morning," Lynch said. "You are to travel as quickly as you can without endangering the men. There will be wagons waiting at Dix's to take the badly wounded men to the hospital in Halifax. Once they are safely deposited, get back with whatever provisions you can put in the wagons."

"Yes, sir," Henry answered. When Lynch turned to leave, Henry called out, "Colonel."

Lynch turned around. "Yes?"

"I'm taking Jake Thomas," Henry said.

Lynch hesitated a few seconds, then nodded. "I understand," he said, before turning and walking away.

~~~
~~~

Greene poured hot rum into a tin cup and carried the cup over to Washington, who had just entered the little house where the general had established his headquarters. "You're soaked, Colonel," he said, handing Washington the cup. "This might help warm you up."

"Thank you, sir," Washington said, taking it from him.

Greene took a seat in one of two chairs before the fireplace and gestured for Washington to take the other one. "Sit down a minute, Colonel," he said.

Washington took a seat and for a few minutes the men sat silently, sipping their rum and warming themselves.

Greene broke the silence. "How is your command, Colonel?"

"We lost some good men, General," Washington answered. "Three known killed. And we left some good men behind, wounded on the field and now at the mercy of the enemy. The rest of us are in good spirits and ready for duty."

Greene stared into the fire for a few minutes, then said, "Nothing but blood and slaughter prevail here, Colonel, and we are operating in a country little short of a wilderness."

Washington nodded. "I am grateful it was not worse. I believe we did grievous damage to the British. Their losses must have greatly exceeded our own."

"The result was unfortunate, but by no means decisive," Greene answered. After a pause he turned to face Washington and said, "You were magnificent, Colonel Washington. You and your men displayed remarkable valor."

"Thank you, sir," Washington answered. "The men fought courageously." He paused, then turned toward the fire. "But I am pained at the thought of leaving those brave wounded men behind. The fight did not end as I had prayed it would."

Greene turned and looked pensively toward the fire. "We fight, we get beat, we rise and fight again," he said.

Washington nodded. Gazing into the fire, he sipped his rum silently.

106

Guilford Battlefield
Guilford County, North Carolina
March 18, 1781

"Fallen man's capacity for cruelty seems limitless," John Robinson said, as his team of oxen trudged along the muddy New Garden Road, pulling a creaking wagon. He and his son Thomas, along with several other of their Quaker neighbors, had come out that morning to search the battlefield. "How many of these poor souls," he said, gesturing to a gruesome stiff corpse nearby, "must have survived the fight, only to perish in the storm."

Thomas swallowed hard and looked away, his stomach turning at the thought of so many wounded men, left unattended to suffer and die slowly and miserably in a cold torrential two-day rainstorm.

"The wages of sin, Thomas," Robinson said. "Let this be a lesson to thee. That is what thee sees before thee now—the wages of sin." He sighed and pulled back on the reins, stopping the oxen. "These men must be buried. Let us begin loading them."

Thomas hopped down off the wagon. Queasy at the

thought of loading the bodies, he walked toward a nearby oak, trying to settle his stomach. As he drew closer to the tree, he noticed a man's leg protruding from behind it. Approaching cautiously, he stepped around to the other side. At the sight of the man leaning against the trunk, he gasped. "Goliath!" he exclaimed.

~~~

With great difficulty, Thomas and his father managed to lift Peter Francisco into the wagon bed. Breathing but unconscious, the wounded man's clothing was soggy, and both of his hips and legs were thickly caked with dried blood.

Sarah rushed out to meet them when they arrived back at their house in New Garden. She peered over the rail into the wagon, then threw her hand over her mouth. "Have mercy, Lord!" she exclaimed.

She turned to face her father. "I'll make a pallet for him by the fireplace," she said, before hurrying back into the house.

With the help of neighbors, Robinson and Thomas carried Francisco inside. As they lowered him onto the pallet, he began to revive. They stepped back and when they did Francisco's eyes opened and he glanced around, confused.

Sarah dropped to her knees beside him and gently rested her hand on his arm. "Peace, good soul," she said sweetly. "Thou art with Friends."

As Francisco's eyes darted around the house, his gaze landed on the mutilated face of a young man sitting up in a bed on the other side of the room. When the two men made eye contact, they both recognized
~~~

instantly that they were enemies.

The young man turned to face the wall and Francisco turned and stared up at the ceiling. A few seconds later Sarah lowered a cup to his lips and said, "Take a sip of this soup. It will refresh thee."

Francisco swallowed obediently.

"Now rest quietly," she said softly, "My father will cut away thy breeches so I may clean and dress thy wounds."

Francisco returned his gaze to the ceiling.

"Perhaps our village will finally have some peace," Robinson said as he began cutting.

"What do you mean?" Sarah asked, while gently peeling the blood-caked cloth off Francisco's legs.

"General Cornwallis is leaving," Robinson answered. "The camp followers say he is marching his army to Wilmington."

Startled, the mutilated young man's eye flew open.

~~~

The next morning, as dawn was beginning to break, Sarah quietly approached the bed, carrying a candle. "Wake up, Jeremiah," she said gently. "It is time for me to dress thy wounds."

She threw the light of the candle upon the bed and was surprised to discover that it was empty. Lying atop it was the slate and chalk. Tilting the candle, she saw scrawled on the slate, barely legible, the words "Thank you."
~~~

107

On the road to Dix's Ferry
Guilford County, North Carolina
March 20, 1781

Songbirds sang cheerfully in the bright sunshine, and along the roadside wildflowers joined them in announcing the coming of spring. But in the gloomy column of men trudging north on the muddy road, the only thing joyful was the thought of home.

Henry and Will were marching silently at the head of the column, their rifles shouldered, scanning the woods and fields around them for any sign of danger. From the wagons behind them came an occasional groan, as the wounded men were bumped and jostled along the rutted road.

"Look, Pa," Will said, gesturing toward a field to the east. A few hundred yards away, a saddled but riderless horse was coming toward them, at a trot.

"Be alert," Henry said, readying his gun. He raised his right hand and brought the column to a halt.

Will brought his rifle to the ready, his eyes darting rapidly around the field and surrounding woods as the horse continued to approach. When it was less than a hundred yards away, he said, "That horse looks just like Caesar."

Henry swung around and looked quickly at the approaching horse, seeing that his son was right, then resumed scanning the distance. "Pay attention, Will. Keep an eye on those woods yonder."

Without pausing, the horse trotted directly to Will, coming to a stop when he arrived. Will reached out and touched the animal's head. After a few seconds, he exclaimed, "Pa, this *is* Caesar!"

Henry glanced over his shoulder at the horse, then turned nervously back toward the woods along the road, swinging his gun in that direction. "Can't be," he said, peering into the woods. "Just looks like him. Don't let him distract you, son."

At that the horse stepped past Will, lowered his head, and began to nudge Henry's coat pocket. Astonished, Henry turned slowly around and looked the animal directly in the eyes. Then he relaxed his grip on his gun and, bewildered, walked slowly around the horse, dragging his hand gently along the animal's sides and flanks. After a complete circuit he stopped, scratched the horse behind an ear, ran his hand across its mane, then rubbed it on the forehead. The horse answered with a snort and a nod, then nudged Henry's coat pocket again. "Well, I'll be," Henry said, amazed.

At that moment an officer, with one of his arms in a sling, rode up. "What is the reason for this delay, Sergeant?" he barked.

For a few moments, Henry continued staring at the horse in astonishment. When the fog cleared from his mind, he turned to face the officer. "This horse just came up from that field yonder," he said.

The officer looked quickly at the horse, then out

across the field. "Any sign of the rider?"

"None, sir," Henry answered. As the officer continued searching in the distance Henry continued, "Sir, this is *my* horse."

The officer looked at him. "Your horse? What do you mean?"

"I mean this horse belongs to me," Henry answered. "To our family in Bedford County. How he came to be here, or who this saddle belongs to, I have no idea."

The officer looked at the horse, skeptical. After a few seconds he said, "Well, unless someone else shows up to claim him, we can use him." He turned in his saddle and called out, "Wells! Coleman! Take the van!" Two militiamen came forward. The officer turned back to Henry, "Put the horse to use, Sergeant," he said. Turning back to the wagons he shouted, "Resume the march!"

Henry led Caesar down the line of wagons. As he neared one of them, he called out brightly, "Jake, you're not going to believe this!" Beaming, he looked over the railing into the wagon.

His smile disappeared instantly when he saw Arthur sitting up in the wagon bed, cradling Jacob's head on his lap. The boy looked up at his father, his eyes filled with tears. "He's gone, Pa," he said.

108

Dix's Ferry
Pittsylvania County, Virginia
March 21, 1781

When the column reached the Dan River there were a half dozen boats waiting to ferry them across. Word had been sent ahead that the men were coming, so on the north side of the river they were being awaited by their anxious families, along with wagons that would transport to the hospital in Halifax the men too badly wounded to go home.

Once across, Henry led Caesar off the boat and onto the shore, Arthur and Will by his side, and into the crush of people—some searching for loved ones, others in the midst of bittersweet reunions. As they were gingerly trying to make their way through, Martha suddenly burst out from among the crowd, her arms outstretched, and her face streaked with tears. She ran straight to Arthur, smothering him with kisses while battling the impulse to hug him. "Oh, my son. My precious son," she repeated between kisses.

Henry and Will stood by patiently, their hats in their hands. After a few minutes of devoted attention to

Arthur, Martha turned and wrapped Henry in a powerful hug, weeping. Then she released one arm and pulled Will in as well. "My prayers are answered," she said, choking with emotion, pulling them both tightly to her. "Thank you, Lord. Thank you. Thank you."

Just as Henry felt his heart would burst, he heard words that sent a chill up his spine.

"Where is Jacob?"

Martha relaxed her hug and turned around to face Ann Thomas, who was scanning the boats, a distressed look on her face. Martha turned quickly to her husband and read the answer instantly on his face. Her eyes widened and she threw her hand over her mouth.

Henry stepped toward Ann. "Where is Jacob, Henry?" she said, her eyes darting now, her tone more frantic.

Henry reached out and took her hand, trying to make eye contact. "Ann," he said gently.

"Where is he?" she said, urgently and more loudly. "Where is Jacob?" She pulled her hand away. "Where is he? Where is he? Where…."

Suddenly Ann fell silent and looked into Henry's eyes. He turned his gaze slowly toward Caesar and then to the litter the horse was pulling, and Ann's eyes followed his. As he turned back slowly to face her again, he said, softly, "Ann…"

Before he could speak another word, she let out a shrieking wail, dashed forward, and threw herself onto the litter, onto the tightly wrapped body of her husband.

Henry lowered his eyes as they filled with tears, then turned again to face his wife. For a moment she stared back at him, tears streaming down her face. Then she turned away and hurried to Ann's side, falling to her knees, and weeping alongside her.

~~~

The pain of the grieving women reopened the wounds on Will's heart. He turned his head to hide his tears, and when he did he noticed Lucy, standing back, fearful of intruding. He bolted toward her, and she met him halfway. They wrapped each other in a tight hug, Lucy whimpering, bathing his shoulder with tears while he fought to keep his composure. They were interrupted by the voice of Abraham Soblett.

"Welcome home, Will," he said, as the young couple embraced. "I've been reflecting on this campaign, the logistics of it I mean. It is interesting to compare how the two commanding generals have…."

Will suddenly released Lucy and turned to face her father. "Mr. Soblett," he said abruptly, interrupting him, "I want to marry Lucy."

Soblett seemed surprised by the interruption. "Well, young man, as we have discussed in the past, when Lucy is a bit older…"

"No, sir," Will said firmly. "I want to marry her now. Immediately."

"Immediately?" Soblett replied, seemingly confounded. "Well, that isn't…," he stammered, at a loss for words for perhaps the first time in his life. "I mean to say, at some point in the future… Some reasonable time, I mean…"

"Mr. Soblett," Will said. "We've waited long enough, sir. Lucy and I want to be married now. Not later."

"This all seems rather impulsive, rather impetuous. The emotion of the moment has perhaps…" Mr.
~~~

Soblett stopped, arrested by Will's determined stare and the imploring plea on the face of his daughter. Taken aback, he turned toward his wife. "My dear…," he began, stopping cold when he saw her resolute stare. "Well, um, I see," he said.

He furrowed his brow and looked carefully into the three faces awaiting his answer. He opened his mouth to speak, then stopped. He bit his lower lip and turned his gaze away for a few seconds. When he looked back at them, he was smiling.

"Immediately?" he said. "A wonderful suggestion. It will be a joy and honor to have you join our family, son," he said, extending his hand to Will.

~~~

Alice Lightfoot wandered among the thinning crowd, searching for her son with increasing concern, her heart racing as it rose into her throat. She had been told that Dodd had been wounded, and that he would be among the men arriving at Dix's that day. About his condition, about the nature of his wound, she knew nothing.

She had watched anxiously as the boats unloaded, and all around her in the crowd she had witnessed both tearful reunions and heartbreaking grief. But she had seen no sign of Dodd.

Finally, behind her, she thought she heard someone say his name. She looked around frantically. Where had the voice come from? She rushed ahead in one direction, then stopped and turned in another. Where? Becoming increasingly distressed, she noticed two men loading a wagon nearby. She pushed her way toward them and as she drew close, she saw what they were
~~~

loading. She gasped and began to sob, as the men carefully lowered another body onto the wagon bed. She felt herself growing faint and dizzy, her heart being rent apart. Then she heard a voice call out from behind her.

"Ma," Dodd said.

Alice spun around, bursting into tears at the sight of her son, propped up on crutches, one of his legs wrapped in bloody bandages. With a wail, she wrapped her arms around his neck and wept with joy and relief.

109

Martin's Tavern
Peytonsburg
Pittsylvania County, Virginia
October 20, 1781

As he rode slowly into town, Bayard felt as if he was enveloped in a despondent cloud. He had come to get the latest news from Yorktown, but he had already resigned himself to expect the worst.

The long ride had given him time to reflect, not just on the impending disaster on the coast, but on all the mistakes and tragedies of the year—a year that had begun with so much hope.

Cornwallis was a fool. Of that he was now sure. The seeds for the siege at Yorktown had been sown at Guilford Courthouse. What folly! What madness! To march his army deep into hostile and barren territory, without provisions, without a base of supplies, and without any realistic hope of reinforcement—it had been a monumental blunder. And then to issue an arrogant proclamation, announcing a "complete victory," with a quarter of his army killed or wounded and many of the survivors starving and barefoot—how could the man have been so deluded?

But it wasn't Cornwallis's mistakes that tormented him the most, it was his own. How many times had he failed? How many fatal errors had he made? He couldn't even count them.

Of all his mistakes, the one that haunted him the most was his decision to send Gus Johnson to Benedict Arnold. How stupid it seemed in hindsight. He had sent that young man to his death.

And yet, there had been so much optimism at the time. The King's forces were victorious and on the march. The rebels were reeling. The end seemed near. He shook his head. He saw now that the optimism had been unwarranted and that he had allowed himself to be swept up in it, with tragic consequences.

And now, he thought, as he dismounted and tied his horse to the hitching post, the Loyalist rising that he had spent years planning and preparing for would never occur. All that remains now is the denouement, he thought, the final degrading and ruinous scene. He pushed open the door and stepped into the tavern.

Bayard donned his cheerful mask upon entering. "Good day, John," he said to the tavern keeper as the approached the bar. "Has the express arrived?"

"Not yet, Reverend," Martin answered, filling a tankard with ale and sliding it across the bar to Bayard. "We're expecting him any time now."

"With momentous news, let's hope," Bayard answered, as he took the tankard, turned, and walked toward a table in the rear.

As soon as Bayard turned his back, Martin pulled a young server over and whispered something in his ear. The boy nodded and dashed out the door.

Bayard settled onto a bench at a table and took a

long drink. Am I doomed to spend the rest of my life acting out a lie? he thought.

After sitting quietly for a few minutes, brooding while pretending not to be, he heard a voice call out to him. "There you are!" He looked up, to see Charles Clay coming through the tavern door and striding toward him.

Oh Lord, spare me from this blowhard, Bayard thought, while affecting a warm smile.

Clay sat down at the table, directly opposite Bayard, his face somber.

"Have an ale on me, Mr. Clay," Bayard said.

Clay shook his head. "I'm here on business, Wynn. Very serious business."

As Clay was speaking, Bayard saw the tavern door open again. Colonel Wilson and Colonel Boyd entered, accompanied by a militia officer Bayard didn't recognize. Behind them, Bayard could see that a sentinel had been posted outside the door. The men closed the door and approached.

"We have been discussing you all morning, sir," Clay said, as Wilson and Boyd took seats on either side of Bayard. The other officer stood behind Clay, his hands on his hips.

"Recent events have caused us to make a very careful examination of your past actions, sir, as well as of your opinions, both expressed and implied," Clay said grimly.

Bayard shot a glance around the room, seeing immediately that he had no chance of escape.

Clay leaned forward, locking eyes with Bayard.

"Our investigation has led us to a conclusion, sir," he said. "A conclusion we should have reached much sooner."

Bayard sighed. It will be a relief to finally stop lying, he thought.

Clay looked sternly at him for a second, then broke into a wide smile. "We want to put you up as a candidate for the legislature, Wynn," he said. "Now more than ever our country needs men like you."

"Hear, hear!" Boyd and Wilson exclaimed, clapping him on the back.

110

Sandy Hill Plantation
Charleston District, South Carolina
February 20, 1810

Ransom was staring up at the wall in the foyer, entranced, when he was interrupted by a woman's voice. "How may I be of service to you, sir?"

Lowering his gaze to the woman, he recognized her instantly. Instead of the riding habit of a spirited 17-year-old, Jane Elliott now wore a tasteful peach dress, ruffled on the collars, with a string of pearls around her neck. The long flowing auburn hair he remembered was now tied up neatly atop her head. The beautiful girl he remembered from 30 years earlier was now an elegant woman.

"I regret that I had no calling card to present to your servant, Mrs. Washington," Ransom said, bowing slightly, holding his hat in his hand. "I am an old comrade of your husband. I recently learned of his illness and have come in hopes of seeing him."

She answered him cordially, but firmly. "I am sure the general would be delighted to see you, sir," she said, "but unfortunately his illness prevents him from receiving visitors."

Ransom nodded, deeply disappointed. "I understand, ma'am," he said. Pausing to consider what message to leave, his eyes, seemingly involuntarily, returned to the item on the wall.

When Jane turned her head to see what he was looking at, Ransom sputtered, apologetically, "Please pardon me, Mrs. Washington. It's just that that flag is very dear to me. I haven't seen it in many years."

Jane smiled, looking up at the 18-inch square piece of crimson cloth affixed to the wall. "I was a silly young girl, sir. When I told the dashing Colonel Washington that I would anxiously await news of the triumph of his flag, he replied that he had no flag. So, I rushed inside our home, cut that square from the drapery, and presented it to him."

"I remember that day well, Mrs. Washington," Ransom replied, his eyes misting at the memory.

"We call it our Eutaw Flag, in memory of the battle where my husband was captured and grievously wounded," Jane said. "It flew at our wedding."

"I was by your gallant husband's side at Eutaw Springs, Mrs. Washington," Ransom answered, facing her. "It was there that I was transformed into the monstrous sight you see before you. I hope you were forewarned."

Jane looked back at him, pleasantly. A black patch covered one of his eyes and two jagged scars crossed his face, one through a badly misshapen and incomplete nose.

"I see nothing but evidence of valor, honor, and patriotism, sir," she replied with a gentle smile.

Ransom bowed his head slightly. "Thank you, ma'am," he said, touched. After a moment he said, "I will take my leave now. Will you please be so kind as to tell your husband that Ransom Wiatt came to wish him well?"

He turned to leave, then paused. Turning back and gesturing toward the flag, he added with a smile, "We called it 'Tarleton's Terror.'"

Turning away again, Jane suddenly stopped him.

"Wait, sir!" she exclaimed. "My servant mispronounced your name. Are you Captain Wiatt?"

"Yes ma'am, I am," Ransom answered.

"Oh, my," she said, her face lighting up. "I think it would do William a great deal of good to see you, sir. I think he will be very pleased.

"Come with me, sir," she said, leading Ransom down a hallway. He followed her, walking with a pronounced limp.

She stopped at a doorway, turned and, with lowered voice, said, "Regrettably, your visit will have to be brief, sir. And you must avoid overly exciting him."

Ransom nodded his understanding and he followed Jane into the room.

The room was shuttered, dimly lit by scented candles. A nurse, who had been sitting by the bed in the center of the room, rose when they entered. After a signal from Jane, she curtsied and exited.

Jane approached the bed, Ransom cautiously following her. "William," she said pleasantly. "You have a visitor. One of your dragoons has come to see you."

Ransom drew closer.

The man lying on the bed opened his eyes, as Jane bent over and adjusted the pillow upon which he was propped. Even though pale-skinned, thin, and cadaverous, seemingly drained of his vigor and vitality,

Ransom instantly recognized his colonel. He was struck immediately and simultaneously by a strange combination of sadness and joy.

"Good day, sir," Ransom said.

Washington looked back at him, studying his face for a few moments, until his eyes suddenly widened and brightened, his face flooded with emotion. "Ransom??" he said, his voice raspy. "Ransom Wiatt?"

"Yes, sir," Ransom answered, with a smile. "I'm surprised you recognize my face in its present condition."

"Of course I recognize you!" Washington said, struggling to sit up.

Jane bent over again, put a hand behind his back and helped him sit up.

"Of course I do!" Washington said, smiling broadly and extending his hand. "It is so good to see you, my friend."

Ransom shook his hand, cold and skeletal.

"I am very pleased to see you as well, sir," Ransom answered. "It's been a long time."

"Yes," Washington replied. "Yes, it has." He turned his head and coughed, then turned back to Ransom. "You must excuse me for not getting up, my friend, and for my wretched condition. I am, for now, confined to this miserable bed."

"I understand, Colonel," Ransom answered, then quickly corrected himself. "Pardon me, sir," he said. "I should have said 'general.'"

"Bah!" Washington said, with a dismissive wave of his hand. "They made me a general, but I have never had a greater title than lieutenant colonel of the Continental dragoons." He paused, looking intently into Ransom's face. "I wondered if I would ever see you again, Ransom. The last time I laid eyes on you was during that catastrophe at Eutaw Springs."

Ransom's face turned somber. "I never would have left you there, sir. Had I been able I would have brought you out. I have wanted to tell you that for nearly 30 years.

"When I was shot," Ransom continued, "the ball passed through my ankle and into my horse. The horse fell and pinned me to the ground. While I was struggling to get free, a British officer did me the favor of sabering me in the face, as you can see.

Then, to my great surprise, the horse, a noble creature, got back to her feet, dragged me back to our lines, then promptly expired."

"I thought we were all done for," Washington said. "My horse went down too. The bastards bayoneted me before I could get out from under it."

Ransom nodded. "I saw it happen, sir," he said. "I was trying to get to you when I was shot."

Washington chuckled, shaking his head. "Our luck finally ran out that day, didn't it, Captain?"

Ransom smiled. "I suppose it did. But Providence is mysterious. Our misfortune brought you back to Miss Elliott."

Washington smiled and turned his eyes to his wife, who smiled sweetly back at him.

"Yes, it did. That it did," he said. "Jane was a wonderful nurse. She sweetened my captivity." He turned back to face Ransom. "What of the old troopers? Do you keep up with any of them?"

"No, sir," Ransom said. "I'm afraid not. I found a woman willing to marry the ugliest man in Virginia and we moved to her family's farm in North Carolina, not far from where we fought at Guilford."

"Jennie?" Washington asked.

"No," Ransom said with a slight smile, shaking his head. "I'm surprised you remember that. I was heartsick for Jennie for many years, but God brought me a woman who took all that away. We have five children."

"Ha!" Washington exclaimed, cheerfully. "That's the style, Captain!" he said with a laugh, then he began coughing roughly, turning his head, his shoulders shaking. Jane hurried to his side, wiped his face with a handkerchief and reached for a glass on the bedside table, casting an imploring look at Ransom as she did.

"Perhaps I should go now and let you rest, sir," he said.

Washington raised his hand and shook his head, his face reddened but his coughing subsiding. "No, not yet," he said, his voice cracking. He took a sip from the glass and returned it to Jane. "Please stay a little longer."

Ransom glanced at Jane and interpreted her expression as reluctant consent.

"So, what happened to Jennie?" Washington asked.

"When the Tories in our community were being exposed, she fled with some of them to Wilmington," Ransom answered. "After the war was over, I went there to look for her. I turned over every rock in that town but could find nothing. I was ready to give up when I finally found a woman who remembered her. She said that right after Cornwallis left for Virginia, Jennie took a ship to England. She said Jennie was traveling with a man whose face looked even worse than mine, if you can imagine that."

Washington nodded. "But it all ended well for you, Ransom."

"It did, sir," Ransom replied. "I've been blessed."

Washington changed his tone, his expression becoming more serious. "I've had a lot of time to think, while stuck in this blasted bed. I often wonder if it was all worth it. What do you think, Ransom? Was it worth it? All we did? All we suffered?"

"Worth it?" Ransom said, surprised by the question. "Of course it was. We have our independence."

"Yes, but what are we making of it?" Washington asked, scowling. "Squabbling, bickering partisanship is all we hear now. Federalists versus Republicans, East versus West, North versus South. We have no unity. I fear our cause may be destined to die."

Jane shot an urgent look at Ransom, and he saw her meaning instantly—do not discuss politics.

Before Ransom could speak, Washington continued, "And I fear our struggle is being forgotten, Ransom. When we forget the cost of our independence, we render it less valuable." He shook his head, sadly. "The youth of today know little about the war and they care even less. Who remembers Cowpens now? Or Guilford? Or Eutaw? It seems to me that for most Americans today it was just Bunker Hill, then Valley Forge, then Yorktown. If that. Will we even be remembered at all in another few years?"

Jane reached out and laid her hand tenderly on Washington's shoulder. "Do not allow yourself to become excited, dear. Remember what the doctor said."

"Yes, yes, yes," Washington said, with a wave of his hand. "I know, I know."

Ransom saw the concern on Jane's face and saw that the conversation was fatiguing Washington.

"I regret that I must be going now, sir," he said.

"But I will answer your question first. Yes, Colonel, I choose to believe that we will be remembered. *Omnia fert aetas, animum, quoque.* 'Time bears away all things, even our minds.' In time our countrymen may forget our names. They may forget our deeds. But they will never be able to forget what we earned for them. Our memory will live on in what they possess—what they have because of what we did. Their liberty will be our legacy."

Washington closed his eyes for a few seconds, then smiled and reached out his hand. Ransom gripped it warmly.

"God bless you, Ransom," Washington said.

"And you, sir," he answered.

Dramatis Personae

Benedict Arnold left Virginia shortly after Cornwallis arrived. He led a raid that burned New London, Connecticut, adding to his infamy in America. In December 1781 he traveled to England, where he lobbied to be given command of the British army in America, while continually complaining that he had not been adequately compensated for his defection. Spurned and distrusted, he died in England in 1801 at age 60, deeply in debt.

Wynn Bayard was elected to the Virginia House of Delegates in 1782. He was unopposed. Relying on his service to the cause, several of his descendants have since been proud members of the DAR.

Edward Carrington served as General Greene's quartermaster for the rest of the war. After the war he served as a delegate to the Continental Congress and was appointed the first U.S. marshall in Virginia by George Washington. One of the founders of the Society of Cincinnati, he died at age 62, having had no children. He was buried at St. John's Church in Richmond, where at age 27 he had heard Patrick Henry deliver his famous "Liberty or Death" speech.

Charles Clay retired from the ministry and served as an anti-Federalist delegate to the Virginia Constitutional Convention of 1788. In 1790 he ran unsuccessfully for Congress. In his old age he managed his farm and frequently visited his friend Thomas Jefferson.

Charles Earl Cornwallis marched his army to Virginia, after it rested and was reprovisioned in Wilmington. There he was trapped at Yorktown and forced to surrender to a combined U.S. and French army commanded by George Washington and French general Rochambeau. He was received with honor on his return to England, generally not regarded as being at fault for the surrender. In 1786 he became Governor-General of British India and commander in chief of British forces there. After his victory over the Kingdom of Mysore, he was elevated to Marquess in 1792. Afterwards Cornwallis was appointed Lord Lieutenant of Ireland and commander in chief of British forces there, defeating both the Irish rebels and a French invasion force. He returned to India as Governor-General in 1805, dying soon after his arrival at age 66.

George was bequeathed to Will Lawton in Henry Lawton's will. At age 24 he married, and he and his wife had several children together. He and his family remained the property of the Lawton family all their lives. George died in 1850 at age 84.

George Dudley moved to Kentucky. In 1832 he applied for a pension, citing his service at the Battle of Guilford Courthouse. His application was approved.

Joseph Eggleston served in the Virginia House of Delegates for 13 years before serving a term in the United States House of Representatives. He died at his home in Virginia at age 56.

Lawrence Everhart became a Methodist minister. He died at his home in Maryland in 1840, at age 85.

Peter Francisco was nursed back to health by the Robinson family. On his way back to his home in Virginia he encountered and killed several of Tarleton's dragoons, adding to his already legendary status. After the war he married three times and fathered six children. He died in Richmond at age 70, having spent the last three years of his life as sergeant at arms of the Virginia Senate. A monument on the battlefield at Guilford Courthouse credits him with having slain 11 British soldiers in the battle. In an 1820 letter to the Virginia General Assembly he wrote, "I never felt satisfied, nor thought I did a good day's work, but by drawing British blood."

Joseph Graham served as a brigadier general of North Carolina militia during the War of 1812. A delegate to the North Carolina constitutional conventions and a member of the first board of trustees for the University of North Carolina, he earned great wealth as an iron manufacturer.

Nathanael Greene led his army back into the Carolinas, where he repeatedly fought, was beaten, rose up, and fought again. By the end of 1781 he had recovered nearly all of North Carolina, South Carolina, and Georgia. Regarded as one of the greatest heroes of the Revolution, after the war he relocated to a plantation near Savannah, a gift to him from the state of Georgia. There he died of sunstroke in 1786 at age

43.

John Eager Howard was seriously wounded while leading a bayonet charge in the Battle of Eutaw Springs, forcing him to retire from the army. After the war he served in the Maryland legislature and in the United States House and Senate. He was elected to three terms as governor of Maryland and was the Federalist vice presidential candidate in 1816. He died in 1827 at age 75.

Isaac Huger was shot in the hand at the Battle of Guilford Courthouse but later returned to duty with Greene's army. After the war he served in the South Carolina legislature and was the first U.S. marshal in the state. In 1785 he fought a duel with Founder and fellow South Carolinian Charles Cotesworth Pinckney, shooting Pinckney in the leg with his third and final shot, all three of Pinckney's shots having missed. Afterwards both men advocated for the abolition of dueling. General Huger died in 1797 at age 54.

Duncan Jones and his sons continued to serve under Andrew Pickens for the remainder of the war, rejoining General Greene's army when it returned to South Carolina. All survived the war, afterwards returning to their family farm on the Pacolet River.

Robert Kirkwood was never promoted above captain, despite the valor of he and his famed "Blue Hens," being denied advancement because promotions were doled out by state and his small state of Delaware had no vacancies. He moved to Jefferson County Ohio in 1787. Commanding a company of regulars, he was killed at St. Clair's Defeat in 1791 during the Northwest Indian War, at age 35. In Henry Lee's history of the war he wrote, "It was the thirty-third time he had risked his life for his country; and he died as he had lived, the brave, meritorious, unrewarded, Kirkwood."

Arthur Lawton lost the use of left arm permanently as a result of his wound at Guilford Courthouse and was granted a small pension from the state of Virginia. In 1787 he married and moved to a farm in Raye, Virginia, where he and his wife built a house and raised two children. Hampered by his disability, Arthur was not a successful farmer. He died in 1818 at age 58, substantially in debt.

Will Lawton married Lucy Soblett on April 1, 1781. He served two more tours of duty before the war ended and was present at the siege of Yorktown. After the war he and Lucy moved to Pittsylvania County and had seven children together. He died in 1846 at age 85. Lucy's application for a widow's pension was denied because she could not prove the exact dates of her husband's service.

Henry Lawton died in 1796 at age 61, a year after the death of his wife Martha.

Henry Lee commanded his legion with distinction for the remainder of the war. In the post-war years he served in Congress and as governor of Virginia. He was promoted to the rank of major general by George Washington in 1798. Lee twice married wealthy women, squandering the estates of both wives through a series of speculative investments. While in debtors' prison he authored a successful history of the war in the Southern Theater. Seriously injured in 1812 by an anti-Federalist mob while defending a Federalist newspaper in Baltimore, he traveled to the Caribbean to recover and to escape his creditors. In 1818, while on his way home to Virginia, he died in Georgia at age 62, being cared for in his final days by a daughter of Nathanael Greene.

Jennie Lewis was seen boarding a ship to England in April 1781, accompanied by a badly disfigured man. Nothing more is known of either of them.

Dodd Lightfoot's wound left him disabled the rest of his life. Nevertheless, he became a farmer in Maple Grove, married, and fathered eight children. He died in 1848.

Archibald McArthur was transferred to the 60th Regiment of Foot, after a prisoner exchange, where he served for the balance of the war. He joined in a petition to Cornwallis, in which the signatories declared their refusal to ever serve under Banastre Tarleton again. Later promoted to brigadier general, he served in Canada, the Caribbean, and Europe. After marrying a German woman, he retired from the army at age 60. He died in Germany at age 75.

John MacLeod was presented to the King by Cornwallis, in honor of his service at the Battle of Guilford Courthouse. In a long and distinguished career, he served all across the empire, rose to the rank of lieutenant general, and became the highest-ranking artillery officer in the British army. He married the daughter of a marquess and fathered nine children. He died in London at age 80.

Daniel Morgan recovered from his sciatica sufficiently to return to the army when Tarleton launched a raid across central Virginia in the summer of 1781. This time Tarleton carefully avoided Morgan and his army. General Morgan was called up to help suppress the Whiskey Rebellion and he was elected to a term in Congress, but he chose to spend most of his final years managing and enjoying his Virginia estate. In 1792 President Washington nominated him to be second in command of the United States Army, but Morgan declined the offer. He died in Winchester in 1802. Because Morgan never revealed any details of his childhood, including his birthday (which he may not have known), his exact age at death is unknown, but he was likely about 65.

John Morton recovered from the wound he received at the Battle of Guilford Courthouse. In 1791 he and his family moved to Wilkes County, Georgia, where he died at age 60.

Charles O'Hara recovered from his wounds. It was he who officially surrendered to George Washington at Yorktown, Cornwallis having claimed to be too ill to attend the ceremony. After the war he rose to the rank of lieutenant general and twice served as Governor General of Gibraltar. Captured during the Napoleonic Wars, he became the only man personally taken prisoner by both George Washington and Napoleon. After two years in prison, he was exchanged for Count Rochambeau. He died in Gibraltar at age 62, of lingering complications from the wounds he received at Guilford Courthouse.

Andrew Pickens commanded South Carolina militia for the rest of the war, participating in the battles at Augusta, Ninety-Six, and Eutaw Springs, where he was wounded. In 1782 he led a campaign against the Cherokee. After the war he served in the state legislature and the United States Congress. He died in 1817 at age 77.

Rebecca was able to keep her Loyalist past hidden. She and her family made their living as small farmers and market gardeners. She died at her home in North Carolina at about age 66.

John Robinson and his family emigrated to a Quaker community in Ohio, to distance themselves from slavery and slaveholding. In the next generation, their home became a well-known stop on the Underground Railroad.

Walter Robertson went on to become the sheriff of Pittsylvania County and in 1829 he helped 65-year-old Dodd Lightfoot obtain a small pension. Robertson died at age 80, less than a year after the death of his wife, leaving behind eight children.

Squire recovered from his wound and returned to the Lawton farm. Under the terms of Henry Lawton's will, Squire became the legal property of Arthur Lawton upon Henry's death in 1796. Squire passed away ten years later, at age 70. He never shared a household with his wife.

Edward Stevens was in Charlottesville, recuperating from his wound, when he was nearly captured during a raid by Banastre Tarleton. Rescued by Jack Jouett, General Stevens went on to command troops during the Siege of Yorktown, having erased at Guilford Courthouse the disgrace he felt after the Battle of Camden. He died in 1820 at age 75.

Banastre Tarleton lost two fingers as a result of his wound at Guilford Courthouse, but nonetheless continued to command his troops for the rest of the war, leading a raid in the summer of 1781 that nearly captured Thomas Jefferson. He was received as a hero on his return to England, but later fell into disfavor after publishing a history of the war that many regarded as self-serving and unfair to his old mentor and supporter Lord Cornwallis. Tarleton married the daughter of a duke, rescuing himself from chronic debt, and was later made a baronet. He served for many years in Parliament, where he was mostly known as an ardent opponent of abolition. He died in 1833 at age 78.

William Washington was wounded and captured at the Battle of Eutaw Springs. A prisoner for the balance of the war, he was nursed by Jane Elliott, a wealthy heiress. They married in April 1782 and lived afterwards in Charleston and on the South Carolina estates she inherited. Although he was occasionally active in Federalist politics and was promoted to general during the "Quasi-War" with France, Washington preferred to live quietly, devoting much of his time to breeding and training racehorses. He died in 1810 at age 58, two weeks after Ransom's visit. Jane survived him by 20 years, but never remarried.

James Webster, grievously wounded during the Battle of Guilford Courthouse, died painfully on the march to Wilmington. The location of his grave has since been lost to history.

Ransom Wiatt was shot in the ankle and sabered in the face at the Battle of Eutaw Springs, leaving him disfigured and disabled for the rest of his life. In 1785 he married and moved to Rockingham County, North Carolina, where he and his wife raised five children, his mother Tabitha having died shortly after the end of the war. When Ransom applied for a pension in 1819, the examining officer expressed doubt that the scars on his face were from combat and required him to remove his stocking to prove he had been wounded in the ankle. After those indignities, he was granted a small pension.

Otho Holland Williams was promoted to brigadier general in 1782 and served with General Greene's army for the duration of the war. Afterwards he served as commissioner of the port of Baltimore. In 1792, after General Morgan turned down the offer, President Washington offered to make Williams second in command of the United States Army. Williams also declined. He died in 1794 at age 46.

Author's Note

This is a work of fiction. Many of the characters in this novel are, therefore, products of my imagination (the Bayards, Lawtons, Lightfoots, Lewises, Wiatts, Walter Robertson, Squire, George, and Rebecca, for example), though almost all of them were all inspired by and derived from actual historical persons.

But while my purpose was primarily to tell the imagined stories of fictional characters, I have attempted to locate those stories within the true history of the time. So, the events described in this book have been carefully researched and I have attempted to be historically faithful, albeit with some caveats. Sometimes my story has necessarily intruded on the historical record. For example, Caesar is fictional, and so therefore is the Peter Francisco horse-swapping episode. Likewise, I have often used in dialogue words taken from letters written by the historic figures, enabling me to capture their actual words without burdening the text with correspondence. In a few cases, for the sake of the story (and sometimes to avoid having to introduce new characters) I have attributed actions and words of historical figures to someone else. Thus, for example, it was actually Captain Duncanson of the Highlanders, not Major McArthur, who told Colonel Howard they had orders to give no quarter at Cowpens. Likewise, it was General O'Hara who wrote "it was resolved to follow Greene's army to the end of the world." There are several other such instances. Likewise, I have on a few occasions shifted events slightly for the sake of the story. General Greene's letter to Jefferson described in Chapter 46, for example, was actually written at Boyd's Ferry on February 15th, rather than at Halifax Courthouse on the 16th. Similarly, I have allowed Major Giles to arrive in Peytonsburg with news of the Battle of Cowpens a couple of days earlier than he actually did. Finally, in a few instances I have compressed the timeline, such as, for example, when I have Cornwallis ordering the march to Wilmington on the night of the battle at Guilford Courthouse, and when I have Captain Watkins and his cavalry combining with Colonel Lynch's regiment at Ward's Ferry. No doubt the story also contains historical errors that were unintentional. Of course, as is the prerogative of an historical novelist, I have often filled in gaps in the historical record using my imagination or my best guesses.

Much of the history of these three months remains controversial today. What happened on the first American line at the Battle of Guilford Courthouse? Are the traditional accounts of atrocities by Tarleton's Legion exaggerated? Did Cornwallis order his artillery to fire into his own troops at Guilford Courthouse? In this story, when I depict these and other uncertain or disputed events I have chosen the account that seems most plausible to me, but without making any claim that my account is historically definitive. For example, my depiction of the episode at the Battle of Guilford Courthouse when Lord Cornwallis ordered his artillery to fire into the melee is mindful of both Henry Lee's account and Lawrence Babits' skepticism of that account and reflects my own opinion after a careful review of the historical record.

Two instances of significant deviation from the historical record deserve explanation. Although at least two veterans' pension applications place Washington's dragoons at Pyle's Defeat, the historical record is clear that they were not there. So, I have invented a plausible explanation for how my fictional character Ransom Wiatt came to be there. The description of how his presence caused Lee's ruse to be exposed is, of course, entirely from my imagination. But I kept in the narrative the actual event that triggered the fighting, so that my invented tale does not materially alter the history and seems to me to be well within an historical novelist's prerogative.

More likely to be objectionable is how I have conflated Collin, the trumpeter hero of Cowpens, and James Gillies, Lee's trumpeter who was killed by some of Tarleton's dragoons at Bruce's Farm. I have done so reluctantly and remain uncertain whether I should have. I am aware that doing so may be an injustice to James Gillies, a hero who deserves to be remembered and honored by name. What actually happened after Cowpens to the boy traditionally remembered as "Collin" is unknown.

Note that throughout the book, places are described according to their names in 1781, which do not always match their names today. Campbell County, Virginia, Rockingham County, North Carolina, and Alamance County, North Carolina, for example, did not yet exist, and were still parts of Bedford, Guilford, and Orange counties, respectively. Likewise, some of the towns and communities mentioned either no longer exist (as in the case of Peytonsburg and Halifax Courthouse) or today have different names (as in the cases of Pittsylvania Courthouse, Guilford Courthouse, Gilbert Town, etc.).

Finally, this is the place where I should give thanks to all the people who helped me on this project.

Unfortunately, however, while doing the research for this book I did a poor job of keeping a record of all the people who provided help. Consequently, I am embarrassed to admit that I am unable to produce an accurate and complete list of everyone who deserves to be thanked. With sincere apologies to those omitted, thanks to Ralph Alderson, Nathan Black, T.K. Blackwood, Reve Carwile Jr., Kyle Griffith, Cherie Guerrant, Will Guerrant, Mike Hudson, Henry Hurt, Bruce Jennings, Bobby Ricketts, the late Danny Ricketts, David Roach, Thorntonius Velox, and the ranger staffs at Cowpens National Battlefield and Guilford Courthouse National Military Park. Of course, I have benefitted from the work of many other historians, amateur and professional, and to all of them I am grateful. Needless to say, none of those folks are to blame for my errors. Finally, I am deeply indebted to the persons whose stories inspired this book.

Made in the USA
Middletown, DE
28 September 2022

11419472R00335